James Craig has worked as a journa[...] than thirty years. He lives in London [...] ous Inspector Carlyle novels, *London* [...] *Never Explain*; *Buckingham Palace* [...] *We Die*; *A Man of Sor[...] Shoot to Kill*; *Sins of the Fathers*; *Nobody's Hero* and *Ac[...] of violence* are all available from Constable & Robinson.

For more information [...] www.james-craig.co.uk or follow him on Twitter: @byjamescraig

Praise for *London Calling*

'A cracking read.' BBC Radio 4

'Fast paced and very easy to get quickly lost in.' Lovereading. com

Praise for *Never Apologise, Never Explain*

'Pacy and entertaining.' *The Times*

'Engaging, fast paced . . . a satisfying modern British crime novel.' *Shots*

'*Never Apologise, Never Explain* is as close as you can get to the heartbeat of London. It may even cause palpitations when reading.' *It's A Crime! Reviews*

Also by James Craig

Novels
London Calling
Never Apologise, Never Explain
Buckingham Palace Blues
The Circus
Then We Die
A Man of Sorrows
Shoot to Kill
Sins of the Fathers
Nobody's Hero
Acts of Violence

Short Stories
The Enemy Within
What Dies Inside
The Hand of God

All Kinds of Dead

James Craig

Constable • London

CONSTABLE

First published in Great Britain in 2017 by Constable

3 5 7 9 10 8 6 4 2

A CIP catalogue record for this book
is available from the British Library.

ISBN: 978-1-47212-218-6 (paperback)

Typeset in Times New Roman by TW Type, Cornwall
Printed and bound in Great Britain by CPI (UK) Group Ltd, Croydon CR0 4YY

Papers used by Constable are from well-managed forests and other responsible
sources

Constable
is an imprint of
Little, Brown Book Group
Carmelite House
50 Victoria Embankment
London EC4Y 0DZ

An Hachette UK Company
www.hachette.co.uk

www.littlebrown.co.uk

For Catherine and Cate

This is the eleventh Carlyle novel.
Thanks for getting it done go to Krystyna Green,
Clive Hebard, Joan Deitch and Michael Doggart.

PROLOGUE

CONFIDENTIAL: Not for onward circulation

The incident took place in Uruzgan Province, Afghanistan, approximately twenty-three months ago. A group of Taliban fighters were intercepted approaching a settlement on the outskirts of Deh Rawood, an area approximately 400km south-west of Kabul.

The group were engaged by an Apache helicopter gunship before the troops on the ground, members of the Ground Task Force of the Special Operations Expeditionary Force conducted a damage assessment. During that process, six officers discovered two combatants. Both had been hit and seriously wounded by cannon fire from the Apache. The officers are accused of denying the unidentified prisoners first aid. Dragging them under the cover of some trees, the soldiers allegedly waited until the helicopter had left the area before both men were executed.

Soldier A, the commander of the patrol, is accused of having fatally shot both wounded men in the chest.

The incident was recorded with a head-camera worn by another of the accused, Soldier B.

The third accused man, Soldier C, is allegedly heard asking if he can shoot one of the captives in the head.

All three men have begun a court-martial at Upper Moldean Military Court Centre in Northamptonshire. The case hinges on the contents of the helmet-camera video. According to the prosecution, this shows that A, B and C conspired to murder the injured insurgents.

All three men deny murder.

All three have an otherwise unblemished military record. They have received strong testimonials from their Commanding Officer, as well as from other senior military figures, several of whom have spoken out in the press. Each has been awarded the OSM (Operational Service Medal) for the Afghan Campaign. Soldier A is one of only four soldiers to have been awarded the Victoria Cross for bravery during the current campaign in Afghanistan. He is the only recipient who currently remains in service.

Three other soldiers – D, E and F – feature in the transcripts. They are not facing trial.

The investigation into the incident was conducted by a team from the Special Investigation Branch (SIB) of the Royal Military Police, led by Captain Daniel Hunter. Judge Desmond Dunne, Judge Advocate General, has ruled that the SIB report, along with the video itself, should not be publicly released, on the grounds that it could be used as propaganda by terrorists, both in the UK and overseas. However, in response to the massive media interest – and to stall the risk of a leak – a heavily edited written transcript of the video (see below) has been made available online at the MoD's website.

The court-martial is approaching its conclusion. It has been adjourned for further psychological reports to be completed.

Key:
Square brackets [ ] are the speech analyst's marks.
Round brackets ( ) signify that the analyst has a lower confidence in the words recorded.
Three dots . . . denote unintelligible speech.
?Soldier B – question mark denotes lower confidence in attribution.

2

Glossary

AH – Apache helicopter.

Browners – dead (as in the rhyming slang, 'brown bread').

FFD – First Field Dressing.

HIIDE – A HIIDE camera takes images of fingerprints, irises and other details.

Nine-liner – request for helicopter casualty evacuation.

PGSS (Persistent Ground Surveillance System) – British observation balloon.

Ugly – Apache helicopter.

The footage starts with the patrol waiting at the edge of a field of tall crops. An Apache helicopter is audible overhead. The soldiers are heard complaining about being ordered to carry out a damage assessment after the helicopter attack on a group of insurgents who had been spotted approaching a village through a partially cultivated field.

The wounded insurgents had been shot at with 139 30mm anti-tank rounds. Lying on the ground, covered in blood, they were seriously injured but still alive when discovered by the patrol. The patrol dragged the two men across the field and into a wooded area nearby before the alleged executions took place.

The figures record the elapsed time from the beginning of the recording. The transcript begins with unintelligible speech and radio traffic before a man, thought to be Soldier B, begins to talk.

00:00:03   ?Soldier B: Come on.

D: . . .

B: Bollocks.

E: . . .

00:00:09   D: . . .

F: . . . shit . . .

D: . . .

00:00:11   A: . . . any more of this?

E: [coughs].

C: . . . cunt.

00:00:18 D: Fucking bastard.

E: [coughs].

00:00:19 A: That, ladies and gentlemen, is what a direct hit looks like.

F: [laughs] You know when you've been Tangoed.

A: An FFD ain't gonna help them.

E: You are fucked, boys.

D: Fucking browners, the pair of them.

00:00:32 B: How long will we have to wait for these fuckers to die?

A: We've got time.

E: . . .

[Vocalizations, probably from insurgents].

00:00:40 D: Fucking whining bastard. Not much of a fucking suicide bomber, are you?

[Laughter]

B: Dickhead.

00:00:47 C: We got a PGSS on us?

A: Move them both over there.

E: Come on.

00:01:05 D: . . .

E: That'll do. That'll do.

F: Mm.

00:01:18 D: . . .

E: . . . waste of fucking time.

00:01:32 C: Anybody wanna offer first aid?

D: No.

00:01:34 B: No.

E: . . .

00:01:36 C: I'll put one in his head, if you want.

D: [laughs]

E: [laughs]

00:01:40 A: Like that wouldn't be fucking obvious.

F: You'd have to give back your OSM.

4

D: [Laughs]. They might give you another one.

00:01:54 *D:* Want me to send a nine-liner?

B: . . .

[Radio].

00:02:02 *B:* We're waiting for [name of comrade] to er – . . . may well be dead. [Speaking on radio].

C: . . .

00:02:05 *F:* . . . stopped breathing.

B: For fuck's sake.

D: Don't. Yeah.

00:02:08 *E:* . . . just . . . him.

[Laughter]

F: Yeah. That might . . .

?E: Yeah.

00:02:13 *A:* Fuck it, he's done.

D: Yeah.

C: You're dead, son.

00:02:19 *A:* Hello, one zero, one four. [Speaking on radio].

B: . . .

00:02:25 *B:* Cunt shooting at us.

00:02:28 *D:* Twats.

00:02:33 *A:* Administering first aid to these er – individuals, they're er – passed on from this er world, over. [Speaking on radio].

00:02:46 *A:* . . . Okay, er we'll try to biometrically enrol these guys as best we can and we'll gather what er – intelligence we can before moving back. [Speaking on radio].

?E: [Clears throat].

D: . . .

00:03:12 *A:* Right, get the – get the HIIDE camera out, see if you can get a picture of him, minus all the – stuff.

00:03:16 *C:* Where's the Ugly?

B: Headed north.

?A: Yeah?

B: Deffo.

00:03:28 [GUNSHOT #1 – This is the moment when A allegedly shoots the first prisoner].

F: Fuck. [Distant voice].

E: (What was that?) [Distant voice].

D: (Don't know) [Distant voice].

00:03:29 *F:* . . .

00:03:35 *E:* . . .

00:03:59 [GUNSHOT #2 – This is the moment when A allegedly shoots the second prisoner].

00:04:05 *A:* Shuffle off this mortal coil, you cunts.

D: . . .

E: Fuck.

00:04:20 *A:* Obviously, gents, this doesn't go anywhere.

B: Roger that.

A: I've just broke the Geneva Convention, big time.

C: What happens in Vegas.

D: . . .

B: Their numbers came up.

F: . . .

D: . . .

00:05:08 *A:* Yeah, they're, er – fully dead now [Speaking on radio].

A: (Yeah, roger.) . . . [Response from radio].

00:05:14 *B:* [laughs] All kinds of dead.

E: Stupid fuckers.

F: Dead, dead, dead.

ONE

'Why is that dog trying to shag the grass?'

'Huh?' Dominic Silver made a point of finishing his newspaper article before looking up. A group of soldiers were being court-martialled, accused of killing a couple of Taliban terrorists. Wasn't that what they were supposed to do? Frowning, he struggled to make sense of the story.

'That dog . . .' John Carlyle, Metropolitan Police Inspector and all-round animal-phobe, took off his glasses and began wiping the lenses with a paper napkin.

Looking over the top of the *Daily Mail,* Silver took a moment to locate the mongrel in question. The sorry-looking animal appeared to be some kind of terrier. Whatever its lineage, the mutt was squatting down on the tattered lawn, ten yards or so from where they were sitting, and was vigorously thrusting its private parts into the ground, with what looked like a cheery grin on its face.

'You gotta get it where you can,' Dom reflected, quickly returning to his newspaper. 'One more reason why you should never sit on the grass. Fuck knows what you might catch.'

Carlyle finished cleaning his specs and placed them back on his nose. 'It shouldn't be allowed,' he harrumphed.

'Maybe,' Dom casually suggested, 'you should go over there and arrest the dog for public indecency.'

'Ha fucking ha.' Retrieving the paper cup sitting next to him on the bench, Carlyle poured the last of his green tea on to the

7

ground. Careful not to get any drops on his coat, he tossed the cup towards the rubbish bin situated at the end of the bench. For once, his aim was true. However, the bin was full to overflowing so the cup simply bounced off a discarded 2-litre Coke bottle and landed on the tarmac. With an exaggerated sigh, Carlyle struggled to his feet, picked up the cup and stuffed it as far into the mound of waste as it would go. Returning to his seat, he eyed the dog, which still appeared to be pleasuring itself. 'Maybe I should call the RSPCA.'

'And what would they do?' Dom asked, hiding his grin behind the pages of his paper. 'Send a dog-catcher?'

'It's his sunburn,' said a voice.

'Eh?' The inspector looked round to see an elderly-looking bloke trundling towards them on a chestnut-brown mobility scooter. The guy was wearing a bush hat and a pair of outsized sunglasses. His grubby yellow T-shirt bore the legend *Stop the War*.

Which particular war are we talking about? Carlyle wondered as he clocked the two large bottles of Strongbow cider bouncing about in the wire basket perched on the front of the scooter.

The man came to a halt three feet in front of the bench. His sunburned knees stuck out from the bottom of baggy green Bermuda shorts. A pair of red Crocs finished off the ensemble nicely.

Taking one hand off the scooter handle, the man gestured towards the rutting dog. 'Joey was lying out in the sun too long, last week,' he explained, 'and got badly burned; he's in quite a bit of discomfort.' One cue, the dog finished whatever he was doing and wandered over to inspect the newly planted flowerbeds.

'He looked like he was enjoying himself,' Dom pointed out.

The man shook his head. 'He's in pain. His skin underneath, it's really sensitive.'

'Sometimes it's hard to tell the difference.'

'You should keep him under control,' Carlyle muttered, sounding a bit like *Disgusted of Tunbridge Wells*. 'Grumpy old man' was not a very appealing persona but one that he was effortlessly growing into. 'Someone's bound to complain about such *lewd* behaviour.'

Lewd behaviour? Dom stifled a titter.

'He's only a dog,' the man objected.

'You,' Carlyle said, 'are responsible, as his owner.'

The man frowned. 'He's in pain.'

'This is Berkeley Square, not . . .' Carlyle tried to think of a more appropriate venue for Joey's performance. Nowhere came to mind. 'It's Berkeley Square,' he repeated.

The old guy looked genuinely offended. 'Don't be so bloody heartless. You wouldn't call the Rozzers over a poor sick dog, would you?'

Before Carlyle could respond, Dom stuck out a thumb. 'He *is* the police.'

'Yeah?' The man looked him, unconvinced.

'I am the police,' Carlyle said solemnly.

'Haven't you got better things to do than harass my poor Joey?' Shifting in his seat, the man looked around, as if searching for some assistance in dealing with the two jokers making fun of his dog. But the end of lunch hour had largely emptied the park, and none of the remaining visitors showed any interest in coming to his aid.

No, not really. Carlyle watched Joey stop what he was doing and head towards a pair of Chinese tourists eating their lunch on a bench in the mini-pagoda that stood in the centre of the park. Taking up a position in their line of sight, the dog waited expectantly for a morsel of hamburger.

'He's begging now,' Carlyle spluttered.

'Leave the poor little sod alone.' Dom stood up. 'Everybody gets hungry after sex. It's all the calories you burn.' He turned to the man on the scooter. 'I bet that must be sore.'

The man nodded. He looked genuinely upset. 'Joey's really been suffering.'

Carlyle rolled his eyes. He hadn't schlepped halfway across town for a discussion regarding a dog's sunburned privates.

Ever the humanitarian, Dom was far more sympathetic. 'I'm sure you can get some kind of ointment for the problem,' he told the man. 'Ease the discomfort. He needs to leave it alone.'

So do we, Carlyle observed.

The guy looked round the square. Expensive office space rose up on all sides, broken only by the occasional gentleman's club and luxury car dealership. 'And where am I going to find a vet round here?'

Dom turned and raised an enquiring eyebrow to the inspector.

'Don't ask me,' Carlyle huffed. 'How would I know? Animals are not my thing. I've never owned so much as a goldfish in my entire life.'

Shaking his head, Dom pointed in the direction of Oxford Street. 'Just take Joey to Superdrug. There's one at the top of Davies Street. I'm sure that the pharmacist will be able to give you something for his . . . problem.'

With a grunt, the man put the scooter into reverse, sending it shooting across the grass. Conducting a wide U-turn, he went off in search of his four-legged friend.

'I quite fancy one of those.' Carlyle nodded at the scooter. 'It looks quite nippy; handy for getting around.' Turning towards Dom, he realized that his mate was already heading towards the park exit. 'Hey!' he shouted, jumping to his feet. 'Wait for me!'

'I've got to get back to the Gallery,' Dom replied, over his shoulder. 'Fiona will be wanting her lunch.'

Fiona? Carlyle wondered. Who's Fiona? 'Fair enough,' he said, jogging after him.

What the hell was that beast doing? Discarded newspaper on one side of him, empty coffee cup on the other, Daniel Hunter tried to take up sufficient space to deter anyone else from joining him on the bench. After the best part of half an hour sitting in the park, the only thing that had caught his attention was the eccentric dog. Daniel watched with wry amusement as the uninhibited animal finished its . . . rutting on the grass and then went off in search of other diversions. No one else in the park seemed to bat an eyelid. That was the thing about London, everyone was wrapped up in their own little world. No one paid the slightest attention to what was going on around them. The city was a funny place; as a country boy, he wasn't sure if he would ever really get used to it.

By now, lunchtime was over. The office workers had gone back to their desks and only a handful of folk remained loitering in the square. Daniel quickly pegged the old guy on the electric scooter as the dog's owner. No one else looked like they would have the time or inclination for looking after a dog. Of course, the mutt could be a stray but he doubted it. As a rule, you didn't see many strays roaming the streets of Mayfair.

Scooter-man finished his conversation with a couple of guys on a bench on the far side of the park and headed for the pagoda-type building where the dog was now being fed titbits by a couple of tourists. Trundling across the gravel, the man manoeuvred his scooter next to the dog. From his hand gestures, Daniel could see that he was making a half-hearted attempt to scold the dog for its shameless panhandling. Bowing its head, the animal looked suitably contrite. After a nod in the direction of the tourists, the man reached down and scooped up his pet. Placing it in the basket on the front of the scooter next to a couple of bottles of cider, he drove off, making for the exit on the west side of the park.

As he watched the unlikely duo traverse the zebra crossing leading to Hill Street, Daniel caught sight of Mel coming the other way.

'At last!' He gave her a wave but, head bowed, marching forward, she had yet to notice him. Her determined strides underlined that she was the best part of fifteen minutes late. Tutting like an old woman, Daniel let his hand drop back by his side.

Timekeeping was not one of his wife's strengths. It drove him mad. Whereas he would always be five minutes early for any rendezvous, Mel was never knowingly on time. Daniel simply couldn't comprehend her mindset. How hard was it to be on time for things? All it required was a bit of thought and some forward planning.

When they had been courting, Melanie Ward had never been less than twenty minutes late for a date. Once, she had made him wait an hour and twenty-five minutes outside the local picture house. When she finally turned up, Mel smiled sweetly and claimed that he had got the time wrong. Daniel had been furious – he had never done that in his life. They were supposed to be going to see *Avatar*. To this day, he had never seen the film and never would. Mere mention of the title made him bristle with frustration.

Ten years and two kids later, she was still always late. He had never been able to shake the idea that she did it on purpose, just to wind him up. It was something that caused more than a few arguments between them.

Now, however, was not the time for a row. Daniel was only going to be home for a short time. Tonight would be the first time he had slept in his own bed for almost a week. And the last too, for God knows how long.

Walking through the gates, Mel finally looked up. Spotting him, she upped her pace, an embarrassed grin on her face. As she came closer, he could see fatigue etched into her face. Her skin was deathly pale and the rings under her eyes were so dark it looked like her mascara had smudged. Bloody hell, Daniel thought, you need a break. His wife looked completely knackered. That was not so surprising. To all intents and purposes, she had been playing the role of single parent for the last two years, with minimal support from friends and family.

Not for the first time, Daniel felt ashamed. He knew that he hadn't pulled his weight at home for a long time now. Mel deserved better. So did the kids. So did he, for that matter. What was the point of having a family if you never saw them?

Pushing the jumble of unhappy thoughts to the back of his mind, he got to his feet and stepped towards her, holding out his arms. 'Hey.'

'Hey, yourself,' Mel smiled, stepping into his embrace.

Pulling her towards him, Dan closed his eyes, breathing in her perfume, as she kissed him gently on the lips.

'Sorry I'm late,' she said, once they slid apart.

'Are you?' Daniel tried to sound nonchalant as they sat back down. 'I hadn't noticed.'

She gave him a gentle punch on the arm. 'Liar.'

'It wasn't that much.' By your standards, at least.

'There was a security alert on Oxford Street.'

'Anything serious?'

'I doubt it,' Mel said. 'At any rate, I haven't heard a bang. It's probably just some traffic problem or other. Whatever it was, it was a right pain. I had to go all the way round by Regent Street. Otherwise, I would have been on time.'

'Mm.'

'Well, just about.'

'Don't worry. My train was late, anyway,' he fibbed again. 'I've only just got here myself. How long have we got? What time is pick-up?'

Mel checked the time on her phone. 'Don't worry, we've still got half an hour.'

'Fine. Want to get a coffee?'

'Nah. I'm okay.' She took his hand and gave it a squeeze. 'It's nice just to be able to sit down for a moment, without having to rush about.'

'Yeah.' He gave her a squeeze back.

'The kids will be thrilled to see you when they come out of school.'

'You didn't tell them?'

'I wanted it to be a surprise.' Now it was Mel's turn to fib. The truth was that she didn't want to get the kids' hopes up; it wouldn't be the first time their father had let them down at the last minute. It wasn't that he was an unreliable man, far from it. It was just that his job was ultra-demanding and the Army made no allowances for family life. 'You should have worn your uniform.

13

You know they get a kick out of seeing you in it. I'm sure it would have gone down well with Mr Fry too.'

'The headmaster? I thought he had retired last summer.'

'No, not till the end of this year. You know how impressed he was that you were a Redcap.'

'Yeah. It certainly helped get us through the interview.' It was a conversation they'd had many times before. Bagging not one but two places at any Central London school required ruthlessly exploiting any connection or asset you had. When Daniel had walked into Dr Alfred Fry's office in his Royal Military Police uniform, the old fella's face had lit up. Even before they had shaken hands, Daniel had known the kids would get in.

'I'm sure he'll be at the gates. It would have been nice if you'd had it on.'

Irritated, Daniel tugged at the collar of his North Face jacket with his free hand. With the fleece lining, it was a bit too warm for the time of year but he would wear it on all but the hottest days; it was his off-duty uniform. 'I don't like wearing the uniform when I don't have to,' he mumbled. 'Too conspicuous.' Britain had long since stopped being a country where members of the military were shown proper respect. He was fed up with being accosted by wankers who felt they had the right to walk right up to you to give you a piece of their mind about everything from the 'so-called War on Terror' to the 'dictatorship of the military-industrial complex'.

Mel nodded. She had heard it all before. 'I understand.' She gave his hand another squeeze. 'The kids'll just be happy to see you. That's the main thing.'

'Yeah.'

For a while, they sat in silence, each simply enjoying the pleasure of the other's presence.

TWO

Groaning inwardly, Hunter watched as the dosser came towards them, an expectant grin on his face. He was a tall guy, in his thirties perhaps, with a thick beard and eyes that lacked focus. In one hand was a bottle of cheap Australian red wine. It was as close to empty as made no difference.

Jimmy Gallagher eyed the couple sitting on the bench and smiled to himself. Jimmy knew every type of person that turned up in the square. He could calibrate the likelihood of each one putting their hand in their pocket down to a fraction of a percentage point. The bloke wouldn't want to know; the woman, however, was a racing certainty.

Seeing the scowl on the bloke's face, Jimmy addressed his remarks to his good lady wife. 'Spare a few pence for a cuppa, love?' The accent was more West Country than West End.

Before Mel could stick a hand in her pocket, Daniel waved him away angrily. 'Sorry, mate,' he muttered with a robotic insincerity, meaning, *Bugger off.*

Sensing the woman's hesitancy, Jimmy stood his ground. Every second of compound embarrassment was money in the bank.

'Here you go.' Mel fished a few coins out of her pocket and handed them over. She didn't know precisely how much it was but it certainly wouldn't come close to covering the cost of a latte in the Starbucks across the road.

'Thank you.' Jimmy gave Daniel a small smirk of triumph

before shuffling off in search of his next target. 'Have a nice day.'

'What did you do that for?' Daniel asked as he watched the dosser line up his next target. 'He'll just use the money to stay pissed.'

'Poor bloke.'

'Poor bloke, my arse.'

'Daniel Hunter,' she admonished him. 'How do you know he's not an ex-serviceman?'

'Pfff.'

'You're the one always pointing out how ex-soldiers are more likely to end up homeless than normal people.'

Normal people. 'Okay, okay.' He watched the dosser get short shrift from a guy in a suit with a copy of the *Financial Times* under his arm. Presumably used to such rebuffs, the tramp wandered off without any protest. 'You're right.'

Satisfied with the admission of defeat, Mel graciously moved the conversation on. 'How was Hereford?'

'Hereford,' he sighed, 'was fairly routine.'

'Must have been nice to have a simple one, for a change.'

'You can say that again. Three SAS guys went out for a night on the tiles and put a couple of the locals in hospital. No one disputed what happened. I handed the report over to the Camp Commandant all signed, sealed and delivered. Job done.'

'So what happens to the SAS guys?'

'They'll get three months in MCTC, something like that.' The Military Corrective Training Centre in Colchester was England's only military prison. It was built to house 500 service personnel convicted of various offences; the current population was 782, and rising. Daniel had spent a decent part of the journey back to London trying to work out how many of the buggers in there he'd put inside personally. His best guess was eighty-four, give or take. 'Then it will be back to active service.'

'They always take them back, don't they?'

'Not always.'

'No, but most of the time.'

'Why wouldn't you? A lot of time, effort and money goes into recruiting and training these guys in the first place. If you throw them back on to the streets, all that goes to waste.' He looked up, trying to pick out the tramp, but the man had disappeared from the park. 'Plus, they'll probably cause more trouble out here than if they stay in uniform.'

'But they broke the law.'

'I suppose so.'

'There's no suppose so, Dan, it's black and white.'

'Is it?' He made a face. 'They were provoked. The civilian "victims" were the ones who kicked everything off.'

'But still—'

'It's always the ones who retaliate who get the blame. The blokes who started it all, they're sorted. They'll get their compo from the government, along with a formal letter of apology, plus their fifteen minutes of fame in the local paper.'

'So, job done.'

'Yes. Apart from the three off to the MCTC, everybody's happy. And even they didn't seem that bothered, to be honest.'

'You're just doing what you're supposed to.' Mel was used to her husband's somewhat cynical tone. As far as she could see, it helped to keep him sane in a job which revolved around cleaning up other people's mess.

'Everybody's happy,' Daniel repeated. 'The whole thing's more a PR exercise than anything else.'

Mel edged closer on the bench, slipping her arm through his. 'So what's next?'

'I was thinking we'll pick up the kids and maybe take them to the Giraffe up the road, grab a burger and a Coke. What do you reckon?'

'Okay.'

Registering the uncertain tone, he turned to face her. 'You don't seem too sure.'

'Giraffe's fine. But you know that's not what I meant. What's your next investigation going to be? How long will you be home for this time?'

The killer question.

Daniel stared up at the grey sky. 'That depends on what comes up. I need to check in with the CO later on.' He could not face telling her that he was already booked on a Hercules leaving Mildenhall for Kandahar the day after tomorrow.

If only the RAF did 'air miles'. In the last eight months, Hunter had handled three investigations in Afghanistan. This time around, an Afghan civilian had been shot in the neck while praying in a field. His death had caused protests that had left another three locals dead and a further sixteen injured. Two Welsh Guards accused of the initial killing languished in the brig at Camp Leatherneck. Each was blaming the other for firing the fatal shot.

The fact that Daniel was being flown in showed that the powers-that-be recognized that this would be a difficult investigation and also a political nightmare. For sure, the case was far more serious than some handbags outside the Queen Victoria in Lugwardine. And far more complicated too. The preliminary enquiries into the Leatherneck killing had seemingly managed to uncover no weapon and no usable forensics evidence. How could that be possible? Daniel felt a spasm of frustration. The investigator inside him knew that he should be there already. Every hour that passed made it less likely that he would ever get to the truth of the matter.

But sitting here, next to his wife, waiting for his kids to get out of school . . . did he really want to go? There was a limit to the amount of other people's shit that any man could deal with. After twelve years in the RMP, Daniel fancied that he was getting very close to that limit.

'You're a captain now,' Mel said. 'That should make a difference.'

'Maybe.'

'Perhaps you'll get a choice of assignments.'

Yeah right. 'I dunno about that, love.'

'Surely, this time?'

'You know as well as I do, we've been saying that for the last year or so. But the RMP ain't big on choice, whatever rank you wear on your shoulder. They tell you where to go and you say, "Yessir". Simple as.'

She gave him a sad smile. 'Chain of command.'

'That's right. It's the Army. You have to respect the chain of command. Anyway, there's bugger all below me at the moment. A lot of blokes are saying now is the time to get out. There are cuts everywhere. The politicians won't stop trimming budgets, so the brass are trying to convince themselves that we're running out of people to fight.' The irritation in his voice was clear, but did he really care? 'Three of the guys in my team have gone in the last six months and another two are angling for redundancy. At this rate, I shall be the only one left.'

'Smithy's still there though, isn't he?'

Daniel smiled. Sergeant Giles Smith was the only comrade whose name Mel ever remembered. Right now, Sergeant Smith, a fifteen-year veteran with a wife and three kids of his own, should be about 27,000 feet above Croatia, heading for Kandahar, the advance party of their murder investigation. Hopefully, Smithy would have started to bring some order to the Leatherneck investigation by the time Daniel got there. Maybe even found a bit of bloody evidence. 'Yeah, he's still around. Run off his feet, like me.' Depressed by the conversation, he glanced at his watch. 'School will be out soon. We should get going.'

'We've got a little more time.' Mel reached into the pocket of her coat and pulled out a thin brown envelope. 'This arrived yesterday.'

'Fuck. Not another one.' Taking it from her hand, he looked at the address. The usual careful handwriting in blue ink, all capitals: MRS DANIEL HUNTER, 36 MORRISEY GARDENS, WC2M 5RG. 'I thought all this shit had stopped.' With a sigh, he tore open the envelope, even though he knew what would be inside. 'Why didn't you tell me?'

19

'I didn't want to worry you.'

Daniel pulled out a single sheet of A4 paper. 'You should have said.' He scanned the contents and offered it to Mel. 'It's just the usual: *Lay off Andy Carson. We know where you live.*' She waved it away. Daniel re-folded the sheet of paper and placed it back in the envelope. 'Of course you know where we live, you dicks, you sent us a bloody letter!' He shoved the envelope into the pocket of his jeans.

Mel stared into the middle distance. 'I thought this was all over.'

'It is. The investigation finished months ago. With that bloody video footage, the court-martial is a formality. The only question is how long he gets. And that's nothing to do with me.'

'It's been all over the papers.'

'I know. Andrew Stephen Carson – aka Soldier A – come on down.'

'So why bother to send us another letter?'

'I don't know.' Looking around the park, he saw that the tramp had reappeared and was sitting on a bench with a can of lager in his hand. At his feet was a blue plastic bag, doubtless containing more cans. Daniel shook his head. 'Carson's got a couple of brothers. They're not necessarily the sharpest tools in the box.'

'You said we would get away from all of this.' She fought back a sob.

'We will, I promise.'

'It's one of the reasons we came down to London, after all.'

'Yes.'

'So how did they get our new address?'

Good question. 'How many letters is that now? Four? Five?'

'Six. We had five before we moved.'

'Fuck.'

'Daniel!' She gave him a gentle shove. 'Don't use that language. The kids pick up everything.'

'The kids aren't here.'

'You don't want to get into bad habits.'

'Fair enough.' It was an easy thing to concede.

'Dr Fry would have a fit if he heard you using language like that at the school.'

'Don't worry,' Daniel smiled. 'I'll be on my best behaviour.'

'Good.' Levering herself up, Mel began fussing with her coat. 'Now come on, let's get going. We don't want to be late.'

THREE

The two men were turning into Cork Street by the time Carlyle got round to explaining the reason for his appearance in the West End. 'I need a favour,' he said, stepping off the pavement in order to dodge some scaffolding.

'Big surprise,' Dom grunted, not slowing his pace in the face of the building works. 'There's no such thing as a free lunch, even if it's only a Pret sandwich.'

'It's about Alexander,' Carlyle added, jumping back out of the gutter.

'Your dad?'

Carlyle nodded.

Reaching the Molby-Nicol Gallery, Dom stopped in front of a large poster in the window advertising his latest exhibition, 'Mega-Dams', and turned to face Carlyle. A look of genuine concern appeared on his face. 'That must be a bastard. How's he doing?'

'Oh, you know.' Carlyle stared at his shoes and noticed that the soles were coming away from the uppers. 'He's okay, under the circumstances.'

'It's been, what – three months now?'

Five, Carlyle thought, nearly six. 'More or less.' Feeling a hand on his shoulder, he looked up. 'I mean, cancer – what can you do? I think he'd known for a while that something was wrong; it was almost a relief when the diagnosis confirmed the worst.'

'After your mum going, as well.'

'Yes,' Carlyle nodded. 'He's got the right mentality for it though. Very stoical. No wailing and gnashing of teeth. He just keeps going about his business. Taken it all in his stride, really.'

'And you?'

'Me?' Carlyle frowned. 'I'm fine.'

'The whole thing must be taking its toll though.'

The inspector shrugged. 'It's something we all have to go through.'

'Yeah, but still.' Dom waited as an elderly couple shuffled out of the gallery. Giving them a polite smile, he caught the door before it shut and ushered Carlyle inside. 'C'mon, we can talk in my office.'

The gallery space consisted of a single large room with white-washed walls. On the far side of the room, halfway towards the back, a tall elegant young woman, dressed all in black, sat behind a desk on which were piled a number of exhibition catalogues. Busily tapping away on a MacBook, she did not acknowledge the new arrivals.

On the walls were hung a series of massive photographic prints. Carlyle glanced at the image closest to the door, a large colour photograph of a group of jackbooted soldiers goose-stepping through a building site next to a river. A small notice next to the picture explained what he was looking at: *Chunqiao Dam. Number 6 Chromogenic print, 122×162cm, 48¼×64in. Edition 22. Multiple sizes available.* Carlyle knew better than to enquire as to the price.

Dom noticed him taking a look and automatically slipped into salesman mode. 'This is the mega-dams project. You know that the Chinese are building more than a hundred and thirty of them at the moment?'

'I had no idea,' Carlyle confessed.

'It's the next great environmental disaster – *one* of the next great environmental disasters. And this is a chronicle of that folly.' Dom mentioned the name of the photographer. 'It's a vast, ten-year undertaking. Quite remarkable. It has won loads of awards all over the world.'

'Nice,' Carlyle responded, somewhat disconcerted by the speed with which Dom moved from environmental catastrophe to photographic awards in the space of a single breath.

'The exhibition here's been a great success. Best we've ever had. It's going to go over to a gallery I work with in New York next month.'

'Mm.'

Dom turned towards the desk. 'Sorry I'm late, Fiona.'

Without looking up, the girl pushed back her chair and stood up, hoisting an oversized tan bag over her shoulder as she did so. 'I'm just off to Tutti's for some lunch.' She smiled unconvincingly. 'I won't be too long.'

'Er . . . could you give me another ten minutes, please?' Dom asked, rather apologetically, Carlyle thought, considering he was supposed to be the boss. 'I just need to sort something with Insp— er, *Mr* Carlyle out in the back.'

'Very well.' Dropping her bag back on to the desk, Fiona's shallow smile evaporated and she sat back down with a bump. 'That's no problem.' Unzipping the bag, she fumbled inside for a moment, before produing an apple. 'Don't forget that you've got Mr Spargo in half an hour.'

Did the inspector imagine it, or did Dom's shoulders sag a little at the mention of his imminent meeting? Spargo. Unusual name. Instinctively, the inspector filed it away in his cranial Outlook.

'His office confirmed this morning,' the receptionist added. 'They said half an hour should be fine.'

'I bet it is,' Dom muttered.

The girl scrunched up her face, making her look about twelve years old. 'What?'

'Nothing. Thanks.' Head bowed, Dom shuffled off before Fiona could ask any more questions or, worse, change her mind about further delaying her lunch. Careful to avoid eye contact with the hungry receptionist, Carlyle followed on in his wake.

At the back of the gallery, off to the right, a door led to a small space, maybe ten feet by twelve. This was Dom's office and storeroom. Carlyle regularly ventured inside and was always distinctly unimpressed. The room had no windows, just a small skylight in the ceiling, leaving it in a permanent state of twilight. Worse, it was always cold. The temperature was at least five degrees lower here than in the gallery proper and there was a strong smell of damp. For a man who was supposed to be worth somewhere north of £20 million, Carlyle didn't understand why Dom was happy to spend so much time in here.

On three sides, large canvases cocooned in bubble wrap stood against the wall, leaving just enough space in the middle for a small desk and two chairs. Even then, Carlyle had to remove three boxes of catalogues from the chair nearest the door before he could sit down.

'Still the same old hole, I see.'

Dom carefully pulled the door shut. 'It's home.'

'Don't the customers expect better?'

'The customers,' said Dom, slipping behind the desk, 'expect a Cork Street address and some traditional English hospitality.'

'Eh?'

'Polite but relentless ass-kissing,' Dom explained.

'I didn't think that was your kind of thing,' Carlyle chuckled.

'I don't mind,' Dom grinned. 'I find that as I get older it's easier to fake these kinds of things.'

'I don't,' Carlyle grumped.

'Which is why you will never make it past Inspector, my friend, even if you were to stay in the Force for fifty years.'

'As you've always told me.'

'As I've always told you. Not that I would want you to change now. It's part of your great charm.'

'Ass-kisser!'

'Guilty as charged.' Dom held up both hands in mock surrender. 'Like I said, I'm getting quite good at it. You have to be if you work in the service economy. Not all of us can suck on the tit of the public finances, you know.'

'Ha!' Carlyle gestured back in the direction of Berkeley

Square. 'You could still do all your brown-nosing in one of those nice new developments up the road.' He shivered theatrically. 'I'm sure they have central heating, for a start.'

'Very expensive central heating.' A pained expression crossed Dom's face. 'The rents they are proposing are totally unbelievable. They are putting up 80,000 feet of new space – with the threat of more to come – and think that they can charge more than double what anyone has ever charged before. It's insane. The only people who can afford costs like those are private equity firms and the kind of retailers who sell handbags for three grand a pop.'

'Yeah,' Carlyle nodded. It was a common theme you heard these days: Central London neighbourhoods being turned into homogeneous ghettoes for the super-rich. It was a kind of ethnic cleansing, less violent than the versions that you saw in the Balkans or in Rwanda, but ultimately just as effective.

'I would be bankrupt within six months,' Dom continued. 'Probably less.'

Carlyle raised an eyebrow.

'I know that you – suspicious little sod that you are – think that the gallery is just a hobby, or some money-laundering scam, but it's not. It's what I do now. I enjoy it – but only because it's a proper business. It has to stand on its own two feet. Do you understand?'

No. 'Yes.'

'Plus, when I bought it I made two promises to the previous owners, Mr Molby and Mr Nicol. One, I wouldn't change the name, which was fine by me anyway; and two, I wouldn't move from this location, which also makes sense. The gallery has been here ever since it was founded in 1947. They exhibited Bacon in the 1950s, Hockney in the 1970s.' He mentioned the name of a famous American painter. 'Twenty-odd years ago, he turned up at an opening totally off his face. They found him in this very room getting a blow job from one of the waiters.'

'I don't see a commemorative plaque anywhere,' said Carlyle wryly.

'There's a famous photograph of him stumbling out of the gallery at the end of the night. If you look closely, you can see that his fly's still undone.'

'Nice.'

'It's all just part of the legend. The point is that you can't take that history with you. I reckon that if we moved – even if we just moved to the other end of the street – I would lose maybe twenty per cent of my clients straight off the bat.' Dom tapped determinedly on the desk with an index finger. 'They like coming *here*.'

A phone started ringing in the gallery. Carlyle counted eight rings before the caller gave up. 'You could get yourself a new receptionist, at least.'

Dom smiled. 'Fiona's a very nice girl. She can be a bit highly strung but the clients like her.'

'How highly strung do you have to be, to be unable to answer the telephone?'

'She's just hungry.'

'Mm.' As the sustaining effect of his cheese and pickle sandwich began to wear off, Carlyle was beginning to feel a bit peckish himself.

'She's very bright.' Dom kept his voice low, as if he was worried that the lovely Fiona might be listening on the other side of the door. 'And I'm very lucky to have her.'

'I would have thought she's lucky to have you,' Carlyle snapped. 'Isn't everyone under thirty supposed to be out of work these days?' His thoughts turned to his own daughter. Alice would need to start working on her CV soon. Maybe Dom might be able to give her a Saturday job or, at least, some work experience. He thought about mentioning it then checked himself. Asking for two favours in one day would be a bit much.

'Fiona would never have a problem getting a job,' Dom explained. 'I know for a fact, she's been offered jobs in at least three other Mayfair galleries.'

'Good for her.'

'She's currently doing a PhD on Contemporary Chinese Art at

27

the Courtauld.' Dom gestured at a poster taped to the wall behind his head. It was a smaller version of the one in the window, advertising the gallery's current exhibition. 'Which is perfect for me. Half of my artists these days are Chinese. And almost as many of my buyers.'

Carlyle nodded, trying to feign interest. The truth was that he had found Dom's previous career far more engaging than his reincarnation as a respectable art dealer. After more than twenty years as a successful – and discreet – London drug dealer, Dom had cashed in his chips and pursued a new vocation. From the inspector's point of view, the modern art market was harder to understand – and less professionally relevant – than illegal narcotics.

'The flipside is, I can't afford to piss her off.' Dom glanced nervously at his watch. Carlyle couldn't remember the model, but he knew it had cost roughly the equivalent of three months of his salary. *Before* tax. 'I've had three assistants in the last twelve months. None of them ever stay. Eva says that I have to keep hold of this one.'

Carlyle allowed himself a rueful smile. Dom was the one person he knew who was as under the thumb as much as he was himself. Eva Hollander, aka Mrs Silver, kept him on a short leash.

'She says it is a test of my management skills.'

'From what I remember,' Carlyle said drily, 'your management skills were quite good.'

'Keeping my crew in line was a piece of cake compared to the girls that waltz through here. They all think they can wrap you around their little finger.' Dom grinned sheepishly. 'And they do.'

'I bet.'

'Anyway, about your dad . . .'

'Alexander is doing okay,' Carlyle started up where he'd left off. 'But we're talking months, rather than years.'

'Treatment?'

Carlyle shook his head. 'He's decided against it. And I can see his point. Tests, surgery, doctors will only mess about with

28

whatever quality of life he has left, and for what? It might buy him a little more time. Then, again, it might not. Better to have six months living a relatively normal life than nine sitting in a hospital bed, surrounded by sick people.'

Dom nodded. He had a fair idea as to what was coming next, but he waited patiently for his friend to come out with it.

'So . . . the matter in hand is pain relief. It gets pretty bad at times. And it's only going to get worse. Alexander is adamant that the stuff they are giving him at the Royal Marsden is pretty shit. He needs some help. So, I wondered . . .'

He was interrupted by a knock at the door. Turning in his seat, he saw Fiona's head appear.

'Mr Spargo's here.'

Dom glanced again at his watch. 'For fuck's sake. He's twenty minutes early.'

The assistant shot him a look that said, *There's not a lot I can do about that.* 'Anyway, I'm off to lunch. Be back soon.'

'But—'

Before Dom could protest, the head disappeared and the door clicked shut. Carlyle listened to the young woman say, 'Mr Silver will be with you in a minute,' followed by a reply which was inaudible.

'Bollocks,' Dom hissed.

'Not a valuable client then?'

'No, no.'

Carlyle realized he had to get on with it. 'Alexander.'

'C'mon, John, you know I don't dabble in any of that these days.'

'As I recall,' Carlyle said flatly, 'you never "dabbled". You were one of the most successful dealers in London for a couple of decades at least.'

'Flattery will get you nowhere,' Dom told him.

'I'm just saying. I know that I'm asking for a big favour.'

'Not the first, is it?'

'No,' Carlyle admitted, 'and probably not the last. Then again, I've done my share of favours for you, over the years.'

29

Dom gave a grunt of acknowledgement.

'Under the circumstances, what I am looking for doesn't seem that unreasonable. You were very good at what you did. You can sort us out.'

'I was always professional,' Dom agreed. 'But when you're out of the game, you're out. This is my world now.'

'You must still have plenty of contacts from the old days.'

'A few,' Dom conceded, 'but it's been more than a couple of years now. As you know, not many people survive for long—'

'You were the exception.'

'That's right, I was the exception.' Shifting in his seat, Dom glanced nervously at the door.

Not so much at the door, Carlyle realized, but at what was behind the door. Or, rather, *who* was behind it. This guy Spargo, he wondered, why is he freaking you out so much?

'I had a good run, hell, I had a great run and I got out on my own terms. I wanted to make a clean break and I made a clean break. It's different now.'

'I know, I know. But my old fella really needs some help.' The inspector gestured towards the gallery proper with his thumb. 'A photograph or a painting isn't going to be much use to him.'

'I've got to get on.' Dom pushed himself out of his seat. 'Does Helen know you're here?'

Carlyle nodded. 'It was her idea.'

Standing upright, Dom raised an eyebrow. 'Yeah?'

'It's true. She said it was the obvious solution to the problem.'

'Your wife,' Dom grinned, 'is a very smart woman.'

'She is that,' said Carlyle, with more than a hint of pride. 'And she said that if you don't sort us out, she will take it to Eva.'

'Unfair!' Dom protested.

'I know. But what can I do? Helen calls it the hegemony of the matriarchy. We do what we're told, or else.'

'Okay, okay,' Dom sighed. 'If that's the way it's gonna be, let me make a few enquiries.'

'Thanks.' Carlyle got to his feet.

'How much will Alexander need, d'ya think?'

The inspector stared at his hands. 'No idea. Enough pain relief for maybe three to six months. How much would that be?'

'How the hell should I know? Apart from a couple of the dope smokers, my clients tended to be recreational rather than medicinal users.' A thought popped into Dom's head. 'By the way, dope will be easier to get, and cheaper.'

'No, no, no.' Carlyle realized he hadn't even considered the question of cost; he would worry about that later. 'We are talking about terminal cancer here. This is no time to be fucking about with soft drugs. It's only the best quality Class A we're interested in. He's not going to be spliffing up here for a casual smoke. As the bitter end approaches, I want him coked up to the eyeballs with a smile on his face.'

'Heroin's probably better than coke,' Dom mused. 'Opiates are your best bet for pain relief.'

'Heroin?' That was a bit of a shock. 'I can't really see the old man chasing the dragon.'

'No need. We can probably do tablets.'

Carlyle thought about it for a moment. 'Tablets would be good. Easier for him to take.'

'You really are the dutiful son,' Dom observed.

'Yeah, I think I am. Under the circumstances, isn't this precisely what a dutiful son should do?'

'I suppose so.'

'Isn't it what *you* would do?'

Dom stared at a point on the wall above Carlyle's head. 'My dad's dead.'

Ah. 'Sorry.'

'You knew that, didn't you?'

'Yes, sorry,' Carlyle groaned. 'Me and my big mouth.'

'Don't worry. It was a long time ago now. He wrapped his Lancia around a lamppost in Brixton. It was a shock at the time but at least it's saved me from the type of situation you've got now.'

'There's no good way to go,' Carlyle mused.

'No. And you're right, I should help. Let me see what I can do.'

'Okay.' Carlyle exhaled, relieved. 'How much do you think he could get through in six months?'

'How long is a piece of string?' Dom headed for the door. 'We'll get him started and take it from there. Apart from anything else, you don't want him sitting on a big stash,' he giggled, 'just in case the police were to come calling.'

'Sounds like a plan,' said Carlyle, happy that his friend had finally stepped up to the plate. 'Thanks.'

'No problem,' Dom smiled as he reached for the door handle. 'I'm sure we can sort something out. Just leave it with me.'

FOUR

Carlyle emerged from the back room to find two men standing in the gallery, one towering over the other. They were inspecting one of Dom's photographs in silence. The black and white image showed a small group of people watching impassively as a trio of bulldozers went about demolishing a row of houses. In the foreground, a small child waved a stick while it chased after a dog. Overhead, dark rain clouds gathered ominously.

Fiona had made good on her promise to bolt for lunch, which presumably meant that the two men were not clients or otherwise deserving of her continued attention. The tall guy looked up as the inspector approached. Wearing black jeans and a long leather coat, he had a shaven head and the square frame of a bodybuilder. His expression oozed malice.

Muscle.

Keeping his gaze on the picture, the second man took a step backwards. He was obviously the boss; squat, overweight and balding. He wore a creased, navy pinstripe suit and a cream shirt. A grey tie hung limply around his neck. Even from the best part of six feet away, Carlyle could see that it was badly stained.

Mr Spargo, I presume.

The man yawned as he turned to face Carlyle, inspecting him for a moment before deciding that he was a nobody, unworthy of any further attention.

Dom appeared at Carlyle's shoulder. 'Mr Spargo. Sorry to keep you waiting.'

Spargo lifted a meaty finger and pointed at the photograph he had been inspecting. 'How much is this one?'

'Er,' Dom seemed momentarily thrown by the question. 'Which one is that?'

The bodyguard stepped forward and bent down to read the description on the wall. '*Relocation of Residents on the Golden Sands River.*' Carlyle was surprised to hear a West Coast accent. London seemed so full of Chinese, Russians and French these days that Americans seemed almost exotic by comparison.

'How much?' Spargo repeated.

'Well . . . it depends on the size.'

Spargo pointed again. 'That one.'

'Well, er . . .' Dom grabbed a catalogue from the desk and began flicking through it. There was an awkward pause while he tried to find the correct page. 'Ah, yes, right, Golden River—'

'Golden Sands,' the American heavy corrected him.

'Golden *Sands*, yes, right.' Irritated, Dom glanced up at the image. 'So . . . the one on the wall there is £12,300 plus VAT.'

Spargo let out a low whistle. 'And people pay that? For a photo?' He shot an ironic glance at the bodyguard.

'That's what,' the American mused, 'twenty thousand bucks?'

'Something like that,' Dom agreed.

'That's a lot of cash.' Stepping past Carlyle, Spargo gave Dom a pat on the shoulder. 'Business must be good.'

'The exhibition has been a great success.' The way in which the words came out, Dom sounded almost embarrassed by the admission.

What is going on here? Carlyle shot his friend a quizzical look but Dom, focused on the man in the suit, didn't respond.

'Are you ready for me now?' Spargo asked.

Dom gestured towards the office. 'Please, come in.'

With a grunt, Spargo marched past Dom and into the office. Watching his boss disappear, the bodyguard moved on to inspect the next picture.

A weary look passed across Dom's face. 'I'll see you later, John.'

'Yeah. Thanks for your time.'

'Why don't you take this?' Dom handed over the catalogue. 'Helen might be interested. Alice too, for that matter.'

'Thanks.' Taking the book, Carlyle was surprised by its weight.

'Tell them to come in and say hi sometime. I'd be very interested to see what they think.'

'I will.'

'Good. And I'll be in touch soon over the other thing. I'm sure we can get it sorted out quickly.'

'Okay.' Carlyle watched his friend slip into the back room, closing the door behind him. Opening the catalogue, he checked the price printed on the inside front cover. £40. 'Forty quid,' he muttered. 'Bloody hell!' Shoving it under his arm, he headed for the door. The bodyguard, still engrossed in the exhibition, paid him no heed.

Muttering to herself, Becky Carson inspected her nails, wondering if she might be able to fit a manicure in before her trip to the airport. It was just one more thing to add to her 'to do' list. Becky bridled at the thought of the rising levels of stress she was enduring; life was spinning out of control and she didn't like it. Five yards away stood the person responsible. Hands in pockets, head bowed, Andy Carson stared at his trainers, oblivious to his wife's withering glare.

What a useless lump, Becky thought bitterly. It would have been better if those bloody terrorists had shot *you*, rather than the other way round. Playing the role of the grieving widow for a couple of months would have been a doddle, compared to this.

My husband, the killer.

Wasn't killing people what soldiers were supposed to do?

It wasn't shame she felt, exactly, having her old man banged up for shooting some blokes in cold blood, more a sense of profound annoyance. It was a feeling that had been impossible to shake,

35

ever since that Army cop, Daniel Hunter, had arrived at the house and taken Andy away in handcuffs. The kids had watched in stony silence; Becky had been profoundly pissed off. Walking out of the door, Hunter had handed her a business card, like he was a bloody double-glazing salesman or something. She had wanted to slap him; she had kept the card though. Right now, it was nestling in the bag at her feet. Just in case she ever needed it.

Taking a drag on her Benson & Hedges, Becky tipped back her head and sent a stream of smoke into the dull, grey sky. A hundred yards off to her left, the solitary guard on duty waved a woman in a red hatchback through the gate and into the camp. 'You could probably walk right out of here if you wanted to,' she mused.

'What's the point of that?' Lifting his gaze from his feet, her husband scowled. 'I would get maybe a mile down the road and then they'd pick me up, still stuck in the middle of nowhere. Anyway, they know I won't try anything while you're here. That's why they let us come outside.' He looked around as if enjoying the view. 'Nice to get a bit of fresh air.'

'It's going to rain.' Becky watched the woman pull into the car park and bring the vehicle to a halt. 'You sure you don't want a smoke?'

'Nah.' Andy Carson shook his head. Even though there was no one within fifty yards, he lowered his voice. 'I wouldn't mind a quick shag though.'

Becky made a gagging sound. 'Don't be stupid.'

'We could go back to the cell,' he ventured.

'Dream on.' She ended his faint hopes with a dismissive wave of her nicotine wand.

Carson's face crumpled like a six year old who'd just seen his ice cream fall on to the pavement. For a moment, Becky thought he might actually start to blub, which only made her hate him more.

After a couple of moments, however, he managed to compose himself. 'How are the kids?'

'They're fine.' Becky took a final drag on her cigarette before tossing the stub away. 'Lucinda says my mother is driving her up the wall, which I can well believe. But Liam seems happy enough. I think he's hooked up with that local girl again, so he's not been around the house that much.'

I bet he's getting his end away, Carson thought enviously, the little bugger.

'Mum says it's all fairly quiet.'

Carson nodded. His mother-in-law had taken the children to the family holiday home, near Sitia on the island of Crete, weeks ago now. Even there it was hard to get them away from all the publicity of the court-martial but at least they didn't have a bunch of tabloid hacks standing on their doorstep. The headmaster of their school wasn't very happy about the kids going AWOL, but it wasn't like he could just nip over there and bring them back. 'When are you going over there?'

'I already told you,' Becky said irritably. 'You never bloody listen, do you?'

'I have got rather a lot on my mind at the moment,' he snapped back.

'Jesus!' Becky stomped her foot. It was at times like these that she seemed more like a teenager than Lucinda, her husband thought. 'I leave Gatwick at ten tonight; get in to Heraklion at four in the morning.'

Carson winced. 'Killer.'

'It was all that was available. I need to get out of there or I'm gonna go mad.'

'Yeah.' His attempt to sound sympathetic was feeble, at best. 'Did you speak to the Commander?'

'Yeah.' Becky smiled lecherously. 'I think he fancies me.'

Don't flatter yourself, Carson thought.

'He kept talking to my chest.'

You should stop wearing those push-up bras then. 'What did he say about my request?'

'He says you're allowed your right of ... whatchamacallit ...

37

religious expression the same as everyone else, and he'll see what he can do.'

'Good,' Carson nodded. 'Glad to hear it.'

Sergeant Kelvin Smith stood by the dirty window, a clipboard in one hand, a badly chewed biro – attached to the clipboard by a length of string – in the other. Outside, a group of squaddies wandered past, laughing and joking about something. In the distance, at the entrance to the facility, a freshly laundered Union Jack waved frantically in the strong wind. He had been here almost ten years now. The place never changed; he liked that.

Most of the time.

Extending his arm, Smith tapped a cracked windowpane with the nib of the biro. 'Shouldn't someone have washed these?'

'What?' Private Anastasia Harries stopped picking her nose and frowned.

'The windows.' Tap, tap, tap. 'They're a bloody disgrace. Someone should have been round here with a bucket of water and some shammy leather.'

Harries looked at him blankly. 'Dunno, Sarge, were they supposed to?'

Smith tried not to wince at his colleague's adenoidal Black Country accent. 'Yes, they bloody well were.'

Harries shrugged.

Tutting to himself, Smith turned his attention to the timesheets attached to the clipboard. 'Nothing gets done around here, does it?'

'No, Sarge.' Feeling vaguely guilty, Harries blushed. Staring at the floor, she had a flashback to her not so distant days at Cyril Regis High School in Smethwick; being carpeted by Mr Douglas for smoking in the Rec Room. Mr Douglas had been quite dishy, only twenty-five or something. Old, but not that old. All the girls fancied him, including Anastasia herself. Still, she'd had the shock of all time when she'd seen him on the telly, large as life, earlier in the year. The silly sod had run off to Bulgaria with one of the fifth-formers. End result: two years in jail and a listing on the Sex Offenders Register. His wife must have been hopping mad.

'Harries!'

She looked up to see Smith smear his scrawl across the page. 'Sarge?'

'Wakey, wakey, girl.' The sergeant gestured towards the metal door at the far end of the corridor. 'Have you checked on our special guest?'

Harries nodded. 'Yeah. He's fine, Sarge. Seems to be very relaxed, all things considered. He's treating the place as a holiday camp, if you ask me. Asked could I get him a copy of *Top Gear* magazine.'

'And you told him to fuck right off, I hope.'

Not exactly. 'Yes, Sarge.'

'Good.' Smith carefully hooked the clipboard on to the nail that protruded from the brickwork and checked his watch. 'Where's young Turpin – any idea? Run off to join the circus, or the Foreign Legion perhaps? I know which I think would be the most appropriate, given his so-called skill set.'

Harries raised her eyes to the ceiling. Once the sergeant got started, he could go on a bit. 'Rob might be running a bit behind schedule,' she ventured. 'You know what he's like.'

'Always bloody late,' Smith harrumphed. 'Why he ever joined the Army I'll never know.'

'No, Sarge.'

'He'd be better off stacking shelves in Aldi.'

'Yes, Sarge.'

'Anyway,' Smith belatedly realized he was sounding like an old fart, 'you go and get a cuppa. I can hold the fort until the useless sod turns up.'

'Thanks. It's been like Piccadilly Circus in here today.' Harries gestured back down the corridor. 'The guy has been holding court. People coming in and out all the time.'

'With the press all over it, the brass are scared of him. For the moment, he can have all the visitors he wants.'

'More work for us.'

'Not for much longer. Mr Carson should be out of here in a couple of days. We'll get him off our hands for good this time.'

Harries scratched her nose. 'Won't he be back here to do his sentence?'

Once again, Smith tried not to cringe at his colleague's whining Birmingham accent. 'Nah. The MCTC only takes people doing a stretch of two years or less. He's going to get a lot more than that – life maybe – so he'll be straight into a regular prison. Once that happens, and the media interest dies down and life around here goes back to normal, no one will give much of a fuck about Andy sodding Carson when he's sitting in a prison in bloody Wales or somewhere.'

'His wife isn't going to like that,' Harries observed.

'From what I've seen of Becky Carson, there's lots of things she doesn't like.'

'Tell me about it,' said Harries with feeling. 'It's not right that she's been allowed unlimited access to see 'im. She swans around here like she owns the ruddy place.'

'I'll be glad to see the back of both of them.'

'She spouts the Service Custody rules like she's learned them off by heart. Marched right into the Commander's office this morning and demanded that her husband be allowed to practise his religion.'

'Do what?'

'He's to be allowed to go to the chapel to give his confession, would you believe it?'

'I didn't know he was a Catholic.'

'Well, apparently he is. Maybe he found God when he realized he could be facing the rest of his natural behind bars.'

'I suppose we should be grateful that he hasn't converted to Islam.' Smith's eyes narrowed. 'The whole thing sounds like a scam to me.'

'Why would it be a scam?' Harries objected. 'It's not like it's going to do him much good now, is it?'

'Mm. Maybe not.'

'Whether it is or not, Father Thornton is due to hear his confession at four o'clock. We have to present Carson at the chapel at no later than five to.'

'Why can't he do it in there?' Smith gestured over his shoulder.

'Come again?'

'Why can't we just escort Father Thornton to Carson's cell, rather than have to traipse the bugger all the way over to the other side of the camp?'

'Don't ask me,' Harries replied, starting down the corridor, heading towards the canteen, 'I just do what I'm told.'

'I bet this is gonna take a while.' Private Rob Turpin slid along the pew, leaving space for Anastasia Harries to take a seat.

'Why's that?' Not wishing to expose herself to Turpin's wandering hands, which were almost as legendary as his time-keeping, Private Harries chose to stay on her feet. Placing a hand on the end of a pew, she looked back down the length of the MCTC Ecumenical Chapel. Built in 1964, the low brick structure had been due to be knocked down, until the local council had slapped a preservation order on it, much to everyone's surprise. This was the first time that Harries, a confirmed agnostic, had ever been inside. She knew, however, that the various services on offer were popular with many of the inmates, keen to exploit any opportunity to get out of their cells.

Staring at the cross-shaped blue glass window at the far end of the building, above the central altar, she wished she hadn't scoffed that bacon sandwich at speed in the canteen. She hadn't been really hungry and now the food sat uncomfortably in her stomach, waiting to be properly digested.

'He's got a lot to confess, hasn't he?' Turpin pointed to the confessional boxes off to his left, underneath the sloping gull-wing roof.

41

'I suppose.'

'For sure.' Turpin pulled a smartphone from the breast pocket of his tunic and began tapping away on the keys.

'I wouldn't let Smithy see you playing on that, if I were you.'

'The sergeant's probably already on his first pint in the Dog and Duck down the road,' Turpin grunted.

Harries had to acknowledge that the little scrote had a point. Kelvin Smith liked his ale, whatever time of day it was.

'And even if he's not, he's hardly gonna sneak up on me in here, is he?' Turpin nodded towards the entrance to the chapel with the back of his head. 'Keep an eye on the door.'

Harries was miffed that Turpin felt he could tell her what to do, but she complied anyway.

An explosion came from Turpin's phone. 'Fuck! I'm outta lives.'

'Shame.'

'I'll have to buy some more credits.' He looked up from the screen. 'Do you think he's guilty?'

'Carson? He's certainly guilty of being stupid,' Harries huffed. 'Imagine shooting someone when you know you're being recorded on a bloody helmet cam. That's not very clever, is it?' As far as she could see, this was pretty much the consensus view among the ordinary troops when it came to 'Soldier A' and his court-martial. No one was particularly bothered by the idea that he had wasted a couple of terrorists. Being dumb enough to allow yourself to be videoed doing so was another matter entirely.

'No,' Turpin conceded, 'I suppose not. Everybody does it these days though, don't they? It's the digital age. Cameras are everywhere. Ubiquitous.'

Ubiquitous? Who would have thought in a million years that Turpin knew a word like 'ubiquitous'? Maybe the boy had hidden depths. Very well hidden. Harries giggled at her own joke.

'What's so funny?'

'Nothing.'

'Maybe he just forgot about it.'

'Forgot about it?' Harries asked. 'How does that work? You

shoot two guys to death and then just let one of your team wander off with the evidence? Come on.'

'I heard that the Redcaps only found it by accident,' Turpin pointed out. 'They came across it when they were investigating something else entirely. The bloke who shot it tried to erase the video, but the stupid sod made a right pig's ear of the whole thing. Carson was dead unlucky. It was just Sod's Law.'

'All the more reason he should have made sure it had been deleted,' Anastasia. 'That way he would have been covered.'

'Schoolboy error,' Turpin agreed, returning his attention to the screen.

The door at the far end of the chapel opened. Harries watched as two uniformed men entered and began walking towards them. One of them had a small day sack slung over his shoulder. Turpin quickly shoved the phone back into his pocket and slid out of the aisle. Taking up a position behind Harries, he whispered in her ear: 'They don't look like they're here to light a candle, do they?'

'Sshh!' Harries waved him away as she acknowledged the new arrivals. As they got closer, she could see that each man had two pips on his shoulders: lieutenants.

The shorter of the two stepped in front of Harries.

'Where is the prisoner?'

'He's in the confessional, sir,' Harries said quickly, cursing inwardly that she had forgotten to offer a salute to her superior officers.

Neither man seemed in the slightest perturbed by the breach in etiquette.

'How long has he been in there?' said the shorter man. Under his cap, his blond curls reached down dangerously close to the collar of his jacket.

You need a haircut. 'I don't know,' said Harries.

'There's no time-limit on these things,' Turpin tittered, 'when you are cleansing your immortal soul.'

Bloody idiot. Harries aimed an elbow at his ribs but caught only fresh air. The shorter man glared at Turpin.

43

'Stand to attention, Private!'

'Sir!' Turpin barked, clicking his heels together.

Not waiting to be told, Harries followed suit. Head back, chin up, she watched out of the corner of her eye as the taller guy shrugged off the backpack and dropped it on to one of the pews. Bending over, he unzipped the bag and rummaged inside. Harries' eyes grew wide as she saw him pull out a black semi-automatic. Attached to the end of the barrel was a silver silencer.

Disbelieving, Harries watched the man lift the gun and point it at her chest. Instinctively, she took a step backwards, forcing Turpin to jump out of her way.

'Fuck me!' He let out a girlish giggle. 'That's a Glock 17 Gen 4 with a titanium silencer.'

Harries felt her heart-rate go into overdrive. How do you know this shit? she wondered.

'Is it?' The gunman looked at his colleague. 'I can't say I've noticed.'

'I've always wanted one of those,' Turpin said.

The gunman laughed. 'Maybe I'll let you have a go later.'

'Cool,' Turpin chirped.

No, Anastasia thought, it's not cool. It's not cool at all.

FIVE

'Forgiveness must come from within. You must forgive yourself, so that others may forgive you. Only in that way can we allow the quality of mercy to triumph.'

'Yes, Father.' Sitting in the gloom of the confessional, Andy Carson tuned out the gentle drone of the priest coming from the other side of the screen. Tilting his head towards the door, he picked out the sound of a familiar voice in the chapel outside. There was a short discussion, followed by two gentle but distinct thuds. Carson smiled.

Game on.

'Are you still there, my son?' Still focused on the quality of mercy, Father Frank Thornton didn't seem to be aware of the developments beyond the confessional.

'Sorry, Father, what were you saying?'

'Is there anything else you wanted to confess, my son?'

Carson rubbed his hand across the stubble on his chin. 'No, I don't think so. What about you?'

There was a pause. Carson imagined the priest frowning on the other side of the screen.

'Me?'

'Yes.'

More silence.

'Why would I want to do that?' These bloody soldiers, smart alecs and chancers the lot of them. What did he have to confess to any of them? The priest stopped just short of letting his irritation show. 'That's not actually how this works, Andrew, as I'm sure you know.'

Carson listened to the approaching footsteps on the stone floor. 'I just thought that you might want to take advantage of this last chance to unburden yourself.'

'Last chance? But—' The door to the compartment flew open before he could finish his sentence. Looking up, Frank Thornton barely had time to cross himself before setting off to meet his Maker.

Stepping out of the booth, Carson allowed himself a stretch as he watched the men in the lieutenants' uniforms drag the bodies of the guards between the pews.

Job done, the taller of the two men picked up a rucksack from one of the benches and looked over at Carson. 'You okay, Andy?'

Carson took a quick peek inside the confessional. The late Father Thornton was still sitting on the bench, with his head slumped against the latticework of the screen, as if he had been caught listening to a particularly lengthy and boring confession. The expression on the priest's face betrayed neither surprise nor dismay. A trickle of blood ran from his temple all the way down to his jaw. It had already begun to dry.

Carson crossed himself. 'Remember,' he muttered, 'you must forgive yourself, so that others may forgive you.'

'Andy?'

Stepping away from the confessional, he closed the door with the toe of his boot. 'You were a bit quick on the trigger there, Ryan.'

Ryan Fortune dropped the Glock into the day sack. Zipping up the bag, he asked: 'How do you reckon that?'

'You shot him too quick.' Carson turned to his liberator and grinned. 'He didn't get the chance to give me my penance.'

'You'll definitely need to do a few more Hail Marys and How's Your Fathers now.'

'I suppose so.'

'Anyway, there'll be plenty of time for all that later.' Hoisting the bag over his shoulder, Fortune turned and headed towards the door. 'After all, I know how important your faith is to you.'

'Bless you, my son,' Carson cooed, echoing the sarcasm in Fortune's voice.

'Save it for later, Andy,' Fortune repeated. He turned and headed towards the door. 'C'mon. We need to get going.'

Sitting on the sofa, Helen flicked through the Mega-Dams catalogue. 'This stuff is really good.'

Carlyle, trying to veg out in front of *Sky Sports News*, struggled to muster a response.

'I might go and have a look at the exhibition.'

'Dom will be happy to see you. Just don't let him sell you one. The prices are eye-watering. Even the bloody catalogue cost forty quid.'

His wife raised an eyebrow. 'You didn't buy it, did you?'

'Nah. Dom gave it to me.'

'That was nice of him.'

'Mm.' With the TV on mute, the inspector focused on the SSN ticker, sighing as an update on Fulham's latest injury worries rolled across the bottom of the screen. The football club was having a particularly poor season and relegation was a real possibility. Carlyle felt torn between a sense of guilt at not going to more games and relief that he didn't have to endure the torture of watching ninety minutes of failure, regularly repeated, leading to an inevitable, painful conclusion. He felt physically unable to subject himself to such masochism any more. A line from The Wire bounced around in his brain: *You can't lose if you do not play.* The older he got, the more he tried to make that his mantra.

Alice wandered in from the kitchen, mobile phone glued to her ear. 'That sounds very nice,' she was saying blandly, 'but I just can't make it. I'm going out with Edward that night.' Without acknowledging her parents, she continued her conversation, slipping out of the opposite door into the hallway. Carlyle waited until he heard her bedroom door slam shut.

'Edward? Who's Edward?' He could just about make out the strains of the Ramones' 'Pet Sematary' coming from behind Alice's door. 'I thought she was supposed to be going out with a kid called . . .'

'Oliver,' Helen reminded him. 'Yes, she is.'

'So who is Edward?'

'Edward,' Helen explained, turning a page, 'is her *imaginary* boyfriend.' She looked at her husband, to see if he understood. However, the concept was beyond him. 'Alice is stepping out with Oliver, but she wants to keep it low-key. When another boy asks her out, she uses this Edward as an excuse. He goes to Magwitch Secondary in Islington, by the way, and is a black belt in karate.'

'Who? Oliver or Edward?'

'Edward.'

'Good for him,' Carlyle responded, still more than a little confused. 'And how often does this imaginary squeeze get wheeled out to fob off real live boys?'

'About once a week, as far as I can see.' Helen placed the catalogue on the arm of the sofa and snuggled up to him. 'Alice is a good-looking girl. And very popular. She has quite a few suitors.'

'Mm.' Keeping one eye on SSN, Carlyle placed an arm around her shoulders.

Helen dropped a hand on his chest. 'I would have thought you would approve.'

'I do . . . I think.' An uncomfortable idea popped into his head. 'Did you ever have an imaginary boyfriend?'

'Me?' Helen chuckled. 'Sadly not. I wish I'd thought of it, back in the day.' Sensing Carlyle's discomfort, she mimed conjuring up a distant nirvana in her imagination. 'Paolo. A Vespa-driving fashion design student from Milan.'

'A bit less credible than a kid from Magwitch Secondary,' Carlyle scoffed.

Helen gave him a gentle poke in the stomach. 'A girl can

dream. Anyway, I think Paolo would have been very handy . . . especially when you came sniffing around.'

'Ha bloody ha.'

Squirming round, she gave him a peck on the cheek. 'Only joking, sweetie. No imaginary boyfriend could ever hope to be a match for you.'

'Glad to hear it,' Carlyle mumbled, only partially mollified.

'Anyway,' said Helen, moving the conversation smartly on, 'it's good that Dom can help Alexander out.'

'He's going to try. We'll have to see if he actually delivers.'

'Still, it's good of him to make the effort.'

'I suppose so.' An advert appeared on the TV. Grabbing the remote, Carlyle found the BBC's News Channel. A young female reporter was standing in the road, in front of a large metal gate, grinning away as she talked into the camera at a rapid rate. Behind her was a sign that said *MCTC: AUTHORIZED PERSONNEL ONLY*. The strapline on the story read: MILITARY DEATHS. 'What's all that about?'

'Dunno,' Helen yawned. 'More bad news.' She pointed to the reporter, still gabbling away on the screen. 'I just don't understand why they are always so cheery about it.'

'It is a bit ghoulish,' Carlyle agreed.

'So why do we watch it?' Releasing herself from his embrace, Helen struggled to her feet. 'I think I'll have a bath. Want to join me?'

Carlyle smiled. 'Why not?' Switching the off button, he watched the screen go black before getting up and following her out of the room.

Mel switched off the TV as Daniel walked into the room. 'Are the kids asleep?'

'Just about,' Daniel nodded. 'At last.'

'They're just excited to see you.'

'I know.' His heart soared and sank at the same time. 'But it's a school night, and—'

She shuffled along the sofa to make some space. 'Come and sit down.'

The living room was dark, save for the light from the lava lamp Mel had bought from the market at Brick Lane when they'd first arrived in London. While he was distracted by the red blobs floating around inside, she picked up his wine glass from the coffee table. 'Here, have another drink.'

'Thanks.' Taking the glass, he saw that she had refilled it almost to the brim. 'Are you trying to get me drunk?'

Grinning, Mel said, 'It's always worked in the past.'

'It's like that, is it?' He carefully lowered himself down beside her. Outside, the omnipresent background hum of traffic noise was interrupted by the harsh sound of a siren. The noise got louder until the emergency vehicle stopped somewhere on the street outside. Daniel made to get up, but his wife placed a hand on his arm.

'Leave it, Dan. That's someone else's drama.'

'Good point.' He settled back into his seat and took a sip of the wine. 'Ahh! Not bad. What is that?'

'Some Chilean red or other. It was on special offer at Tesco.'

'Nice.' A couple of glasses of wine, on top of two beers in Giraffe, meant that he was nicely relaxed. The central heating had made the room over-warm and he was beginning to feel a little drowsy. Laying his head back on a cushion, he closed his eyes. 'The kids did well in the restaurant.'

'They're always good.' Mel lifted her feet and draped her legs across his lap. 'Even when you're not here.'

'Mm. Do you think they miss me? When I'm not here?'

'Of course they miss you.'

'I'm away a lot.'

'They know that it's just the job.'

Opening his eyes, Daniel took another mouthful of the wine. 'I was thinking about that.'

Swinging her feet back on to the floor, Mel sat up. 'About what?'

He took a deep breath. 'About the job. I was thinking it's time

50

to pack it in – do something else. If I don't do it now, it will be too late. Every time I come back after a couple of weeks away, I can see changes in the kids. If I leave it too much longer, they'll be grown up and I'll have blown it. I really have to find something that doesn't mean being away from home.'

She was watching him carefully now. 'Like what?'

'I was thinking maybe a teacher?'

'A teacher?' Mel stifled a giggle.

He frowned. 'Why not?'

'Sorry, love. But you left school at sixteen. How many exams did you get?'

They both knew the answer to that one: none.

'I can get retraining as part of the exit process. I've got enough time under my belt that they'll give me a decent lump sum and pay for me to go to college. And I'll still have my pension.' The words tumbling out of his mouth made it sound like he'd given it some serious thought. The reality was that the idea had only just popped into his head while sitting in the park, earlier in the day.

'It's a bit early to be thinking about your pension.' Mel reached down and recovered her own wine glass. 'That's a long way off yet.'

'I know. But you've got to think all these things through. The point is, we'll keep the pension if I leave. Financially, we won't lose out.'

'You've really thought about this, haven't you?' She began turning the idea over in her head.

'They're desperate to get rid of people.'

'Not someone like you, surely?'

'They're happy to wave bye-bye to anyone, if they can get the costs down.'

'Okay, so if you did do it . . .' Her voice edged higher and he could tell that the idea was beginning to excite her. 'What would you teach?'

'Er . . .' His gaze fell on the fat tome sitting underneath the coffee table. Max Hastings' history of World War Two – *All Hell Let Loose* – had been a Christmas present from his mother. He had been meaning to start it for the past two and a half years. 'Maybe history.'

'History? Like Margaret Thatcher and stuff?'

'I think it started a bit before that,' he grinned.

'Mm.' Mel looked dubious. 'I was never any good at that at school. It was dead boring.'

'I could make a decent history teacher – bring it to life. Make it exciting for the kids.'

Mel appeared less than convinced.

'Don't you think?'

'Well . . .'

In the hallway, the phone started to ring.

'Who the hell is calling at this time of night?' Mel grumbled.

'Your mother?'

'Hardly.' She gave him a gentle push. 'Go and answer it quick, before it wakes up the kids.'

Colonel Trevor Naylor didn't waste any words. 'Carson's escaped.'

'What?' Hunter coughed. He didn't want to sound under the influence while talking to his CO. 'What happened?'

'He was sprung from the MCTC just after 4.15 this afternoon.'

'Fuck.'

'My sentiments exactly. They left three bodies in their wake – two young soldiers and a priest. The place has been locked down but it's a proverbial case of shutting the stable door—'

'Yes.' Hunter stuck his free hand into the back pocket of his jeans. The anonymous letter was still there.

Lay off Andy Carson. We know where you live.

The message seemed rather more significant now.

'The media are going to go crazy over all this,' complained Naylor.

That wouldn't be my main concern right now. 'Yes.'

'A driver should be outside your front door in the next twenty minutes. You need to get up there right now.'

Hunter lowered his voice, in case Mel had started taking an interest in the conversation. 'What about the Leatherneck?'

'Smith will have to take care of that on his own.'

'But—'

'Look, Dan . . .'

Hunter sighed. Whenever Naylor called him 'Dan' it meant that he was being ordered to jump into a swimming pool filled with shit.

'This is a potential disaster of career-altering proportions,' Naylor went on.

'Yeah, I can see that – but not for us, surely?'

Naylor let out a brittle laugh and Hunter wondered if he had been drinking himself. 'If we don't get Carson back – and quick – there will be more than enough to go round on this one.'

'True enough.' Suddenly, a trip to Afghanistan was looking very appealing indeed. 'But why me?' Hunter reeled off a couple of names of possible alternative investigators.

'They're busy,' was the curt response.

'I thought—'

'The car will be there in twenty minutes,' Naylor repeated. 'No one knows Carson better than you. Give me a call when you get up there. Find the bastard. And find him quick.'

Hunter listened to the dial tone for a moment before putting the handset back on the cradle. Turning, he saw Mel standing in the doorway. She had the two-thirds-empty wine bottle in one hand, her glass in the other.

'I take it that wasn't your mum?'

'No.'

'Work?'

He nodded.

'This teaching idea is beginning to make a lot of sense.'

'Glad to hear it,' he grinned, relieved that she was being so cool about it.

She flicked her eyes towards the bedroom. 'When I was in the fifth form, I had a fantasy about bedding one of the teachers.'

Hunter's heart sank. 'There's a car coming for me in twenty minutes.'

Gesturing for him to follow, Mel started down the corridor, slightly unsteady on her feet. 'We'd better not hang around then.'

SIX

Six years at university, an MBA from the Technical University in Padua and then another twelve years working like a slave in this grim city where all it did was rain. And for what? Balthazar Quant stared morosely at the number he'd written down on the pad in front of him and felt a very real stab of physical pain in his intestines. His estimated net worth, down to the nearest thousand dollars. Underlining it did not make it any bigger. Even taking into account a number of relatively optimistic assumptions, the fucking number was a complete joke.

Balthazar had always been a man with a plan. Arriving in London, that plan had been to squirrel away twenty million dollars and retire to somewhere far more pleasant – Tuscany, perhaps, or maybe Switzerland. Five years ago, he had massaged the figure down to ten million. Now, forcing himself to confront the figure scrawled on the page, he was forced to admit that he was nowhere close. Worse, the numbers were going backwards.

Tapping his pencil on the pad, he stared at the name embossed along the side. The gold capitals stood out against a black background, proclaiming the name of the firm's latest set of legal advisers. They were getting through lawyers at an alarming rate. The latest advisers were one of the so-called 'Magic Circle', home to some of the best legal minds in London. Balthazar let out a hollow laugh; their fees certainly were amazing enough. With eight outstanding suits in three different jurisdictions, legal costs were one of the many reasons that MCS, Macroom Castlebar Salle, was haemorrhaging cash. Almost £150,000 in billings in the last month. And what they did get for their money?

A pencil.

A lousy fucking pencil.

'Well?' Gerry Durkan stood at the window on the thirty-first floor, watching a jet that had just taken off from nearby City airport rising towards him. Most of the competition had based themselves in the West End, but Gerry preferred an office in the adult Legoland of the East.

Apart from anything else, the sense of irony always made him smile. The woman he had once tried to kill was now in the ground and he was the closest thing she had left to a disciple. Being here, in her spiritual home, gave Gerry a buzz that he'd just never get in Mayfair. The Docklands was Margaret Thatcher's Gotham City. Even the building he was standing in bore her name. It was one of a series of seven huge tower blocks that some megalomaniac property developer was building in anticipation of London's latest growth spurt.

And, almost as important as appealing to his sense of humour, the rents were much cheaper than in the West End.

'Well . . .' Quant stabbed his notepad with the pencil and the lead promptly snapped. With a sigh, he let it bounce off the pad and roll across the boardroom table.

Watching the plane pass in front of him, so close that he could almost reach out and touch it, Durkan started listening to Elvis Costello in his head. The vista in front of him disappeared as he focused on a video in his head of Elvis singing 'Tramp the Dirt Down', articulating each word with such venom that you could see the spittle flying from his mouth.

Oh, the passion! That was what being young was all about. Losing that passion was the first stage of the dying process.

A small tremor of never quite forgotten hatred rippled deliciously through his body while Durkan waited patiently for Balthazar to come up with a half-decent response to his query.

That was the problem with MBAs – so-called Masters of Business Adminstration – they could never give you a simple answer to a simple question. Everything had to be over-engineered to the *nth* degree. It was a wonder they managed to make it out of bed in the morning.

Fortunately, patience was something that Gerry had mastered over the years. These days, he liked to think of himself as something of a Zen Master. There was hardly a relaxation, meditation or well-being retreat within fifty miles of London that he had not tried out in the last decade or so. Of course, the twelve years spent in Long Kesh, five of them in solitary, were probably a contributing factor to his never-ending search for peace and tranquillity. So too was the ageing process. Pushing sixty, it was a long time since he had been able to tap into the reserves of energy and hate that had driven him as a young man.

Whatever the reasons, Gerry Durkan was now one mellow fucker. He had trained his brain to stay calm in the face of any kind of frustration, upset or provocation. Which, right now, from Balthazar's point of view, was just as well. The boy wouldn't be much use on the slopes of Gstaad without his feckin' kneecaps.

'The numbers are only provisional . . .'

'Yes, yes, I understand that.'

'But redemptions last month were slightly up on the month before, at £28.7 million.'

'Net or gross?'

'Gross. But there's not much difference. Inflows were negligible, just under £300,000.'

'Three hundred grand?' Gerry watched the reflection of his grimacing face in the bulletproof, earthquakeproof window. 'That's less than *nothing*.'

Head bowed, Balthazar did not move to correct the factual inaccuracy.

'What the feck are the sales team *doing*?'

Even a Zen Master has his limits.

'Some of them are on the road. And you know how it's been

when people saw what the bonuses were like, a load of them walked.'

'No one got a bonus,' Gerry muttered, 'not even me.'

Not that you needed one, given you pocketed £12 million from special dividends and consultancy fees. Balthazar kept that thought to himself. Picking up a sheet of A4 paper from the desk, he stared at the row of numbers that the Chief Financial Officer had reluctantly given him the night before. 'What we expect to see going forward—'

'Bottom line,' Durkan growled, finally turning to face his associate. 'Just gimme the bottom line.'

'The bottom line is that, on current projections, Macroom Castlebar Salle faces a funding shortfall of £183.2 million by the beginning of next year.'

Point two? thought Durkan. How the feck do you calculate the point two?

'That is based on the expectation of continued redemptions and also a recognition that there are a number of obligations falling due, notably the next tranche of the £105 million we are contracted to provide to the Hydra SPV.'

Which I am on the hook for personally, Gerry thought glumly. With the benefit of hindsight, the Special Purpose Vehicle had been a mistake. Getting into bed with a bunch of Indian spivs who were involved in everything from trading gold and diamonds to developing infrastructure projects in Africa and the Middle East had been somewhat risky; which was a Zen way of saying that the SPV had been a disasstrous clusterfuck from day one. It was the sucking chest wound that would bleed him dry if he didn't manage to come up with a way to close it down quickly.

Gerry knew that this was a mess of his own making. He had gotten way too greedy. And with the £££ signs flashing in his eyes, he had forgotten the number one rule of business: *always gamble with someone else's money.*

'We're in a hole,' Balthazar observed.

'I can see that.'

'We're not the only hedge fund to be feeling the pain at the moment. Investor redemptions caused Boson Briggs to close most of its funds last week.'

'I saw that.' Head bowed, Durkan paced the carpet. 'But we are not going to go belly up. I won't allow it. I can't.' That was true enough. Closing up shop and retreating to his mansion in Epping to count his money and lick his wounds was one thing, but Gerry knew that if he closed up now, he would be penniless, bankrupt. An image of himself closing out his days, a broken old fella sitting in a freezing bedsit above the Sultan's Fish Bar on Carrickfergus High Road flashed through his brain.

No, no, no!

'It will not happen.'

Balthazar continued to look gloomy. 'I spoke to Bianca earlier.'

'Oh, yes?' Gerry's face brightened at the mention of MCS's Chief Marketing Officer. 'Where is she?'

Balthazar mentioned the name of a city that Durkan had never heard of.

'Eh? Where the hell's that?'

'Indonesia.'

'Indonesia?' Gerry frowned, genuinely confused. 'What's she doing in Indonesia?'

'What do you think? Looking for investors for you.'

Okay, Gerry thought, Indonesia. Fine. The global economy and all that. He wasn't sure he could find the place on a map, but what the hell. Presumably they had money there, or Bianca wouldn't have gotten on the plane. That woman could sniff out money a thousand miles away. 'And?'

'Early days.'

'Early days. Meanwhile, we're losing almost thirty million a *month.*'

'Maybe . . . you could go and talk to Nat.'

Nathanial Ridley, scion of the Ridley Cranes empire, had inherited his father's portfolio when the old man had unexpectedly keeled over at the blackjack table in the Caspian Casino on

Chelfont Square. MCS had been looking after £200 million of Daddy's investments at the time.

'*You* go and talk to him,' Gerry snorted. 'The boy's an idiot.' He thought back to the old days, when he could have gone round with a baseball bat. That would have done the job. These days, he had to play by different rules. 'How much has he cashed in already?'

'Almost half. He's taking it out as quickly as he can.'

'Well,' Gerry sighed, 'you go and talk to him if you want, but I think it's a waste of time.'

'Maybe Joe could have a word?'

Gerry raised an eyebrow. Joseph Isaacs, his security consultant, was not the kind of guy you put in front of investors . . . not unless they owed you money. 'Why?' A measure of hope crept into his voice. 'Has he got something on Nat that we could use?' Over the years, Joe had proved a dab hand at ferreting out embarrassing information on clients that could be deployed in support of his fundraising efforts. Gerry liked to see him as the company's Black Ops division.

'Not as far as I know,' Balthazar said lamely.

'Shame,' Gerry muttered. 'You almost got my hopes up there.'

'We need to do something.' It was the whine of a man who had never once in his life got his hands dirty.

'You reckon? God knows what I'd do without an MBA as my right-hand man.' Gerry tutted in mock dismay. 'I would doubtless be losing even more money than I am already.'

Balthazar looked at the number on the pad showing his tiny net worth and stifled a sob. 'There's got to be some kind of Plan B.'

There was a polite knock at the door. Gerry turned to see Delia Sansom, his Executive Assistant, poke her head inside the room. Even from five yards away, it was clear that she looked pale and exhausted. Gerry shook his head. Despite being easily the wrong side of forty, the woman sure liked to party. Hanging on the door for dear life, it looked as if she might retch on the carpet.

Gulping some air, Delia waited for her nausea to pass.

The Zen Master focused on his own breathing.

'I've got a call for you, Mr Durkan,' she said eventually. 'They didn't give a name.'

'That's fine.'

Balthazar raised an eyebrow. When did Gerry Durkan ever take a call without knowing who it was on the other end of the line?

'They said that you were expecting it, but there's nothing in the day book.'

'That's fine,' Gerry repeated. 'I'll take it.' He gestured towards the star-shaped telephone sitting in the middle of the table. It looked like a bit of kit that had been pinched from the *Starship Enterprise*. 'You can put it through to me in here.'

'Of course.' The secretary made a better show of hiding her surprise than Balthazar had done. 'Will do.'

'And get me some coffee, please. Black.'

'The Ethiopian or the Costa Rican?'

He couldn't have told the difference between the two if his life had depended on it. Still, Gerry weighed the question carefully before plumping for the Ethiopian. 'As strong as you like.'

'Yes, of course.' Delia tried to smile through her hangover, not quite able to manage it, before retreating behind the door.

Turning to Balthazar, Gerry said. 'I need to take this. Are we done here?'

'Er, yes.' Not used to being summarily dismissed in such a fashion, Balthazar hesitated in his seat.

'Good, good.' Gerry waved him away as the conference phone began to ring. 'We can talk later. Let me know if there are any developments . . . positive developments.' Reaching across the table, Gerry pulled the phone towards him and hit the receive button. 'Hold on a sec, Delia.' He watched Balthazar belatedly lift his ass from the chair, gather up his papers and slink away. 'Okay, put them through. And don't forget the coffee.'

'Yes, Mr Durkan. Putting you through now.'

Balthazar had left a broken pencil on the table. Grabbing it, Gerry tossed it in the direction of the bin, punching his fist in the air when it bounced on the rim and fell inside.

'Gerry.'

Gerry? Why couldn't they call him Mr Durkan, like everybody else? Was that such a big thing to ask? 'Yeah, I'm here. Did everything go okay?'

'Did you not see the news?'

'No.' Flipping open a compartment on the top of the desk, he picked out a TV remote and began flicking through a succession of news channels on the 55-inch plasma screen at the far end of the room. By the looks of things, it was shaping up to be a very boring news day: flooding in the provinces; the Archbishop of Canterbury moaning about the evils of capitalism; pro-democracy protests somewhere or other. The sort of stuff that failed to excite even the most hardened news junkie.

Finally alighting on one of the business channels, Gerry hit the 'mute' button. On the screen, a dour blonde previewed the US employment figures, which would come later in the day. They were forecast to be mediocre, at best. 'Looks like you didn't make it on to CNBC,' he observed drily.

'CNBC?'

'Never mind.' Delia reappeared with a mug bearing the legend *SHOOT TO KILL*, along with a small plate containing four Jaffa Cakes. Gerry mouthed '*Thank you,*' stuffing one of the cakes into his mouth while he waited for her to leave. Chewing quickly, he swallowed before speaking again into the phone. 'So, did it all go according to plan?'

'More or less.'

More or less? 'What does—' Stopping himself, Gerry realized that he didn't want to know. Changing tack, he asked, 'Are you guys ready to go?'

'Good and ready,' came the firm response.

'Fine.' Gerry took a sip of his coffee and winced with pleasure. Acutely bitter and scalding hot, it was just the way he liked it. Delia might be a bit of a dipso, but she knew how to make a decent cup of coffee which, after all, was 90 per cent of the job. 'The timetable remains unchanged. You have everything you need?'

'Yes.'

'Good. Let me know when it's done.'

'Will do.'

'We have to move quickly.'

'We will. We are very comfortable with the timetable.'

A seed of doubt began to sprout in his mind. 'Are you sure you've got everything nailed down?'

'Don't worry about us, Gerry. We're all *very* focused.'

'Mm.' He chewed his bottom lip, running through in his mind the various different ways in which they could fuck this up or, worse, screw him over.

Not very Zen.

He exhaled. To hell with it, it was too late to worry about all that now.

A low chuckle came out of the telephone speaker, as if the man on the other end of the line was reading his thoughts. 'Nervous?'

'Me? Hardly.'

'No, I suppose not. The great Gerry Durkan. Never lost it, eh? Still got the old skill sets.'

I bloody hope so, Gerry thought. 'Yeah.'

'Don't you wish you were coming with us tonight?'

Yeah. 'We've all got our jobs to do.'

'That's right. Quite the team we are. And to think, forty years ago we would have been trying to kill each other.'

Were you even born then? 'Times change.'

'Yes, they do. It's all the same game though.'

'That it is.'

'Good to get the old blood racing.'

'Just stay focused.'

'We will.'

'Okay. Good luck.' Gerry ended the call with a stab of his

finger. Plan B was finally swinging into action. To his surprise, he felt a shiver of excitement, the like of which he hadn't experienced for decades. There was a jolt in his chest as if he'd just done a line of speed. 'That cheeky bastard is right,' he said to himself. 'This is going to be fun.'

SEVEN

'Hey, they've announced the release date for the new *Grand Theft Auto*. That's a result!'

'Good to know.'

'Haven't you played *GTA*? It's fucking brilliant.'

'Games are for kids.' Ryan Fortune tossed his mobile into the plastic bag on the table. Like everything else in the bag, the phone and its sim card would be destroyed and dumped in a drain, en route to the job.

'Don't be so boring.'

'Andy, we've just popped three people for *real*. Why would I want to shoot people in a game?'

'It's just not as much fun in real life,' Carson reflected, 'as it is in the game.'

'You should know,' said Fortune glumly.

'I'm gonna pre-order it.'

'That might not be so easy,' Fortune said quietly, 'where you're going.'

'What do you mean?' Carson looked up from his copy of *T3*, genuinely confused. 'You can get *GTA* in Greece, I would have thought.' He dropped his head back into the magazine. 'If not, I'll get it on Amazon.'

'For fuck's sake,' Fortune said, exasperated. 'You are gonna have to lie low for ever, sunshine. At the very least, for the next few years. In the meantime, the villa in Crete is out.'

'But that's where Becky's taken the kids.'

'And they should be getting a visit from the local plod, right about now. Use your loaf, son. That's the first place they'll look for you.' He watched impassively as the penny slowly dropped. 'It's off-limits.'

'So what's the plan then?'

'Watch this space.'

'I don't want that damn cop coming after me.'

'Hunter? Don't worry about him.' Fortune's face hardened. 'He's got a family, kids. He won't put them at risk just to nail you.'

'He did last time.'

'This time will be different.'

'I bloody hope so,' Carson muttered. 'The stupid bastard just couldn't leave things alone. If he'd looked the other way, we could have deleted that video properly and none of this crap would have ever happened. Instead, he walked straight into my bloody house and snapped on the handcuffs, right in front of the bloody kids. Marched me out into the street and pushed me into the van, watched by all the sodding neighbours.' He seemed genuinely shaken by the experience. 'The git got a big kick out of the whole thing.'

'He was a man on a mission,' Fortune agreed. 'But that mission's been terminated. Don't worry about that.'

Carson tossed the magazine on the floor. 'I'd like to put a round right between his eyes.'

'Not a good idea.' Fortune picked up the mag and dropped it in the plastic bag. 'Look at what happened last time. Put it behind you. For now, we've just got to do the job, get the fuck out of Dodge City and then keep a low profile.'

'What about Hunter's family?'

'What about them? Once we're free and clear, they'll be cut loose.'

Carson made a face. 'Sounds like a half-arsed plan to me.'

'This is about making some money, Andy. Not about you getting some payback for your hurt *feelings*.'

'It's not about that.'

'No? Then what is it about?'

'Hunter's a wanker. He needs to be taught a lesson.'

'He's already had his lesson.' Fortune gestured towards the door. 'If you don't like it, you can walk out of here.'

Carson looked at the door, as if thinking it through.

'I won't stop you. Your face will have been on every TV news bulletin by now. It's odds-on you'll get recognized before you reach the end of the road. I reckon they'll have you back in jail in time for tea.'

An idea popped into Carson's head. 'If that happens, I could give you up.'

'Yes,' Fortune nodded, 'you could. But in that case you'll be dead before breakfast.'

'Okay, okay.' Carson held up his hands in mock surrender. 'So, on reflection, your plan does have its attractions.'

'Yes, it does.' Fortune smiled thinly. 'Get yourself together. We'll have to get going soon.'

'We've got almost twelve hours yet,' Carson yawned. 'Plenty of time.' He rose to his feet. 'Who was that you were rabbiting on to on the phone?'

'That's the bloke who's paying our wages.'

'Yeah, but who is it?'

'Need to know, Andy, old son.' Fortune tapped his temple. 'Need to know.'

Fortune walked over to the window. He was already beginning to regret his decision to spring Andy Carson from the Military Corrective Training Centre. After a few months inside, the guy's brain seemed to have gone to mush. It was too late to do anything about it now though. After the job, however, was another matter altogether. Outside, it had started to drizzle in the early morning gloom. He watched as Adrian Colinson dropped the last of their gear in the back of the SUV.

'I want to know,' Carson insisted.

'Yeah, but you don't *need* to know.'

67

Carson followed his comrade over to the window. 'How can you expect me to trust this guy if I don't know who he is?'

'He sanctioned me and Ade getting you out of the nick, didn't he?'

'Hardly the Great Escape,' Carson huffed.

'No, maybe not. But it should be more than enough to put him in your good books. You could have totally buggered this whole mission. More than nine months of work down the drain. Not to mention the rest of your natural in jail.'

'Even *if* they'd found me guilty – and that's a big "if" – I wouldn't have got life.'

You would now. 'You fucked up, big time.'

'How was I to know they'd find that bloody video?' Carson retorted.

'No, but they did, didn't they? So we're heading down to D-Day and not only are you banged up but you are fucking public enemy number one.' Fortune ran a hand over his recent buzz-cut. 'Maybe I should have left you there. I could have got Steve Thomson to come on board. Or maybe that big bastard we hung out with in Malta that time, John Harverson.'

'Ha!' Carson gave him a playful punch on the arm. 'They're not in my league and you know it. Anyway, they're past their sell-by date. The last I heard, Tommo was busy getting stoned on a beach in Thailand. And Jock Harverson was re-training as a sports teacher.'

'Bloody hell!' Despite himself, Fortune let out a cackle. 'I know who got the better deal there.'

'Tell me about it,' Carson agreed. 'But neither of them are still in the game.'

'Unlike you.'

'Unlike me. You need me to pull this off.'

'Yes, I do. So get your fucking game-face on. And I don't mean your computer-game face.'

'What the hell is going on here?' Standing in the entrance of

Charing Cross police station, Carlyle stared at the empty space where the front desk used to be. It had been replaced by a pile of rubble, with a few papers scattered about on the floor. A collection of wires hung from a hole in the ceiling, awaiting attachment to the security camera which sat in its box by the door that led into the station proper. To his right stood a noticeboard on which a sheet of A4 paper had been pinned, informing members of the public that the station would not be receiving their complaints for the next week. Anyone with a pressing concern was invited to call 999 or schlep over to the Holborn station on not-so-nearby Lamb's Conduit Street.

''Scuse me, guv.'

'Sorry.' Jumping out of the way, the inspector looked on as a group of four workmen wheeled in a prefabricated cubicle on a small trailer. The thing looked like a smaller version of one of the theatre ticket booths in Leicester Square. On the glass window was a large sticker that proclaimed: *CLERKENWELL GLAZING SERVICES, Ballistic Bullet-Resistant Glass.*

There's optimism for you. As far as he could recall, no one had ever tried to pull a gun on the duty sergeant. There had been the one time when Dennis Buscombe had been assaulted by a mentally disturbed woman, armed with a baguette from Tesco's, but that was about as dangerous as it got. It wasn't exactly Fort Apache; this was twenty-first-century Covent Garden, not the South Bronx, circa 1975.

Bringing the trailer to a halt, the men began carefully levering the box into the space where the desk had been.

'Welcome to the future.'

Carlyle turned to find Sergeant Alison Roche standing by his shoulder. Her face was free of make-up and her red hair was pulled back into a ponytail. She looked extremely tired. In her hand was the kind of outsized coffee cup that could only have come from Starbucks. Momentarily mesmerized, Carlyle had to fight to suppress a familiar Pavlovian response. Upping her campaign to reduce his weekly coffee intake, his wife was trying to restrict him to a couple of Flat Whites at the weekend. They were in week two of Helen's latest programme; the inspector knew he would succumb sooner or later but, in the meantime, having temptation thrust in his face hardly helped.

'They're finally putting in the facilities upgrade at last.'

'Looks like it,' Carlyle agreed, none the wiser.

She gave him a nudge. 'You didn't read the email, did you?'

'No, of course not.' For the inspector, it was a badge of honour that he deleted all management emails unread as a matter of principle.

'There's going to be a set of turnstiles as well, to stop just anyone wandering in. We'll need a swipe card to get into the rest of the building.'

'Jolly good.' Carlyle wondered how long it would be before he lost his card. Maybe he could blag multiple copies from HR, or whoever happened to be the card monitor. 'I didn't realize we had been at risk all these years.'

'Health and Safety wasn't such a big issue then.'

'Mm. What happens if someone gets caught in the turnstile? That could be very nasty indeed.'

'I'm sure appropriate turnstile training will be made available to all members of staff,' Roche grinned.

Carlyle sucked in a breath. 'What a total waste of money.'

One of the workmen bent forward, giving them both a view of his arse crack. Roche wrinkled her nose in disgust. 'If it's in the budget, it's in the budget. The reality is we are just playing catch-up. Haven't you seen this stuff in the other stations?'

Carlyle thought about it for a moment. The only other station he could remember being in recently was Savile Row. He vaguely recalled seeing a set-up along the lines Roche had described. 'I suppose so.'

Roche waved her cup in the direction of the workmen. 'Charing Cross has – *had* – the last traditional front desk in the whole of London. The only reason they kept it so long was for the tourists.'

'A bit like the last few Routemasters on the 38 route?'

'Exactly,' Roche said cheerily, pleased that, for once, her boss was able to keep up. 'They obviously saw us as the Dixon of Dock Green Experience.'

'Ha!' Carlyle was impressed that his sergeant had heard of Dixon of Dock Green. He was also genuinely chuffed that she had returned to Charing Cross, to work with him, after an extended spell on other duties.

'The desk itself was a bit of a collector's item. I think they're going to sell it on eBay.'

'I liked it where it was.' Carlyle had never considered himself a sentimentalist but the feeling of dismay, mixed with irritation, was palpable.

Roche pointed at the booth with her cup.

'Everyone else got one of these years ago. There was one in Mile End even before I started there.'

'It's rough in the East End,' Carlyle observed. 'But do we really need bulletproof glass?'

'We can't put any of our contractors at risk. Apart from any-thing else, Minerva would sue the Met's arse off.'

Minerva? The name vaguely rang a bell.

'Minerva Support Services,' Roche continued, 'has held the "customer engagement contract" with the Met for the last few years. As of next week, when a punter walks through our doors, they will take a number and wait for a Minerva operative, dressed suspiciously like a police officer, to see them.'

'Listen to them complain, you mean, and then tell them, in not so many words, to bog off?'

'You've got it.' Roche lifted the cup to her lips.

'So what happens if they've got a genuine problem?'

'Good question. As far as I can tell, the company's Key Performance Indicators are to do with waiting times, forms filled and boxes ticked. Actually dealing with problems? That's some-thing else entirely.'

'It's a long way from solving crimes and protecting victims.' Carlyle knew he was sounding hopelessly old-school. The reality, however, was that there wasn't much he could do to change things, so what was the point in getting worked up about it?

'It's just the way things have been going for a long time now, with more to come,' Roche said.

'What else can they outsource?'

'Lots. The Met's looking to hand over another five hundred million pounds worth of work to private companies, to take care of things like finance, custody healthcare, and catering.'

Catering? Now she had his attention. Carlyle gestured towards the stairs leading down to the basement. 'They're not going to mess with the canteen, are they?'

''Fraid so. The dinner ladies have already been told that they could end up being put on "no hours" contracts. They'd effectively be turned into casual workers, not knowing at the start of any week how much work they're going to get.'

'Jesus. That sucks.'

'It's always the little people that suffer. The Met says it has to save another twenty per cent from its budget, due to cuts in government spending.'

Carlyle eyed the Starbucks cup enviously. 'How do you know so much about all this?'

'I read the memos from Simpson – unlike you, obviously.'

'Obviously,' Carlyle grinned. 'I wouldn't have thought Simpson would be in favour of all this though.' Over the years, the inspector's opinion of Commander Carole Simpson, his immediate boss, had changed dramatically. Whereas once he had dismissed her as a vapid careerist, he now cast her in the role of compassionate and engaged leader.

'I'm sure the Commander is sympathetic to your point of view. But she won't have a say in these things, any more than we have.'

'I suppose not.'

As the conversation petered out, one of the workers started up with a drill, sending the two officers scurrying for the stairs.

EIGHT

Reaching the welcome calm of the third floor, the sergeant dumped her bag and promptly disappeared into the lift. Carlyle fired up his computer and started deleting the contents of his inbox.

After a few minutes, Roche reappeared, a mug of green tea in each hand. Placing one on Carlyle's desk, she switched on the TV that hung from the ceiling.

'Thanks.' Carlyle wished it was an espresso but at least Helen would be happy with his reduced coffee intake. Taking a sip of the tea, he glanced up at the screen. As usual, it was muted, tuned to the News Channel. Slowly, he realized that it was the same story he'd seen last night: same strapline, same metal gates, just a different reporter. This time it was an earnest-looking bloke who couldn't have been much older than twenty-two or twenty-three. The poor guy appeared cold, tired and hungry. Rather unfortunately, his ears stuck out to the extent that he looked like one of the Bash Street Kids.

A good face for radio, Carlyle mused.

'Got much on today?'

Carlyle shook his head. 'Nah. You?'

Roche perched on a nearby desk. 'I've got to go and interview David Howard.'

The name didn't ring any bells.

'He's the cyclist who was knocked off his bike and had his wallet lifted by one of the passers-by who went to help.'

'What's that got to do with us?' the inspector grumbled. 'It didn't happen anywhere near here.'

'He reported it here,' Roche shrugged, 'and no one volunteered to take it off our hands.'

Carlyle grunted. He had little sympathy for London's cyclists. Most of them rode like lunatics. As far as he was concerned, they deserved everything they got.

'Apparently, the *Standard* has made a big thing about it. He was in the paper last night, complaining that the police aren't taking it seriously.'

'How very kind of him. Was there much in the wallet?'

'Fifty quid. Something like that. The usual cards and stuff.'

'Fifty quid! Definitely worth your time and attention.'

'Tell me about it,' Roche sighed. As she stood up, Carlyle noticed a distinct thickening around her midriff. The sergeant had always been very lean but now there was a distinct bulge over the top of her jeans.

Catching him staring, she frowned. 'Beginning to show, is it?'

'What?' Carlyle stammered, feeling himself blush.

Roche looked around, confirming that the rest of the room was deserted. 'The baby bump.'

Baby bump. 'You mean, you're—'

'Yes.'

'But how?'

Now it was Roche's turn to blush. 'What do you mean, "how"? How do you think?'

'But what I mean is . . .' What *did* he mean? The inspector had no idea.

'The time was right,' said Roche firmly. 'So I decided to get on with it.'

'And the father?' Carlyle tried to think back to the last time Roche had mentioned a boyfriend of any sort.

'I'm going to be a single parent,' was her rather terse comment on the matter.

'Well, er . . . great.'

She carefully scrutinized his facial expression. 'It'll be tough, but I'll be able to cope.'

'I have no doubt,' he said sincerely. 'Congratulations.'

'Thanks.' She smiled sheepishly from behind her mug.

'When is it due?'

'Don't worry,' she laughed. 'You don't have to worry about finding a replacement for me just yet.'

'I didn't mean it like that,' he fibbed.

'I know, I know. But it is early days, so I'll still be around for a while. I wanted you to be the first person at work to know.'

Bloody hell. 'Well, that is fantastic. Good for you.' Getting to his feet, the inspector gave her a brief, awkward hug.

'Thanks, John.'

'Can I tell Helen and Alice?'

'Of course!'

'They'll be chuffed too. And, of course, if there's anything we can do to help. A friend of ours is a doctor at UCH, so—'

'That's very kind.' Roche put her mug down on the desk. 'My mum will be coming down to help, closer to the time. But at the moment, it's business as usual.'

Yeah, right. 'Okay.'

'So, I'm off to do the Howard interview.' Roche grabbed her bag and slung it over her shoulder. 'See you later.'

'Okay, see you later.' Watching her go, Carlyle felt a stab of irritation. He had fought hard to secure Roche's return and now she would be off again. How long would the maternity leave last? A year? Maybe longer. Maybe she would never come back. Either way, he was back to square one.

I'm the one going to be left holding the sodding baby here, he thought.

A large part of his annoyance was down to his inability to hold on to colleagues for any length of time. The inspector had to admit that his recent track record with sergeants was very poor indeed. As soon as he thought he'd got it cracked, the wheels came off.

Roche's predecessor, the occasionally brilliant but routinely irritating Umar Sligo, was a perfect example. Umar had resigned from the Force, jumping ship before he had to face a disciplinary hearing which would have almost certainly led to him being found guilty of gross misconduct and being summarily sacked. At the time, the inspector had been happy enough to see him go. Now, he would have welcomed the stupid bugger back with open arms. That, however, was a complete non-starter. Umar would never be allowed back on The Job. Last heard of, he had been working as a 'security adviser' for a Sloaney pimp called Harry Cummins.

Returning to his chair, Carlyle placed his hands on his head and stared dolefully at his computer screen. He should call Simpson; the last thing he wanted to do was have to break in a new side-kick, but maybe the Commander could help him come up with someone who would be relatively low maintenance. Springing into action, he picked up the phone and punched in the number for her office in Paddington.

'Good morning!' The hyper-cheery voice of Simpson's PA, Michael Hastings, almost caused him to drop the handset.

'Michael, it's John Carlyle in Charing Cross.'

'Good morning, Inspector.'

'Good morning to you too. I was wondering if the Commander was around this morning.'

'I'm afraid not. She's out for the next couple of days.'

'Okay. I'll try her on the mobile.'

'Her phone will be switched off,' came the instant reply. 'She's on a management course.'

Carlyle's antennae started to twitch. The Met was famous for wasting money on fatuous training sessions. What nonsense were they peddling now? 'A course?'

'A course,' Michael repeated, worried now that he had already divulged too much.

'What kind of a course?'

There was a pause. Then: 'I don't know.'

You're not much of a liar, Carlyle thought. 'Okay. No problem. If you speak to her, can you let her know I was after a word?'

'Of course,' the boy replied, happy that he wasn't going to be pushed any further on his boss's whereabouts.

'Thanks.' Ending the call, Carlyle immediately dialled Simpson's mobile. As Michael had predicted, the call went straight to voicemail. Hanging up without leaving a message, the inspector chortled to himself. 'A course, eh? What nonsense have they got you on now?' Taking a mouthful of his rapidly cooling tea, he wondered what to do next. In the absence of any pressing police work, the sensible option would be a trip to the gym. Looking down, the inspector contemplated his stomach, which was at least as large as Roche's. How long was it since his last visit to Jubilee Hall? At least a week, probably nearer two. A thirty-minute blast on the cross trainer would do him a power of good.

On the other hand . . .

Hovering over the computer keyboard, his fingers started to type in *Spargo Cork Street*, and he hit Search. In an instant, a host of results appeared on the screen. At the top was a link that said *Petition Westminster Council – Save Cork Street*. Clicking on it, he was taken to an article entitled *Art & Culture Being Strangled by Foreign Cash*.

SAVE CORK STREET!

For nearly 100 years Cork Street has been recognized as one of the most important, if not *the* most important street in the world for art. It has launched more careers in the art world than any other street. Small independent dealers mean diversity and innovation. Cork Street is known and loved not only in Britain but internationally, and provides a major draw to London and the UK throughout the course of a year. The history and atmosphere of this street, as well as its close proximity to the Royal Academy of Arts, make this a unique place to visit for collectors, art enthusiasts, students and tourists alike.

Now, we face being thrown out of our home so that a developer can turn it into a new version of Bond Street, a characterless mix of luxury shops and office developments. Already, five galleries have been given notice to leave their premises as part of a massive redevelopment of a site that stretches right through to Old Burlington Street. And what a developer! Spargo Developments is owned and run by Lucio Spargo, a man who has always shown himself to be ruthless in dealing with anyone who gets in his way. Ask the family of Sally-Anne Mason.

Ignoring the 'Save Cork Street' petition, Carlyle typed in *Sally-Anne Mason* next to *Spargo* in the search engine. A couple of seconds later, he was reading a twenty-year-old article from the *Daily Telegraph*:

Controversial property developer Lucio Spargo was released without charge last night as police said they were closing their investigation into the death of Sally-Anne Mason. Mrs Mason, 79, was found dead in her St James's flat three weeks ago. Police are refusing to say if they are treating the death as suspicious. The widow was the last remaining resident of Mathias Mansions who was holding out against a redevelopment of the property by Mr Spargo's company, Spargo Developments. Mrs Mason's family condemned the decision not to charge Mr Spargo. Helen Parsons, 52, Mrs Mason's daughter, said: 'My mother has been harried to her grave by greedy men, obsessed by money.' Mr Spargo was unavailable for comment.

The piece was illustrated by a picture of the block of flats. Carlyle estimated that the location had to be little more than a two-minute walk from Dom's gallery.

'Haven't moved far over the years,' noted Carlyle. Then again, why would they? There could have been few better locations around the world to have been a property developer than smack in the centre of London.

Closing the story, the inspector delved into the PNC. The Police National Computer system was rather unwieldy at the best of times, particularly when you started looking for data that was more than a decade old. Therefore, it wasn't much of a surprise that Spargo's profile wasn't on the National DNA Database, nor his prints on IDENT1, the fingerprint database. There was, however, an Arrest Summons Number, relating to an incident only eleven months earlier. The ASN had been generated by an officer in the West End Central station. Once again, Carlyle picked up the phone.

The number rang for what seemed like an eternity.

He was on the point of hanging up when a bored female voice finally answered. 'Which station, please?'

'Eh?'

'You've reached the Control Rooms and Enquiries Department,' said the woman, who sounded like she'd already had her quota of idiots on the line today. 'Which police station do you want to speak to?'

Carlyle gritted his teeth. CR&ED was the Met's outsourced call centre. Another cost-saving initiative, which meant it was now impossible just to pick up the phone and call a colleague direct.

'Which station?'

'West End Central,' he said quickly, before she decided to cut him off.

'Putting you through.'

It took the best part of another five minutes before he found the direct line he wanted. However, any hope he might have harboured that his quest was over was crushed when a recorded message kicked in: '*You have reached the voicemail of Inspector Sarah Ward . . .*'

Aaargh! Resisting the temptation to smash the handset into small pieces, Carlyle took a deep breath and then left a vaguely coherent message. That done, he jumped to his feet and headed for the exit, thinking that maybe he would go to the gym, after all.

NINE

Alison Roche watched a steady procession of kids troop through the school gates. Some of them were hand in hand, heads bowed in earnest conversation, others were focused on waving goodbye to their parent or nanny, all of them seemingly happy enough to be going to school on this grey, featureless morning. It had rained heavily overnight and Roche groaned inwardly as she stepped off the kerb, straight into a large puddle of dirty rainwater that had collected in the depression of an incipient pothole. Shaking her damp foot, she crossed the road.

An old-looking guy, wearing a tweed jacket under a garish red waterproof, greeted each of the new arrivals. One of the teachers, she assumed, or possibly the head. According to the board next to the gates, the headmaster was one Dr Alfred Byron Fry OBE. Byron! Roche wondered if he had been interviewed about the bicycle incident. There was nothing about it in the original report. Then, again, that had been a masterpiece of box-ticking brevity, little more than the victim's statement and a crime reference number for the benefit of the insurance company.

Waving at a departing woman, the man briefly caught the sergeant's eye. A faintly quizzical look passed across his face as he tried to place her, before he was distracted by a couple of small boys who were engaging in a spirited bout of shoving and name-calling before they made it into the classroom. By the time that had been sorted out, Roche had been forgotten. A solitary woman hovering outside a school was not going to invite much scrutiny; a man, of course, would be another story entirely. Roche grinned at the thought. In some ways, a woman's relative invisibility was a benefit when it came to being a cop.

The sergeant's gaze alighted on a well-dressed thirty-something blonde woman waving animatedly to a smiling girl as she skipped across the playground and disappeared inside the rather tatty-looking redbrick building. As soon as the child was inside, the woman pulled an iPhone from her bag and started tapping on the screen. Clamping the device to her ear, she began a vital conversation while marching down the street in the direction of Park Lane. That'll be me in a few years from now, Roche thought, trying to juggle the work-life balance, keep the show on the road. Happily, it was not a daunting prospect. She had always been an organized and practical creature and was looking forward to the challenge. Schools, of course, would be a big issue. Roche wondered what kind of ranking Dr Fry's establishment enjoyed. She made a mental note to check out its performance results online when she got home in the evening. Her child might not have been born yet but everyone knew that, when it came to securing a decent school place in London, you had to start as early as possible.

The blonde woman disappeared round the corner. The flow of new arrivals was starting to slow now, as most of the kids were dropped off in good time. A group of boys were chasing each other in the playground, but most of the kids had gone straight inside, ahead of registration. Hovering on the kerb, Roche brought her thoughts back to the reason for her visit. Ten yards down the road was a zebra crossing. It was here that David Howard had been knocked off his bike. The cyclist had agreed to meet her at the scene to talk her through the incident and the subsequent theft of his wallet. As Carlyle – always very good value when it came to stating the bleedin' obvious – had been quick to point out, the police investigation was little more than a PR stunt. Simpson, however, had been adamant; cyclist abuse was a hot topic and Mr Howard was keen to exploit his moment in the media spotlight. As a result, they had to show they were taking the matter extremely seriously.

Roche looked at her watch and uttered an annoyed cluck. For his part, Mr Howard was demonstrating the seriousness with which he was treating the matter by being twelve minutes late and counting. The sergeant gave her damp foot another shake. How long should she wait? If she left now, all it meant was that she would have to come back again later. The bloody public. As far as they were concerned, they paid your salary and that gave them the right to waste as much of your time as they liked.

For want of anything better to do, she pulled out her phone and snapped a couple of pictures of the crossing.

'What are you doing?'

Roche looked round.

'What are you doing?' This time the question was accompanied by a tug on her jacket.

Roche looked down into the face of a pretty girl, maybe five or six. In one hand was her school bag, in the other a half-eaten *pain au chocolat*. 'I'm taking some pictures of the crossing,' she explained.

The girl looked puzzled. 'Why? It's not very pretty.'

'No, it's not. But I work for the police. A man got knocked off his bike here the other day.'

'I saw that!' the girl said brightly.

'Oh yes?'

'There was a load of shouting and an ambulance arrived. Everyone crowded round the window, till Ms Milton made us all sit down and get back to our verbs.'

Verbs. Urgh.

'Did he die?' Seeing Roche's confusion, the girl added, 'The man on the bike.'

'No. He's fine. His bike got a bit bashed though.'

83

'Mm.' The girl took a bite of her pastry and chewed thought-fully. 'My mum says cyclists are a menace.'

'She should meet my boss,' Roche grinned. 'He thinks pretty much the same thing.'

The girl shoved the last of the pastry into her mouth. 'Are you really a policeman?'

Roche winced as the child wiped a chocolate-covered hand on her bright red blazer. 'I'm a policewoman, yes.'

'Can I see your badge?'

'Sure.' Stuffing the phone back in her pocket, Roche fumbled with her warrant card. Flipping it open, she handed it to the girl. 'Here you go.'

'Wow!' For several seconds, the girl stared at the photograph on the card, occasionally looking up at Roche, as if she was struggling to reconcile the two. 'You look a lot younger in your picture,' she said finally. 'It must have been taken a long time ago.'

Thanks a lot.

'Amy!'

The sergeant looked round to see a harassed girl in her late teens or early twenties standing by the gates, holding the hand of a younger child. Younger than Amy.

The nanny, Roche thought.

'What are you doing? Hurry up!'

Amy handed the warrant card back to Roche and trotted off without another word.

'Nice to meet you too,' Roche huffed, sticking the ID in the back pocket of her jeans.

'Sergeant Roche?'

'That's right.' A young man was pushing a bike along the pavement towards her. He was wearing a hi-viz yellow jacket and a crash helmet, along with a pair of Lycra shorts and expensive-looking trainers. Attached to the side of the helmet was a video camera that looked like a small torch.

'David Howard?' She resisted the temptation to point out that he was fifteen minutes late.

He gave her a nod.

Roche belatedly noticed the guy hovering behind Howard with a video camera.

'That's Serge – he's shooting some material for my vlog.'

Serge waved his camera by way of greeting.

Roche raised an eyebrow.

'My video blog.' Howard gave her a patronizing *You are too old to understand this kind of stuff* smile. 'It's on YouTube. I put up a couple of posts a week on cycling and the trials and tribulations of being a cyclist in a totally car-centric city like London.'

What a wanker. Roche's heart sank.

Howard's bland features edged towards a scowl. Everyone knew that the average plod was a bit thick, but this one surely took the biscuit. 'I've had almost a million hits since I got knocked off my bike. If I get enough subscribers I'm going to give up the day job and do the vlog full-time.'

Not wanting a starring role in his next post, Roche persevered with the small talk. 'What is the day job?' she asked, trying to sound remotely interested.

'I'm a Planning Officer for Westminster Council.'

Nodding, Roche gestured towards his helmet as casually as possible. 'Is that thing on?'

Howard reached up and pressed a button on the camera, activating a red light. 'It is now,' he grinned.

Great. 'But it wasn't working the other day?'

'This is a new one. The old one was broken in the accident. I think whoever nicked my wallet stomped on it on purpose. The casing was smashed to bits, although the memory card was okay. I got some great footage of me slamming into the van but then it goes blank.'

Roche tried to discreetly step out of shot. 'Are they expensive?'

'Nah.' Howard's face brightened as the conversation turned to his new toy. 'This only cost sixty quid and it more than does the job. Works a treat.'

Great. 'And what about Serge?'

'He's going to get some extra footage,' Howard explained. 'We're planning to do a follow-up special on what happened. You should check it out; maybe we'll make you a star.'

And maybe I'll make you eat that fucking camera.

'I'll start shooting once you've sorted out the set-up,' Serge told them.

Set-up is exactly right, Roche thought grimly. How was she going to get out of this?

Howard looked at her expectantly. 'So, Sergeant, how would you like to proceed?'

'Well . . .' Roche glanced towards the school, in search of some inspiration. The man in the red waterproof was in the process of closing the gates when he was distracted by a shout. He looked up to see a red-faced woman jogging along the pavement towards him, a couple of young kids, a boy and a girl, in tow, struggling to keep up. She waved a hand and called out something that Roche didn't catch. Smiling, the teacher waved back, signalling that he would wait. A look of relief crossed the woman's face as she realized that the kids would just be able to duck inside before the gates were shut for the morning. Another school-run success-fully completed.

The woman slowed her pace to a walk, allowing the chil-dren to catch her up. As they reached her side, she came to a halt to hand each child its bag. Bending down, she kissed the boy on the forehead and then the girl, offering some final encouragement before the working day began in earnest. Setting off again, the little group were almost level with the zebra crossing when Roche noticed two well-built, shaven-headed men slip out of the back of an ancient Transit van that had been parked by the service entrance of the office block adjacent to the school. As the men ran up behind the woman, one of them said something, causing her to turn. The moment she did so, he lifted a small aerosol and sprayed something into her face. When she started to scream, he grabbed the collar of her coat and began dragging her towards the van. The children were wailing now, making quite a racket as they tried to cling on to their mother. With a minimum of fuss, the second man gripped each one by the collar. Sticking the girl under one arm and the boy under another, he marched briskly back to the van.

The abduction lasted less than ten seconds. Still holding the gate open, the man in the red waterproof looked on, bemused. Howard and Serge, fiddling with their technology, didn't even look up.

'What the fuck?'

As the van doors slammed shut, Roche stepped off the kerb.

'Eh?' Belatedly realizing something was wrong, Howard started after her.

'Stay here,' Roche commanded. Striding towards the van, she saw the driver, skinhead number 3, reach forward and turn the key in the ignition. The engine reluctantly spluttered into life. 'Call 999. Tell them an officer needs assistance.'

'But—'

'Do it now!' Roche was conscious of Serge bringing the video camera up to his face. She would have to take that off him later. The van edged out into the road and turned towards her. Grabbing her ID, Roche flipped it open and held it above her head. 'POLICE!' she screamed. 'Stop the vehicle and take the keys out of the ignition.'

The driver released the handbreak and rolled the van slowly forward. When Roche stood her ground he came to a halt barely six feet in front of her, a bemused grin on his face.

'POLICE!'

Half turning in his seat, he kept his hands on the steering wheel as he had a brief confab with his colleagues in the back about this latest development.

Stepping up to the driver's door, Roche flattened her warrant card against the window. The driver studied it, unimpressed.

'Get out of the fucking van!'

After a moment, there was a click. Roche took a step backwards, stuffing the ID back in her pocket, as the driver pushed the door open.

'Okay, officer,' he smiled. 'I'm getting out of the van.'

TEN

In the cold light of day, things didn't look any better. A couple of forensics technicians remained working in the chapel but Daniel Hunter knew that there would be nothing much left to find. Wishing he was still in London, he looked at his watch. He should have been dropping the kids off at school about now. Once this crap was sorted out, he was definitely packing it in. Whether he ended up becoming a History teacher or not, his Army days were over.

The lack of sleep did nothing to improve his mood. A couple of hours laid out on one of the back pews had left him feeling stiff and profoundly weary. Yawning, he pointed to the CCTV camera positioned on the wall high above the altar.

'How long has it been out of order?'

'Oh, it's working all right, we had to switch it off.' The MCTC Commander, Brigadier William Soames, gave a helpless smile. 'One of the men who used the chapel complained that it infringed his Human Rights. Freedom of religion, or some such. His lawyer threated to take it to the European Court, so . . .'

'So you switched it off.'

'Yes.'

Brilliant.

'Commander.'

Soames and Hunter turned to see a red-faced young recruit, who saluted the pair of them as he walked up the aisle. Soames returned the salute; Hunter didn't bother.

'Nigel Drinkwater has arrived, sir. They've put him in the Goose Green Room.'

'Drinkwater . . .' Soames struggled to place the name.

'Soldier B,' Hunter reminded him.

'Ah, yes. Very good. Let's go and speak to him then, shall we?'

'I think I need to speak to him alone.'

Soames started to protest, then thought better of it. Frankly, the less he had to do with this mess, the better. Running the MCTC was a thankless job at the best of times and these were most definitely not the best of times. The sooner the Brass found him something else to do, the happier he'd be. With a grunt, he signalled for Hunter to do as he pleased. The Captain, already halfway to the door, did not acknowledge the concession.

The Goose Green Room was basically one half of a prefabricated building that had been divided in two. The other half bore the moniker the Darwin Room, both names being a nod to the Falkland Islands military campaign. After a quick diversion to the canteen, Hunter flashed his ID at the two guards by the door and stepped inside. The room was dominated by a large square table, which took up maybe 80 per cent of the available floorspace. Hunter counted sixteen chairs. Only one was occupied. Drinkwater sat in front of the only window, which looked out on to a car park. He watched Hunter pull out a nearby chair and sit down.

'How's it going, Nigel?' Hunter placed two paper bags on the table. 'I thought you might want some breakfast – I know I do.' From the first bag, he pulled a couple of cups of coffee, placing one in front of Drinkwater and taking a sip of the other. Aaah! 'There's milk and sugar in the bag.'

'Black's fine.' Removing the lid, Drinkwater left the cup sitting on the table.

Delving into the second bag, Hunter produced a couple of rolls wrapped in greaseproof paper. Placing one next to Drinkwater's cup, he began unwrapping the other. 'Bacon sarnies.' He took a bite. 'I don't know about you, but I'm fucking starving. It's been a very long night.'

'Tell me about it,' Drinkwater said with feeling as he reached for the roll. 'They dragged me out of bed at three o'clock this morning to drive me down here.' Pulling off the wrapper, he took a large bite.

'Bummer,' said Hunter. 'Where were they holding you?'

'Bolton.' Drinkwater heaved a sigh. 'I've been moved three times in the last week. No one has any space.'

Hunter nodded.

'They sent Dern to bloody Stirling.'

'I know.' Bryce Dern was Soldier C, the third man being court-martialled for the alleged murder of the terrorists. 'He's on his way, apparently,' Hunter said. 'God knows what time he'll actually get here.'

'So, once we've had our little chat, I'm going straight back, am I?'

Hunter shrugged. 'Don't know. Nothing to do with me.' Stuffing the last of the food into his mouth, he reached into the bag and took out a second roll, along with a fistful of napkins and a sachet of tomato sauce. Having got what he wanted, he tossed the bag over to Drinkwater. 'Two each.'

For a couple of minutes, they sat in silence, enjoying their food. Hunter, feeling his mood improve as his stomach filled, ran through in his head what he knew about Nigel Drinkwater. Twenty-four years old, seven-year veteran, grew up in Brixton, a smart kid, with six A-levels from the Pimlico Academy. Quite the athlete too: he had walked out on a professional contract with Charlton to sign up for the Army. He had been on his second Afghan tour when he had hooked up with Andy Carson. Never been in any kind of trouble before.

Being honest, Hunter was hoping that Drinkwater escaped punishment from the court-martial. As far as the captain could see, Carson had simply gone a bit crazy on the day and the others had just not been able to stop him. It would be a crying shame if

91

Drinkwater's career ended up being destroyed because the Army was spooked by the PR fall-out from the incident.

Wiping the grease from his fingers, Hunter swallowed the last of his coffee. Gathering together all his rubbish, he shoved it into one of the paper bags.

'Right. That's better! Now, where will I find Andy Carson?'

Drinkwater pushed his chair back from the table and stretched. 'No idea, sorry, Captain.'

'C'mon, Nigel. You know I'm going to track the stupid bastard down sooner or later. Do yourself a favour.'

Placing his hands on the table, Drinkwater looked slowly around the room. 'Is this being recorded?'

Hunter shook his head. 'Nope.'

Unconvinced, Drinkwater scratched at the stubble on his jaw.

'I'm not even taking any notes.' Hunter held up both hands. 'And nothing that gets said here will appear in any report.'

Drinkwater stared at the remains of his breakfast on the table. 'This is nothing to do with me.'

'No.'

'Andy is a crazy bastard, a real nutter. And some of his mates, they're even worse.' When Drinkwater looked up, Hunter could see real dismay in the man's face. 'Nasty.'

'I'll keep you out of it,' Hunter repeated.

Drinkwater bit his lower lip. 'So . . . I got a message yesterday evening. They told me to deliver it to you face-to-face, when we had our meeting. I was to tell you to ring your wife.'

Hunter frowned. 'You were to tell me to call my wife?'

Drinkwater nodded.

'Who told you that?'

'No idea. Some guy just came up to me in the canteen. One of the warders.'

'What did he look like?'

'I dunno.' Drinkwater thought about it for a few moments before his face broke into a grin. 'He was white.'

'Right. You can do better than that.'

'You know what it's like if you come from Brixton, man. All you white boys look the same – know what I mean?'

More questions started thudding through Hunter's mind. Ignoring them, he got to his feet, fumbling for his mobile as he headed outside. Stepping on to the tarmac, he hit Mel's number. It rang three times before a male voice answered.

'About time. We were beginning to think that you weren't going to call.'

'So, what happened? Are you okay?'

Sitting on the edge of a bed, Roche dangled her feet a couple of inches off the floor. 'I'm fine.'

'Are you sure?' Other than the bandage on her cheek, Carlyle had to admit the sergeant looked pretty much the same as she had at Charing Cross a few hours earlier.

'Yes I'm sure,' she insisted, more than a hint of irritation clearly evident in her voice.

'Does it hurt?' The question sounded more voyeuristic than concerned.

'I've had worse hangovers.' She lifted a packet of ibuprofen from the bed and waved it in her hand. 'They told me to take a couple of these if it gets worse.'

That's doctors for you. 'Did they do any tests?'

'I don't need any tests.'

'Shouldn't you have a brain scan, or something?'

She waved away the suggestion. 'Don't be daft. You're worse than my mother.'

'Err on the side of caution, that's my motto. You read so many horror stories, about people being sent home with a few pills and then dropping down dead the next day because a stomach tumour was misdiagnosed as indigestion.'

Roche gave him a hard look. 'Since when did you start to believe stories in the papers?'

'Fair point.' Carlyle backed against the wall as a nurse skipped past carrying a stack of folders. 'You would have thought they

93

could have done better than plonk you in a bloody corridor though.'

'Everyone's been very nice. It's the NHS. They're doing the best that they can.'

'Mm.' The inspector let his gaze slide towards her stomach. 'And the—'

'All good,' she said sharply. 'The baby's fine. Nothing to worry about.'

'Phew!'

'Tell me about it.' She gave him a rueful smile. 'The way it all happened was really quite fortunate.'

'That's one way of looking at it.'

'The scary thing is, I didn't stop to think, "I'm pregnant". I just waded in.'

'Acting on instinct.'

'Worse. Acting on *cop* instinct,' she groaned.

'Think of it as a learning experience.'

'It bloody better be.' Roche dropped the painkillers into the pocket of her jacket. 'Did becoming a parent change the way you handled things like that?'

Carlyle knew he should say 'yes' but Roche deserved an honest answer. 'Not really. Not in any quantifiable way, at least. It's not like we go taking undue risks, is it? It's just part of The Job. As you get older, the way we do The Job changes. Becoming a parent may be one factor in that, but there are lots of others.'

He could see in her face that he wasn't making a lot of sense, so he changed tack. 'I think you can be a good parent and a good cop. In my opinion, the people who are irresponsible are those who have kids and then go off and get themselves killed climbing mountains or skydiving – shit like that.'

'I never was much of a skydiver,' Roche chuckled.

'No, but you know what I mean. It wasn't as if you went out looking for trouble this morning.'

'I should have seen it coming though.'

'What else were you going to do? Ignore it?'

'I could have just called it in, rather than confront them. In the end, I held them up for maybe thirty seconds. The guy just stepped out of the van, smacked me with a left hook and that was that. I was right out of the game. Fortunately, I landed on my arse on the pavement. The next thing I remember, I was sitting against a wall, waiting for the ambulance.'

'Thank God it turned out so well.'

'Yeah. We've got to be thankful for small mercies. From what I understand, the other guys didn't come off so good.'

'No.' Carlyle consulted the notebook in his hand. 'David Howard and Serge . . . Aubry. I spoke to them on the way in. Howard has two broken fingers and a broken wrist. Aubry has a fractured jaw.'

Roche said, 'I didn't have them pegged for have-a-go heroes.'

'They weren't coming to your aid,' Carlyle pointed out. 'From what I can tell, they just stood around like complete lemons; didn't even have the sense to run away. The guy in the van clocked their cameras and was worried about what they might have filmed. When they refused to hand the cameras over, he slapped them about a bit and then took their kit.'

'But they didn't film anything, I don't think.'

'That's what they told me. According to our two "heroes", they didn't shoot a single frame.'

Grinning, Roche pulled her phone from the pocket of her jacket. 'I did though.' Flicking through a series of images, she held one up for Carlyle to inspect.

'A picture of a zebra crossing,' Carlyle deadpanned. 'Nice.'

She gave him a gentle smack on the arm. 'There – in the background. You can distinctly see them.' Tapping the screen, she zoomed in until the front of the van dominated the screen. The man behind the wheel was just a mess of pixels, but the licence-plate was clear enough.

'Bugger me,' Carlyle beamed, scribbling down the details. 'Might be a fake, or stolen, but I'll see where it gets us.'

'Okay.' Roche put the phone back in her pocket and slid off the bed.

'Where are you going?'

'I've got to get out of here.'

Carlyle looked around for an authority figure in a white coat who could come wafting down the corridor and counsel caution; perhaps insist that his sergeant be whisked off for an immediate MRI scan. But Holby City this was not. Scanning the corridor with a plaintive look on his face garnered no response whatsoever. When he glared at a bunch of orderlies chatting happily in front of a vending machine selling different kinds of junk food, they ignored him completely.

'I've sat in this bloody corridor long enough,' Roche grumbled.

'Okay,' he said resignedly. 'I hear you.'

'I hate hospitals.'

It was a sentiment Carlyle could easily relate to. Hospitals always made him feel ill. Knowing better than to try and stop her, he offered her his arm. For a moment, Roche looked bemused but then she slipped her arm inside his and let him walk her to the door.

Out on the street, he hailed a black cab. 'Okay, here's the deal. You head for home and put your feet up for the rest of the day. I'll go back to the school and sniff around. And I'll chase up the van. I'll give you a call later on and then we can decide what to do next.' As the taxi drew up to the kerb, he pulled open the passenger door and gestured for her to get inside. Roche hesitated, then did as he requested.

'Thanks.'

'No problem.' Carlyle slammed the door shut. 'I'll call you later.'

Reaching for his phone, he watched the cab pull out into the traffic. Hitting Simpson's number, he listened to it ring for what seemed like an eternity before her voicemail kicked in. This time he did leave a message: 'Boss, it's me. I know you're tied up on a course, but there have been a few developments. I just wanted to keep you informed. Give me a bell when you get the chance. Bye.'

Satisfied that Simpson couldn't now complain that he wasn't keeping her in the loop, Carlyle rang another number.

'Well, well, well, if it isn't Inspector John Carlyle. What do *you* want?'

'How are you?' Carlyle chuckled. 'And what makes you think I'm after something? It could be a social call.'

'I'm more likely to get a social call from George Clooney.'

'Sheelagh,' he protested, 'be fair.'

'I am being fair. You'd think I was the only person in Scotland Yard dumb enough to do you favours.'

You are, the inspector reflected, more or less. He had first met data analyst Sheelagh Buttimer on a mandatory training day, five, or maybe six, years ago. Like Carlyle, she was a second-generation Celt. Whereas his parents had arrived in London from Glasgow, hers had originated in Cork, ending up in a flat off the Fulham Palace Road, less than half a mile from the Carlyle home. It turned out that they shared a love of Fulham FC and a deep distrust of the Met management. Sitting in an office on the fourth floor of Police HQ, she had access to every database known to man, and quite a few that weren't. As such, Carlyle had not been averse to co-opting Sheelagh into his own informal professional support network.

'What did I get last time? A bottle of cava and a box of bleedin' Milk Tray!' Her tone was more amused than outraged. 'Talk about a cheap date.'

'Proper champagne this time,' Carlyle promised.

A heavy sigh came down the line. 'What are you after?'

'Can you check a numberplate with the DVLA for me?'

'Can't you do it yourself?'

'I would, but I'm a bit tied up at the moment.'

'What about that glamorous sergeant of yours, can't she do it?'

Glamorous? 'That's why I'm a bit tied up.' Carlyle talked up Roche's run-in with the van driver.

'Oh, bloody hell. Is she going to be okay?'

'She should be fine.'

'Give me the licence-plate.'

Carlyle obliged.

Sheelagh read it back to him and added: 'I'll check it right now. Just need a couple of minutes.'

'Thanks.' As he put the phone back in his pocket, the inspector's stomach started to rumble. On the other side of the road, he spied a Greggs offering a tempting selection of takeaway treats. Waiting for a break in the traffic, he licked his lips. 'Food first,' he muttered to himself, 'then school.'

Standing outside the shop, he was just shoving the last of a ham sandwich into his mouth when Sheelagh called him back.

'The van was reported stolen in Peterborough, two days ago.'

'That looks like a dead end then.'

'Sorry.'

'Not your fault. Thanks for checking. It's one thing I can tick off the list.'

'No problem. I'll email you the details.'

'Thanks.'

'I hope Roche is okay. Give her my best.'

'I will.'

'Speak later.'

'Yeah.' Making a mental note to get Sheelagh a bottle of something nice, he turned his attention to the selection of cakes in Greggs window. 'Time for dessert.'

ELEVEN

By the time he finally made it to the school, the lunch hour was in full swing. Arriving at the gate, Carlyle watched a swarming mass of kids rushing around in all directions, squealing and squawking with delight. Aside from a couple of teachers standing by a bike shed, playing on their mobile phones, it was an almost timeless scene.

Envious of the children's energy and good humour, the inspector watched the ebb and flow of a game of football for a few moments before pressing the buzzer and identifying himself. Several minutes later, a young woman with a severe bob haircut appeared through the throng. Dressed in a grey trouser suit and a red blouse, with a pair of sensible shoes, she looked like a management trainee from Marks & Spencer.

'I'm Melissa Foreman, one of the administrative assistants.' After carefully checking his ID, she released the lock and let him inside.

Pushing open the gate, Carlyle gave her one of his winning smiles. 'I'm here to—'

Not interested in his explanation, the woman turned on her heel and began marching across the playground, expertly side-stepping little turbo-charged bodies as she went. 'I'll show you to the headmaster's office.'

'Thanks.' Carlyle had to break into a jog to catch up.

'We've had quite a morning,' she said over her shoulder.

'I can imagine,' Carlyle replied to her back.

'Poor Mrs Hunter,' she clucked. 'Was she really kidnapped? And her kids! What kind of a world are we living in?'

The same one as always, the inspector thought.

'What's going on?'

'That's what we're trying to find out,' Carlyle said blandly. 'I'll need to see all the relevant papers on the children.'

'Your colleague is already upstairs.' Slowing slightly, Melissa pointed to the top floor of the school building.

My colleague?

'She has the files for Susannah and Robert.'

'What kind of kids are they?'

'I wouldn't know,' she said snootily. 'We have more than three hundred and fifty children here. I don't know them all personally.'

'No, I suppose not.' Carlyle was suddenly distracted by a football hurtling towards his face. Thrusting out a hand, he managed to push it away, avoiding another pair of broken specs in the process.

Melissa scanned the sea of faces, looking for the rogue footballer. 'Tommy Wilson,' she scolded, 'you're even worse than Bobby Zamora.'

The kid looked at her blankly.

Before your time, Carlyle thought. Chasing after the ball, he passed it back towards the suitably shamed tousle-haired kid. To the inspector's chagrin, the ball squirted off his toe and veered off to his left, almost decapitating a girl playing hopscotch before smacking harmlessly into a wall.

Oops! Happily, Melissa, almost at the entrance to the school building, had not witnessed his lack of technique. Blushing, he chased after her. 'Are you a West Ham fan then?' he asked, referencing one of the well-travelled Zamora's former clubs.

She shook her head. 'My family's from Shepherd's Bush; they all support QPR.'

'Mm.' Carlyle decided to keep his Fulham allegiance to himself. The only team Fulham fans liked less than Queens Park Rangers was Chelsea.

Pulling open the door, she ushered him inside. 'I'm not into football myself but I've had to listen to my dad and my brothers moan about poor old Bobby often enough over the years.'

'I'd forgotten he played for them.'

'I wish my lot would,' the woman griped. 'Even now, they still go on about him.'

Unable to offer much sympathy, Carlyle pointed at the lift. 'Is it upstairs?'

'Yes.' Melissa stepped forward, pressed the call button and the doors shuddered open. 'Go to the third floor. Mrs Ray, Dr Fry's secretary, will meet you there.'

'Thanks.' Carlyle stepped into the lift and waited for the doors to close.

'Good luck,' Melissa said, and smiled weakly. 'I've got to go and get ready for 3c's trip to Seymour Leisure Centre. You don't know what stress is until you've had to take thirty six-year-olds swimming.'

'I can imagine,' Carlyle lied, watching her disappear down the hall as the doors closed.

The headmaster's office was little more than a large cubbyhole. With two people already inside, Carlyle could barely get through the door. Declining Mrs Ray's offer of a coffee, he turned his attention first to the blonde woman sitting in the overstuffed armchair pushed up against a set of floor-to-ceiling shelves, filled to overflowing with books. On her knee rested a pair of blue files, presumably the records of the Hunter kids.

'Inspector John Carlyle,' he introduced himself.

The woman lifted her backside a couple of inches out of the chair, reaching forward to offer a perfunctory handshake. 'Sarah Ward. West End Central.' The look on her face said, *What are you doing here?*

'I work with Sergeant Roche. I'm just back from the hospital – she's going to be fine.' The woman said nothing; it appeared she could not have cared less. The inspector turned his attention to the grim-looking man perched on the edge of a tiny desk. He was a big bloke, dressed a bit casually for a headmaster, Carlyle thought, in jeans and a North Face fleece, but obviously in good physical shape. His handshake was as firm as the woman's was limp.

'Dr Fry?'

The man's face darkened. 'No. I'm Daniel Hunter.'

'The husband,' Ward explained.

'Ah. Okay.'

Her eyes narrowed. 'Carlyle . . . Didn't you leave me a message about something?'

'Er . . .' It took a moment for his mind to click into gear. 'Ah, yes. Lucio Spargo.'

Ward's expression became even more pained. 'What do you want with that nasty piece of work?'

'If you don't mind, do you think we could focus on the matter in hand?' Pushing himself off the desk, Hunter occupied almost all the remaining available floorspace. He was at least six inches taller than Carlyle and considerably wider. The inspector took an involuntary step backwards, so that he was almost standing in the corridor.

'Mr Hunter,' Ward said wearily, 'we are taking all available steps—'

Hunter swatted away the empty words. 'I've told you already, I know who is responsible for this. We need to move fast. My wife and kids are in serious danger.'

'And I've told you already that we are deploying all available resources on this,' the woman snapped. Hunter started to say something else, but Ward pointed towards the open door. 'If you could step outside for a moment, please, *sir*,' she said, adopting a tone so official that it was almost a sneer, 'I would like to consult with my colleague.'

Glaring at each of them in turn, Hunter ducked out of the room. Carlyle listened to him stomp off down the corridor, wondering what Ward had in mind. He had never come across the inspector before, but his first impressions weren't good.

'Close the door.'

Carlyle did as he was told, taking up Hunter's position by the desk. He scanned the bookshelves, looking for something familiar. Sadly, they all seemed to be textbooks of one sort or another. The latest Robert Crais masterpiece was not in evidence.

'That guy is really getting on my tits,' Ward snapped, 'and now you turn up.' She smacked the files on her lap angrily.

'We are talking about the kidnapping of his wife and kids,' Carlyle said reasonably. 'It's not that surprising that he's a bit stressed.'

'Humpf.' Ward shifted in her seat. 'He should know better.'

'How do you mean?'

Ward didn't seem to hear the question. 'It wouldn't surprise me if it was some kind of domestic.'

'A domestic?'

'Stranger things have happened. Maybe he was beating her up and she faked her own disappearance.'

'That's a bit far-fetched, don't you think?'

'Not at all.' She shot him a hard stare. 'Or are you one of those old-school coppers who don't think domestic violence is a serious issue?'

Don't put words in my mouth. Carlyle was about to fire back a barb of his own, but thought better of it. It was more important that he go and speak to the husband than get involved in a pointless row. 'My sergeant seems to think it was for real,' he said evenly.

'It's far more likely to be a domestic than his cock and bull story.'

'What story?'

Ward shrugged. 'Ask him yourself. I know a bullshitter when I see one.'

She was interrupted by the clanging of a bell, loudly signalling the end of the lunch break. It was followed by the sound of children stampeding down corridors and back into their classrooms. Waiting for relative quiet to return, the inspector was about to

103

continue with his question when there was a knock and a rather peeved-looking man stuck his head round the door. He regarded Ward and Carlyle in turn, before addressing neither one of them in particular.

'I was wondering if you were finished with my office yet?'

Ward gave the headmaster what appeared to be her standard pissed-off look. 'If I could just take a couple more minutes of your time, Dr Fry, to check a few things with you. I gather you witnessed the abduction.'

'If you must.' Slipping into the room, the headmaster removed his red waterproof and hung it on a peg on the back of the door. 'If we could make it as quick as possible though, I would be very grateful.' Stepping round Carlyle, he squeezed behind his desk, settling into a ratty office chair that looked like it had been rescued from a skip. 'I have a paper to complete and a finance committee meeting that's due to start in forty-five minutes. What a trying day!'

Tough at the top, Carlyle thought, sarcastically. Very inconvenient, the abduction of two of your pupils and their mother.

'This won't take long,' Ward said flatly.

Leaving them to it, Carlyle slipped away. Taking the stairs, he went out of the building and crossed the playground – empty now, apart from the husband, who was standing by the gate, drawing hard on a cigarette.

Watching Carlyle approach, Hunter took a final drag on the fag before tossing it on the ground and stubbing it out with the toe of his boot. Then, thinking better of it, he reached down and recovered the flattened stub. 'I don't reckon much to your colleague.'

'Ward's not really my colleague.' Carlyle gestured in the direction of the school building. 'I only just met her up there. We've never worked together before.'

Hunter flicked the stub over the gate. It bounced once on the pavement and disappeared into the gutter. 'So why are you here? I need something to happen – and soon. God knows what those bastards are doing to my family! Are you going to help me?' The big man's face was ugly with tension.

'Yes, I am. It was my sergeant who tried to stop them and got a smack in the face for her trouble.'

Hunter nodded and rubbed a hand over his face. 'So what do you think?'

Carlyle grimaced. 'That's what I was going to ask you.'

TWELVE

Leaving the school, they found a greasy-spoon café on North Audley Street, a block south of Oxford Street. The lunchtime rush was over and the place was empty apart from a couple of students sitting in the back, hunched over their iPads. Stepping up to the counter, Carlyle contemplated the range of cakes and pastries on offer. The girl behind the counter waited patiently while he wrestled with his conscience. After several moments, he chose the side of the angels, settling for a small pot of green tea.

'Anything to eat?' the girl enquired, her accent suggesting that she hailed from somewhere east of the Oder-Neisse Line – the border between Germany and Poland.

Carlyle hesitated. 'No.'

With a brisk nod, she turned her attention to Hunter.

'Double espresso, please.'

Waiting patiently at the counter, each man kept his own counsel as the girl banged away at the coffee machine. Once they had retreated to a table by the window, Hunter slipped a small wallet across the table. 'That's me.'

Carlyle inspected the warrant card and handed it back. 'So you're a cop?'

Hunter nodded. 'Military Police.'

'Must be interesting.'

'It has its moments.' Looking edgy, Hunter downed his coffee in a single gulp.

'I bet.' Removing the tea bag from the pot, the inspector

dropped it on his saucer. Half-filling the cup, he took a cautious sip. Basking in the imagined approval of his wife, he made a mental note to point out his reduced caffeine intake when he got home. Then he thought how he would feel if his own wife and daughter had been kidnapped, and his guts cramped involuntarily.

'It can be quite tricky.' Hunter was holding it together like a pro. 'You've got to be a bit of a politician and a diplomat, as well as a cop.'

'Tell me about it.' Carlyle, who was neither, chuckled knowingly.

'I've been doing it a long time,' Hunter said quietly. 'And I like to think I'm good at it. But now . . . it's the reason Mel and the kids got snatched.' So saying, he pulled a crumpled envelope from the front pocket of his trousers and dropped it on the table.

Eyeing Hunter, Carlyle made no move to touch it.

'Go on, take a look.'

Carlyle obliged. Picking up the single sheet of paper, he scanned its simple message. *Lay off Andy Carson. We know where you live.* The inspector frowned. 'Who's Andy Carson?'

'Aka Soldier A.' Hunter slowly talked Carlyle through the Andy Carson investigation, the court-martial and Carson's violent escape. Once he'd finished, he signalled to the girl behind the counter that he'd like another coffee.

Putting the paper back in the envelope, Carlyle poured the last of his tea from the pot into the cup. 'I didn't know that the Army had its own prison.'

'The Military Corrective Training Centre is not officially a prison.' Hunter parroted the official line.

'Sounds like a prison to me.'

'It exists to detain personnel of the three Services and civilians subject to the Armed Forces Act, in accordance with the provisions of the Service Custody and Service of Relevant Sentences Rules 2009, and provide them with corrective training while they're there.' Hunter paused and looked Carlyle in the face. 'I've sent quite a few soldiers there over the years, as you can imagine.'

107

Carlyle scratched his chin. 'It's a bit late to be trying to warn you off Carson.'

'That's what I thought. Mel and I have been getting these notes for ages, since the beginning of my investigation. They were hardly the most sophisticated of threats but enough to spook the wife a little bit. I just ignored them. They stopped before the court-martial got underway. Anyway, we'd moved off base by then and were given a flat in London, so I thought they wouldn't be able to trace us and that it was all over.' Hunter took the letter and shoved it back into his pocket. 'Then this one turns up. To be honest, I thought it was a joke. Carson's family, some of them are a bit dim, know what I mean? Looks like I should have taken it more seriously.' A murderous look crossed his face. 'When I get hold of them . . .'

'Inspector Ward thinks it's a domestic. Did you explain all of this to her?'

'Her eyes glazed over after about two seconds. She obviously thinks I'm spinning her a line. In her mind, the most likely explanation is that it's just some marital row that's got way out of hand.'

'It's a not unreasonable assumption,' Carlyle mused, surprised to find himself in the position of defending the hatchet-faced Ward.

'Who would fake a kidnapping, for God's sake?' Hunter's control was slipping. He took out his pack of cigarettes and put them on the table, obviously dying for a smoke.

'Stranger things have happened. When people get desperate, normal judgement goes out the window.'

'If that's the story you want to create . . .'

'I'm just trying to see it from Ward's point of view. She lands this case, which is a bit strange. And then you turn up with a story that makes it a whole lot stranger.'

'I can see that.' Hunter nodded, but his leg was jiggling up and down.

'She doesn't want to swallow anyone's line.'

'Naturally suspicious.'

'Not a bad thing in a cop,' Carlyle pointed out.

'No,' Hunter agreed. 'I see quite a few cases of domestic violence myself. When guys come home, a lot of them find it hard to adjust.'

Carlyle looked across the table, expressionless. 'Do you beat your wife?'

'No!' Recoiling from the question, Hunter sat back and put his hands on his head.

'Any domestic problems?'

'Other than the fact that I'm away all the bloody time? No, not really. I don't think so.' Sitting up, Hunter folded his arms.

'Are you on the road a lot?'

'Yeah. The investigations we get could be anywhere: Afghanistan, Cyprus, the Falklands – you name it. I would say that I spend almost half my time out of the country. On average, I only get to sleep in my own bed four or five nights a month.'

'It must be tough.'

'Yeah. Do you have kids?'

Carlyle nodded. 'One.'

'I've got two. Susannah is eight and Robert is almost six. You know what it's like. They're growing up fast. What I do, it's not a job for a family man. I've got to pack it in before it's too late. Otherwise I'm going to walk through the door one day and there'll be no one there.'

Looks like that day's arrived. Carlyle was startled by his phone squawking into life, with the blast of some techno track – Alice's idea of a joke. 'Sorry, my daughter's been fiddling with my phone again.' Checking the screen, he was even more surprised to see Sheelagh Buttimer's name. He lifted the handset to his ear.

This time, Sheelagh was all business. 'That van you were asking about. It's just been found abandoned.' She gave him an address a little way north of the Westway. 'I thought you'd want to know.'

'Great. Thanks.' He signalled to Hunter for a pen. 'Could you give me that address again?'

'Bell Street. Ironically enough, it's only about two minutes from Paddington Green.'

The captain took a biro from his pocket and handed it over.

'Ta.' Carlyle grabbed a *Metro* that had been discarded on the next table and scribbled the address down. 'Thanks for the heads-up, Sheelagh.'

'Just don't get me any Milk Tray this time,' she warned him. 'I'm on a diet at the moment.'

'Okay,' he said, genuinely grateful. 'Speak soon.'

Finishing his tea, he tore the address from the newspaper.

'A development?' Hunter asked.

Getting to his feet, Carlyle made a snap decision. 'They've found the van. C'mon, let's go and take a look.'

Arms folded, Hunter's impassive expression faltered as a technician emerged from the back of the parked van, a small backpack in each hand. On the other side of the road, a couple of scruffy old blokes in cardigans stood in the doorway of a second-hand bookshop, occasionally sipping from large mugs of tea as they watched the proceedings.

'Are these your children's bags?' Returning from a fruitless recce, Carlyle appeared at Hunter's shoulder.

The captain nodded.

'The van can't have been here for very long. We were lucky.' The inspector lifted his chin in the direction of the bookshop. 'They left the back doors open. One of those two had a snoop around, saw that it had been hotwired and called it in.'

Hunter kept his bloodshot eyes on the empty van as if he was trying to absorb any information it contained via some kind of ESP. 'Did they see anything?'

'Sadly not. They rarely open up before lunchtime. It was here when they arrived.'

Hunter nodded. 'Anyway, we know who did it.'

More or less. 'They're dusting for prints now but it looks like it's clean.'

'It will be.'

'Maybe not. You said that Carson's mates were a bit dim. They could have left something.'

'His family, not his mates. Some of his family are a bit thick, particularly his brother. Five foot four and he wanted to take me down an alley for a scrap.' Hunter shook his head at the memory. 'I would have killed him.'

'People usually mess up,' Carlyle observed.

'This wasn't his family.'

'No?'

'No.' Hunter's voice was clear; his statement definitive, if not very illuminating. Beginning to feel confused, Carlyle started to review the wisdom of showing some faith in Hunter. Just because he was a cop didn't mean he couldn't be a flake; a wife-beating flake at that.

His only interest in this was Roche. Roche was okay. Why had he felt the need to jump in and stick his nose in Ward's case? *You berk*, he admonished himself. *You can never just leave things alone, can you?*

'The people who got him out – the people who did this . . . they're professionals. No one in the Carson family could do this.' Hunter stared at Carlyle as if challenging him to disagree.

'So who did?'

'Military guys.' Hunter scratched his cheek. He was weary and he needed a shave. 'Military guys who need Carson for something. They wouldn't go to all this trouble for nothing.'

Really? Carlyle gave an indistinct grunt.

'Carson kept some interesting company. It came up in my investigation but wasn't really relevant to what happened to some Taliban muppets in a field in the middle of nowhere. There's a murky world of servicemen, ex-servicemen and gangsters that most people don't know about.' Hunter corrected himself. 'That most people don't *want* to know about.'

Carlyle nodded. This was a world of which he was well aware. It was his pal Dominic Silver's preferred labour pool, back in his

111

drug-dealing days. Dom's long-time lieutenant, Gideon Spanner, had come out of the Army with an exemplary service record and an excellent contacts book.

'Carson was plugged into that world.' Hunter mentioned a few names that meant nothing to Carlyle. 'I know for a fact that he had done a couple of freelance jobs, quite big too. He was part of a gang that knocked off a bookmakers at York Racecourse and took off with nigh on a million quid.'

'I read about that. I thought they were never caught?'

'They weren't. Not my problem. I was running a murder investigation.'

'Fair point.'

'It's my problem now though. I reckon that Carson's crew needed him for a job.' Hunter lifted his gaze towards the end of the road and the traffic hurtling in the direction of Heathrow on the Westway. 'It must be one hell of a job for them to go to this much trouble to scare me off.'

Carlyle kicked a small stone down the road. 'Well, they picked a good place to dump the van. They could have gone anywhere from here.' He gestured in both directions. 'And this must be just about the only street in London with next to no CCTV. Perfect.'

Hunter nodded. 'Like I said, these are serious guys. Smart. Organized. Disciplined.'

'Speaking of which,' Carlyle said, 'we should get out of here before Ward turns up.'

'Too late.' Hunter pointed to the hunched figure striding towards them. A mobile phone was clamped to her ear; as she got closer it was clear that she was having an argument with the poor sod on the other end of the line.

'Shit,' Carlyle muttered. He already had more than enough women in his life, bossing him about; he didn't need another one. Looking around, he searched in vain for an escape route.

'Uh oh,' Hunter smirked. 'You are so *busted*.'

Ending her call, Ward caught sight of the two men. Her eyes

narrowed and Carlyle could have sworn that her hands instinctively balled up into fists.

I'm busted all right. Taking a deep breath, Carlyle braced himself for the inevitable bollocking.

'What are you doing here?' she demanded, addressing the pair of them simultaneously.

Carlyle shrugged. 'I heard that they'd found the van.'

Coming to a halt a couple of yards in front of them, Ward pointed at Hunter with the phone. 'And what the fuck is *he* doing here?'

'I thought he could come and have a look.'

Now her hands were definitely balled into fists. 'Why did you think that?'

'Why not?' Carlyle edged backwards. He didn't want to find out how good Ward's left hook might be. At the same time, he knew that he couldn't lift his hands under any circumstances. If he were to give in to temptation and belt the stupid woman, even in self-defence, he would be out of a job in less time than you could say *'gender equality has its limits'*, or something similar.

'And *I* thought that this was *my* investigation.' Ward jerked a thumb over her shoulder in the direction of Paddington Green police station on the other side of the Edgware Road. 'Maybe I should nip back and have a word with Carole Simpson. See what she has to say about all this.'

You know the Commander? Carlyle smiled weakly. 'She's not around at the moment. She's on a course.'

'And while she's on this course, did the Commander give you a green light to stick your nose into my case?'

'She knows what I'm up to.' The truth was that Simpson had not returned his call. Carlyle hoped that she had at least listened to her voicemail. The message he had left did give a fig leaf of credibility to his statement.

They had reached a stand-off. Placing her hands on her hips, Ward turned her attention to Hunter. 'Well?' she demanded, 'Have you seen anything interesting – anything that supports the version of events that you outlined to me at the school?'

Eyes fixed on the van, Hunter shook his head. 'Nope.'

'Okay. Well, you need to come with me now, so that we can take your formal statement.'

Hunter glanced at Carlyle, the annoyance on his face clear. Being a soldier, however, he knew when to pick his battles. 'Very well,' he said meekly.

'Fine.' Ward did a pirouette and began marching back in the direction from which she'd come. 'Let's go.'

Before Hunter could follow after her, Carlyle quickly fished a business card out of his pocket and offered it to the soldier. 'Give me a call on the mobile when you're done. I'll do a bit more digging in the meantime.'

Ward was already the best part of ten yards down the road. Nodding, Hunter took the card and jogged slowly after her.

Carlyle watched him catch her up. Reaching the end of the street, they had disappeared into the hustle and bustle of the Edgware Road before he remembered why he'd wanted to speak to Ward in the first place. 'Bollocks,' he said aloud. 'She still hasn't told me about Lucio Spargo.'

THIRTEEN

The middle-aged woman standing at the front of the class nodded in appreciation of her charges. 'Good! Very good.'

An uncomfortable silence descended on the room. The teacher then used an extendable baton to point at the mantra which had been scribbled on to the whiteboard in green pen.

'One more time, ladies and gentlemen – with *feeling*!' The cheery desperation in her voice suggested she was well aware of the deep pools of scepticism within her audience. 'You have to really believe it, if you are going to make it work.'

A low groan went round the classroom, mixed with a few mutterings of discontent, which reluctantly, painfully morphed into the grim chant that the group had been repeating for the last ten minutes or so.

'Positive energy will flow from my being. I will destroy negative energy with empathy and compassion. I will promote social good through my professionalism and dedication.'

'Good!' A rictus grin plastered on her face, the facilitator placed her free hand on her stomach. 'Remember, I want you to breathe from the diaphragm. *Feel* what you are saying. Let the words flow from your inner depths.' She surveyed the blank faces in front of her and ploughed on. 'This is a very serious business. It is about transforming the way that you live your lives in a positive and empowering manner. I want the words to connect with your innermost self. I want you to *become* the words.'

A number of bemused looks were exchanged, quickly followed by the sound of the baton tapping on the board.

'Last time! *Positive energy will flow from my being. I will destroy negative energy with empathy and compassion. I will promote social good through my professionalism and dedication.*'

It sounded more like a dirge than an outpouring of optimism.

Sitting at the back of the classroom, Commander Carole Simpson mumbled the words into the palm of her hand. Despite nine hours' sleep, a series of back-to-back 'empowerment sessions' had left her feeling exhausted, not to mention seriously depressed. Struggling to stay awake, Simpson imagined she had gone back in time and was sitting in Mrs Campbell's Advanced French class, wondering if she should let the dishy Steve Bucknell take her to the Scala on Saturday night.

Steve Bucknell. Whatever happened to him? Almost forty years on, that didn't really bear thinking about. Simpson tried to drag herself back into the here and now. How long was this torture going to go on? Careful not to make eye contact with the teacher, the Commander scanned the room. Sitting in front of her were some of the Metropolitan Police's brightest and best. Each one of them had been hand-picked by the Commissioner to attend the three-day course on *Happiness, Focus & Decision-Making.* Sitting behind their desks, out of uniform, they all looked rather dazed.

Gazing out of the window, Simpson watched another group of senior police officers as they went about the 'bonding with nature' module of the event. Unfortunately, the skies had darkened, so that the bonding exercise meant a dash for the shelter of the nearest elm tree before the heavens opened. At least I'm not getting rained on, Simpson thought smugly. One of the last officers to make it under cover was a Deputy Assistant Commissioner from Leyton called Anna Arendt. Arendt was one of the Met's 'super-women'. Married with four kids, a husband who was a lawyer and a Labrador called Eddie, she was seen as a plausible medium-to-long-term bet for the first female Commissioner.

Irritatingly, she was also one of the most stable and happy people that Simpson knew. What does Anna make of all this, the Commander wondered, as her colleague disappeared into the trees in an attempt to escape the downpour.

According to the gossip, this whole fiasco was costing somewhere in the region of seven grand a head. Apparently, the Commissioner had been persuaded that it was a good idea by his wife. That wasn't such a surprise – the woman ran a PR company for health spas and holiday resorts. What were the odds, Simpson asked herself, of the comedians hosting this course being one of her clients? For the police force, however, it was a shocking amount of money to be spending on such nonsense at the best of times, never mind at a time when operational budgets were being cut and public-facing staff being reduced.

Biting her lower lip, Simpson realized that she was genuinely ashamed to be taking part in this circus. 'Let that be a lesson to you, Carole,' she mumbled to herself. 'You need to pay more attention to what's going on around you.' The Commander wished that she'd enquired about what the event actually involved, when her PA, Michael, had slipped it into her diary several months earlier. With a bit of foresight and planning, she could have booked a holiday instead; or organized a session of the Women in Policing Forum, in order to create an unfortunate but unavoidable scheduling clash. Under her breath, the Commander cursed Michael for not having properly flagged what precisely she was signing up *for*.

As it was, the Commander had already been on the train from Paddington before she checked the actual agenda for the course: positive thinking; happiness and decision-making; constructive leadership. By then, it was too late to do anything about it. The Commissioner had decided that everyone at the rank of Commander or above should attend 'happiness lessons', in order to become 'happiness activists' within the Force. The end result was that Simpson and forty colleagues had been sent on this three-day retreat at Cobb Hall, a decaying stately home in the

Home Counties, which served as the HQ of something called the Brighter Smile Organization. Brighter Smile promised to teach 'better management through happiness'. In practice, the course involved learning meditation techniques to help students live in the present and not to brood about the past. Tutors helped them focus on their breathing and also on allowing their minds to wander. By learning 'mindfulness', the officers were supposed to improve their 'personal resilience' at critical periods in their lives and increase their leadership potential.

A new slogan appeared on the whiteboard. Simpson's eyes refused to focus on the words as she realized that it was going to take all of her 'personal resilience' to get through the three days without murdering the stupid bitch at the front of the class. The Commander held on to the hope that one of her colleagues might take matters into their own hands and off the facilitator for her. However, most of them looked too shell-shocked to make a move. Far more worryingly, a few looked as if they were actually enjoying themselves; doubtless those officers were headed for great things in the new, laid-back Met.

'Now, we want to move to the next level . . .'

Simpson tried to tune out the woman's inane utterances. God help them if the media ever found out about this nonsense, she thought glumly. The *Daily Mail* would have an orgasm if it uncovered the story.

Shifting uncomfortably in her seat, the Commander accidentally kicked her bag, which was sitting on the floor. Looking down, she caught a glimpse of her mobile phone blinking inside. Refusing to switch it off had been a small act of insubordination. For the duration of the course, all phones had to be switched off; participants were supposed to have no contact with the outside world. The enforced isolation was intended to help them build up their reserves of happiness. It was another thing driving her mad.

'Now,' said the teacher, barging her way back into the Commander's consciousness, 'we're going to look at how we focus on thoughts, feelings and bodily sensations.'

118

Oh sweet Jesus. Grabbing the bag, Simpson gently pushed back her chair, careful not to let it scrape against the wooden floor. Getting to her feet, she bolted for the door.

Outside the classroom, Simpson stood in a long, empty corridor which smelled strongly of damp. After a moment's hesitation she headed left, slipping round a corner and ducking into the ladies' toilets. Happily, it was empty. Locking herself in a stall, Simpson put down the toilet lid and sat with her bag on her lap before taking out her phone and checking the screen.

Six missed calls.

Three of those were simply her answerphone calling to tell her she had a message. That left three actual messages from real people. Simpson felt a stab of disappointment; she would have hoped for more than that after almost a day and a half away from her desk. That was another thing that was so profoundly depressing about these kinds of events – they reminded you just how effortlessly the world kept turning when you were removed from it. A meteorite could land on top of Cobb Hall, taking out a large swathe of the Force's 'brightest and best' and it would matter not a jot. Everything would go on exactly as usual. Indeed, there was a 50:50 chance that the crime rate would go *down*.

Giggling at the thought, she turned her attention to the three bona fide calls. The first was from her financial adviser, an excitable young man called Jonathan who was trying to get her to invest in an Emerging Markets Investment Fund. Simpson had foolishly shown an interest in the thing a few weeks earlier when she had visited his offices in St James's to have her annual financial health check.

'You could easily afford to retire,' Jonathan had told her.

'I'm not thinking about that right now,' Simpson smiled. 'I like my job.'

For a moment, the boy looked flummoxed, unable to compute the sentiment. 'Lucky you,' he said finally.

'Yes,' she agreed, 'lucky me.' That, of course, had been before she had arrived at Cobb Hall. Just for a moment, the Commander tried to think about what retirement might look like. Nothing came to mind.

Jonathan could wait.

Simpson hit the delete button, confident that the financial adviser would ring her back in the next few days.

The second voicemail was more cryptic. A message from Sarah Ward: 'There's something I need to ask you about. It relates to an ongoing investigation. If you could give me a call as soon as possible, I would appreciate it.'

Simpson sighed. Ward was an inspector from West End Central; she had first met her at one of the Women in Policing events a year or so earlier. Without quite knowing exactly how it had happened, the Commander had turned into something of a mentor to her younger colleague. Increasingly, Ward had proved to be hard work. A pessimist, depressive and generally high maintenance, she was the type of person who might conceivably benefit from this damn happiness course. One thing was for certain: speaking to the woman right now would do nothing to improve the Commander's own happiness quotient. Deleting the message, she made a mental note to call Ward when she was safely ensconced back in Paddington Green.

Which left call number three.

John Carlyle.

'Boss, it's me. I know you're tied up on a course, but there have been a few developments. I just wanted to keep you informed. Give me a bell when you get the chance. Bye.'

'I just wanted to keep you informed?' Ha! Simpson had known Carlyle long enough to understand that the inspector liked to give the *impression* of sharing information, the better to allow him to go off and do whatever the hell he wanted, without paying due attention to the chain of command i.e. herself. Normally, she did not have the time or energy to bring him to heel. Now, however, was different. It was time to call her tiresome underling's bluff.

* * *

Seeing Simpson's number flash up on the screen, Carlyle hesitated before deciding to take the call.

'Boss!' he said cheerily. 'How's it going?'

'I'm out of town.'

'Why are you whispering?'

Simpson dropped her voice even lower. 'It's a long story.'

Sensing she was on the defensive, he kept probing. 'You're not in any trouble, are you?'

'No, no,' she muttered irritably. 'Why would I be in any trouble?'

'No reason. It's just that you sound a little stressed.'

'I'm fine,' Simpson snapped.

'I heard you were on a course.'

'That's right.'

'Ah, well. It's good to know they've still got money for that sort of thing.'

'Mm.'

'What kind of course is it?' he asked innocently.

'A management course.'

'Oh.' Carlyle smelled a rat. 'Anything interesting?'

'It's about happiness.' She knew he was fishing, but the words just kind of slipped out before she could stop them.

'A happiness course?' Predictably, he chuckled. 'What the hell is that?'

'It's about how to develop a positive frame of mind, in order to boost your decision-making and leadership skills.'

'Come again?'

'It is about,' she repeated, exasperated, 'trying to keep focused on the positive, so that you can do your job better.'

'I see,' said Carlyle thoughtfully. 'And is it any good?'

'Not really,' Simpson admitted.

'Ha! I can see how being sent on something like that could really piss you off.'

'Yes, well. Keep it to yourself.'

'Don't worry, boss, you know me. The soul of discretion.'

Yes, thought Simpson, when you want to be. Regretting having let the cat out of the bag, she struggled to remember why she'd called him in the first place. 'So what's going on? You said you wanted to keep me informed about something or other.'

'Ah yes. There's been quite a bit going on here. None of it happy.' He explained about the apparent abduction of Mel Hunter and her kids and the assault on Roche.

'Fuck,' Simpson hissed. 'I sent her over there to see that cyclist.'

'That's okay,' Carlyle said cheerily, 'he didn't manage to video any of it.'

'Eh?'

'The guy who smacked Roche took the cyclist's cameras.'

'That hardly seems to be our most pressing concern right now,' Simpson said, her voice sharp.

It would be if we had a starring role on YouTube, Carlyle thought sourly. Aloud, he said, 'Anyway, Roche is going to be fine. She'll probably be back at work tomorrow.'

'Good, good.'

'In the meantime, I'm making a few enquiries of my own.'

Simpson started to protest then thought better of it. Carlyle was a law unto himself. By now, she knew better than to try and micromanage him. 'Okay. What else have you got on your plate at the moment?'

Carlyle mentioned a couple of routine cases. The clear implication was that they were ongoing; in reality, he had wrapped them both up the week before.

'Fine,' Simpson conceded. 'As long as those are put to bed, you can try and chase down Roche's attacker.'

'Thanks, boss.'

'Just remember though, that it's part of a wider investigation. *Someone else's* investigation. Don't go wading in and start causing aggravation.' Even as the words were coming out of her mouth, the Commander knew that they were wasted.

'No, boss.'

'Who is the lead investigating officer in the Hunter case?'

'An inspector out of West End Central by the name of Ward,' he said casually. 'I've never come across her before, but she seems all right – a bit touchy.'

Simpson's heart sank. 'Sarah Ward?'

'Yeah. She mentioned that she knew you. Any good?'

'Highly thought of,' was all Simpson could think of by way of reply. 'Just make sure you don't get in her way.'

Ending the call, she pulled up her knees and hugged them to her chest. Here she was, a grown woman hiding in a toilet stall. Out in the real world, her troublesome charges were being – well, troublesome. Rarely had she felt as unhappy as she did in that moment. 'Bloody hell, Carole,' she said to herself. 'How on earth did you end up here?'

FOURTEEN

'Who was that?'

Scratching his ear, Carlyle gave a rueful grin. 'The boss.' Tipping back his head, he drained the last drops of Jameson's from his shot glass. Should have got a double, he thought, or maybe even a treble. His bum had barely reached his seat and already he needed to get back to the bar.

'They should leave you alone when you're not at work.'

'You know what it's like. There's no such thing as off-duty these days.'

Alexander Carlyle nodded. 'Checking up on you, eh?'

'Something like that.'

Alexander looked at his son. John was more than a little worn around the edges, but still a boy in his old man's eyes. 'You're not in any trouble, are you?'

'No, no, of course not.' Carlyle placed the empty glass on the table, next to his mobile, a pile of change and a copy of the *Standard*.

'Good.' Alexander watched a couple come in from the street. 'How much longer is it until you can retire?'

Carlyle waved a hand airily. Retirement wasn't something that he wanted to think about. 'That depends.'

'You wouldn't want to mess things up before you got your pension.'

'There's no chance of that.'

'You have to be careful,' his father insisted.

Like you would know.

'It's the same everywhere, these days,' the old man grumbled. 'They'll always try and do you if they can.'

'You know me, Dad,' Carlyle chuckled, 'always one step ahead. There's no worries on that score.'

The inspector stared across the table at his father. The old man was deathly pale, with a clammy look to his skin, like a vampire, perhaps; hiding away from whatever weak sunshine London had to offer in the back snug of the Salting House. I wish you were a bloody vampire, Carlyle thought unhappily. At least then I wouldn't have to worry about you keeling over any time soon.

Come to think of it, I wouldn't mind being a vampire myself. It would make life simpler in a lot of ways.

What a ridiculous line of thought! He tried to physically shake the frivolous idea from his brain.

Alexander gave him a funny look. 'You okay?'

'Yes, fine.'

'What are you shaking your head like that for?' He looked around the pub, genuinely embarrassed at his boy's behaviour.

'Like what?'

'Like a nutter.' Alexander tried to shrink further into his seat. 'People will think you're soft.'

'Don't be daft,' Carlyle tutted. Of the dozen or so other afternoon drinkers present, none was showing any interest in the gathering of the Carlyle clan in the corner.

'I'm just saying,' Alexander sulked.

'Rubbish,' Carlyle snorted.

For several moments, they sat in uncomfortable silence.

'Your boss is still that woman, is it?' Alexander asked, attempting to return the conversation to a more neutral topic.

'Yeah,' Carlyle replied, happy to go along with it. 'I've been working with Carole Simpson a long time now.'

'I suppose you're used to her then.' Alexander frowned, as if still coming to terms with the various changes in gender equality that had occurred in his lifetime.

'It doesn't bother me.' Carlyle was aware he sounded rather stiff and defensive. 'She's a good cop.'

'Mm.' Alexander Carlyle rubbed a hand over his chin. Two days' growth covered his jaw, the grey stubble crawling up his sunken cheeks in an irregular line. 'Strange business though, wasn't it?'

'What?'

'Wasn't her husband a crook?'

Carlyle nodded. Joshua Hunt, aka Mr Carole Simpson, was indeed a convicted fraudster. 'That was a long time ago.'

'So how can you stay in the police force if your husband is bent? Surely that's not on?'

'The stuff he got up to – that was nothing to do with her,' Carlyle said evenly. The last thing he wanted to do now was get into a discussion of Simpson's unfortunate marriage.

'He died though, didn't he?'

'Yeah.'

'Cancer?'

Ah.

'I don't know,' Carlyle lied. Joshua Hunt had been diagnosed with cancer of the colon while in prison. He had been released on compassionate grounds, so that he could die in his own bed.

For a moment, his father was lost in thought. Through watery eyes, he watched a girl feed a succession of pound coins into a slot machine in the far corner of the room without any reward. 'Did she ever remarry?'

'No,' Carlyle replied. 'Not that it's any business of mine.' Or yours. 'Why do you ask?'

'Just making conversation, son. Just making conversation.' The girl finally gave up on her gambling spree and slouched back to the bar. 'Maybe that's why she doesn't trust you.'

'Eh?'

'That business with her man. That kind of thing would leave you suspicious of anyone.'

'She trusts me,' Carlyle said defiantly, 'professionally speaking.'

A flicker of amusement spread across Alexander's lips. 'Hardly. Not if she's checking up on you in the pub.'

'I rang her earlier. She was just returning my call.' Feeling his hackles rising, Carlyle glanced at the newspaper. It took considerable force of will not to pick it up and start reading.

'Mm.' The dark rings under his father's eyes glowed with malevolence. The eyes themselves, however, seemed almost to have disappeared into their sockets. Carlyle always remembered his father's eyes as sparkling with possibilities; now they appeared to have closed down. The lights were off, even if someone was still home.

What's more, Alexander's traditional dress sense seemed to have deserted him. Under a suit jacket he was wearing a grubby grey sweatshirt, with a couple of large sauce stains prominently displayed on the front. Carlyle had to admit that the old fella didn't smell too good, either. How long was it since he'd taken a shower? The inspector knew that he should say something but couldn't quite bring himself to offer any advice on personal hygiene.

Uncomfortable with his son's scrutiny, Alexander reached for the untouched pint of Guinness in front of him. It took an eternity for him to grasp the pint and lift it to his lips, taking a sip that barely made a dent in the head.

'Not fancy it tonight?' Carlyle asked, nodding at the pint.

Placing the glass carefully back on a beermat advertising a pole-dancing club that had recently opened up down the road, Alexander made a face. 'Ach, you know how it is.'

'How's it going?'

'I know I look like death warmed up but the last couple of days have not been so bad,' he answered, his voice so low that Carlyle had to lean almost all the way across the table to make out what he was saying. It wasn't just the rasping whisper. His father had lost his Scottish accent decades ago, soon after arriving in London; it only reappeared on the few occasions when the old man took too much drink. Now, however, it was making a comeback – or, at least, a cod version of it, mutated by fifty years of living in London – as he stared death in the face. Carlyle couldn't help but be amused.

Alexander noted the stupid look on his son's face. 'What's so funny?'

'Nothing.' A moment passed. 'Do you want to go home?'

'Eh?' Alexander pointed at his pint. 'I've still got my drink.'

'No, not back to the flat. I mean back to Scotland.'

'Scotland?'

'Yes, you remember. The country of your birth. Rains a lot.'

'Why would I want to go back there?'

'I just wondered.'

Alexander looked at him. 'D'you mean before I check out? Or after?'

Carlyle shrugged.

'Why would I want to go back?' Alexander repeated, signalling the end of that particular topic of conversation.

'So you're feeling a bit better?' Carlyle asked, returning to less controversial ground.

'A bit. The pain comes and goes but most of the time it isn't so bad. There have even been a couple of days this week when I've been able to forget about it altogether.'

'That's good,' Carlyle said, and he meant it.

Alexander stared him in the eye. 'For a while, anyway. It's not going to go away, is it?'

'No, it's not.'

'I spoke to the GP again yesterday. He's a nice lad. Originally from Swansea. Very young.'

'They all are, these days. Just like coppers.'

Alexander raised an eyebrow. 'Some coppers, at least.'

'Aye, well.' Fuck, where had that Scottish accent come from? Stop sounding like a dick, Carlyle admonished himself.

'He's still trying to find me something better for the pain.' The old man gestured towards the unsupped pint on the table. 'Says I need to give up the drink though.'

Carlyle was baffled. 'What's the point of that?'

'You can't mix the drink and the drugs.'

'Bollocks.'

'That's what he says. But I need something, son. When it's bad . . .' His voice trailed off, making Carlyle recoil in shame.

'I know, Dad. I know.'

Alexander gave him a look that challenged the veracity of that statement.

'It's just that dealing with the NHS is so bloody annoying,' Carlyle said, relieved that his mouth had reverted to using the Queen's English. 'Pain relief is the one thing that they *can* do. Why don't they just give you the strongest stuff available? It seems crazy that they make it all so complicated.'

'What are they going to do?' Alexander coughed. 'Give me a big bag of smack and send me off down the road?'

Funny you should mention that. 'I'm trying to sort something out,' Carlyle whispered. 'You can't just sit back and accept what you're given, or not given.'

'I've no complaints.'

'If you don't stand up for yourself, they'll just fob you off with any old rubbish. That's the way it works.'

'Don't worry about it.'

Carlyle felt miffed at his father's lack of enthusiasm for his efforts. The blue-collar stoicism was irritating. The inspector himself had effortlessly slipped into the ranks of the moaning middle classes over the years. That meant playing the game, stamping your feet, knowing your rights, exploiting your contacts. That was what it was all about. 'No,' he persisted, 'seriously. You should be getting more help.'

'You get what you get,' Alexander responded philosophically.

'There's no harm in asking.'

A flicker of curiosity passed across the old man's face. 'Asking who?'

'I have contacts.'

'Mm. I hope you're not discussing my business with the world and his wife.'

'I'm just seeing what might be available,' Carlyle said firmly. In truth, he was fed up with the whole business. As well as being irritated by his father's passivity, he was annoyed that Dom had not yet been in touch. With Lucio Spargo in his face, the art dealer no doubt had a lot on his plate. But even so, it was just a question of a couple of phone calls. Dom was a very organized and focused kind of guy; the whole thing should have been sorted out in less than ten minutes.

'You do that,' said Alex gruffly, as if nothing his son could get up to could in any way have an impact on the short-term suffering that was inevitably heading his way.

No need to say 'thank you', thought Carlyle peevishly.

Alexander stared into his pint but made no effort to pick up the glass. Instead, he shoved a hand inside his jacket and pulled out a tattered manila A5 envelope. Placing it on the table, he turned it around so that Carlyle could read the spindly scrawl on the front: *Inspector J. Carlyle.*

'It's for you.'

'I can see that,' said Carlyle, making no effort to pick the envelope up. 'What is it?'

'The arrangements.'

Oh fuck. Carlyle's heart sank. Here we go. He braced himself for yet another unwelcome conversation. 'What arrangements?'

'The arrangements,' Alexander snapped, swatting away his son's obtuseness as best he could. 'Everything you will need when the time comes is in there. Take a look.'

Still Carlyle sat back.

'Go on.'

'Jesus, Dad.'

'Don't be such a big Jessie. I'm saving you a load of aggravation here. Your mother was always the one for forward planning. Well, this time, I've taken a leaf out of her book. You should be chuffed.' He picked up the envelope and offered it to his son. 'Take a look and see.'

'Fuck!' Reluctantly, Carlyle took the envelope. Carefully tearing it open with his thumb, he pulled out a sheaf of papers which had been folded in two. Straightening them out, he began sifting through the pile: utility bills, tax statements, pension details. All the necessary bits of paper required to officially close down a life; or, rather, to close down a *former* life. At the bottom was a receipt from V&H Hannah on the Fulham Palace Road. Blinking, Carlyle stared at it for several moments before looking up at his father. 'Christ Almighty,' he said. 'What have you done?'

For the first time that evening, Alexander looked vaguely apologetic. 'I know it seems a bit strange—'

'I'll say,' Carlyle cut him off. 'Organizing your own funeral? What kind of weirdo does that?'

'Lots of people do it, apparently. So the undertaker said.'

'Yes, the kind of bampot who wants to have a vegan funeral and a cardboard coffin.'

'Folk who want things sorted out.' Alexander pointed at the bill. 'See there, down at the bottom. Says *"paid in full".*'

Thank God for that, Carlyle thought. Funerals were expensive these days and his savings, last time he'd dared to look, barely made it into four figures. 'How much was it?'

Alexander reeled off the figure, down to the last penny.

'Bloody hell!'

'Comes out of your inheritance, of course,' Alexander reflected, 'but there's nothing I can do about that.'

'Don't worry,' Carlyle chuckled. 'I wasn't expecting anything.'

'When the time comes, you just call them up and quote the reference number on the invoice and they'll come right round.'

How efficient.

'I've known Vincent Hannah since before you were born. We used to go to Fulham together in the sixties.'

Carlyle made a face; he didn't remember the guy.

'He died about seven years ago. His son, Henry, runs the place now. Nice lad. Younger than you.'

131

A thought popped into Carlyle's head. 'We should go and see a game.'

'Yeah. Why not?' Alexander smiled, but his voice betrayed his lack of interest.

'I'll see what's coming up.'

'Okey dokey.'

As the conversation waned, Carlyle flicked through the papers a second time.

'Everything's there,' Alexander repeated. 'Bills, rent agreement. There's even a council number you can ring – a kind of one-stop shop. They'll cancel my pension an' all that.'

'Handy,' Carlyle nodded.

'And the will, of course.'

'Yes.' Carlyle found the relevant document.

'There's not much left after paying for the funeral and stuff,' the old man explained, 'but there's a few bits and pieces I'd like to leave to Alice and I thought Helen might sort out the rest for me.'

'Helen?'

'Yes, well. She's good at that sort of thing, isn't she?'

And I'm not? 'Yes.' Folding up the papers, Carlyle forced them back into the envelope. 'That's a good effort, well done.'

'Thanks. Of course, I knew the drill from when your mother died.'

'I suppose,' said Carlyle stiffly.

'It's interesting, sorting out all the papers and stuff. I found the whole thing quite comforting really. It gave me something to do. It's just a shame that there are some things that'll have to wait until I'm, you know . . . well, dead.'

'That's bureaucracy for you,' was all Carlyle could stammer. Placing the envelope back on the table, he scooped up the change. 'Well, I certainly need another drink after that.' He gestured towards Alexander's largely untouched pint. 'I'm assuming you're okay?'

'Fine,' the old man nodded. 'Perfectly fine.'

FIFTEEN

'Jesus, woman! You really know how to wind me up!' Ignoring the stream of invective coming from the handset, Gerry Durkan hurled his mobile at the window. The handset bounced off the reinforced glass and landed on the carpet, apparently undamaged.

How was it that he was still tied to Rose Murray? Shouldn't he be on his third wife by now? Or even his fourth? Instead, Rose had been driving him insane for more than three decades. While Gerry had been on a long and winding personal journey that had taken him from administering kneecappings on the Falls Road in Belfast to dishing out the Dom Perignon in Docklands, Rose had essentially remained unchanged, a gangster's moll. Her total inability to evolve as a person was something that pained Gerry greatly. Over the years, he had bought into the idea that personal growth was an essential component of a life well lived; it was an idea he embraced as fervently as the Fenian shibboleths of his youth.

Taking a succession of deep breaths, Gerry stared into the night sky, trying to remember exactly what it was that they had been arguing about. With Rose it really didn't matter. For something like the ten-thousandth time in his life, he made a vow that he would finally bring the world's most dysfunctional relationship to an end; trade in his own Bonnie Parker for a nice Sloaney girl with an easy smile and not an idea in her head.

Or maybe a Russian hard body. The kind of girl who took no

shit and could siphon £5k from his credit card in Typhoon Joe's in less than an hour.

No, no. Definitely the Sloane.

Thinking through the possibilities for Mrs Durkan number two calmed him considerably. Walking over to the window, Gerry recovered his phone and checked that it was indeed still working. Giving heartfelt thanks for the wonders of modern technology, he made another call.

After several rings, he got a reply.

'What?'

What do you fucking think? Gerry thought crossly. Why was it that everyone was so focused on giving him shit? 'Is it done?'

'Not yet. The flight was delayed. Don't piss yourself. I'll call you when it's done.'

The line went dead. 'Yeah,' Gerry spat at the handset. 'And fuck you too.' Maybe, when the job was done, he should give these boys a taste of what the old days were like. See how hard they were with a gun stuck in their faces. But his anger quickly passed. Putting the phone back in his pocket, he caught a glimpse of himself in the window. He had to acknowledge that it wasn't a pretty sight. 'The good old days are long gone,' he told his reflection, 'and don't you forget it. You don't want to be goin' round makin' a fool of yerself now.'

'Who was that?'

'The boss.'

Andy Carson grinned. 'Tense, is he?'

Lifting his eyes to the arrivals board at London's City airport, Ryan Fortune said nothing.

'I still want to know who we're working for,' Carson continued. He had a QPR baseball cap pulled down low over his eyes. That, along with a day's stubble and a pair of rimless glasses offered a fairly effective disguise. In the forty minutes they had been hovering around the terminal, no one had given Britain's Most Wanted a second glance, not even when his ugly pixilated

134

mug appeared on the large screens showing the Sky News Feed. According to the ticker, police believed that Carson had fled the country. Fortune allowed himself a chuckle at that one; hiding in plain sight had a lot to commend it.

'It's a perfectly reasonable question,' Carson whined.

Fortune shook his head in exasperation. When was this fucking plane going to land? He was beginning to think that the job might be cursed. But if it got called off, that would leave everyone in a bind, not least Durkan. Ryan had worked with Gerry Durkan on half-a-dozen jobs over the last four years and had always found him to be reliable, professional and, above all, a man of his word. This time, however, things were different. Gerry had seen some investments go tits up and now he was desperate for a quick cash injection. Desperate was not good. Desperate was what led you to spring Andy Carson from jail because you didn't have time to find anyone else.

'What does it matter who he is?'

Carson scratched his head under the baseball cap. 'Maybe we should just do him.'

Fortune watched as an armed police officer strode slowly past, cradling a machine gun in his arms. He tried to ignore the signals from his brain inviting him to turn round and just walk out of the arrivals terminal, slip into the Range Rover stolen from long-term parking, and tell Colinson to drive them into the night. If only. 'Will you shut up, you total scrote?'

'Why not?' Carson grinned. 'It's an idea; save the whole score for us.'

'And who would fence the gear?'

'How hard can it be?'

'Everybody has their jobs to do. That's his. Anyway, he's no mug. I wouldn't fancy your chances if you went up against him.'

'I very much doubt that,' Carson harrumphed. 'Apart from anything else, the bloke's too scared to let me to know who he is.'

Fortune turned to face his mate. 'Andy, for the last time, you don't want to possess that information. And that's me talking. The man himself couldn't give a flying fuck whether you know who he is or not. I'm not tellin' you his identity for your own good. The less you know, the better.'

'Stupid cunt,' Carson snorted.

Fortune looked like he was about to give him a smack.

'Not you,' Carson said hastily. 'Our Mr Big.'

'There's nothing stupid about him,' Fortune informed Carson. 'And he's not the kind of bloke who scares easily. Back in the day, he was quite the man.'

'Back in the day?'

'In the seventies and eighties.'

'That's a long time ago. Was he in the Army?'

Fortune chuckled. 'Not exactly. Take it from me though, he still has it. And he's not a bloke you should mess with. He's put far more people in the ground than you have – and none of them were illiterate sheep-shaggers who had already surrendered.' Once again, he looked up at the arrivals board. 'Thank fuck for that.' The Antwerp flight had finally landed. He gave Carson a gentle punch on the shoulder. 'Game on, my son. The fun's about to start.'

Trying to look as casual as possible, they positioned themselves at the front of the Essex Pasty Company franchise, just two regular guys waiting for the return of friends or relatives. While Fortune scanned the terminal building for another of the sporadic police patrols, Carson consulted the menu.

'Beef in red wine sauce sounds good.'

'Fuck's sake, Andy,' Fortune hissed. 'Focus on the matter in hand.'

'But I'm starvin'. We've been standing around here like numpties for more than an hour.'

'Shouldn't be long now.' Fortune felt the reassuring presence of the Glock in his jacket pocket. Fantasising about saving the last round for Carson, a smile played at the corner of his lips.

'What's the joke?'

'Nothing.' According to the board, it looked like four flights had arrived more or less at the same time. As waves of travellers started spewing out of the customs area, Fortune focused on making his breathing deep and regular. Now he had to be calm and decisive. Everything must flow as he ordained it. Letting his shoulders loosen, he recalled the mantra from the Focus & Decision-Making class that he'd taken on the recommendation of one Gerry Durkan Esq.:

'Positive energy will flow from my being. I will destroy negative energy with empathy and compassion. I will promote social good through my professionalism and dedication.'

'There's loads of people coming out of here,' Carson whined. 'How the hell will we find our guy in the middle of all this?'

Fortune sighed. 'Don't worry about that.' With the slightest tilt of his head, he gestured towards the line of seven or eight taxi drivers standing by the stairs, waiting for their fares. Each man had the same bored expression on his face as he stared vacantly into the middle distance. In each set of hands was a board with a name scribbled on it in marker pen. 'The guy on the far end in the Spurs shirt. The one with the ginger hair.'

Taking a step forward, Carson squinted at the sign the taxi driver was holding under his chin. 'Go-pal Ullal . . . math? What kind of a name is that?'

'The name of a man who is just about to say goodbye to a fortune in diamonds.'

Gopal Ullalmath wished he hadn't had that last beer on the plane. A nervous flier at the best of times, he didn't like taking to the skies in anything smaller than an Airbus A320. At least in one of those you could try and forget that you were actually 30,000 feet in the air with only the thinnest of sheets of metal between your ass and . . . nothing. By contrast, the Fokker that plied the Antwerp–City route only carried fifty passengers. Every time Gopal caught sight of the turbo-prop engines, he thought he was about to throw up. Worst of all, as the plane circled over London

137

on its descent into City, he imagined them smacking into the top of one of the skyscrapers that lined the Thames. Not so long ago, a helicopter had done just that. Gopal considered it almost inevitable that, one day, a plane he was on would do the same.

The most annoying thing about the whole experience was that it was so unnecessary. Gopal regularly begged his uncle, Bob Biswas, to be allowed to take the Eurostar. This plea was routinely rejected on grounds of cost and/or convenience. Biswas ran a tight ship; one that made full use of the delights of low-cost airlines wherever possible.

Working for Uncle Bob was something of a mixed blessing. Biswas Trading Services offered relatively relaxed hours and good pay. Career prospects were hard to define, however, and if asked, Gopal would be hard pressed to offer up a job description for his role. His mother was still on at him to become an accountant. After a trip like this, Gopal wondered if she might not be right.

Where Bob refused to help with Gopal's travel problems, there was always Heineken. However, self-medicating with lager was never a good idea. Gopal had a limited capacity for alcohol and a smaller bladder capacity. At the end of the flight, he found himself slouching through customs with an aching groin and a restless stomach. The prospect of a car ride across London did nothing to improve his mood. The city's traffic was a complete lottery: the journey could take forty minutes or it could take the best part of two hours. As he stepped through the sliding doors, to be confronted by a sea of faces and a blast of icy air, he turned to his travelling companion. 'I need to use the toilet,' he said. 'Find the driver and I'll catch up with you outside.'

Ignoring the fact that this would already be Gopal's second comfort break since getting off the plane, Giles Brix gave a curt nod. Lifting a meaty finger, he gestured towards a sign hanging from the ceiling off to his left. 'The rest rooms are over there.'

'Thanks.'

Keeping a tight hold on his case, Brix watched Gopal scuttle off towards the facilities. Why the guy couldn't save his drinking until after the conclusion of business, Brix didn't know. Stepping away from the doors, he scanned the line of waiting drivers until he spotted the one with the right name-board. Catching the eye of the driver, a scruffy-looking bloke in a football shirt, Brix gave him a thumbs-up. The guy clocked the attaché case, catching a glimpse of the handcuffs that attached it to Brix's wrist. His mouth opened as if he was about to say something then he clamped it firmly shut.

Brix gestured towards the exit. 'Let's go.'

'Mr Ullal . . .' the guy took a quick look at his board, 'math?'

Close enough. Brix nodded. 'He's just coming. He'll meet us outside.'

From across the concourse, Carson watched the big white bloke with the case approach the ginger-haired guy he had now come to think of as 'his' taxi driver. 'Are you sure that's him?'

'Must be,' Fortune shrugged.

'Big bloke.'

Not quite what I was expecting, Fortune thought, but said aloud: 'Nothing we can't handle. The gear will be in the case.'

'Handcuffed to his wrist,' Carson pointed out.

'He can keep the case,' Fortune observed, 'as long as he opens it.'

An unhappy thought suddenly occurred to Carson. 'Supposing he can't?'

'Worst comes to the worst,' Fortune grinned, 'you chop his arm off.'

'Eh?'

'Only joking. Adrian's got some bolt-cutters in the back of the motor. Don't worry though, it won't come to that. These guys are told to give the stuff up, rather than have any trouble. That's what insurance is for.' Sticking a hand inside his pocket, Fortune let his fingers close round the grip of the Glock. 'Now remember, we let them get outside into the car park, and then we take the stones, nice and easy. No muss, no fuss and no fucking drama. We're not in some paddy field in Shitsville now. I can't have any of your *dogs of war* shit goin' on.'

'It wasn't a paddy field,' Carson huffed. 'And he would have done the same to me.'

'Mm.'

'Or maybe he would have made a video of his mates chopping my head off and stuck it on the internet.'

Sounds like an idea.

'Imagine the family watching that!'

'Horrible,' Fortune agreed. But he was sure that Becky would be able to take her old man losing his head in her stride. The formidable Mrs Carson was a force of nature. Indeed, he was beginning to wish he'd brought her along and left her old man in the nick. 'Have you spoken to them yet?'

'Left a message.' Carson caught Fortune's sideways look. 'Nothing silly.'

'Good.'

'Said I was in Dublin.'

'That'll throw them off the scent,' Fortune said drily.

'It's thirty-two degrees in Sitia today.' Carson's voice was wistful.

'I dunno what you're bothering to check the weather forecast for,' Fortune retorted. 'You won't be going there. I told you, Greece is off the agenda. Get used to it.' He watched as the taxi driver stuck the name-board under his arm and led his fare through the milling crowd, heading towards the exit. On the far side of the concourse, a couple of coppers were slowly making their rounds. A man and a woman, both in their twenties, walking in step, stony-faced; both of them heavily enough armed that they could pass for extras in a Schwarzenegger movie.

Carson followed his gaze. 'What about the plods?' he asked.

'We knew they would be here.'

'But—'

'The guns're just for show,' Fortune scoffed. 'I bet they couldn't hit a coconut from ten yards.'

Carson looked doubtful. 'Whatever happened to the great unarmed British bobby?'

'Ancient history. Even Inspector Morse would have a Heckler & Koch MP5 these days. Instead of a Jaguar, he'd be driving a bloody tank.' He laughed briefly at his own joke.

'Those two have got enough firepower to start a small war,' Carson said moodily.

'Only if they know how to use it.'

'Either way, they could make a hell of a mess.'

'Which is precisely why they'll never take the safety off,' Fortune reasoned. 'Those cops wouldn't want the risk of shooting somebody innocent by mistake. The danger of taking down a few bankers – or even a handful of ordinary taxpayers – far outweighs the need to stop a couple of minor-league crims like us.' He watched the taxi driver disappear through the exit and into the darkness, closely followed by the man with the case. 'Anyway, by the time they make it outside, we'll be halfway to the Blackwall Tunnel.'

'Let's hope so.'

'Christ!' Fortune complained. 'How did a few months in prison manage to turn you into such a total pussy? That's one of the great things about doing a job at an airport – there are plenty of escape routes.' He gave his comrade a nudge towards the exit. 'C'mon, let's go. Ten minutes and it will be job done and time to get the beers in.'

They strode towards the exit like two men without a care in the world. Fortune was in no particular hurry; he knew where the diamonds were going. The airport only had the one car park – a couple of football fields' worth of freshly laid tarmac by the side of the terminal building. It would be impossible to lose their target while he was still on the premises. Stepping into the phosphorus glow of the street lights, Ryan was hit by a wave of freezing air. For some reason, it always seemed colder in East

London. Zipping up his jacket, he took a deep breath, conscious of Carson at his shoulder, bouncing around like the Duracell bunny.

'Where are they?' Carson asked.

Fortune pointed in the direction of the car park as he picked up the pace. Swerving past a couple of returning holidaymakers, he tuned into a fragment of their conversation.

'*Lanzarote was a lot warmer,*' observed a fat, lobster-coloured woman as she tried to steer an overloaded trolley in something approximating a straight line.

'*Well,*' mused the tiny bloke following on behind her, '*it's gonna be, innit?*'

Leaving the pair behind, Fortune strode purposefully towards the car park. As he passed the first line of parked vehicles, he could see the driver and his fare about fifteen yards up ahead. The driver was waving a hand in the air as he talked. No doubt he would be apologizing for the walk, explaining that he couldn't get any closer to the building '*because of all the bloody security*', trying to build up a bit of a rapport in the hope of a decent tip at the other end. Behind them, illuminated against the inky black sky, Tate & Lyle sugar refinery offered a reminder that a few examples of the capital's industrial past still survived.

Just about.

Reaching the second row of cars, Fortune slowed his pace, waiting to determine precisely where the taxi was parked. As he hovered by the side of a burgundy Lexus, Carson appeared at his shoulder, gun in his hand.

'Put that fucking thing away!' Fortune ordered.

'But—'

'Put it away! It's only for show – *if* we need it.'

Carson reluctantly did as he was told.

The taxi driver was still leading the fare past another row of parked cars. Letting his eyes dart towards the exit, Fortune saw the stolen Range Rover sitting just outside the illumination cast by a streetlight. The headlights were on. Fortune could make out a pair of hands on the steering wheel but not the face of the driver. Adrian was ready to go.

A high-pitched beep told him that the driver had found his cab. 'Right,' he said to himself. 'Let's get this thing done.'

SIXTEEN

Stumbling out of the airport terminal, Gopal buttoned up his jacket and shoved his hands deep into his pockets. Contemplating the sea of butts strewn across the pavement, he suddenly fancied a smoke. He let the fingers of his right hand close around a packet of Marlboro Lights, only to confirm what he already knew – that it was empty; he had smoked his last cigarette before getting on the plane in Antwerp. Should he go back inside and get a fresh packet? He cursed himself for not stocking up in Duty Free. The bloody English made them so expensive – all that tax – it was like bloody Communism or something! Whatever happened to freedom of choice?

The other issue was time. Gopal glanced at his watch. They were already more than an hour behind schedule and Uncle Bob was a stickler for good timekeeping. *'Never keep the client waiting,'* he would say. *'Always show them that you value their time as much as they do themselves.'* He also liked to quote Shakespeare on the subject: 'Better three hours too soon than a minute too late.' Then again, the Merry Wives of Windsor had probably never had to use City airport.

Gopal vowed not to give in to his nicotine craving. Veering left, he began marching towards the car park. Skipping over a small pothole, his mind turned to the question of how he might spend the rest of his evening, once the work part of proceedings had been dealt with. All of London and its multitudinous delights were stretched out in front of him, but Gopal had the nagging sense that he wasn't making the most of the opportunities they presented. This was the sixth time he had come over from Antwerp in the last year or so. Each time, it was the same routine: make the delivery, then check into a Travelodge somewhere in the middle of the city before rising early to catch the 10.15 a.m. flight back to Belgium the next day.

On his first ever visit, Gopal had headed for the red-light district of Soho in search of smut and debauchery, only to be sorely disappointed. It was clear to even the most casual visitor that whatever seediness the place was supposed to contain had been cleaned up long ago. Other than a drab-looking 'sex shop' and a couple of obvious clip joints that only the most stupid or desperate would venture into, the place was just a familiar jumble of cafés and offices that could be found almost anywhere. Soho made the Schipperskwartier, Antwerp's own red-light district, look like the very heart of Sodom and Gomorrah. After wandering up and down Berwick Street for an hour, a disappointed Gopal had ended up in the Trocadero, a down-at-heel shopping centre on the south side of Shaftesbury Avenue, eating desiccated pizza and playing vintage arcade games. That had pretty much become the template for his subsequent trips. Tonight, he promised himself, he would do something different.

But what to choose?

'Christ Almighty, Gary. He's got a gun.'

Gopal looked up. A few feet ahead of him, an improbably fat woman, rather underdressed for the night's chill, was tugging at her trolley, trying to pull it back towards the terminal. Her companion, a small man in a red Adidas T-shirt, was gawping at something in the middle distance. Stepping behind an Audi, Gopal too looked – and saw two men standing in front of Giles and the taxi driver. Even at this distance, Gopal could see that they were engaged in what appeared to be a heated, if rather one-sided debate. One of them, the smaller of the two, was pointing a gun at Giles.

Shit. Grabbing his mobile, Gopal hit Bob's 'hotline' number that he was under strict instructions to use only in the direst of emergencies. Like this. After several moments, it started to ring.

'He's got a gun,' the woman repeated.

'Police!' the little man shouted. In truth, it was more like a question. Cowering behind the woman's not inconsiderable bulk, he said to her, 'C'mon, Tina. Let's get back inside. Leave the trolley and let's make a run for it.'

'The gear,' the woman pleaded, still gripping the trolley tightly. 'We can't leave our gear.'

'It's just stuff.'

'It's *my* stuff,' the woman argued. For a moment, the couple stood frozen by indecision. 'Go and get the cops,' she said finally. 'They're inside.'

The man didn't move.

The phone kept ringing. So much for an emergency hotline, Gopal thought crossly.

The woman called Tina gave her companion a hard poke in the ribs.

'Ow!'

'Stop being such a wanker, Gary. Go an' get the Old Bill.'

Gary stopped being a wanker and finally did what she asked.

'I told you we should have stayed for a second week,' the woman bawled after him. 'It was only an extra hundred and fifty bleedin' quid.'

Trying to ignore their squabble, Gopal listened to Bob's voice-mail kick in. Exasperated, he ended the call without leaving a message. He glanced back at Gary, who wasn't breaking any world records as he headed for the terminal.

Still gripping the phone tightly in his hand, Gopal stepped off the pavement and started walking towards the man with the gun.

He was less than ten metres away from the confrontation before his presence was noticed.

'What are you doing?' Gopal addressed the gunman, ignoring his larger colleague.

'Piss off, kid,' the gunman snapped, keeping his weapon trained on Giles as his eyes darted between the briefcase and the new arrival. His voice tried to exude authority but it had a brittleness to it that only added to the tension.

Gopal glanced at Brix, who was standing stock still, apparently unconcerned by developments. Behind him, the taxi driver fidgeted nervously with his car keys, shifting his weight from foot to foot as he tried to calculate the chances of finding some cover behind the boot of the BMW parked in the space next to his cab.

'*You* piss off,' Gopal shouted, surprised by his own audacity. Off to his right, there was a mighty roar as a plane took off from a nearby runway. Clearly, news of an armed man on the site had yet to make it to the control tower. For a moment, all further debate was put on hold.

'The police are coming,' Gopal shouted as the noise died away. And if they don't get you, he thought, my uncle will crush you like bugs.

'Fuck off,' the gunman countered. His larger associate shook his head, his eyes sparkling with delight, as if he was amused by the exchange.

'I would be careful, kid,' the big guy advised. 'He's armed and dangerous.'

The gunman swung his arm round. 'And I don't give a monkey's about the bloody police.' As he trained the gun on Gopal, Giles saw his chance. Jumping forward, he swung the case at the man's head. But the gunman easily ducked away from the blow. Gopal closed his eyes just as there was a loud explosion from the muzzle of the gun. He kept them tightly shut as the sound of the gunshot reverberated in his brain, followed by the sound of Giles whimpering on the tarmac.

Gopal half-opened his eyes.

'It's just a flesh wound.' The bigger man stepped over to Giles and pressed down on his blood-soaked trousers with the toe of one of his shoes.

147

'Awww!' Giles screamed. 'Fuck!'

'Unlock the handcuffs.'

'He can't,' Gopal quickly explained. 'We don't have the keys.'

The man frowned, but lifted his foot, releasing the pressure on Giles' wound.

'And we don't have the combination to unlock the case either,' Gopal added, anticipating his next question. 'He can't take it off or open it until we get to our meeting. That's just the way these things work.' It was true enough. Uncle Bill's security basically boiled down to the mantra: '*If they want it, they can chop your bloody arm off.*' At the time, Gopal had found this an amusingly quaint approach; now, not so much. Glancing back at the terminal, he saw Gary the holidaymaker emerge with two police officers. One was shouting into her radio, while the other lifted his machine gun to his shoulder and began walking slowly towards them.

Gary's wife was still stuck in no-man's-land, clinging on to her trolley for dear life.

The cop with his weapon raised was shouting something at them but he was too far away and his words were lost on the wind. He continued to approach them with all the speed of a pall-bearer. Clearly, the officer wasn't the have-a-go hero type. At his current rate of progress, he would be with them in about fifteen minutes. Where were the reinforcements? Gopal listened for the sound of sirens. Then he looked to the heavens for the reassuring whine of a police helicopter heading to the rescue.

Nothing.

The moment seemed frozen in time. Then the tableau was interrupted by a Range Rover which roared up and came screeching to a halt at the end of the row of parked cars.

'Keys,' the man demanded again.

Brix groaned.

'We don't have them,' Gopal insisted.

A pained expression crossed the man's face. 'Can't you unlock the case?'

Gopal shook his head.

The man looked at Brix.

Brix shrugged as best he could.

The seconds ticked slowly past. Word had obviously reached the terminal of an incident in the car park as no one had ventured outside in the last few minutes. The policeman with the machine gun was still closing in on them, inch by inch. Dancing forward like a batsman planning to hit a six, the gunman lifted his weapon and fired a warning shot over the cop's head. Immediately, the officer ducked behind a parked van; the advance had been halted.

'Hey!' the large guy shouted. 'No shooting!'

The gunman gave his accomplice a *no big deal* look and gestured towards the getaway car. 'Want me to get the bolt-cutters for the handcuffs?'

'No time.' The big man grabbed Brix by the collar and pulled him to his feet. 'We'll have to sort this out en route.' He began marching Brix towards the car.

'What about the other two?' the gunman asked.

Gopal glanced at the taxi driver, who was now sitting on the tarmac, mumbling to himself. In one hand, he grasped the crest on his football shirt as if that higher deity would help him escape this disaster unscathed.

'Just leave 'em,' the big man instructed.

'But—'

'Fucking hell, Andy! Just fucking leave them, all right? Enough with the cops and robbers already. We need to vamoose. Unless you want to go straight back to fucking Peterborough, let's go.'

Fortune pushed the man with the case towards the back door of the Range Rover. 'What's your name?'

'Giles. Giles Brix.'

'Okay, Giles. We're going to get this little problem sorted out.'

Brix looked unconvinced. He was hobbling badly, wincing every time he put any weight on his injured leg.

'You and me are just the hired help here, am I right?'

'Yeah,' Brix agreed. 'That's right.'

'Neither of us wants to end up face down on the tarmac in a squabble over someone else's diamonds, do we?'

'No.' Brix nodded, his accent blanketed by a concentrated mixture of pain and fear. 'That's true enough.'

'Good. As long as we're on the same page, there's no problem. Just stay cool and everything will be okay.'

As they approached the motor, Colinson reached into the back and pushed open the door.

'Get in,' Fortune ordered. When Brix hesitated, Fortune gave him a glimpse of the Glock. 'Just because I don't wave it around like the moron over there doesn't mean I won't use it.'

Brix nodded and a fleeting look of professional understanding passed between the two men. Grabbing the door, Brix pulled himself inside and slid across the back seat. Fortune slipped in behind him, cursing as his ears were assaulted by a blast of hideous thrash metal that was pouring from the car's stereo.

Colinson drummed his hands on the steering wheel in time to the music. 'Hurry up!' he shouted. 'We should have been gone already.'

'Turn that shit off,' Fortune shouted.

Still hitting the wheel with one hand, Colinson smacked the stereo with the other. The silence was instant and almost overwhelming. It felt so good that Fortune nearly smiled. Slamming the door closed, he looked back for Carson. 'Andy . . .'

A shot rang out, followed by a second.

'No,' Fortune growled as he contemplated the two bodies sprawled on the tarmac. *'No, no no.'*

Carson turned and ambled towards the car, as nonchalant as a man heading to the pub on a Sunday lunchtime, not quickening his pace even as the first sirens sounded in the distance.

As the sirens got louder, Carson finally broke into a jog. Climbing into the front passenger seat, the blood splatter on his face made his child-like grin seem totally deranged. Colinson stomped on the accelerator and they shot forward, heading in the direction of the A1020.

Resisting an urge to splatter Carson's brains all over the inside of the windscreen, Fortune fumbled for his seatbelt. Clicking it into place, he nudged Brix, who was sitting with the case on his knees, eyes front.

'Buckle up,' Fortune advised. 'This is gonna be a bumpy ride'

SEVENTEEN

After seeing his father safely home, Carlyle headed back to Covent Garden. Feeling rather the worse for wear, he struggled to make sense of their situation. It was hardly unique. Nor was the fact that he was soon to become an orphan the greatest tragedy the world had ever seen. But he was conscious that he was moving into a new phase of his life and rather disconcerted that he didn't feel much about it, one way or the other.

Muttering to himself about '*circle of life shit*', he wandered down Endell Street. It was still early and the post-work crowds were out and about. The energy and enthusiasm coming up from the pavement made him feel a little better as he tried to shake the woolly feeling from between his ears. Even sipping at a slow pace, the inspector had managed to work his way through five shots of Irish whiskey in the time that Alexander had managed to drink approximately half of his pint of Guinness, spilling most of the rest when he knocked the damn thing over.

As Carlyle had been busy mopping up the mess, the auld fella had jumped to his feet and announced that he was calling it a night. Carlyle had returned the sopping bar towel to a less than impressed woman behind the bar, finished the last of his Jameson's and stumbled after him – not drunk exactly, but not entirely sober either.

'You shouldn't drink so much,' his father counselled as Carlyle tripped over a rogue paving stone and almost headbutted some random piece of street furniture which seemed to serve no obvious purpose, other than to turn a routine walk into an assault course.

'At least I managed to put it in my mouth,' Carlyle countered, rather unkindly.

'Good for you,' was all Alexander offered in retaliation.

They walked the rest of the way in silence. Reaching Alexander's flat – the family home on a small Fulham council estate where Carlyle had grown up – the inspector braced himself for the invite to come in for a cup of tea, but to his relief it was not forthcoming.

'Night, Dad.'

'Night, son.'

Carlyle watched him trudge towards the stairs. At least the old man was back in the family home. It was only a few years ago that his parents had divorced and Alexander had been banished to a nearby bedsit. Carlyle's mother had died not so long after that, and his father had quickly moved back in before the council could reclaim it.

'I'll let you know if I manage to get anything for the pain relief.'

'Aye,' said the old man, his tone indicating a complete indifference one way or another. 'You do that.'

Back in Covent Garden, Carlyle decided that he didn't want to arrive at his own home too obviously under the influence. He wasn't much of a drinker, and Helen was tolerant of his occasional indulgences, but his wife would not appreciate him turning up clearly intoxicated.

'Better get something to eat.' Reaching the corner of Betterton Street, the inspector went to try and soak up some of the alcohol in his stomach with a visit to the Rock & Sole Plaice. The fish and chip shop was something of a tourist trap, being the only establishment of its kind in the neighbourhood, but the food was good for all that. After queuing for an age behind a family of Italian tourists, he emerged with an open bag of chips, smothered in vinegar and ketchup. Crossing the road, he speared a fat slab of fried potato with a tiny wooden fork and poked it into his mouth. As he did so, he felt his mobile phone begin to rumble in the breast pocket of his jacket.

'Bollocks.' Should he answer? The call might prove to be important. Then again, shouldn't a man be allowed to have his dinner in peace?

What to do? Dropping the fork into the bag, he cautiously lifted the phone between his thumb and forefinger. On the screen was a local landline number which he didn't recognize.

'Mm.'

The phone kept ringing. Allowing alcohol-fuelled curiosity to get the better of him, Carlyle lifted it to his ear. 'Yes?'

'What took you so long?' Dominic Silver sounded irritated.

'Just be grateful that I picked it up at all,' Carlyle shot back cheerily. 'You know what I'm like with phones – if you had gone to voicemail, I might not have got to it until some time next week.'

'Next month, more like,' Dom pointed out, his annoyance tempered by a sense of surprise that he'd got through.

Carlyle suddenly let out an unguarded burp.

'Are you drunk?'

'Me?' Carlyle came to a halt in front of a poster advertising the latest edition of a style magazine. On the cover was a picture of a leading manager, a bullshit merchant of the highest order. The smug bastard was wearing his usual shit-eating grin, while the cover line explained that inside was an exclusive interview explaining in great detail the man's innate genius. Grunting, the inspector instinctively wanted to flick a V-sign at the offensive creature, only to be prevented from doing so by the lack of a free hand.

'You sound pissed,' Dom persisted. 'Have you been drinking?'

'Just a few,' Carlyle offered. 'I was out with my dad.' Wedging the phone between his ear and his shoulder, he tried to recover his fork from inside the chip bag. Failing, he picked up a couple of chips with his fingers. 'Which reminds me,' he said, shoving the chips into his mouth. 'I've been trying to get hold of *you*. Where are you?'

'West End Central,' Dom said flatly.

Carlyle frowned and chewed at the same time. 'The police station? What are you doing there?'

'What do you think? I've been bloody nicked.'

Sitting on a bare mattress, Dom looked up as the cell door opened and Carlyle stepped inside. 'You took your time.'

'Nice to see you too,' Carlyle smiled. 'I came straight here when I got your call.'

Dressed in a pair of jeans and a cashmere sweater, Dom gestured at the door with one of his Nikes. 'The service in here is bloody terrible,' he grumbled. 'I asked for a Flat White an hour ago.'

'I'll have a stern word with Customer Service.' Carlyle glanced over his shoulder, waiting for the door to close behind him. He listened to it being locked, followed by the sound of feet receding down the corridor before continuing: 'Sorry it's taken so long. It took me a while to blag my way inside your lovely abode.' He gestured around the graffiti-ridden cell. 'Seems you can't just turn up and walk right in.'

'Who knew?' Dom was trying to be cool about it, but it was clearly a struggle.

Carlyle tutted in mock dismay. 'They're a right suspicious bunch round here.'

'I should have called my lawyer,' Dom said.

Carlyle frowned. Barry Fagen was a corporate lawyer. He firmly belonged to Dom's current life, rather than his past. There was no merit in blurring the lines between the two. 'Barry's no good for a situation like this. Don't worry, I'll get you out, no problem.'

'Mm.'

'Does Eva know?'

'No, no. And she doesn't need to know, either. She's off at her mum's anyway, so that's all fine.'

Carlyle tried to remember Dom mentioning his mother-in-law before. It didn't matter. 'What about the kids?'

155

Dom and Eva had more kids than you could shake a stick at. Sometimes Carlyle – who worried about Alice being an only child – felt jealous about that; mostly he just felt relieved. In his experience, one was more than enough.

Dom thought about it for a moment. 'They're all doing their own thing.'

'All of them?'

Dom shrugged. 'They're not babies any more. They grow up fast.' He saw the doubt in Carlyle's eyes. 'Don't worry, they're all accounted for. I know what they're all up to. Do you want a list?'

'No, 'course not.'

'Well then.' Folding his arms, Dom leaned back against the cell wall. 'What did you tell them at the front desk?'

'I told them that you are a CI and that by picking you up they have compromised a long and expensive investigation.'

'Me?' Dom scoffed. 'A Confidential Informer? Ha!'

'I'll have to put you on the list now,' Carlyle said.

'A bit late for that.'

'Yes, well.' For a couple of moments, the two men contemplated some of the scrapes they'd been in together over the years, all of them strictly off the books.

Those days, they both hoped, were over.

'So, what happened?'

Dom's eyes narrowed as he looked around the cell. 'Are you sure that this place isn't bugged?'

'Come on! That's just the kind of thing they do on the TV.' Carlyle took a half-step into the middle of the room. The residual smell of disinfectant and bodily emissions was beginning to make him feel sick, after the whiskey and chips. 'Apart from anything else, the Met could never afford the equipment.'

'Fair point,' Dom conceded. 'So, I was locking up at the Gallery when—'

Suddenly in dire need of some fresh air, Carlyle held up a hand. 'Bugged or not, that can wait till we get out of here.'

Dom jumped to his feet. 'I can go?'

'Not quite yet.'

'Ah.' He sat back down again.

'I just need to get some paperwork sorted out. You know what it's like.'

'Yeah,' Dom nodded. As an ex-copper, he was well aware of the Met's addiction to form-filling.

'Won't take too long.' Keen to be on his way, Carlyle turned back to the cell door and gave it three quick bangs with the flat of his hand. After a few moments, the duty sergeant idled down the corridor and opened up.

'Hurry up,' Dom hissed.

'Don't worry.' Carlyle smiled blandly as he stood on the threshold. 'Give me ten minutes.'

In the event, Carlyle was uncharacteristically optimistic when it came to his timings. Back upstairs, he was halfway through filling in yet another form when he was confronted by the arresting officer, a rather obtuse young constable, who clearly didn't believe Carlyle's story about Dom being a CI.

'The guy had a bag of illegal tablets sitting on his desk,' the constable harrumphed. In his mid-twenties, he was a ruddy-faced beanpole who couldn't have looked any more pleased with himself if he had just been made Commissioner. 'There was more than enough for a charge of possession with intent to supply.'

Save it for your sergeant's exam, Carlyle thought. The boy was so annoying it was a racing certainty that he would be on some management fast-track as soon as the brass got wind of him.

'Under normal circumstances.'

'Under normal circumstances,' the constable agreed. 'They're releasing your pal now but it's all highly irregular.'

'He's not my pal,' Carlyle lied, 'he's a very valuable contact.'

'It's still highly irregular,' the constable sniffed. 'There's no way he can have the drugs back, even if he does work for you.'

'No, certainly not,' Carlyle agreed. Clearly, Alexander's

pain-relief medicine would have to remain in the evidence locker at the back of the building for a little while longer.

Watching the frown deepen on Carlyle's face, the constable mistook his dismay for confusion. 'Didn't you know your CI was a dealer?' he smirked.

'He's not a dealer,' Carlyle snapped. Not any more.

'He's got a bloody big habit then,' the constable sniggered. 'Maybe you should get him a DRR.'

Dom's the last person who would ever need a Drug Rehabilitation Requirement Order, Carlyle mused.

'Or maybe just find yourself some better sources.'

Carlyle had to resist the temptation to give the little scrote a smack in the mouth. 'What was your name again, son?'

'Templeton.' The scrote's grin grew wider as he realized that he was getting under his superior's skin. 'Noah Templeton.'

Noah? WTF? Carlyle felt his annoyance begin to melt away. No one with a moniker like 'Noah' was going to be able to offer him any serious grief. He gave the youngster the gimlet eye. 'And how did you happen to be in the Molby-Nicol Gallery this evening, Noah?'

The young man stiffened, breaking off eye contact as he stared at a poster behind Carlyle's head advocating the merits of road safety. 'It's on my patch,' he muttered, somewhat defensively.

'But why were you *on the premises*?' the inspector persisted. 'And what gave you probable cause to investigate Mr Silver's office?'

A constipated look passed across the young officer's face as he tried to work out how much information he needed to divulge.

'Well?'

'It was a tip.'

'A tip?'

'You are not the only person with contacts, *sir*,' the constable responded, trying to reassert some control over the conversation.

Carlyle nodded, reasonableness personified. 'And who was the source of this tip?'

Now the constable stood properly to attention, giving him the full 1,000-yard stare. 'I'd rather not say, sir.'

'And I'd rather not make a formal complaint, Constable,' Carlyle said evenly. 'You don't want a black mark against your name at this stage of what is, no doubt, otherwise shaping up to be a very promising career.'

Muttering something incomprehensible, the constable stared at his shoes.

'What?'

'It was a guy called Jimmy Gallagher. He's a local vagrant. Usually hangs around Berkeley Square and Green Park.'

Bollocks, Carlyle thought. 'And how does Jimmy know about Silver?'

'Dunno,' Templeton shrugged. 'He just does.'

'Given you other quality tips, has he?'

'A few.'

'And so you took this tip from Jimmy the wino, and went off on a solo drugs bust. Who do you think you are, son, bloody Serpico?'

'Who?'

The youngster was saved further interrogation as Dom appeared, shoving his wallet into the inside pocket of his jacket. Ignoring Templeton, he gave Carlyle a rueful shake of the head. 'Ten minutes, eh?'

'Stop moaning,' Carlyle replied, embarrassed.

'Let's go and get a coffee,' said Dom, heading for the exit, 'so I can share some of that *confidential information* you were after.'

Ignoring the sour look on the constable's face, Carlyle dutifully followed his CI out of the door and into the chill of the night.

159

EIGHTEEN

Dom skipped down the front steps of the police station, mobile clamped to his ear. Carlyle watched from a polite distance as he made a succession of calls. Taking out his own phone, the inspector checked the time and winced. Deciding it was too late to call, he sent Helen a text.

Sorry, got a problem at work. Home soon. x

The reply was gratifyingly quick.

Ok. Gone to bed. x

Happy that he wasn't in the dog house, Carlyle waited patiently for Dom to finish his calls before leading him across the road to the Arcade Café, an all-night greasy spoon, complete with faded Art Deco interior, that somehow managed to survive in one of the most expensive neighbourhoods in the city while still charging less than two quid for a cup of coffee. Given the insane level of local taxes and business rates, the inspector had long suspected that the place had to be the front for some kind of money-laundering operation. On the plus side, it served an excellent all-day breakfast.

Even at this time of night, the place was still pretty full with an eclectic crowd, ranging from taxi drivers, to late-night shoppers, to a group of young clubbers lining their stomachs before a night out. Carlyle gestured towards a free table by the far wall, under a pretty ropey oil painting of an old Routemaster bus, and they carefully manoeuvred their way towards it.

A pretty waitress appeared at their table even before they had sat down on the uncomfortable wooden seats. Dom ordered a coffee and an egg sandwich, while Carlyle made do with a green tea.

'Helen's still weaning you off the caffeine, eh?' Dom was talking to Carlyle, but his eyes were on the waitress as she slalomed back behind the counter.

Carlyle shrugged. 'I quite like it. Anyway, it's not as if I've given up on coffee completely. It's just that I'm down to a couple of cups a day or thereabouts.'

'You always did drink too much coffee,' Dom observed.

'Hardly.'

'Made you wired.'

'Me?'

'Jumpy.'

Carlyle put on a miffed expression. 'I've always considered myself coolness personified. Anyway, there are worse things to be hooked on than the humble coffee bean.'

'Right enough,' Dom agreed.

Carlyle slipped off his jacket and placed it over the back of his chair. The slight intoxication of earlier in the evening had been replaced by an intense sense of weariness. 'I'm sorry about the palaver tonight.'

Dom waved the apology away. 'It was my own stupid fault. I should have stuck the bloody stuff in a drawer. Or, at least, closed the office door.'

'Yes.' Carlyle tried to sound sympathetic. However, the chips had settled uncomfortably in his stomach and he had to stifle an acidic belch.

Graciously, Dom ignored his comrade's lack of table manners. 'Thirty-odd years in the business and never arrested.' He heaved a sigh.

Carlyle raised an eyebrow. 'Never?'

'Never arrested,' Dom repeated. 'And now this.'

The inspector suspected that there was a bit of airbrushing of history going on, but he let it drop. 'What did you tell Eva?'

'I said that a buyer had turned up unexpectedly, so I had to

161

take him out to dinner.' Dom scowled. Like Carlyle, he didn't like lying to his wife. They were both firmly committed family men, who understood that honesty was the bedrock of a successful, long-term relationship. More to the point, the reverse could get you in far more trouble than you could ever find in a West End Central holding cell. 'I could have gone through what happened,' he reasoned, 'but now is not the time. There's a lot going on at the moment and this would only stress her out more.'

More?

'There's no need for that,' Carlyle agreed.

'No.' Dom looked at Carlyle.

'When you talk about her being stressed, you mean the problem with Lucio Spargo?'

Dom nodded. 'Eva was very involved in setting up the gallery – everything from the finances through to choosing the artists we would exhibit. She even hired the girl Fiona on reception.'

Not her finest hour, Carlyle reflected.

'She really enjoyed it,' Dom continued. 'Obviously, she was happy about my change of career but above all, I think it gave her something to focus on as the kids started becoming more independent. And I think she liked the fact that it was something we could do together.'

'I'm not sure Helen and I could work together,' Carlyle commented.

'It isn't like it's a nine-to-five thing.'

'No, but still. She'd probably kill me after about a week.'

'You do tend to have that effect on people,' Dom grinned.

The waitress appeared with their drinks. After placing them on the table, she gave Dom a big smile and told him, 'Your sandwich is coming.' She clearly wasn't English, but Carlyle had long since given up playing the game of *guess the accent*. Aside from all the usual foreigners, London was chock-full of people from places you'd never even heard of. That was one of the things that made it such a great place.

'Thanks,' Dom smiled back. Taking a sip of his coffee, he

waited for her to leave before continuing. 'Then, one day, she was in the gallery alone when Spargo and his henchman turned up. She hasn't been back since.'

'They threatened her?'

'Duh?' Dom widened his eyes. 'You reckon? You know, it's amazing that they never made you Commissioner.'

Carlyle didn't rise to the bait. 'When was this?'

'I dunno. About four months ago maybe – when it became clear that we wouldn't go quietly and accept Mr Spargo's plans for redeveloping the street.'

'Four months ago? Bloody hell! Why didn't you tell *me* about this?'

Dom picked up a sachet of sweetener between his thumb and forefinger, waving it around aimlessly before tossing it back on to the table. 'What's to say? I didn't want to bring my troubles to your door.'

'I had no compunction about bringing mine to you,' Carlyle shot back.

'That's a bit different though.'

'How's that?'

'Well, when it came to your dad, there *was* something specific that I could do to help.'

The inspector bridled at the suggestion that there was nothing he could do when it came to the Spargo problem. Realizing, however, that there was more than a smattering of truth to that assessment of the situation, he kept schtum.

The waitress reappeared with Dom's sandwich. 'Here you go,' she said pleasantly.

'Thanks.' Reaching for the ketchup bottle, Dom added some sauce before taking a dainty bite and chewing vigorously. 'Spargo's a canny operator. The police haven't been able to touch him.' Taking a napkin from the dispenser, he wiped the corner of his mouth. 'The word is that he's got political contacts, along with some pretty senior friends on the Force.'

Carlyle raised an eyebrow. 'Anyone we know?'

'I didn't get any names. The point is that Spargo knows how to play this game. He's been doing it for decades – operating in that rather large grey area between what is legal and what can be proven to be illegal.'

'That's a very large area,' Carlyle observed. 'And a very grey one too.'

'Quite.'

'You, on the other hand, preferred to go straight into the black.'

Dom conceded the point with a slight lift of his chin. 'That's very true. Then again, making people homeless was never part of my business plan.'

'I suppose not.'

'Not that I'm trying to claim the moral high ground.'

'God forbid!'

'This project on Cork Street is supposed to be Spargo's crowning glory. A new, luxury "destination address" in the heart of Mayfair. Local businesses and long-term residents out. Absentee owners and international brand names in. No little gallery owner is going to be allowed to prevent that from happening. It's just the way of the world. It's odds-on that he'll get what he wants.'

Carlyle sipped his tea. 'So why the need for violence, or even the threat of violence?'

'You can take the boy out of the ghetto . . . Spargo grew up on a tough estate in Elephant and Castle.' Dom took another bite of his sandwich. 'He was picking pockets before he was ten, robbing houses at twelve. It's claimed that he killed a man in a dispute over money when he was seventeen.'

'But there's no criminal record,' Carlyle said. 'It sounds like an urban legend to me.'

'Maybe so, but the man has a taste for other people's pain, both physical and emotional. Believe me, I know what I'm talking about.'

Carlyle did not demur.

'Eva described him as a torturer in a suit.'

Carlyle grimaced. 'Did he hurt her?'

'She says not.'

'You think she wouldn't tell you?'

'She will always try to protect me,' was Dom's cryptic response.

'Well,' Carlyle let out a long sigh. 'You know people. You could always have him taken out.' The irony of a policeman talking like that was not lost on him. However, where family was involved, lines could be crossed. He had crossed them himself. They had crossed them together.

Dom shook his head. 'Not worth it. Why risk everything for what is essentially a glorified hobby. Better just to walk away.'

Dismayed by his friend's defeatist talk, Carlyle changed tack. 'How long is your lease?'

'There's a little less than twenty years left to run,' Dom told him. 'Spargo is happy to buy me out, but the cost of finding somewhere else would be prohibitive . . . unless I run the place at a loss, which I won't do on principle, or we move to Walthamstow or somewhere.'

Carlyle shivered at such a grim prospect. 'So, what *are* you going to do?'

'Dunno.' Dom finished his sandwich. 'I can hold out for a while, but Spargo will withdraw his offer and I'll basically be left sitting in the middle of a building site. Then, one night, the place gets robbed, or accidentally burns down . . . you know what it's like.'

'You have insurance,' Carlyle pointed out, somewhat feebly.

'Yes. But I'd effectively be out of business.' Dom wiped his hands on another napkin. 'Apart from anything else, what kind of artist wants to exhibit in a gallery that might get firebombed?'

'Fair point.'

'Anyway, that's not what I'm really worried about. Suppose Eva or Fiona were to find themselves in the wrong place at the wrong time?' The pained expression on his face was genuine. 'I wouldn't want them to end up like that granny up the road.'

'No.' Sally-Anne Mason, aged seventy-nine, Mathias Mansions. Carlyle was surprised that he could remember the details. 'Do you think Spargo killed her?'

'Directly or indirectly.'

'Either way, he got away with it.'

'Like I said, he has some useful friends and allies.'

'I'll see what I can find out, but even friends in high places wouldn't have saved him from a murder charge.'

'Maybe, maybe not.'

'No way.' Although Carlyle liked to think of himself as supremely cynical when it came to all things relating to law and order, even he didn't believe that fellow Met officers would look the other way when it came to murder.

'Spargo knows how to get what he wants,' Dom repeated. 'And what he wants is me out.' Taking a mouthful of coffee, he caught the eye of the waitress and ordered another sandwich. 'Anyway, we're not going to do anything about that tonight. How's Alexander?'

'He's doing okay, under the circumstances. I have to say, he's being very stoical about the whole thing. This is the kind of situation where his Calvinist fatalism really comes into its own.'

'Good for him,' Dom chuckled. 'Don't worry about his pain relief, by the way. It'll be no problem to get some more. And this time, I won't leave it lying around where the local plod can spot it.'

'What did you make of that kid?' Carlyle asked. 'I got the sense that there was something off about him.'

'I've seen him around a few times. Turned up just before closing and said he was investigating some local robberies.'

'Mm. He told me that he'd had a tip-off from a local tramp that you had the stuff.'

'He'd been tipped off, all right.' The waitress quickly returned with a second egg sandwich. Once again, Dom added ketchup and started to nibble around the edges. 'Your dad's stuff was sitting on my desk in a takeaway bag. He walked right up to it and peered inside. He's not going to get that kind of gen from some dosser though, is he?'

'Spargo?'

Dom looked sceptical. 'How would he know?'

'Maybe he knows about your past. Maybe he's got Templeton on a retainer to help him deal with local problems.' Carlyle knew it was thin but, as his dad liked to say, you had to speculate to accumulate.

'A constable?' Dom snorted. 'I doubt it.'

'I don't like him,' Carlyle announced.

'John,' Dom chuckled, 'you don't like anyone.'

'Harsh.'

'But fair.'

'I like to think of myself as a good judge of character. In my experience, most people, if you give them a chance, turn out to be complete tossers.'

'I agree with you about Templeton – he seems like an officious little prick. Don't worry about it though. We could drive ourselves mad trying to unravel imaginary conspiracy theories. Give me a couple more days and I'll get your dad sorted out.'

A worrying thought occurred to Carlyle. 'How much did the stuff cost?'

Dom mentioned a figure that was rather more than the balance of the inspector's current account.

'Christ!'

'Don't worry about it; it's my shout. More useful than getting your old man a wreath later on.'

'No, no.' Pushing back his chair, Carlyle jumped to his feet. 'Sit tight. I'll be back in ten minutes.'

'Where have I heard that before?' Dom grinned. 'If you get arrested, just remember – don't call me.'

NINETEEN

The Evidence Room in West End Central was located at one end of a long, dingy corridor on the first floor. At this time of night, the offices on either side of the hallway were empty, save for members of the cleaning crew. As Carlyle walked under the harsh strip-lighting, he listened to the soles of his shoes squeaking on the linoleum. The only other noise came from the sound of a vacuum cleaner being operated with unnatural vigour by a tiny woman in an office that bore the title *Public Liaison & Customer Complaints*. As he walked past, Carlyle gave the cleaner a friendly nod. Responding in kind, she smacked the side of a desk with her machine, sending a discarded cup of coffee tumbling to the floor. Not wishing to cause any more trouble, the inspector moved swiftly on.

Reaching his destination, he contemplated the large metal door, painted in battleship grey, with the warning *NO UNAUTHORIZED ACCESS* stencilled on it in fading red letters. Next to the door was an Access Control System and, for those without the required electronic fob, a large green buzzer. Carlyle hit the buzzer with the palm of one hand, using the other to show his ID to the lens of the inevitable security camera hanging from the ceiling.

'This is where it would be good to have a plan,' he mumbled to himself. Back down the corridor, the cleaning lady moved into the next office. Inside Fort Knox, however, no one stirred. Carlyle responded with three further sharp blasts on the buzzer.

A few moments later, there was the sound of the lock releasing. Pulling open the door, the inspector stepped into a small lobby, not much bigger than a lift. Directly in front of him was another door. Next to the door was an unmanned counter. Behind the Perspex screen he could see into the depository proper; rows of different-sized lockers, like safety deposit boxes, lining the back wall, from floor to ceiling. Taped to the screen was a small notice, written in biro: *RING FOR ASSISTANCE.*

'Fuck me,' Carlyle grumbled, 'I thought I just did that.' Glued to the counter was a small white button, like someone's front-door bell. 'How very hi-tech!' He stabbed it with his index finger and was immediately assailed by a shrill, high-pitched bell. He was still in shock when a small, silver-haired man shuffled into view behind the counter.

'That's a bit loud, isn't it?' Carlyle said.

'Wakes me up if I doze off,' the man explained, without any obvious sense of embarrassment. He tossed his newspaper on to a chair and addressed Carlyle. 'What can I do for you?'

The inspector looked at the man's navy and grey uniform. A name badge pinned to his chest bore the moniker *Ben Wilkins.* A casual observer might not realize it, but he wasn't a policeman at all. Rather, the tiny logo on the badge indicated that Mr Wilkins worked for a 'servicing and outsourcing company' that had more than 150,000 employees and held public sector contracts for everything from rubbish collection to atomic weapons research. Evidence Management was just another of the Met's services that had been efficiently and effectively outsourced. Carlyle wondered how long it would be until his job was handed to some bloke off the street earning £12.50 an hour. Hopefully not until after he had retired.

'Well?'

'Er . . . I need the evidence on the Sally-Anne Mason case.' The inspector cringed when he contemplated the extent of his cunning plan: blag his way inside and then improvise. Anything relating to the Mason case – if there was anything relating to the

Mason case – would have been dumped in a distant storage facility a very long time ago.

Wilkins ran a hand across his well-past-five-o'clock shadow. For someone who had such a stress-free job, his nails were badly chewed. 'Reference number?'

'Er . . .' Carlyle tried to look even more clueless than he felt. 'No idea, I'm afraid.'

Typical, Wilkins thought. The crap that he had to put up with was unbelievable. These cops, they were all halfwits, the whole lot of them. 'You'll need to look it up on the database.'

'How do I do that?'

Wilkins opened a small window above the counter and pushed through a grubby sheet of paper on a clipboard. 'Sign in and you can take a look at the computer. But hurry up, I go off shift in fifteen minutes. If it's gonna take any longer than that, you'll have to come back in the morning. We open at eight.'

Scrawling his details on the sheet, Carlyle offered up his friendliest smile. 'Fifteen minutes will be more than enough.'

'Just as well,' Wilkins replied as he watched Carlyle complete the form.

'There you go.' Carlyle pushed the clipboard back through the open window. Without looking at it, Wilkins hung it on a nail on the wall. Then he padded over to the door, released the lock and ushered the inspector into the inner sanctum.

With one eye on the clock on the wall, Wilkins hovered at Carlyle's shoulder. 'Don't you know how to use the system?'

The inspector tapped the keyboards aimlessly. In front of him was a sea of data that added up to a whole heap of nothing. 'This is not usually my area,' he admitted. Finding a search box, he typed in MASON, trying to look interested as seventeen different items came up. It was no surprise that none of them related to the widow from Mathias Mansions; there was nothing on the list that was more than two years old.

'Looks like you're out of luck,' Wilkins commented, not sounding too disappointed about it.

'Haven't you got something to do?' Carlyle muttered. Like file your nails or something?

'Not really,' Wilkins said cheerily. 'It's been very quiet today. All I've had is a wallet that was found on the street by a member of the public and a pair of specs that were taken from a pickpocket.'

A pair of specs? Carlyle recalled how much he had spent on his last pair of glasses. As he mused on the vagaries of opticians, another idea seeped into his brain. 'What time did you come on shift?'

'I started at three,' Wilkins told him. 'Why?'

Not furnishing an answer, Carlyle jumped up from the computer and grabbed the clipboard hanging from the wall. It confirmed what Wilkins had said: aside from J. Carlyle, only two officers had visited the locker in the last seven hours.

Neither of them was Noah Templeton.

'You cheeky little wanker,' Carlyle chuckled.

'Eh?'

'Not you.' Putting the clipboard back on its nail, he hit the lock release and pulled open the door. 'Thanks for your help.'

'But you didn't find anything.'

'It's okay,' Carlyle said, already halfway to the outer door. 'Thanks anyway. Now you can call it a day.'

When he made it back across the road to the café, Dom was busy chatting up the waitress.

'I wouldn't believe a word he says,' Carlyle told the woman as he took his seat. 'He has a wife and a dozen kids.'

'Don't exaggerate,' Dom laughed. 'There's only ten of the little buggers.'

Not sure what to make of their comedy double act, the waitress went off to empty the dishwasher.

'I suppose that was closer to "ten minutes" than last time,' Dom said philosophically.

'You know what they say,' Carlyle shot back. '"Life is short, but the day is long".'

171

'This day certainly is bloody long.' Dom glanced around the nearby tables before lowering his voice. 'Did you get it?'

'Nope.'

Dom nodded. 'Just as well. It would be a shame for you to get kicked off the Force for nicking drugs out of a police station. I always imagined you would get axed for something a bit more noble.'

'Ha!'

'Well, something a bit less grubby, if you prefer.'

Carlyle folded his arms. 'I didn't get the stuff because it wasn't there. Your local bobby, PC Templeton, didn't turn it in.'

Dom's eyebrows shot up. 'Interesting. Did you ask him about it?'

'Didn't get the chance. He's left for the night.'

A broad grin spread across Dom's face. 'Just as well I know where he lives then, isn't it?'

A liveried taxi barrelled down the road, its driver leaning forward in his seat, like an explorer in search of the next traffic jam. In the back, a banker-type, all slicked-back hair and pinstriped suit, chatted away blithely on his mobile phone. Standing under a sodium streetlight, the inspector stared at the screen of his BlackBerry. 'Bloody web pages take forever to load on this thing.'

'Should get an iPhone,' Dom suggested smugly.

'The Met doesn't run to iPhones,' Carlyle pointed out. 'Anyway, I like my BlackBerry.'

'It'll be obsolete soon.'

'Yeah, but still.' The inspector liked to think of himself as technology neutral; neither an early adopter nor a Luddite. As a man who had spent the first ten years of his career bashing a typewriter, however, the little gadget in his hand could still inspire both wonder and affection.

When it worked.

Leaving the machine to its sedate progress, he kicked a discarded fast-food wrapper towards the gutter and gazed up at the squat, five-storey building on the other side of the street. 'It looks like Hitler's bunker.'

'That's a bit extreme,' Dom countered. 'Hitler's bunker was basically just a hole in the ground.'

'After the Russians arrived.'

'Well, as far as I know, the Red Army never made it to Pimlico.'

Carlyle gestured off to his left, in the vague direction of Chelsea. 'Maybe not, but there are plenty of Russians just down the road these days.'

'That's progress, my friend,' Dom smiled. 'If you're going to become the capital of the world, you have to let the world come and play. Who else would spend millions of their not-so-hard-earned cash on basement swimming pools? It gives them something to do, once they've finished raping and pillaging their own fair land.' Dom waved a hand aimlessly in the air. 'Such a cultured people. I quite like them.'

'Got a load of Russian clients at the Gallery, eh?'

'One or two,' Dom grinned. 'If they see something they like, the old Platinum Amex comes out and it's bish-bash-bosh. All that money changing hands; it's a better rush than any Class A, I can tell you.'

The inspector muttered something to himself before returning to the matter in hand. The relevant Heritage Explorer web page had finally come up on his BlackBerry. 'Darbourne House,' he intoned, reading from the screen. 'A block of fourteen three-bedroom flats, three one-bedroom flats and three studios . . . part of the Blefuscu Gardens Estate, designed in 1962 by Sidney and Hermione Less for Westminster City Council.'

'Less *is* more,' Dom quipped.

Groaning, Carlyle continued: 'Blefuscu was one of the first low-rise, high-density public housing schemes to be built in London. It helped prove that low-rise flats with an interesting design could accommodate as many people as tower blocks. It influenced the style of the city's council housing from the mid-1960s until the early 1980s. The scheme won many awards, including a Ministry of Housing Award for good design in 1971 and a Commendation in the Royal Society of Architects' New Communities Awards Scheme of 1974.' He looked up from the screen at the forbidding structure on the other side of the road. 'Grim.'

'It's not that bad,' Dom reflected. 'Nicer than Winter Garden House for a start.'

'You're right there,' the inspector agreed without rancour. Winter Garden House, where Carlyle lived with Helen and Alice, was a featureless tower block near Holborn tube station. Its only redeeming quality was the location, in the north-east corner of Covent Garden, five minutes' walk from Charing Cross police station; right in the heart of the city, in the heart of the *action*.

'Not really my cup of tea.' Dom, happily camped up in Highgate in a six-million-pound Huf Haus, liked to think of himself as something of an architecture buff. 'Looks like it's stood the test of time well enough though.'

Carlyle finished reading and dropped the BlackBerry back into his pocket. 'There are two thousand folk on the estate. How are we going to find Noah bloody Templeton?'

'There can't be more than thirty flats in Darbourne House,' Dom calculated. 'And Fiona says he lives on the top floor. That narrows it down even further.'

'Good old Fiona.' Carlyle had to admit he felt a grudging respect for the young constable's attempts to chat up Dom's rather forbidding receptionist. 'I still can't believe that she went out with him.'

'It was just a drink in a pub round the corner. When he suggested they get some chips and go meet his mum, Fiona made her excuses and left. For most of the conversation she said that he seemed more interested in trying to get information on me and the gallery than he was in her.'

'That would have gone down well.'

'Fiona was amused, rather than annoyed. Her take on it was

that he was smart enough to realize that she was rather out of his league. That makes him smarter than most blokes.'

'Good for her.' Carlyle shivered at the brutality of the twenty-first-century dating game. It had been hard enough thirty years ago.

'Anyway, Fiona's love-life is more than complicated enough already.'

'Oh?' The inspector tried not to sound *too* interested.

'From what I can gather,' Dom confided, happy to fan the fires of his pal's prurience, 'she is caught up in what you might call a four-way love, er, rectangle with one of her tutors – a married guy in his fifties – a fellow student and a Dutch girl she met on holiday in Ibiza.'

Sticking out his bottom lip, Carlyle contemplated this state of affairs for several moments.

'Like I said,' Dom grinned, 'we are very lucky to have her.'

'I can see how she might struggle to fit young Noah into her busy social schedule.' Off to his right, Carlyle saw an elderly couple emerge from the main entrance to Darbourne House. Slipping between two parked cars, he jogged across the road to catch the iron gate before it slammed shut, waiting patiently while Dom followed after him in a more leisurely fashion.

Eschewing the lift, they took the stairs to the top floor. Half a dozen flats were laid out along an external walkway which was decorated by an impressive collection of colourful hanging baskets and flower boxes.

'Very nice,' Dom observed, bending down to smell some lavender.

Carlyle, who wasn't really a flower man, grunted as he went from door to door, checking the name-plates by the buzzers. 'Here we go.' Ringing the bell, Carlyle stood back from a door that looked like it had been recently painted in a colour that he would describe as Racing Green. The door opened and a woman stood on the threshold.

'Yes?'

175

Her expression was neither welcoming, nor hostile. Carlyle guessed that she was in her fifties, with grey hair, cut short, and a lined face. In her hand was a mug bearing the Metropolitan Police logo.

'Mrs Templeton?' Carlyle took out his Warrant Card and held it up for her to inspect.

'Noah's not in,' she said, not waiting for him to explain his presence on her doorstep. 'He's gone to get some fish and chips. Shouldn't be too long though, I don't think.' Turning round, she disappeared back down the hallway, leaving the door open. Taking that as an invitation, Carlyle and Dom followed her inside.

The Templetons' living room reminded the inspector of the Carlyle family home when he was a kid growing up in Fulham. Clean, sparse and relatively timeless. An old-style cathode ray tube TV squatted in the corner. On top of it was the room's only photograph, a young Noah Templeton standing on a beach, sandwiched between his mum and a bloke, presumably the boy's dad.

Mrs Templeton followed his gaze. 'That was taken in Brighton,' she explained. 'Twenty-odd years ago.'

Carlyle nodded. Although not a great fan of the place, the inspector was a frequent visitor to the seaside town. His mother-in-law had decamped there after separating from Helen's father.

Taking a seat on the sofa, Dom made himself comfortable. 'So how long have you been here, love?'

With Carlyle still on his feet, Mrs Templeton hovered by the empty fireplace. 'Ooh, now, we moved here in . . . ninety-four – something like that. Just after Noah was born, anyway.'

1994! Carlyle hated the little sod for being so young. 'I was wondering, why did you call him Noah?'

'Eh?' The woman was still trying to formulate a reply when the sound of a key in the front door came from the hallway.

'I'm back, Ma!' Noah Templeton appeared in the doorway. In a pair of torn jeans and a grey T-shirt, he looked even younger than he had appeared when in uniform. In his arms, he cradled a paper bag containing his dinner.

'Mum?' Noah's gaze shifted from his mother to Carlyle and then to Dom. For a moment, he froze. Then he threw his fish and chips at the inspector and ducked back down the hall. Dodging the flying food, Carlyle chased after him. As his chest started to burn the inspector wished that he had been a bit more diligent when it came to visiting the gym.

He was about to give up the chase when he heard a crash, followed by a stream of curses.

Jogging over to the stairs, Carlyle started to laugh.

'Fuck off,' Noah hissed. 'It's not funny.' Forcing himself upright, he touched the large gash across his forehead and winced.

Kicking the scattered flowers out of the way, the inspector ventured down a couple of steps and offered him a hand. 'You've got to watch out for those flower boxes,' he observed, pulling the boy to his feet. 'They can be really quite dangerous.'

TWENTY

Noah Templeton trooped disconsolately into the living room, head bowed, looking every inch the naughty schoolboy that he undoubtedly was.

'Try not to bleed on your mother's carpet,' Carlyle advised.

Mrs Templeton had not moved from the fireplace. Looking at her son's face, she exclaimed. 'Goodness, Noah! What happened?'

'He tripped over some of your flowers,' Carlyle told her, 'and fell down the stairs.'

'Fell down the stairs?'

The young constable gave a whimper of confirmation.

'You never learn, do you?' With the air of a woman who had seen it all before, Mrs Templeton shuffled towards the door. 'Let me get some TCP. I hope we've got some plasters that are big enough.' Pausing to peer at the wound on the boy's scalp, she added. 'That looks deep. You might have to go to A and E.'

'Ma!'

'I think he'll be fine,' Carlyle offered. 'Just a bump and a bit of a headache.'

Tut-tutting to herself, Mrs Templeton disappeared in the direction of the bathroom.

'Just take a couple of ibuprofen and have a lie-down.' Rummaging in the parcel on his lap, Dom pulled out a chip and stuck it in his mouth.

'That's my tea,' the boy whined.

'I've only nicked a few chips.' Dom lifted up the greasy parcel and dumped it on the coffee table. 'Stop complaining. After all, it's not as if some little wanker stole your stash and locked you up in a cell for four hours.' There was an edge to his voice that Carlyle didn't like. The inspector wondered if he might not have been better off coming here on his own.

'Where's the stuff?' he asked quickly. 'Let's get this sorted before your mother gets back.'

Noah considered the question for several seconds while he tried to construct a bemused expression. 'Whaddya mean? I don't understand.'

With a theatrical sigh, Carlyle placed a hand on Noah's shoulder. 'Look, son. You fell down a few stairs, you don't want to take a dive off the balcony as well. Then you really would have to go to A and E.'

The boy bridled. 'You wouldn't dare!'

'No,' said Dom grimly, getting to his feet, 'but I would.'

'But only after I tell your mum what you've been up to,' Carlyle added. 'Look at it like this: we're making a problem go away for you. Much easier to hand the stuff over to us than explain to Duty Command why you didn't put it in the Evidence Locker.'

'That would be your career over like that.' Dom snapped his fingers. 'The only reference you'll have will be a criminal record. You wouldn't even be able to get a job as a security guard at the local supermarket.'

'Okay, okay.' With a groan, Noah flopped into the room's only armchair. 'It's in my bedroom. In a bag under the bed.'

'Very original.' Dom brushed past the returning Mrs Templeton and headed out of the room, in search of the drugs. Carlyle tried to ignore the smell of the fish supper as he watched Noah's mother clean his wound with some cotton wool doused in antiseptic.

'I still think you should go and get it seen by a doctor,' she said.

179

'I'll be fine,' Noah harrumphed, his regression to a sullen teenager now complete.

'There's no way that you'll be fit for work tomorrow,' she went on.

'Stop fussing.'

'I think a day off is probably not a bad idea,' Carlyle ventured. 'The Met will be able to cope.'

'See? Your boss agrees with me,' Noah's mother chipped in. 'They won't miss you.'

'He's not my boss,' Noah sulked.

'No?' Mrs Templeton looked enquiringly at Carlyle. 'Who are you then?'

'Just a colleague,' he said blandly.

The woman bit her lower lip; the wheels were slowly starting to turn now. 'And why were you chasing him?'

'It was just a misunderstanding.' Carlyle glanced back down the hall. What the hell was Dom doing?

The woman gestured towards him with the TCP bottle. 'Could you show me your ID again?'

Noah shifted in his seat. 'It's okay, Ma. He *is* a cop. We've worked together on a few things. I just mistook him for someone else when I came in. That's why I tried to leg it.' It was the feeblest of lies and his mother did not believe it for a second. However, she said nothing as she returned her attention to cleaning the boy's wound.

'I wanted to speak to you about Lucio Spargo,' Carlyle said casually, not addressing either one of them in particular.

Mrs Templeton didn't look up as she said. 'What's he got to do with anything?'

'*Mum!*' Noah tried to rise out of his seat, but she pushed him back down with surprising force.

'Stay still!'

'Do you know him?' Carlyle asked.

' 'Course I do,' the woman said calmly. 'Noah's dad worked for Mr Spargo for almost ten years.'

'Why did he stop working for him?' the inspector asked.

'He died,' she said matter-of-factly.

Oh. 'I'm very sorry to hear that.'

'Don't worry about it, love. It was a long time ago now. Got run over by a taxi on the Vauxhall Bridge Road. Died instantly.' She sighed. 'The silly sod never did watch where he was going. Noah took it very hard, of course.'

'Of course.'

'Poor lad. I sometimes think he'll never get over it. I was so pleased when he made it into the police. It's good that he's got a proper job, a career.'

'Yes.'

'Makes me feel a lot happier about things.'

'I can understand that.'

'I can remember the funeral like it was yesterday. The vicar was a right doddery old git. He kept getting the name wrong – calling him Kevin instead of Kelvin. Noah was only little, but he wanted to go up there and sort him out.' The memory seemed to cheer her a little. 'Mr Spargo was very kind. Calmed Noah down during the service and bought him some Smarties afterwards. Smarties were always Noah's favourites. Especially the yellow ones.'

'I liked the red ones when I was a kid,' Carlyle recalled.

'I remember Noah coming home with six tubes of Smarties that Mr Spargo had bought him. I hid them in a drawer and rationed them out. Otherwise he would have eaten them all in one go and made himself sick.'

'That's kids for you.'

'Mr Spargo didn't even need to come to the funeral. Kelvin was just an employee, after all. How many bosses would do something like that?'

'Not very many,' Carlyle agreed.

'He's a very nice man. Always extremely polite.'

'So I've been told,' Carlyle said drily.

'I never believed any of those things about him in the paper. I think that they just make that kind of thing up, don't you?'

'Most of the time, yeah.'

'Anyway, what're you interested in him for?'

Before Carlyle could construct some kind of an explanation, Dom finally appeared at his shoulder. When the inspector looked round, he held up a paper sandwich bag bearing the legend *FitzGibbbon's*, above a line drawing of a trio of cheery-looking Aberdeen Angus cattle.

'Got it!'

Carlyle nodded, before turning to Mrs Templeton and giving her a big smile. 'We can sort all this out later. Right now, I've got to go. Noah, I'll come and have a word with you when you get back to work.'

The boy grunted something that just about managed to convey his combined annoyance and acquiescence.

'Good.' Feeling very pleased with his night's work, the inspector quickly followed Dom down the hallwayand out the door.

Outside Victoria train station, they prepared to go their separate ways. Dom handed Carlyle the paper bag and fumbled in his pocket for an Oyster card.

'Thanks,' the inspector said.

'You do realize,' Dom pointed out, 'that a couple of dozen security cameras have just caught you taking possession of enough Class A to put you away for at least six years?'

'There's nothing like hiding in plain sight,' the inspector inspected the logo on the bag. 'What's FitzGibbbon's, anyway?'

'It's an upmarket burger chain. My kids love it. You should check it out.'

'Not our kind of place, I don't think. Alice has refused to eat hamburgers on principle since she read an article about the use of growth hormones in cattle.'

'Smart girl,' Dom said. 'She'll doubtless go far.'

'Yes, she probably will.' Carlyle enjoyed a small frisson of parental pride as he watched a number 38 bus manoeuvre its way around the omnipresent roadworks that circled the station like barricades put down against an invading army.

Dom gestured at the bag. 'In all seriousness though, do you really want to be carrying that around in Central London?'

'Who's gonna stop me? And even if they did, I'm an officer of the law. I know my rights.'

'Yes, but still—'

Carlyle held up a hand. 'It's got to be safer than letting you keep it. Anyway, I need to get my dad sorted out asap. I'll go and pay him a visit tomorrow.' Carlyle glanced at the clock high up on the station entrance. Assuming it was telling something approximating the right time, it was barely more than five hours since he had been sitting in the pub, watching the old man let his Guinness evaporate. After the evening's main event, it felt like months ago – almost a different lifetime.

'Give Alexander my best.'

'I will.'

'And make sure he uses that stuff sparingly.'

'Of course.'

'No more than two tablets every twelve hours.'

'Okay.'

'If that's not enough, we can review the situation. One step at a time though. Imagine the palaver if he were to OD on us.'

'I'm aware of that.'

'I know you are,' Dom said kindly. 'If he's careful, there's more than enough tablets there to keep him going for the foreseeable.'

'How much do I owe you?'

Dom waved away the question. 'Don't be silly.'

'Thanks.' Carlyle patted him on the arm. 'I really am very grateful for this. And sorry for all the hassle.'

'Pfff. These things happen. Funny old night, huh?'

'Yeah.'

'What do you think that kid Noah's playing at?'

Carlyle related his brief exchange with Mrs Templeton.

'Noah's father worked for Spargo. It looks like the boy is Spargo's stooge.'

'Okay.' Dom thought about it for a moment. 'But how would he know about the drugs? And what was he going to do with them?'

'No idea,' Carlyle said. 'But it was a stroke of luck that he tried to nick the tablets. Otherwise, we wouldn't have got the damn stuff back.'

Arriving home, Carlyle found Helen and Alice asleep and the flat in darkness. Taking off his shoes, the inspector slipped quietly into the kitchen, carefully closing the door shut before filling the kettle and putting it on to boil. He dropped a green tea bag in a white mug bearing the legend *Keep Calm and Support Fulham*. While the kettle laboured towards boiling point, he took his mobile phone from his jacket and plugged it into the charger by the bread bin. As the screen lit up, the inspector was dismayed to see that he had six missed calls. They came from a mobile number that he didn't recognize. 'Fuck it,' he yawned. 'If it's important, they'll ring back tomorrow.'

The kettle finally came to the boil. Placing the charging phone on top of the bread bin, he half-filled the cup with boiling water. Looking around the kitchen, he wondered where to stash the FitzGibbon's bag. Just for a second, he had an out of body experience, as if he was looking down on the scene, laughing at himself as he tried to hide his illegal score.

'What a bloody stupid carry on!' Pulling open a cupboard above his head, the inspector lifted out a large cardboard box containing Helen's breakfast cereal of choice. Removing the cellophane bag inside holding some form of designer organic French muesli, he folded up the paper bag and shoved it into the bottom of the box, replacing the muesli on top. Putting the box back in the cupboard, he took a couple of gulps from his tea before placing the mug in the sink. Then, taking a moment, he gazed out of the window, with its view across the Thames towards the drab flatlands of South London. Under the cover of darkness, the city seemed relaxed enough; it certainly didn't care about his little adventures. Comforted by the thought, he switched out the light and headed for bed.

TWENTY-ONE

A brief rain shower had cleared the air, bringing with it, if not a new sense of optimism, a fresh burst of energy. Hunter glanced at his watch. He had hardly slept in the last two days, feeding on his exhaustion like a bodybuilder gobbling steroids. He would not rest until Mel and the kids had been found, safe and sound. In the meantime, rest was simply not an option.

Neither was standing around like a spare prick at a whore's wedding under the glare of arc-lights that looked like they'd been set up to shoot the latest Docklands gangster B-movie. The only reason for him being here was to get a line on Andy Carson and his crew. Otherwise he was no better than the rest of the gawkers trying to get some interesting shots of the crash on their mobile phones.

It looked like the Range Rover had smacked into the side of the Astra and headed straight into one of the concrete supports holding up the elevated stretch of the motorway above. Even at this late hour the A13 hummed with a relentless stream of traffic doing 70 mph a hundred feet over their heads. Giving the Fire Brigade and the medical staff space to get on with their jobs, Hunter stood well away from the wreckage, contemplating his next move. It was more than three hours since he'd had the call from Colonel Naylor telling him that one of Andy Carson's associates had died in a car accident following a police chase.

One of the firemen, a square-framed Yorkshireman who had been directing the teams trying to cut away the wreckage, walked past. The two black bands on his yellow helmet told Hunter that he was a Crew Manager, while the name on his tunic said Fitton.

'Any developments?' Hunter asked.

Fitton stopped and looked at him suspiciously. 'And who are you, lad?'

'Police.' It was not the time for detailed explanations.

'Aye, well. It's not good.' Fitton went back on his way. Hunter nodded. He already knew the reality of the situation; the pace of activity around the two cars had slowed noticeably in the last twenty minutes. This was no longer a rescue operation. He was still watching the retreating figure of the Crew Manager when there was the crunch of footsteps on his blindside.

'What have we got?'

Recognizing the voice – a perfect mixture of Harrow, St Andrews University and the Guards – Hunter threw back his shoulders and stood to attention. 'Sir!'

Stepping into his line of vision, Colonel Trevor Naylor said gruffly, 'No need for any of that here, Dan. We're in mufti, remember?' He pointed towards the growing group of TV crews who had set up camp behind the police tape. 'We don't want that lot getting wind of our presence.'

'No.'

'There's more than enough for the media to wet their pants about already; it's rumoured that a fortune in diamonds was stolen at the airport. We're talking tens, if not hundreds, of millions.'

Hunter let out a low whistle.

'Diamonds really are a crook's best friend, eh? Portable, basically untraceable and hugely valuable; acceptable currency anywhere in the world. Who needs Bitcoin?'

Not really sure what his boss was getting at, Hunter stared at his shoes.

'If they find out that there's a connection to Andy Carson as well,' Naylor continued, 'they'll go crazy. And I don't know about you, but I don't feel quite ready for my close-up.' For a man pulled from his bed to make a mad dash down the M1, he looked remarkably composed. He'd even taken time for a shave, with his pencil-thin moustache looking like it had been carefully groomed. Dressed in a Barbour jacket and a tweed flat cap, all that was missing was the open Purdy resting in the crook of his arm and the Retriever at his feet. All in all, it wasn't really much of an E16 look.

It occurred to Hunter that this was probably the first time he had ever seen his CO out of uniform. Together, they watched as a body was carefully brought out of the back of the Astra and placed on a gurney.

'So here we are, out in the real world, God help us. What have you found out?'

Hunter began reeling off what he had gleaned while his boss had been speeding down the motorway, trying to pad it out with a mixture of backstory and supposition in the hope of making it sound more substantial than it actually was. 'Adrian Colinson was driving the Range Rover. The irony of it was, I think they were in the clear but it looks like he might have taken a wrong turning.' He pointed in the direction the SUV had been travelling. 'This road would have taken them back to the airport.'

'That's what happens when you rely on bloody satnav,' Naylor muttered. 'People can't do anything for themselves any more.'

'Anyway, forensics estimate he was doing a hundred and twenty when he took out the Astra and hit the pillar.'

'Who was in the Astra?'

'Four teenagers, apparently. They were all dead when I got here.' Hunter felt a wave of cold disinterest pass over him. 'They were just in the wrong place at the wrong time. Not relevant to us.'

'No, suppose not. So what about the Range Rover?'

'Again, four occupants. Colinson is dead, along with the security guard who was couriering the diamonds. Carson, we think, and a fourth man were able to get away – with the stones.'

Naylor looked around at the impressive collection of police

vehicles which had congregated around the scene, while gesturing at the two helicopters circling overhead. 'How is that possible?'

Hunter just shrugged.

'Any ideas on the identity of the fourth man?'

'My guess is that it's Ryan Fortune.'

Naylor grimaced as he played with his moustache. 'Really?'

'I've had plenty of time to stand here and think about it. Fortune is a known associate of both Carson and Colinson. He certainly has the skills – and the balls – to try and pull off a job like this. And he certainly has previous.'

Naylor nodded. He didn't need reminding of Ryan Fortune's sheet; it was longer than a politician's nose. 'Didn't you put him away that last time?'

'That last time' was the robbery of six million pounds of banknotes, fresh from the printer in Malta. Only about half of the cash was ever recovered.

'Yes,' said Hunter. 'He was supposed to do eight years. It was reduced to five and half on appeal. He got out eighteen months ago on parole.'

Naylor shook his head sadly. 'You've got to love our judicial system.'

'The crooks certainly do. Fortune is a hard bastard. He skipped through multiple tours in Iraq and Afghanistan as if it was some kind of holiday. He's the sort of guy I rather wish was on our side, to be honest.'

Naylor was clearly not impressed by the sentiment. 'He's not though, is he?'

'No, not by a long chalk. When he was on active, I'm sure he did a lot worse than Andy Carson; he didn't do it on bloody video, though. He's nobody's fool.'

'So he was the brains behind this diamond job?'

'Maybe the connection between the brains and the brawn. Fortune knew he needed a three-man crew for tonight, so I think he and Colinson went and sprung Carson. They must have been under a bit of time pressure, otherwise they would have surely tried to find someone less high-profile. Fortune knew I would be on the case faster than a rat up a drainpipe, so he tried to scare me off. He only needs the distraction of Mel and the kids for a couple of days and then he's gone.'

'And they're free.'

'Let's hope so.'

On that basis, maybe you should just let it run its course. Don't give these guys any excuse to do something stupid. Leave this one to the police. You can reacquaint yourself with these gentlemen once Melanie and the children are safely accounted for.'

'With all due respect, Sir, you know that's not my style. Anyway, the local plod have been less than impressive so far.' Hunter quickly recounted his run-in with Inspector Sarah Ward of West End Central. 'She was so convinced I'd kidnapped my own family that she interviewed me under caution.'

'She's only doing her job,' Naylor observed. 'If you plan to stay on the case you're going to have to build bridges with these people, whether you think they're half-decent or not.'

'There was another inspector who seemed quite on the ball. But he doesn't answer his bloody phone.' Hunter watched as the Crew Manager, Fitton, reappeared, a paper cup full of steaming coffee in his hand. Ignoring the Colonel, he stepped up to Hunter, the dismay at being stuck in the middle of this mess clear in his eyes.

'Are you the Army guy?'

'I am.'

Fitton gestured towards the wreckage with his cup. 'The cops say those bastards have got your family.'

Hunter nodded. 'That's right.'

Looking around to check that no one was watching them, Fitton jerked out his free hand. 'Here.'

Hunter took the business card, closing his fist around it.

'One of my guys found it on the driver,' Fitton said quietly. He took a sip of his coffee. 'It might be of some use.'

'Thanks.'

'Good luck. I hope that everything turns out okay for you and yours.' Turning away, Fitton emptied the contents of his cup on to the cracked tarmac before tossing it towards the gutter.

Watching him head back to work, Hunter finally inspected the card.

'What is it?' Naylor asked.

'A lettings agency.' Hunter gestured back in the direction of the City proper. 'An address in Old Street.' He was still a relative newcomer to London but he knew that Old Street was located somewhere close to Liverpool Street station and the City of London.

'A lead?'

'I bloody hope so.' Hunter looked at his CO. 'Do you think you could give me a lift back into the centre of town?'

In the chill of the early morning gloom, Andy Carson stood by the open window, sucking down on a Marlboro as he listened to the sound of his own breathing. Uneven and rasping, it made him sound like a little old man. On the plus side, it was a reminder that he was still alive.

A police helicopter scudded past on the horizon, heading west. Carson gave them a cheery wave. 'Happy hunting, you wankers!'

Holding the smoke down deep in his lungs, he casually flicked some ash out of the window. At this hour, there was almost no traffic on the roads below. Carson was surprised to hear the sound of birdsong coming from the rooftops. That was an interesting thing about cities, he mused. However hard people tried, they never managed to obliterate nature completely.

Looking out over the derelict patch of ground on the far side of the Clerkenwell Road, towards the Golden Lane Estate, he shook his head in disgust. London was a dirty city. This part of the metropolis had been heavily bombed during World War Two and even now it had the ramshackle air of a district awaiting proper redevelopment. His parents were genuine Cockneys. They had grown up little more than a mile from where he was standing, moving out to Milton Keynes – before Andy and his brothers were born – in search of cheap housing and green space. Forty years later, it still wasn't home. They never managed to get over leaving the East End.

Andy himself failed to see the attraction.

'What a dump.' Taking a final drag of his smoke, he flicked the butt out of the window, into the garden below. After today, he wouldn't see London again; he wouldn't miss it.

The safe house was an unfurnished warehouse apartment at the top of a former pickle factory. Carson had made it back with Fortune just before dawn. Still buzzing from his latest escape from the forces of law and order, he felt invincible. It was like the best 3D game ever. *Grand Theft Auto* on acid. He was Michael De Santa made flesh. Lighting another cigarette, he ran through the highlights of the last few hours.

As it turned out, Adrian Colinson hadn't been as good a getaway driver as they had imagined. He also made the schoolboy error of not wearing a seatbelt, which meant he was halfway through the windscreen before his airbag had the chance to deploy. After his argument with the concrete pillar, even his own mother wouldn't have recognized him.

Fortune had been cursing and blinding at Colinson but it was just a reflex; their comrade had been dead even before they had exited the vehicle. This was real life, not some crappy Army-sponsored movie, and there was no way they were going to try and uphold the bullshit 'no man left behind' code.

'Clunk click, every trip.' Wasn't that what that old perv Jimmy Savile had always said? This time the advice had paid off, big time. After a combination of the seatbelt and the airbag had done their job, Carson had walked from the wreckage of the Range Rover, dazed but essentially unhurt.

Clearing his head, he recovered the bolt-cutters from the boot. Pulling open the back passenger door, Carson saw the security guard slumped forward, clearly dead, his neck having been broken when the impact of the crash threw him against the headrest of the front seat. Pushing the corpse back into something approximating a seated position, Carson cut the chain of the handcuffs with the clippers. Grabbing the case, he wheeled away, ready to take his leave.

'Hey!'

Looking round, he found Fortune standing in a storm ditch ten metres or so away, the top of his head barely visible.

'This way.'

Carson hesitated.

'Hurry up!'

Off to his left, he could make out a police helicopter heading towards them, its spotlight jerking over the open ground. Needing no further encouragement, Carson ran to the ditch. Diving into it, he was pleased that it was dry. Checking his footing, he chased after Fortune, who was already the best part of 100 yards further on, moving at an impressive lick.

Fucking hell, Carson thought. If he doesn't slow down, I'm gonna have a heart attack.

Reaching the end of the drainage system, they emerged into a small housing estate, populated with the kind of starter box homes that looked like they'd fall over if the wind reached Force 6. Looking back over his shoulder, Carson was amazed that no one seemed to be following them. The helicopter remained hovering over the crash scene and the sirens of the emergency service vehicles were moving further away, rather than towards them. Taking a moment to catch his breath, he reflected that it looked like they'd made good their escape, even if things hadn't quite gone according to plan.

Fortune headed directly to the parking lot of a boarded-up pub. By the time Carson had caught up, he was sitting behind the wheel of an ancient, rusting black cab. Coaxing the engine into life, he flicked off the 'For Hire' sign and invited Carson to jump in the back. Heading out of the estate, they set off on a tour of the back streets of East London, arriving on Old Street just before dawn. Dumping the taxi in an underground car park, they had travelled the last few blocks to the apartment on foot.

'Stop daydreaming,' Ryan Fortune appeared at the edge of his peripheral vision. He was stuffing clothes and weapons into a kitbag. 'We need to get out of here.'

Carson glanced down at the case sitting on the wooden floor between them, a single handcuff still locked around its handle. 'How do we get this thing open?'

'Not our problem,' Fortune said tersely. 'Other people will deal with that.'

Carson stepped forward. Picking up the case, he gave it a shake. A stupid grin spread over his face as he listened to the diamonds bouncing around inside. 'Don't you want to take a look?'

'Andy,' Fortune said tightly, 'put that down.'

Reluctantly, Carson did as he was told.

'You need to *focus*.'

Retreating to the window, Carson folded his arms. 'You sound like my mum.'

'Your mum's right.'

Jerking a thumb over his shoulder, Carson gestured towards the door in the far corner of the room, the key in the lock. 'Okay, so what do you want to do with them?'

Them. Mel Hunter and her kids. The *Get Out of Jail* card they no longer needed.

'Just leave them.' Closing the kitbag, Fortune hoisted it over his shoulder. 'We clear out and then someone can come and get them later.'

Carson caressed the semi-automatic in his jacket pocket. 'Surely we don't want any witnesses?'

'Enough people have died already.'

'So what's a few more then?'

'Andy, Christ! That's a woman and her kids you're talking about, not some little Taliban wankers who were trying to shoot your nuts off ten minutes before you wasted them.'

'They could finger us.'

'Use your noodle.' Fortune tapped his temple with a forefinger. 'It doesn't matter. What can they tell the police or the Redcaps that they don't already know? We're well in the frame for all this already. Plus, you were number one on the Army's Most Wanted list to start with, don't forget. You don't need to be Sherlock Holmes to work out who did it. There's no point.'

'I don't like loose ends.'

'I can understand that,' Fortune said sarcastically, 'what with you being so good at tidying them up and all. Maybe you want me to video it for you as well – add it to your collection? The idea popped into his head that maybe he himself should drop Carson here and now. He wasn't really one for improvising but he could see the attractions. The guy had served his useful purpose. From now on, he was only going to be a liability. He felt the grip on his gun tighten. 'Just leave them alone.'

As if reading his mind, Carson backed off. 'Makes sense,' he conceded. 'And, anyway you're the boss.'

'Good,' Fortune walked over to the door. 'I'll just check on them and then we're out of here. I'll call the lettings agent tonight and she can come and get them.'

'Yeah, that's the best way.' Carson watched Fortune turn the key in the lock before disappearing down the hallway. Flicking off the safety on his own weapon, he slowly counted to five and followed after him.

TWENTY-TWO

Refusing to believe the evidence of his own eyes, the inspector stared blankly at the empty cupboard. 'Where's the muesli?'

'It was past its sell-by date,' Helen said blithely, gently blowing on her white tea as she leaned against the sink, 'so I threw it out.'

'Past its sell-by date?' Telling himself not to panic, Carlyle smacked the cupboard door shut and scowled at his wife. 'What the hell's that got to do with anything? Don't you realize sell-by dates are just a massive conspiracy to get people to throw out perfectly good food?'

'Don't worry,' Helen said evenly, 'I'll get some more on my way home tonight.'

'That's no fucking good, is it?' Carlyle felt the vein in his temple begin to throb. He could feel himself coming over all Basil Fawlty.

'What do you care?' Helen, his very own Sybil, retorted, her patience beginning to wear thin. 'You never ate the stuff before.'

'Because I had stashed my dad's drugs in it.'

'Ah.' Helen rapidly recalibrated her assessment of her husband's sense of humour failure.

Opening the cupboard under the sink, Carlyle contemplated the rubbish bin, a bucket lined with a bright orange plastic bag from the supermarket close to the tube. It was empty. Now was the time to panic. He shot his wife a pleading look. 'Where's the rubbish?'

'Alice took it out when she went off to school,' Helen said meekly.

'*Shit!*' Carlyle glanced at his watch.

'It was only five minutes ago,' Helen pointed out. 'Hopefully it should still be there.'

Please, God, let the woman be right.

'If the bin men haven't been.'

'Aaargh!' A surge of adrenalin sent the inspector hurtling through the door and down the hallway. On the landing, he decided against waiting for the lift, instead taking the stairs, three at a time. Reaching the first floor, he hurtled past Mrs Andrews from 2B, almost knocking the pensioner on her backside as he flew past.

'Where's the fire?' she shouted after him.

'Sorry!' Carlyle shouted back over his shoulder, almost tripping and breaking his neck in the process. 'I can't stop.'

'I can see that,' the woman said cheerily. 'Chasing a criminal?'

'Something like that,' the inspector wheezed as a last burst took him down to the ground floor. Heaving at the front door to the building, he dragged himself out on to the pavement. As his eyes adjusted to the glare of the morning sun, his heart sank. 'What a tip!' An unappealing selection of discarded newspapers, food waste, plastic bottles and other domestic rubbish was strewn all over the place, shifting up and down the street with the eddies of the breeze. The local tramps had been out again – a regular occurrence – slitting open the waste sacks that had been left out overnight, filleting them for whatever choice morsels they could find. Everything else was left to spill out on to the road, waiting for some poor sod with a cart to come along and clean it up.

A faint smell of decay reached his nostrils, further darkening his mood. Looking up at the sky, the inspector hoped that the promised rain would arrive to cleanse the neighbourhood. He watched as a taxi casually headed the wrong way down the one-way street, mashing an over-ripe banana into the tarmac before turning into Drury Lane.

Another day in paradise.

Wasn't that a Phil Collins song?

Bemused by the random meanderings of his own mind, Carlyle kicked an empty baked-bean tin into the gutter, careful not to get tomato sauce on to the toe of his shoe. Not for the first time, he reflected that the bin men provided the most truly essential service of anyone in the capital.

After the best efforts of the dossers, there were still twenty or more bags waiting for collection. Grouped around three different lampposts, they were a mixture of black refuse sacks and re-purposed supermarket bags of different sizes and colours. Carlyle scratched his head. Which one was theirs?

'Think!' he muttered to himself. 'Now is the time to work smart.' Slowly, it dawned on him that the easiest thing was to call Alice and hope that his daughter would answer her phone. Reaching for his mobile, Carlyle belatedly realized that he had left it upstairs. Cursing, he glanced back to the entrance of Winter Garden House. Where was Helen? The least she could do was to come down and help him with his search.

Reinforcements, however, were not forthcoming. Feeling more than a little sorry for himself, the inspector strode up to the first lamppost. Half-heartedly poking at the pile of rubbish with his toe, he tried to identify Helen's out-of-date box of muesli inside one of the bags. As he did so, the familiar noise of a diesel engine heading up Drury Lane seeped into his consciousness.

'Bollocks!'

Looking up, the inspector saw two bin men, a young guy in his twenties and an older man, about the same age as himself, walking towards him as their rubbish truck manoeuvred its way into Macklin Street. Carlyle recognized the pair by sight, often coming across them out on their daily route on his way to work. Indeed, he was on nodding terms with one, the older guy, who lived round the corner, near Dragon Hall.

'Hold on a minute, lads.' Fumbling in his pocket, Carlyle pulled out his Warrant Card and promptly dropped it in amongst the rubbish bags. Picking it up, he let them get a good look at it before adding, 'I'm just checking for something. Bear with me till I find it.'

The two men looked at each other and grinned.

'Police business.'

'What happened?' the older guy asked. 'Your missus thrown out your gun?'

'Something like that,' Carlyle muttered, not seeing the funny side.

'Want us to give you a hand?'

'It's okay, won't be a minute.'

The rubbish truck rolled past and came to a halt five yards further along the road. The smell coming from the loading hopper at the back of the vehicle fair made the inspector gag.

'What are you looking for?' the younger guy asked.

Carlyle tried to smile. 'It's confidential, I'm afraid.'

Mrs Andrews had appeared at the entrance to Winter Garden House. She gave him a funny look and then waved a small plastic bag at the bin men. 'Can you take this?'

' 'Course, love,' the older guy smiled. Jogging over, he took the old woman's rubbish and threw it in the hopper. A silver BMW turned into Macklin Street, the driver's face creasing in dismay as he realized his proposed short-cut was blocked by the truck. Smacking his palm against the steering wheel, he let rip with a long blast of his horn, the better to inform the world of his presence.

'Chill, mate,' the younger bin man advised, annoying the driver even more. 'We're only doing our job.' His colleague gave Carlyle a look that said *Get on with it.*

'Just gimme a second.' The inspector picked up a green M&S bag and tore it open to discover the remains of an Indian ready meal and a copy of the *Telegraph*. Not sure which was the more offensive item, he threw the bag into the back of the truck. Picking up the pace, he went through the drill with a Sainsbury's bag and one of the black bin bags.

'This is great,' the younger bin man laughed. 'Wanna finish the round for us?'

Carlyle caught a glimpse of the driver looking at him in the wing mirror. Only you, he thought to himself dolefully, could draw a crowd hunting for drugs outside your front door. The BMW driver let loose with another blast on his horn.

'Shut up, you wanker!' Grabbing another black bag, Carlyle ripped it open, letting out a small cry of joy when he caught sight of the familiar cereal box design inside.

'Got it!' Clasping the bag tightly by the neck, he quickly retreated to the door. 'Thanks, lads. Sorry for holding you up.'

'Good luck with the investigation!' they chorused.

'Thanks!' Punching in the entry code, Carlyle pulled open the door and darted inside. In the lobby, he pressed the button for the lift, cackling like a maniac at the thought of his latest flirtation with disaster.

Leaning against the fridge, mobile clamped to her ear, Helen raised an eyebrow as her husband entered the kitchen and unceremoniously dumped the sack in the middle of the floor.

'He's just walked in.' Pushing herself off the fridge, she stepped towards him, careful to give the rubbish a wide berth. 'It's for you.'

As she offered him the handset, Carlyle felt surprised that his wife had answered his phone.

'It just kept ringing,' she explained, as if reading his thoughts.

'Who is it?' he asked grumpily, taking the phone from her. The excitement of his drugs run was wearing off and he felt decidedly weary.

'A Mr Hunter.'

Hunter? It took a second for the penny to drop. Given his other adventures, the military policeman had been deleted from the inspector's cache of short-term memory. He lifted the handset to his ear. 'Hello?'

'Why the hell don't you answer your phone?'

'I've been busy,' Carlyle snapped back, in no mood to take any crap from a ruddy soldier. 'Where are you?'

Hunter mentioned the name of a ubiquitous sandwich chain. 'I'm on Goswell Road, just north of Old Street. You need to get over here, right away.'

Oh, do I? It took Carlyle another moment to remember he had skin in the game.

'I've got a good lead on these bastards.' Hunter's words were slightly slurred. Carlyle could easily imagine he'd been on the case all night; the guy sounded like he was running on fumes. 'This thing could all kick off very quickly and I'm going to need some help.'

'Okay, okay. I should be there in about twenty minutes.' Carlyle slipped the phone into the back pocket of his trousers and fished the cereal packet from the rubbish. If Helen was as relieved as he was, she didn't let it show. Instead, she watched impassively as her husband checked that the tablets were still inside before putting the box back in its place in the cupboard.

'You're not going to leave it there, are you?'

Carlyle patted the phone with the palm of his hand. 'Duty calls. I need to go and sort something out.'

'But I don't want it in the house,' Helen wailed.

Carlyle lifted a hand to the back of his neck, trying to massage away the incipient headache brewing at the top of his spine. Helen really did pick her moments. Wasn't this whole caper her idea in the first place? Knowing better than to try and point any of this out, he opted for conciliation. 'I'll be back as soon as possible,' he said gently, 'and then I'll take the stuff straight over to Fulham. It'll be out of here before the end of the day. Dad needs to have it as soon as possible anyway.'

'But what happens if someone comes round?'

'Just don't offer them any muesli,' Carlyle suggested. He was halfway through the door when she called him back.

'John!'

'What?'

Helen gestured at the rubbish bag on the floor. 'Don't leave that there, at least. Take it out with you.'

Ending his call with the policeman, Hunter checked in with Naylor, who confirmed that there had been no significant developments since their parting of the ways in the early hours. Stifling a yawn, the captain looked around the cafe and returned to his superficial review of the previous day's paper. After reading about a man released after twenty-five years on Death Row for a murder he did not commit, he was struggling to keep his eyes open, only jerking awake as he watched a tall blonde woman of indeterminate age walk along the opposite side of the road. The shiny silver trainers on her feet did not go well with the formal grey business suit she was wearing, but Hunter assumed that there would be a pair of work shoes nestling in the large bag slung over her shoulder. In her hand was the kind of large paper coffee cup that every other commuter in this city seemed to carry. Hunter did a rough calculation in his head of how much the cost of a daily coffee added up to on an annual basis, frowning when he came up with a total. People down here really didn't know they were born. Everyone talked about London being another country; as far as Hunter could see, it was more like another planet.

Hunter straightened himself up as the blonde woman approached the Silicon Roundabout Lettings Agency, emitting a small croak of triumph as she stopped at its door. From his pocket, he removed the card that the fireman, Fitton, had given him at the scene of the crash, glancing at it as he watched the woman rummage in her bag. After several moments, she pulled out a large set of keys and began going through the laborious process of opening multiple locks. Hunter put the card back in his pocket and slipped off his stool.

Having dealt with the locks, the woman pushed open the door. Planting one foot in the hallway, she quickly disabled the alarm and disappeared inside. Hunter allowed himself the luxury of a stretch while he waited for her to reappear in the office proper, visible through a large plate-glass window – the bottom half of which was filled with the particulars of properties available for rent. He waited patiently for the woman to get herself settled behind her desk before emptying the remains of his cold coffee into the bin provided and stepping out into the street.

The lack of sleep had dulled his reflexes. Crossing the road, Hunter was almost taken out by a delivery van and a cyclist in quick succession. Finally reaching the other side, he took a second to compose himself. Ignoring the Closed notice, he stepped into the office. From behind her desk, the woman didn't seem particularly surprised at his arrival.

'Good morning, sir.' Her smile was impressive, given both his appearance and the time of morning. 'How can I help you?'

Hunter pulled up a seat and sat down. She handed him a business card: *Caroline Batting, Lettings Manager.* He took it with a nod, not mentioning that he already had one sitting in his pocket. Up close, he estimated that she was mid-thirties, not unattractive but rapidly going to seed, the skin under her chin beginning to sag alarmingly. 'I'm looking for a property,' he explained.

'Yes,' she said brightly, already on automatic pilot. 'What kind of thing were you looking for? Do you have a budget?'

'No, no.' Hunter shook his head. 'I don't want to rent anywhere.'

'Oh.' The smile on her face wavered but did not completely disappear.

'I'm looking to track down a property that you let to someone.' Taking his Warrant Card from his pocket, he handed it over for her to inspect. 'A man – or maybe a couple of men – took a short-term rental recently. I need to find them.'

Taking the card, she looked at it carefully. 'So you are . . .'

'Royal Military Police.' He emphasized the first word, knowing from experience that was what civilians usually responded to. The image of a Union Jack fluttering against a clear blue sky would appear before their eyes and they would be falling over themselves to be helpful before he had even asked his first question.

Batting, however, didn't get up and salute. Instead, she handed back the ID and said, 'I'm sorry, but our records are private. We have a duty of confidentiality to our clients, both landlords and tenants. Their information can only be accessed by the police – and even then only upon production of a relevant court order.' The words came out with practised ease, as if she had used them before. Or maybe she just watched too many cop shows on TV.

Hunter stuffed the card back in his jacket. 'I *am* the police.'

She shot him a condescending smile. 'I'm sorry, Mr—'

'Captain . . . Captain Hunter.'

'I'm sorry, *Captain* Hunter, but you will be perfectly well aware that you have no authority out here in the real world.' It was true enough, as a Military Policeman, Hunter did not have any powers over members of the general public. Having called his bluff, she twisted the knife. 'And, no offence, I'm sure you really are who you say you are, but that Warrant Card doesn't prove anything, does it? You could probably buy one of those on eBay for a tenner.'

'You seem to know a lot about it,' Hunter said grimly.

'You need to know about all aspects of the law in this game,' she shrugged, 'otherwise people will mess you about all the time. The nonsense you have to put up with can be unbelievable.'

'I'm not trying to mess you about,' Hunter stressed. 'I am chasing some really bad men who were involved in the airport robbery last night.'

She looked at him blankly. 'What robbery?'

'The theft of some diamonds. A lot of money. People were killed. We have reason to believe that the crew who did the job may have rented one of your flats.'

He had stimulated her interest but she wasn't going to roll over. 'Wouldn't that be a matter for the police?'

'It's a joint investigation.'

'But you have no authority,' she repeated.

'Yes, but *I* do.' Carlyle walked into the office and tossed his ID on the desk. 'You can't buy one of those on eBay.'

'I wouldn't be so sure about that,' Batting scoffed, inspecting this second document with rather less interest than she had the first. 'Anyway, you still need the right paperwork.' Handing the inspector back his card, she bent down and pulled on a pair of black leather shoes. 'Now, you'll have to forgive me, but if I don't get a move on, I'm going to be late for a viewing. If you want to come back with a court order we will, of course, provide every possible assistance.'

'Sorry, love.' Carlyle moved round to her side of the desk, the better to check her computer screen. 'We don't have time for that. The men we are after are very dangerous. We need to track them down, right now.' He glanced at Hunter who looked more than ready to beat the information out of her, gesturing for him to be cool.

The smile had gone now; this was getting very boring. Batting glanced at her watch. Technically speaking, it wasn't even opening time yet. She pined for the days when the nutters wouldn't get out of bed before noon. Her mind drifted to thoughts of her first glass of Sauvignon Blanc at lunchtime. It would be a large one.

'We just need a bit of information,' Carlyle persisted. 'Otherwise, I'm going to have to take you back to Charing Cross police station and book you with obstruction.'

'Nonsense!' she snorted.

'Yes, it is,' Carlyle agreed. 'It'll be a complete waste of a day for everyone.'

Batting took a moment to consider her options. Then she began smacking the keys on her computer keyboard. 'How far back do you want to go?' While she listened to them setting out the parameters of their search, Batting's mind was already in Tommy's Wine Bar. To hell with a glass of wine, today she would be ordering a whole bottle.

TWENTY-THREE

They left Caroline Batting sitting in her office and set off down
the street with six sets of keys and a map covered in crosses. In
charge of the map, Carlyle felt like a bit of an idiot, like a tourist in his own city, unable to find his way around on instinct and
experience alone. At least all of the properties were within easy
walking distance. He let his finger trace a possible route for them
to take.

'How do you want to do this?'

'Start with the closest,' Hunter responded, 'and we can work
outwards from there.'

'Okay.' Carlyle set off in the direction of Moorgate. 'But you
know that they've probably done a runner by now,' he panted,
jogging across the road to avoid the attentions of an onrushing
motorbike. 'They could be in . . .' he tried to think of somewhere
exotic '. . . the Bahamas by now. Almost.'

'That doesn't matter,' Hunter said tightly, 'as long as we find
Mel and the kids. Andy Carson can wait.'

Reaching the far pavement, Carlyle lengthened his stride.
'What's he like?'

'Carson?' Hunter fell in beside him, matching the inspector's
pace. 'Just a fairly normal bloke. Liked his beer, his porn and his
football. An Aston Villa fan.'

At least he didn't support Chelsea, Carlyle mused. That was
one character defect he could never overlook.

'As far as I could see,' Hunter continued, 'Carson was a

perfectly decent soldier. Hardly Sandhurst material, but solid; he did his job and was well enough liked. Had plenty of mates. He could be a bit of a berk when he got pissed up, but you can say that of just about every bloke that wears a uniform. If you had to sum him up in one word it would be "unremarkable".'

'So why did he shoot those guys?'

'Simple – because he had a gun in his hand and he thought he could get away with it.' Carlyle ducked into an alley that provided a short cut. It wasn't wide enough for both of them, so Hunter let him lead before adding: 'He would have done too, if he hadn't been filmed in the act.'

'That's a fairly basic fail,' Carlyle threw back. 'It must have made your life easier though?'

'Yeah. Once the video came to light, he was toast. Even then, he thought that there were absolutely no consequences to his actions. He seemed genuinely offended by the fact that there was even an investigation. When I arrested him he was gobsmacked. I'm sure you've seen the same kind of thing.'

'Many times. People think they can justify anything.'

'Tell me about it.' Emerging from the alley, they fell back in step, two professionals enjoying the simple pleasure of swapping war stories. Going about their business on the quiet streets, they could almost feel like normal guys. For a short while at least, that was something to savour.

The next couple of hours were spent on a Cook's tour, from Moorgate to London Wall and on towards the Barbican. After visiting the first four properties on the letting agent's map, they had done nothing more exciting than walk in on a lawyer enjoying her morning bath. The woman had not taken the interruption well, muttering darkly about legal action as she shooed them out of the door wearing only a towel.

'If you sue anyone,' the inspector said drily, 'make sure it's the Army.' All he got by way of reply was the sound of the door being slammed shut behind them, followed by the deadbolt being firmly thrown into place.

Standing in the corridor, he grinned at Hunter. Gazing into the middle distance, however, the captain did not respond. The look of stony despair on his exhausted face reminded Carlyle of what was at stake and the need to stay focused. 'Let's keep going,' he offered, consulting the last two remaining properties on the map. 'St John Street or Goswell Road, what d'you reckon?'

Heading towards the lifts, Hunter did not express a preference. Scurrying after him, the inspector made an executive decision. 'Let's try Goswell Road,' he said, folding up the map and stuffing it in his pocket.

Hands on hips, Becky Carson contemplated the visitor standing in her kitchen. On the credit side, he was tall, dark and handsome. Fairly handsome, anyway. On the debit side, he was a cop.

The police had arrived at the villa just before 9 a.m. Half a dozen uniformed officers spilling out of the back of a van and then standing around gossiping while she was formally served with the search warrant and signed some papers that consented to them shoving their noses in her knicker drawer.

It was like an episode of *The Bill*, only with better weather. Deep down, she had known that the local police would be paying her a visit. Even so, the timing had been a bit of a surprise, if only because Becky had never come across anyone in Greece who started work before ten-thirty. 'Lazy' was the understatement of all time. It was no wonder that the bloody country was bust. Andy liked to joke that they should just hand the whole thing over to the Germans, lock stock and barrel. That was probably one of the few things that her errant husband was right about.

She looked at the clock on the kitchen wall. 'How much longer is this going to take?'

The officer in command made a non-committal gesture. 'Our orders are to be thorough.'

'Only it's almost lunchtime now. I was planning to go out.'

'I'm afraid you'll have to wait until we are finished.'

'You're not going to find him here.' Taking a packet of B&H from her bag on the Welsh dresser, she rummaged around for a lighter. Coming up empty, she swore in frustration. 'I haven't heard from him.'

'We will be as quick as we can,' the cop said. 'After all, my boys will want their lunch too.'

'Smoke?' Becky offered the open packet to the cop.

He shook his head. 'No. I don't.'

'Suit yourself.' Shoving a cigarette between her lips, Becky tossed the packet back on to the dresser and resumed her search.

Through the open door the sound of police officers roaming freely through the rest of her house set her teeth on edge. They had been going through the house and the gardens all morning. What did they think? That Andy was hiding under the floorboards?

'He's not here,' she repeated.

'I know that.'

'So what exactly are you looking for then?'

The officer smiled politely. 'It's all in the search warrant.' His English was fluent and, disconcertingly, he had no trace of an accent. Becky glanced at the pristine document lying on the middle of the table, making no effort to pick it up. They had given her a copy in English but she wasn't going to read it.

Giving up on the lighter, Becky dropped the cigarette on the dresser. 'What did you say your name was again?'

'Inspector Nikos Jones.'

She frowned. 'Jones? That's not a very Greek name, is it?'

'My father is originally from Weybridge,' the policeman explained, 'in Surrey. My mother comes from the island. He came here on holiday one year, they met up, and he never left. I grew up about thirty kilometres from here.' The boilerplate explanation he had given millions of times already and would give millions of times more.

She waited for him to go on.

'I never wanted to live anywhere else.'

Can't blame you for that, she thought, her hostility towards his presence dissolving rapidly. Nicky Jones, as she already thought of him, maybe wasn't as pretty as the boys who cruised the harbour late into the evenings on their Vespas but she wouldn't kick him out of bed either. She was just about to offer him a drink when an almighty crash came from next door, followed by a short burst of indecipherable shouting. Becky winced. 'Don't they know they have to be careful? What are they doing in there?'

Pushing a loose strand of hair away from his face, the inspector made no attempt at an apology. 'It seems that your husband is really in a lot of trouble.'

'I'm well aware of that.'

'We need to find him before there is any more trouble.'

'But he's not bleedin' *here*, is he?'

Leaning against the doorframe, Jones folded his arms. 'You know where he is?'

'No, I don't.'

Sceptical, the cop raised an eyebrow. It made him look silly. Despite everything, Becky had to suppress a smirk. 'I think women usually like to know where their husbands are, don't you?'

'Not necessarily. Anyway, wanting to know and knowing are two different things.' She checked his hands. No rings. 'As you would understand if you were married.'

The inspector conceded the point with the slightest of shrugs.

Pulling out a chair, Becky sat down, signalling for him to join her. Shaking his head, he stayed where he was.

'I saw him in prison before he – you know – like, escaped. Not that I knew what he was up to, of course. He should have taken his chances at the court-martial. I think he would have got off.' She searched the policeman's face for some sign of agreement. None was forthcoming. 'After all, he was just a soldier doing his job. You're fighting in a war, what are you supposed to do?'

Jones made a vague gesture. He didn't feel the need to venture an opinion.

'Running wasn't very clever.'

If by 'running', Jones thought, you mean breaking out of prison, killing three people in the process, then no, it wasn't. Not in the slightest. 'When you spoke to him, he didn't mention anything about diamonds – a robbery?'

Becky's eyes narrowed. 'What robbery? Andy's no crook. He's just a soldier being hung out to dry by the brass.'

Was she lying? He couldn't tell. 'Do you know a guy called Fortune . . . Ryan Fortune?'

She bit her lower lip, giving the inspector a moment to anticipate the lie that was coming.

'No,' she said. 'I don't think so. Andy has loads of mates though, so, you know, I couldn't say I know them all.'

'You know Captain Daniel Hunter though, don't you?'

' 'Course I know Hunter,' she snapped. 'He was the wan— the cop that nicked Andy in the first place. The stupid sod could have just deleted that video file and none of this bollocks would have ever happened.'

'What about Hunter's family?'

'What about them? I didn't even know that he had one.'

'They've gone missing.'

'Have they? Well, good for them,' Becky snorted, her indifference absolute. 'I wish I could just bloody disappear. What's that got to do with anything, anyway?'

'From what I understand from the British authorities,' the inspector said, casually rewinding the conversation, 'you are seen as a possible accomplice in your husband's escape.'

'Me?'

'Didn't you go and speak to the Prison Commander about your husband being allowed to use the chapel?'

211

'Everybody's allowed to do that,' she countered. 'I was just trying to get him his rights.'

'You were helping plan his escape.'

'No,' she said vehemently. 'I was just getting him his rights. I didn't know he was going to be sprung. Anyway, if he was gonna do it, it doesn't matter whether he was taking confession at the time or not. What kind of prison is it that just lets him walk out anyway?'

'The British Military Police may end up issuing a warrant for your arrest.' The inspector paused to let the point sink in. 'If they don't find Mr Carson soon, I may well be coming back here with an order for your deportation back to the United Kingdom.'

Becky drummed her fingers on the table. That bastard Hunter clearly wouldn't leave them alone until he had destroyed their whole family. She glared at Jones. 'Is that a threat?'

'It is a simple statement of fact, Mrs Carson. I am simply the messenger. If you know anything, you should tell us now. We will pass it on to our colleagues in England and then we can hopefully leave you in peace in your lovely home.' Giving her a rueful smile, he gestured over his shoulder. 'My boys don't like the early starts so much, you know.'

'I don't know where Andy is,' Becky Carson stated again. 'And he's not coming here.' *I hope.*

The cop looked doubtful. 'Where else would he go?'

'I dunno, but he's not stupid. He knows that this is the first place you would come looking. He wouldn't want to drag his family into this mess.'

'I'm afraid, Mrs Carson, he has done that already.'

'It's nothing to do with us.' Looking out of the kitchen window, she contemplated the peaceful delights of her garden under the clear blue sky. Andy, you stupid bastard, she thought, if you do ever turn up here, I swear, I'll kill you myself.

'It really is a nice house you have here.'

Lost on an ocean of self-pity, it took Becky several seconds to realize that he had spoken. 'Huh?'

'You have a very nice house,' Jones repeated.

'I did before your people started trashing it,' she grumbled.

'A soldier's salary must be good.'

Understanding the implication immediately, Becky jerked upright. 'It's my mother's house. She bought it when my father died. You can't touch it.'

'That would be a matter for the courts. Proceeds of Crime legislation is quite rigorous these days, which is good . . . for us.'

A sergeant appeared in the doorway and said something to the inspector in Greek. Jones nodded, replying at length before sending him on his way.

Getting to her feet, Becky went and stood in front of the window, resting her backside against the sink. She was barely four feet from the man now, and lowered her voice accordingly. 'Look, you're not going to find anything here. Take it from me. As far as I know, Andy is still in England. Where, I don't know. London, maybe. But I do know that he's fucked up, big time. And he's not going to get away with it. He'll definitely have to go to prison now, which is fair enough.'

Arms folded, Jones stared at the pristine desert boots on his feet, letting her make her pitch.

'All I want is for me and the kids to be left completely out of it. We've come here to get away from all the crap back at home. The grief they were getting at school was unbelievable. Andy's identity was supposed to be a secret but everybody knew. The bastards all treated us like we was dirt. Criminals. Whatever their dad did, it's not the kids' fault, is it? We just want to be left alone. To have a bit of peace and quiet.'

Still staring at his shoes, Jones nodded. 'Fair enough.'

Becky took a deep breath. 'So, as soon as I hear from him, I'll let you know and tell you where he is.'

'Fine.' Jones stuck a hand in his jacket pocket, fished out a business card and passed it to her. 'You call the mobile.'

'Okay.' Taking the card, Becky stepped over to the dresser. Opening the zipped compartment in her bag, she placed it next to the one for Daniel Hunter. Two cops; Becky realized that she would have to throw her lot in with one of them.

But which one?

Hovering in the doorway, Jones shouted to his sergeant that it was time to leave. There was the sound of doors banging and boots clattering on stone as the policemen jumped back into their van.

'Call me,' Jones shouted over his shoulder as he climbed into the front of the van, next to the driver.

'Yes,' Becky replied. 'I'll call you.' One of you, at least.

Standing at the window, she watched the van disappear down the drive and out into the road.

'He was cute, wasn't he?'

'Eh?' Becky turned to face her daughter. Lucinda was wearing a white T-shirt, which barely covered her bum. The front said *I'd Rather Not* in black letters. Talk about mixed messages.

'That cop who was in charge,' Lucinda grinned, 'I saw you flirting with him.'

'I did not!' Becky pulled open the drawer next to the sink and was relieved and irritated in equal measure to find a Bic nestling alongside a collection of spoons. Taking the lighter, she went to the dresser, retrieved her discarded cigarette and lit up. Taking a deep drag, she let the smoke settle in her lungs, holding it in for a full five seconds before exhaling. 'Ahh!"

'Can I have one?'

'No, you can't. Where's Grandma?'

'Dunno,' the girl pouted. 'She was up early. I think she went into town.'

Thank God for that, Becky thought. The last thing I need is my mum giving me grief as well.

Opening a cupboard, Lucinda took out some Coco Pops. 'Liam didn't come home last night, the dirty little sod.'

Another plus. Becky shrugged as she puffed vigorously on the cigarette.

'Did they take anything?' Lucinda wanted to know.

'I don't think so.'

Lucinda found a bowl and poured some cereal into it, 'What will happen to Dad?' Suddenly she sounded like the child she was.

'How should I know?' Becky said irritably, not interested in offering the girl any comfort. 'We'll just have to wait and see.'

TWENTY-FOUR

Turning the key in the lock, Carlyle quietly pushed open the door. For a moment, the two men stood on the threshold, looking inside. Facing them was a large empty space, maybe thirty feet long and twenty feet wide, with wooden floors and walls that had been stripped back to the original brick. Devoid of furniture, it looked as if its new tenant had still to arrive. Squinting, the inspector glanced at the notes he had scribbled on the back of the particulars he had taken from the agent: *8A Falstaff Court. Rented by a Joseph Isaacs almost a month ago, deposit and 3 months paid in advance.* On the left, a massive window looked out over the rooftops of the neighbouring buildings. Under the window, an attaché case lay open on the floor. In the far corner of the room was a kitchen. Next to the kitchen was a second door. It was shut.

'Through there,' Carlyle flipped over the sheet of paper and consulted the floorplan, 'is a bathroom and two bedrooms.' Folding up the paper, he shoved it back in his jacket pocket. 'Mr Isaacs must have a few bob; he's paying almost eight hundred quid a week for this. Or maybe it's a corporate let or something.' He was about to take a step inside when he felt a hand on his shoulder, staying him.

'This is it,' Hunter whispered.

Carlyle frowned. 'How do you know?' he hissed back.

By way of response, Hunter pulled a semi-automatic from the back of his jeans. Releasing the safety, he racked a round in the chamber. 'Have you got a gun?'

'Me?' Carlyle squeaked. 'No. I'm a fucking policeman, remember?'

'You should carry.'

'Why? I know that this area is a bit rough but, still, it's not exactly the Wild West. It's not even my usual neighbourhood.' As the words left his mouth, Carlyle realized that he should have given his colleagues in the City of London police a heads-up that he was operating on their patch. Oh well, it was a bit late for that now.

'Fuck's sake.' Sticking his free hand in his jacket pocket, Hunter came up with a second, smaller weapon. Holding it by the barrel, he offered it to the inspector. 'Have you ever fired one?'

'No,' Carlyle lied. The truth was different, but it was too complicated and the time for swapping war stories was over.

'Well, these guys have. Take it.'

Carlyle reluctantly did as he was told.

'The safety's on.' Hunter pointed to the small lever above the handle. 'Leave it on unless things get a bit tasty.'

Carlyle nodded.

'Whatever happens, don't shoot me.' Hunter slipped past the inspector, weapon raised, and cautiously moved through the door.

Just as long as I don't shoot myself, Carlyle thought, following on behind.

Standing in the middle of the room, Carlyle carefully took his finger from the trigger of the gun. 'Whoever was here, it looks like they're long gone,' he said hopefully.

'Just keep your eyes on that door.' Hunter made his way over to the empty case. Battered and twisted, there was a large hole where it looked as if someone had shot at it. With his toe, he gestured towards the remains of the handcuffs still attached to the handle. 'The diamonds were in here,' he said. 'The stupid bugger must have shot it open.'

Stepping forward, Carlyle felt something under the sole of his shoe. Bending down, he picked up a small stone about the size of a pea. It resembled a piece of glass. 'They missed one – look.' He held it up for Hunter to inspect. 'God knows how much that's worth.'

'Fingerprints,' Hunter grunted.

'Too small,' Carlyle observed, irritated at being pulled up on procedure by a bloody soldier. 'They'll never get anything off that.' Placing the tiny diamond well down in the front pocket of his jeans, he moved towards the door.

Not wishing to argue the point, Hunter sniffed the air. 'Can you smell that?'

With a terrible sinking feeling in his stomach, Carlyle man-oeuvred himself in front of the Redcap. The odour was faint but nonetheless unmistakable: a mixture of shit and blood, the smell of death. 'Let me go first.'

Hunter tried to protest, but the words wouldn't come. The tension that was so deeply etched on his face had rendered him mute. This was a man steeling himself as he prepared to step into Hell. His breathing was shallow and irregular. Carlyle wouldn't have been at all surprised if he suddenly keeled over, clutching his chest.

The inspector's brain was screaming at him to call for back-up before they proceeded any further. But if they didn't go through that door right now, their legs might fail them entirely. 'I go first. You come when I give the all clear.'

Hunter gave the slightest of nods.

'All right.' Bracing himself, Carlyle raised his gun, trying to ignore the all-too-obvious tremors in his hands as he reached for the door handle.

The bodies were in the final room. Two adults and two chil-dren. Each one had been shot at least twice. Carlyle made a half-hearted attempt to block Hunter's access to his family before quickly retreating from the poor man's howls of anguish. Leaving the flat altogether, he sat on the stairs, tears in his eyes, as he called it in.

* * *

An hour later, he was still sitting, dazed, on the same step. He listened to the buzz of activity inside the flat behind him, the short verbal exchanges between colleagues who were going about their assigned roles, trying to take some comfort from the knowledge that the machine was swinging into action. His machine. The machine that would bring some justice for the victims; and closure for Daniel Hunter.

Or maybe not.

Was he just being a voyeur? Shifting on the cold stone, he knew that he wore the man's pain like a stink. People moved up and down the stairs, giving him a wide berth, lest his smell attacked their nostrils. Even those who did not have any idea who he was knew well enough to leave him alone.

The inspector had long since staunched his tears, wiping his eyes before the first uniforms had come running up the stairs, but still he felt unable to move. Juggling his phone aimlessly, he stared at the blank screen. The overwhelming need to speak to his wife would not go away. For the fourth or fifth time, he tried to ring Helen. For the fourth or fifth time, the call went straight to voicemail. She would be in a meeting, or something. He thought about calling Alice, but she would be in a class. That was okay. He would go home tonight and hug his family. After the horrors he had seen, he would count his blessings, down a couple of large glasses of Jameson's and hope that sleep would come. Tomorrow would be a new day, for him, if not for poor Daniel Hunter.

'Where is he?'

Carlyle broke off from his random musings to watch Inspector Sarah Ward come to a halt on the half landing below him. Dressed in black leather boots, skinny jeans and a battered leather jacket over a figure-hugging grey T-shirt, West End Central's finest looked like she was auditioning for one of those flic dramas so beloved by BBC 4. For once, her hatchet-faced demeanour was fully justified by the scene inside.

'He left.'

'And you let him go?'

'He had a gun, what was I supposed to do?' For the purposes of this conversation, the inspector ignored the weapon Hunter had given him, currently nestling in his jacket pocket. 'I couldn't really stop him, could I?'

The unsatisfactory nature of this reply was written all over Ward's face. Somehow she managed to make her scowl even deeper.

The woman couldn't look any more pissed off if someone chopped her head off, Carlyle thought.

'Where was he going?'

'How the fuck should I know?' Carlyle snapped. 'Off to get shitfaced, probably. I know I would.'

'You seem to be forgetting that he's still a suspect.'

'This is *not* your average domestic.' Carlyle gestured over his shoulder. 'Go and have a look.'

Ward stood her ground. 'I don't need you to tell me how to run my investigation.'

'Wouldn't dream of it,' Carlyle responded prissily.

'You could have made an effort to follow him.'

And you could make an effort to fuck right off, the inspector thought, struggling to keep a hold on his temper.

'He could have done it,' Ward muttered, speaking more to herself than anything.

'Don't be stupid!' Carlyle exploded. 'I was with him all morning. I was here when he found them, for God's sake!'

'You can't be sure though, can you? The time of death won't have been established yet. Maybe—'

'Maybe what?' His patience exhausted, Carlyle sprang to his feet. He could feel his eyes tearing up again, his hands balling into fists. He wanted to smack the moronic, do-it-by-the-numbers, box-ticking drone so that she bounced all the way back down the stairs to the ground floor and out into the street. 'You know what, Ward? I've come across some really fucking stupid coppers in my time, but you—'

'John! That's enough!' Out of the gloom of the stairwell,

Commander Carole Simpson appeared at Ward's shoulder. Behind her was Alison Roche. 'Sit back down,' she instructed him.

Meekly, the inspector did as he was told.

The Commander placed a guiding hand on Ward's elbow. 'Why don't you go and take a look inside, Inspector?' Her polite tone underlined that it was an order, rather than a question. 'Let me deal with . . . this.'

With a curt nod, Ward skipped past Carlyle and disappeared into the flat.

'I would like a full report on my desk by close of play today,' Simpson shouted after her. Lowering her voice, she turned to Carlyle. 'That should keep her busy for a while.'

'I'd like to—'

'Enough. You've had a terrible shock. You just need to calm down for a while.'

'You look terrible,' the sergeant chimed in. 'Are you okay?'

'Better than Daniel Hunter,' Carlyle said. Belatedly he remembered what his sergeant had been through herself. The last time he had seen her, she had just been in hospital. 'How are you?'

'I'm fine,' Roche reassured him, 'and so's the baby. When I went back for a check-up, the doctor said I was fit to come in to work.'

'Good.' Fresh-faced, without any make-up, he realized that she looked lovelier than ever. The thought almost prompted another set of tears.

Get a grip, for fuck's sake!

'You need to explain what exactly you were up to this morning,' Simpson said, gently muscling in on their little catch-up. 'I've had a Colonel Naylor on the phone – Hunter's CO. He's after an update.'

Carlyle rolled his head, trying to release the trauma from his brain. Then, quickly and quietly, he explained everything that had happened since he had first come into contact with Hunter in Dr Fry's office at the school.

When he had finished, Simpson gave him a thoughtful nod. 'Same old John Carlyle, eh? Tilting at windmills as usual.'

'I was just trying to help a fellow officer,' Carlyle protested.

'Well, you did what you could.' Simpson stepped aside to allow a young officer to make his way down the stairs. 'I know I set all this in motion by sending Roche to that school, but this was always Ward's case. I think you should leave it to her now.'

'She's not up to it,' Carlyle argued.

'Yes, she is,' Simpson countered. 'Sarah is a very competent officer. And the fact that she is very different to you is a positive – a *big* positive – in the eyes of the brass. She will go far.'

For the record, Carlyle grunted his disagreement.

'Go home and get some rest. You can give your statement later.'

Wearily, Carlyle got to his feet.

'Let me buy you a coffee first,' Roche offered. 'And maybe a Danish.'

'Nah.' Carlyle shook his head. 'I couldn't face anything at the moment. I think I need to lie down for a bit.'

'Good idea,' Simpson said kindly.

'Thanks, boss.' Starting down the stairs, he remembered her residential course. 'By the way, did you learn the secret of eternal happiness?'

The smile withered on the Commander's face. 'Yes,' she replied. 'If you want to be happy, don't be a cop.'

TWENTY-FIVE

Escaping the prying eyes of his colleagues, the first thing he did was to drop Hunter's gun down a storm drain in an alley off Compton Street, before heading back to the Silicon Roundabout Lettings Agency. The office was empty apart from a young guy in a crumpled suit who was changing some of the advertisements in the window.

'Where's Caroline?' the inspector asked, without preamble.

'Fuck me,' the kid mumbled, 'she's popular today.'

'I just need a quick word with her.'

The youth removed a set of particulars from the display and tossed them on the floor. 'Like I told the other guy, she'll be in Tommy's Wine Bar. She's turning into a right dipso these days. Drinking at lunchtime.' He shook his head in disbelief. 'It's so old school. You just can't do that these days.'

'Where is it?' Carlyle demanded, not interested in the social commentary.

'It's just down the road.' Pointing out of the window, the boy gave him directions. 'If you see her, remind her that she's got a two-thirty and she needs to come and collect the keys first.'

'Will do.'

Arriving at the wine bar, he found Caroline Batting sitting alone at a table, playing a game on her mobile phone. In front of her was a large glass of white wine. The bottle next to it was already three-quarters empty. She didn't look up as he pulled up a chair and sat down.

'Your partner's been here already.' she said. She tipped the phone towards the bottle. 'Wanna drink?'

Carlyle remembered an article he'd read recently on excessive drinking by female professionals. Batting could have been a case study. You're not going to get much work done this afternoon, he thought. 'No, thanks.'

'Shit!' Batting placed the mobile on the table. 'I can never get past the Gates of Sodor. At this rate, I'm never gonna get to level forty-seven.'

Not having the remotest clue what she was talking about, Carlyle watched her take a gulp of her wine.

'Joseph Isaacs paid for the rental of Falstaff Court in cash, up front,' she said, pre-empting his question. 'I checked with the office for the other guy who asked me. That's what you wanted to know, wasn't it?'

'Yeah.'

Batting held the wine glass close to her mouth. 'Your mate seemed very . . . agitated. Like he was totally stressed about something.'

'It's been a tough morning.' Contemplating his next move, Carlyle dived into the depths of understatement.

'Tell me about it. I had Mrs Salamander on the phone for more than half an hour, shouting and swearing, threating to sue the agency and all sorts.'

'Mrs Salamander?'

'The woman you walked in on, in the bath.' Batting grinned.

'Ah, yes.'

'She's a lawyer.'

'I think she mentioned it as we were leaving.'

'Probably the only client we've ever had who has actually read her tenancy agreement. Even the small print. She certainly knows her rights.'

'Sorry.'

'Don't worry. It'll blow over. I think it's more excitement than she's had in years. I know for a fact that she only moved into the

224

place after her husband dumped her and ran off with her sister. I don't imagine she's had a decent shag in at least a decade.'

Carlyle raised an eyebrow.

'You see all sorts in this job,' she added.

'I can imagine.' Surprised to find himself welcoming the warm embrace of idle gossip, the inspector tried to return to the matter in hand. 'My, er, partner – you don't know where he went off to, by any chance?'

Putting her glass back on the table, Batting gave him a quizzical look. 'You're asking me? Don't you two talk to each other?'

'I think his mobile died,' the inspector lied. He had tried Hunter several times on his way over, but the captain was not answering his phone.

'He's quite a good-looking bloke.' Batting blushed slightly. 'Is he married?'

'Sorry?'

'Just asking,' she said defensively. 'There's no point in being shy these days. You have to put yourself out there.'

'I suppose so.'

'Let him know he could give me a call, if he wanted to.'

'He's married,' Carlyle said flatly. 'Two kids.'

'Oh, well, he could still give me a call.' Grabbing the wine bottle, Batting topped up her glass.

'I'll let him know.' Carlyle pushed back his chair and got to his feet. 'Sorry for all the hassle this morning.'

She raised her glass in mock toast. 'Joseph Isaacs paid in cash, but we insisted on a credit card for the security deposit and also for ID purposes.'

'Oh?'

'I remember he made quite a fuss about it before finally handing it over. It was a corporate card for a company called MCS. Billing address in Docklands. Number One, Thatcher Towers.'

'You gave Hunter this?'

She nodded.

'Okay.' Carlyle started towards the door. 'Oh, and your

colleague in the office asked me to remind you of your two-thirty. You still need to pick up the keys.'

Batting made a face that suggested it wouldn't happen. 'Don't forget to tell your partner he can call me,' she shouted after him, reaching for her phone. 'Any time.'

'So this is your office?' Bob Biswas eyed his host suspiciously as he weighed a large glass of fifteen-year-old single malt in his hand. 'Very nice.'

Gerry Durkan gave a modest shrug. 'It's relatively cheap by London standards, and it's very convenient for the airport.'

'You must be doing well.'

'Well enough,' Gerry said, taking a sip of his own Scotch.

Biswas gestured towards the painting hanging on the wall, above the drinks cabinet. 'Is that an original?'

'The Monet? Yes. It was part of a hoard of art stolen by the Nazis that was found in some old guy's apartment a few years ago. It took almost a year to restore it, apparently.'

'Must be worth a fortune.'

'I'm sure. But we don't own it.'

'No?' An amused grin played across Biswas' lips. 'You didn't steal it too, did you?'

'No, it's rented. Just for show. You know, keeping up appearances and all that. Always a talking point for the clients.'

'I should imagine so.'

'Anyway, what can I do for you, Bob? I don't think you came here to talk about art.' The arrival of his erstwhile business partner had been unannounced but it was hardly unexpected. Sitting behind his desk, Durkan stole a glance at the middle drawer on the left. He was confident he could handle their meeting, but if the worst came to the worst, he would let the Walther PPK do the talking. If the weapon was good enough for bloody James Bond, it was good enough for Gerry Durkan.

On Her Majesty's Secret Service!

Well, not exactly.

He couldn't quite manage to suppress his smirk.

'Something funny, Gerry?' Biswas sat up in his chair and crossed his legs. With his carefully manicured beard and three-piece checked suit, he was clearly striving for the Bollywood A-Lister look. Unfortunately, he was at least twenty years too old and ten kilos too heavy to have any hope of carrying it off.

Durkan adopted a more serious expression. 'It's good to see you, despite the circumstances. How can I help?'

'What do you know about the robbery?'

'Only what I've seen in the media. Haven't the police given you a briefing?'

'Ha!' Biswas jerked back his hand in a gesture of frustration which sent most of his Scotch spilling over the arm of the chair. 'The British police are supposed to be the best in the world, yet they make the Mumbai Crime Branch look like world-beaters.' With his free hand, he tugged at the whisky-infused cuff of his shirt, pulling it down over the chunky gold chain on his wrist. 'They have more resources than a small army and still they manage to stand back and let a robbery take place right outside one of London's major airports. And then – then! – they manage to lose the crooks who stole my diamonds, even though they crashed their bloody getaway car into a concrete pillar.'

Durkan gave a sympathetic moue. 'That's what happens in this country.'

'It's shit.'

'It's democracy.'

'Democracy? Don't talk to me about democracy, you bloody terrorist! India is the biggest democracy in the world. Even so, if this had happened at home, everyone involved in this crime would have been shot and unceremoniously left bleeding to death in the gutter.'

'That's one way of dealing with it,' Gerry agreed.

'It's the only way,' Biswas huffed.

'I'm sure that the police will catch them.'

227

'They didn't catch you, did they?'

Gerry bridled at the reference to his past life. 'They did in the end.'

'In the end,' Biswas thundered, 'in the bloody end! How long were you on the run?'

Gerry made a face. He hadn't thought of those days in a while. 'Just shy of a couple of years, something like that.'

'And you were just about the most wanted terrorist in the UK at the time.' Biswas turned to his bodyguard, standing by the door. 'This guy, he was a real hard bastard back in the day.'

The bodyguard said nothing. The look on his face suggested that what might have happened 'back in the day' was of little relevance to the here and now.

'Even then, it was only by accident, was it not?'

'Aye, that's right.' Gerry was rather disconcerted by the amount of interest Biswas was taking in his previous life. 'I was in a car with a girl and she drove through a red light; we got stopped by a traffic cop and she tried to do a runner.' He winced at the memory of another one of Rose Murray's gaffes. 'After a high-speed chase through the streets of Derry, she ended up wrapping the motor round a lamppost. Once the Fire Brigade pulled us out of the wreckage and the RUC realized who we were, it was game over. Go straight to Jail, do not pass Go, do not collect your £200.'

Biswas looked at him blankly.

He's obviously not a Monopoly man, Gerry thought. 'The police are a lot brighter these days though. They've got much more technology on their side, for a start. You can hardly fart these days without some nerdy bastard in GCHQ monitoring its chemical composition.'

'I am taking matters into my own hands,' Biswas stated flatly, clearly not convinced by Durkan's paen to modern policing. 'I can't leave something as important as this in the hands of dis-interested third parties, poorly trained civil servants bobbing around on a sea of lassitude.'

'That makes sense.' Durkan effortlessly changed his tune now it was clear that the conversation was moving on. 'In your position, I would do exactly the same. I really would, no doubt about it.' Taking another mouthful of Scotch, he sat back, waiting for Biswas to reveal his hand.

TWENTY-SIX

Arriving at Thatcher Towers, Carlyle submitted himself to an airport-style security regimen, feeling smug that he had earlier ditched the gun that Hunter had given him. Being allowed to proceed, albeit under the watchful eye of a succession of security cameras, he headed towards a long reception desk populated by a row of smiling young women. The inspector counted six of them in total, all dressed in the same uniforms: crisp white blouse under a grey jacket with green piping around the lapels. It's a bit like being in *The Truman Show*, he reflected, except with more CCTV.

Three of the receptionists were busy processing other arrivals. Two of the remaining trio eyed him warily, as if daring him to step in front of their computer terminals to argue his case for being allowed access to the inner sanctum of their temple. The third girl gave him a big smile which, despite everything that had happened on this terminally shitty day, managed to momentarily lift his spirits. Carlyle smiled back, adjusting his feet to divert himself towards her space on the desk.

'Good afternoon, sir! How may I help you?'

'I'm here to see MCS, please.' A list of tenants on the wall behind the desk told him that Macroom Castlebar Salle occupied floors 26–31; presumably, the man he wanted would be at the top. 'Thirty-first floor.'

'Very good.'

'My name is Carlyle.' A badge on the receptionist's jacket told him that her name was Ella. Her eyes were a bright azure blue and her skin radiated youthful good health.

'How do I spell that, please?'

To his left, a pair of chisel-jawed Americans were anticipating the killing that they were going to make on something called Bruni Bonds.

'Once we go into the market, those cheese-eating surrender monkeys won't know what hit them.'

'Roger that.'

Tuning out of their exchange, Carlyle passed his business card to the receptionist. Ella made no comment as she placed the card beside her keyboard and typed in his details.

'Who are you here to see?'

'Mr Durkan,' Carlyle said firmly, 'the Chief Executive.' Having done some homework on the way over, he was amazed to discover that Gerry Durkan – *the* Gerry Durkan – was still alive and well and, bizarrely, running a hedge fund in Docklands. This was one meeting he was really looking forward to.

'Yes, of course.' Ella made a few more keystrokes before pointing over her shoulder. 'Look into the camera, please?'

What camera? After a moment, he saw it, no bigger than the kind of thing you see on a cyclist's helmet, attached to a pole at the back of her desk.

Ella inspected his image on her computer screen. 'I'm sorry, we'll have to try again. I can't make out your face.'

'Most people would consider that a plus,' the inspector quipped.

Ella smiled weakly. 'Just look straight into the camera, please.'

'Of course.'

'That looks fine.' She hit the save button and reached under her desk. 'Here you go.'

Carlyle took the plastic ID card and inspected the image that had been printed on it, next to his name. It could have been him; equally it could have been a lot of other people.

'You'll need that to get to the lifts.' Ella lifted a telephone to her ear. 'Let me just tell them that you're here.'

'Thank you.' While she called upstairs, the inspector lounged against the desk, checking out the lobby. Interspersed between the low sofas for waiting visitors had been placed a series of large, translucent plastic blocks, maybe ten feet long, three feet high and a foot thick, into which different corporate buzzwords had been carved in large letters.

Integrity.

Transparency.

Trust.

In the far corner, behind *Honesty*, the inspector thought he could make out the back of a familiar figure.

'You don't have an appointment?'

Carlyle turned his attention back to the desk.

'No.' He put an immense effort into trying to out-smile her, failing miserably. 'That's right.'

'I'm afraid—'

Leaning forward, Carlyle let her watch his smile evaporate. 'Look, Ella,' he said quietly, 'I'm not here to cause you, or anyone else, any trouble.'

'You have to have an appointment,' she insisted.

Aware that there was an issue, the other receptionists were beginning to tune into their conversation. 'This is police business.' Carlyle dropped his voice even lower, not wanting to have to bully her any more than was absolutely necessary. 'Tell Mr Durkan's office that I need to come up and see him. I don't want to cause a fuss, but if they keep me waiting, I will speak to Security and get them to take me up.'

She thought about it for a moment. 'Please take a seat. I will give you a call in a few minutes.'

'Thank you.' Turning away from the desk, the inspector walked purposefully past *Trust* and *Honesty* and headed over to Hunter.

The captain was rocking backwards and forwards on the edge of his seat, staring into the middle distance with a murderous look on his face.

'I thought I might find you here.' Carlyle took a seat next to him. Out of the corner of his eye he clocked a couple of security guards eyeing them suspiciously.

'You took your bloody time.'

'They had problems getting my best side for the ID card.' Gesturing towards the X-ray machines by the door, Carlyle whispered, 'What did you do with your gun?'

'It's somewhere safe,' Hunter responded.

'Fair enough.' Carlyle relaxed a little; at least they wouldn't be playing *Gunfight at the OK Corral* on the thirty-first floor. 'Been waiting long?'

'Half an hour,' Hunter grunted. 'I asked to see the Head of Security, but no one's turned up.'

'Hurry up and wait,' Carlyle reflected. 'The Job, in a nutshell.

Hunter glared at one of the hovering security guards. The guard, a pimply kid in a standard-issue black suit, tried to return the look, with interest.

I would leave off if I were you, son, Carlyle thought. My friend here might not be armed, but he sure as shit is dangerous. From the expression on Hunter's face, it looked as if the captain was getting ready to rip the little scrote limb from limb. Carlyle was relieved when the boy gave up on his futile game and went off to continue his rounds.

'Arsehole,' Hunter said.

'Take it easy,' Carlyle advised. 'They'll see us. Just sit tight.'

'Ten more minutes.'

'Fair enough.' Picking up a copy of *The Times* from a selection of newspapers on the table in front of them, Carlyle turned to the sports pages and settled in for what he felt sure would be a short wait.

* * *

Thirty-one floors up, Bob Biswas uncurled a sly smile. Lifting his glass, he gestured towards the tall, well-built man standing by the door. 'Manny here will be leading my investigation.'

Trying to look menacing, Emmanuel Bole said nothing.

'He is under instruction to get it wrapped up in the shortest possible time, with the minimum amount of fuss . . . and by any means necessary.'

'Fair enough.' Durkan glanced at the thug in the leather jacket, unconcerned. He'd seen scarier lads on the Falls Road, boys who were barely in their teens and weighed less than eleven stone, dripping wet. Let this oaf investigate what he liked, he wouldn't be able to scare a confession out of Gerry bloody Durkan. And without a confession, there was no way Biswas would be able to prove a thing. Nor, more to the point, would he be able to find the stones.

'Manny was Indian Special Forces,' Biswas went on. 'The Ghatak Commandos. Saw a lot of action along the Pakistani border. His party piece was beheading terrorists.'

Good for him, Durkan thought. 'Impressive.'

'He will get to the bottom of this – and fast.'

'I'm sure.'

'This time next week, I want this to be nothing more than an unpleasant – and distant – memory.'

'That seems very reasonable.' This time next week, Durkan sincerely hoped that Biswas Trading Services would be out of business. Without the money from the sale of the diamonds, Biswas could not make its next payment to their joint venture business, the Hydra SPV. Hydra would fold and Durkan would consequently be freed of his own outstanding obligations. As a bonus, he would pocket the 15 pence on the pound that his chosen fence, a seriously dodgy Hatton Garden gems dealer called Ron Berblat, was prepared to offer at such short notice. That wouldn't be enough to offset the outflows caused by MCS investors reclaiming their cash, but it was better than a poke in the eye with a sharp stick.

As for raising some serious money, he had spoken to Bianca at the beginning of the day. His top saleswoman was still in Jakarta and spoke confidently of snaring new investors. Durkan smiled to himself; the girl was a force of nature. He had absolutely no doubt that she would come up trumps.

Things were looking up, all round.

Uncle Bob, meanwhile, strapped for cash, would soon be heading back to his roots; running a back-street bookies in Chembur, organizing poker games in 5-star hotels and trying to fix Indian Premier League matches.

Biswas ran a hand across his beard. 'I'm glad you find it all so entertaining.'

'Me?' Durkan quickly composed himself. 'No, not at all.' He gave a small cough. 'I am completely aware of the gravity of the situation.'

'Good. Because we need your help.'

'Of course.'

Biswas adopted the air of a man who had given the matter a great deal of thought, without having managed to come up with a plan. 'The first thing we need to look at is how it was known that Gopal was coming into town with the diamonds.'

'You clearly had a leak.' Gerry brought his hands together, carefully aligning his fingers, as if in prayer. 'By the way, my sincere condolences to you and your family.'

'Thank you.' Biswas' expression suggested a man swamped by irritation and frustration, rather than grief.

'It was a terrible thing to happen to such a bright young man.'

'He was a stupid boy,' was Biswas' unsentimental verdict. 'When the shooting started, he didn't even have enough sense to run away.'

'That happens,' Durkan observed. 'People freeze.'

'It's more than that. Society is making us soft. Children today are so lacking in street smarts, it's incredible.'

'Yes.'

'My sister is not happy about it. Not at all.'

'I can imagine,' Durkan said gently. 'It must be very hard for her.' He could sit here and shoot the breeze all day – just so long as Manny the Sphinx didn't spring to life and try to beat the truth out of him.

'Riyal is most definitely *not* happy,' Biswas repeated. 'Gopal was her only son and even that was a struggle – IVF.'

Durkan felt grateful that he'd never ended up with any kids. Life was gut-wrenching enough without jumping on the biggest rollercoaster ride of them all.

'Three rounds of treatment. It seemed to take for ever – her husband's fault, of course. Morgan had one of the lowest sperm counts ever recorded, according to the specialist.'

'How very unfortunate.' Durkan's opinion of Biswas took another lurch downwards. What kind of man knew about his brother-in-law's jizz?

'I told Riyal she should go to a donor, but she wouldn't have it. She always was a very headstrong girl.'

'Yes.' It's like I've wandered into a Bollywood movie, Durkan thought. Maybe he's gonna break into a song and dance routine.

'Never listened to advice; always thought that she knew best.'

'It sounds like a very difficult situation, right enough.' Durkan made a point of demonstrating his complete focus on every word, even though Biswas seemed to essentially be talking to himself.

'She was blind to the reality. The way she talked about Gopal, you would have thought he was the offspring of Albert Einstein, rather than some Belgian café owner who shot blanks. The lad was competent enough, within clearly defined limits, but soft in both mind and body. I often told Riyal that she should have toughened him up a bit. But did she listen? No. She doted on that child from the very beginning. He left school with hardly any qualifications and, of course, I had to give him a job. Then, whenever something went wrong, it was always my fault.' Biswas stared into what was left of his drink, as if searching for an answer to the tribulations of family life. 'The boy had a place in my organization for life, which was just as well for him. It's not as if other

236

people were queuing up to offer him any kind of position. His own father wouldn't take him on. Not even for a summer job.'

'Oh?'

'Gopal survived less than a week working in Morgan's café. There was a problem with the poison put down for the vermin – he didn't use enough and it took a while for them to die. The patrons were confronted by dazed rats staggering between the tables in their death throes. The place was almost closed down by the Health Inspectors. Morgan nearly throttled him.'

'You did a good thing taking him on.'

'Yes. Yes, I did. Yet when I sent him out on errands, Riyal always complained that I was treating him like a servant. What else was I going to do with him? It was all he was good for.'

If the kid couldn't kill a rat, Durkan wondered, why entrust him with a fortune in diamonds? As he was wrestling with that apparent contradiction, a brilliant thought arrowed into his brain. 'Maybe Gopal did it,' he ventured.

'Maybe Gopal did what?' Biswas slowly pulled himself out of his morass of family issues.

'Maybe,' Durkan offered, trying not to sound *too* keen on the idea, 'your nephew ripped you off.'

'And got himself shot in the process?' Biswas finished the last of his drink and waved away Durkan's offer of a refill.

'You know what it's like, Bob, money trumps family nine times out of ten.' Durkan eased himself down the road of Gopal's imagined treachery, comfortable in the knowledge that he could spout this shit by the yard. 'Maybe the lad saw this as his chance to make a score and he went for it. Yes, he ended up shot – but that could have been an accident, or a double-cross by one of his team.'

Biswas let the idea percolate through his brain for a few moments. Then: 'Gopal didn't have the balls to try and do something like this,' he said finally. 'Or the brains, for that matter. Apart from anything else, he only had a couple of hours' notice that he was making the run.'

'But he'd done it before.' Durkan lifted his arms, weighing the evidence in each hand, all of it circumstantial.

'Gopal had never delivered anything on this scale. Nothing remotely like it.' Biswas' eyes narrowed. 'Only a small group of people knew what was in that case. A group of two, in fact: you and me.'

Studiously ignoring Manny, Durkan kept his eyes firmly locked on his guest. 'Well, if it wasn't Gopal, it looks like you must have a leak somewhere else in your organization then, doesn't it? Someone else must have found out about the run.'

Biswas let out a long sigh. 'I don't think so.'

'It's a possibility.'

'No.'

'So,' Durkan affected a nonchalant air, 'who *do* you think was behind it?'

'Stop playing games, Gerry. I know it was you.' Biswas signalled to Manny. Taking his cue, the man mountain lumbered towards Durkan.

Oh shit, here we go. An image of his head being detached from his shoulders flashed through Durkan's mind. After everything he had been through over the decades, being decapitated in his own office at the behest of an irate business partner felt less than dignified. He held up a hand. 'Look, there's no point in trying to beat it out of me because, I don't know. You've got completely the wrong end of the stick here.'

Jumping to his feet, Biswas sent the empty tumbler flying past Durkan's head. 'You fucking Irish bastard!' he snarled. 'I think I might kill you myself.'

'Hey, hey, now,' Durkan giggled nervously, 'there's no need to bring ethnic references into it. That kind of prejudice isn't allowed these days. You might hurt my feelings.'

'I'm going to hurt a lot more than your bloody feelings!'

Confused by his boss's sudden desire to join in the fun, Manny hesitated in front of Durkan's desk. Savouring the massive jolt of adrenalin surging through his system, the Irishman reached for the middle drawer, chuckling in anticipation of his visitors' reaction when he turned the tables. His fingers were just closing around the grip of the gun when the door opened and Balthazar Quant's head appeared.

'Are you okay, boss?'

Leaving the weapon where it was, Durkan shoved the drawer nine-tenths of the way closed and slumped back in his chair. 'I thought I said that there were to be no interruptions,' he complained, irritated at being deprived of his chance to shine.

'Sorry, it's just there are a couple of policemen downstairs. They want to speak to you as a matter of urgency. They've already been waiting a while.'

'Have they indeed?'

'Yes. Security aren't happy but they don't think they can throw them out without causing an incident.'

'An *incident*?' Durkan arched his eyebrows. 'Well, we wouldn't want that, would we? Do you know why they are here?'

'No,' Quant admitted, before adding, somewhat redundantly, 'it's a police matter.'

'Well, I think you'd better go and get them. Bring them straight in. We can't keep the forces of law and order waiting, now can we?'

'Sure thing.' Quant slipped away, closing the door behind him.

'This isn't going to save you,' Biswas hissed.

Durkan's expression hardened. 'Who says I need saving?' He glanced at Manny. Blissfully unaware of his near-death experience, the henchman had reverted to his statue impersonation, awaiting new orders.

'Where are my diamonds, you fucker?'

Durkan consulted the Rolex on his wrist. 'It takes about twenty-two seconds for the lifts to travel the thirty-one floors, allowing for a couple of stops on the way. The cops should be here in literally one or two minutes. Why don't you stay? I can make the introductions. Maybe they can give you some inside gossip into how the *official* investigation into the diamond robbery is going.'

239

'Fucker!' Biswas' face looked like it was melting with anger.

'I'm sure that they won't take too long and then we can continue our . . . conversation.'

'I don't think so.' Biswas stalked to the door, taking Manny with him. 'But don't worry, we will be back.'

'Any time.' Feeling as giddy as a Bogside twelve-year-old lobbing rocks at the British Army, Gerry waved at his retreating guests. 'My door is always open.'

TWENTY-SEVEN

Five minutes was more than enough time to skip through the various sections of the newspaper. Nothing in its pages lingered in the memory. The whole thing seemed to be no more than a succession of adverts, interspersed by 'thought pieces', written by friends of the government who sought to present the bottomless incompetence and self-serving cant that spewed out of the Westminster village as leadership worthy of Churchill or Attlee. 'Comment' was the new word for propaganda, far more subtle than anything ever seen in *Pravda* but just as relentless. The inspector tossed the paper back on to the table in front of him, glad that it wasn't his £1.50 that had paid for it. The thoughts of Camilla or Tim or Gaby were of no interest to anyone with half a brain. Helen called it 'living in a post-factual democracy'; Carlyle preferred to think of it as 'lying tossers talking shit'.

Profoundly irritated at the crap that was served up as news, the inspector checked his watch. They had almost reached Hunter's unilateral deadline. Carlyle knew that he had to take control of the situation or be dragged along in the captain's violent wake.

God alone knew what might happen once they reached the thirty-first floor. Aware that he would need to be on top of his game, the inspector made a conscious effort to try and clear his mind of all random thoughts and concerns. It was time to focus on the matter in hand.

What was he doing here?
What was the plan of action?

*And why wasn't he trying to get some help for the deeply trau-
matized man sitting beside him?*

Unable to answer any of these questions, he retreated into a
moment of mindless people-watching. A steady stream of corporate cannon fodder came through the lobby, heading in all
different directions. Only a few of them actually went through
the turnstiles that guarded access to the lifts and the building
proper; the rest, presumably, were heading to offices nearby,
almost all of them occupied by different financial service companies. Everybody moved quickly, heads down, as if they were
already ten minutes late for their next meeting. It was like watching one of those sequences in a movie where the film had been
speeded up. All that was missing was the Philip Glass score.

He was trying to pull up some more information on MCS on
his Blackberry, when Hunter suddenly jumped to his feet. 'Fuck
this,' he growled. 'Time's up.'

'Whoa, tiger!' Carlyle pulled him back down before the security guards could intercept him. 'Give it two more minutes.'

'What difference will that make?'

'Two more minutes,' the inspector repeated, playing for time.

Hunter gave a dissenting snort but stayed in his seat. Carlyle
offered him the BlackBerry. 'Macroom Castlebar Salle – MCS – do
you know whose company it is? I Googled it on the way over here.'

Staring angrily into the middle distance, Hunter ignored the
machine. 'Nope.'

'Gerry Durkan,' said Carlyle.

'And who is Gerry Durkan?'

'He was an IRA terrorist, back in the 1980s. One of the Brighton
bombers who tried to take out Thatcher at the Conservative Party
Conference – in eighty-four, I think it was.'

'I would have been in junior school,' Hunter said in a dead
voice. 'Are you sure it's the same guy?'

'How many Gerry Durkans can there be?' Carlyle responded.
'Anyway, according to Wikipedia, he founded MCS, his investment business after getting out of jail.'

Hunter ran his tongue along his lower lip. 'At least he'll be used to someone trying to beat a confession out of him.'

'I'm sure that won't be necessary,' Carlyle said stiffly. 'He's a respectable businessman these days.'

' "Respectable businessman",' Hunter said bitterly. 'That's a term you don't hear much these days.'

'Respectable or not, it's been quite the personal journey for old Gerry. It's a long way from the IRA to MCS, whichever way you look at it.'

'He should still be behind bars,' Hunter offered.

'Maybe.' Not being a *forgive and forget* kind of guy himself, it was a point of view Carlyle had a lot of sympathy for. On the other hand, letting a few dirty little scrotes out of prison early seemed a not unreasonable price to pay so that the rest of the world could forget that Northern Ireland even existed.

'How long was he inside?'

'Fifteen years, something like that.'

'Not a lot, is it?'

'I suppose that it depends on whether you're the one that's locked up,' Carlyle mused.

Hunter got back to his feet. 'We should be grateful that they managed to catch him, at least.'

'He was on the run for quite a while. There was a fiasco where he managed to walk out of a Kilburn pub that was surrounded by coppers.' Carlyle omitted to mention that he was one of the coppers in question.

'C'mon.' Hunter gestured for Carlyle to get up. 'We've been more than polite.'

Doing as instructed, Carlyle eyed a stressed-looking man who appeared from behind the *Integrity* logo and walked towards him, hand outstretched. 'Captain Hunter?'

'That's me.' Hunter stepped in front of the inspector, his stance more suggestive of a right hook than a handshake.

'Ah, yes.' The man let his hand fall to his side.

'I'm just his sidekick,' Carlyle quipped.

The man focused his gaze somewhere between the two of them. 'Balthazar Quant, MCS. Our sincerest apologies for keeping you waiting but Mr Durkan has been stuck in a very important meeting.'

Hunter started to say something, but Carlyle jumped in before him. 'I can assure you, Mr . . .'

'Quant,' the man repeated almost apologetically. His suit looked expensive, but his shirt was as rumpled as his hair and he wasn't wearing a tie. There were dark rings under his eyes and his tan needed a top-up.

You look like you're having a hard day yourself, Carlyle thought. 'I can assure you, Mr Quant, that we are here on a very serious matter. And we are under some *very* serious time pressure.'

'Yes, yes, of course. My apologies again. Anyway, Mr Durkan can see you now. Let's go up.' Quant turned and led them towards the turnstiles. Letting Hunter follow on, Carlyle brought up the rear.

Finally reaching the thirty-first floor, Hunter barrelled out of the lift, almost knocking over a dapper Asian guy who was waiting to go down. Running a hand across his beard, the Indian leaped out of the captain's way like a startled cat. Glaring at Hunter, he said something under his breath. Standing a yard or so further back from the lift doors, a much larger Indian bloke allowed himself a small smile. The amused look on his face did not detract from his extremely muscular presence, which seemed rather out of place, given the surroundings.

Together they made an interesting pair. The inspector's immediate thought was that the big guy was a bodyguard. But who would bring muscle to a meeting in a place like this? Maybe Gerry Durkan's 'personal journey' hadn't taken him as far as it had first appeared.

Ignoring both men, Hunter veered left, heading for the brass name-plate that indicated the offices of Macroom Castlebar Salle.

Following in his wake, Carlyle nimbly stepped aside, in order to let the duo from the sub-continent enter the lift. He waited until the doors had closed and they were hurtling groundward before turning to Quant, who had started fumbling in his jacket pocket. 'Were they Mr Durkan's important meeting?'

'Huh?' Quant retrieved a keycard and placed it on an electronic pad by the doors next to the name-plate. The lock released and he pulled one of the doors open, gesturing for them to head inside.

'Those two guys.' Carlyle jerked a thumb back towards the lifts. 'Are they clients?'

'Er, yes.' Following them through the door, Quant nodded at the receptionist as they swept along the lobby. 'At least, Mr Biswas is. He's a longstanding business partner, a good friend of the firm.'

Pushing out his bottom lip, the inspector tried to look impressed. 'You do business in India?'

'Our clientele tends to be *international*.' Quant stressed the word as if he felt that the concept would be difficult for a humble policeman to understand. 'We operate very much in the wider global economy. Geography is just one of many different considerations when it comes to decision-making and priorities.'

Thank you for the business lesson, Carlyle thought sourly as his expectations of what was to come took a lurch downwards. Durkan himself would need to have a better line in straight talking or Hunter would knock him right into the middle of next week.

'As it happens, Mr Biswas is based in Antwerp, but it could just as easily be Mumbai, or New York, or Beijing.'

Antwerp. What the hell do people do there? Carlyle wondered. 'What does he do?'

Quant's mouth visibly twitched, as if his brain had started signalling that he had already said rather too much 'He's a client.' He hurried to catch up with Hunter, who was waiting impatiently at the next door. Once again, Quant slapped his card on a pad, pulled the door open and invited them inside. 'Go all the way down. Mr Durkan's office is at the far end.'

Sandwiched between Hunter and Quant, Carlyle marched down the central aisle of an open-plan space that was maybe the size of two football pitches. On either side of them, unbroken rows of desks ran next to the floor-to-ceiling windows, which offered a panoramic view of East London, both north and south of the river. A quick calculation suggested workstations for more than three hundred people. The atmosphere on the two sides, however, was completely different. To his right, almost every seat was taken; young men and women sat looking up at as many as six different monitors, let their glaze flit from one to another while talking into their headsets and tapping away at their keyboards at the same time. The low rumble of their conversations suggested a relentless determination to make money. No one looked up from their screens as the visitors walked past.

By contrast, at least half of the desks off to his left were deserted, and most of the people tentatively poking at their keyboards did look up to watch the process towards the boss's office. The inspector caught a glimpse of at least two screens that were given over to games of online poker.

Quant appeared at his shoulder as they endeavoured to keep up with the captain. He was sweating heavily and the inspector caught a whiff of his rather strong body odour. As Carlyle turned his head, trying to locate some fresher air, Quant started waving his arms about like an airline hostess giving the safety demonstration before take-off. 'On the left is research; on the right are our trading desks.'

'Uh-huh.'

'Overhead and profit centre.' With a skip and a jump Quant left Carlyle behind, swerving past Hunter as they bore down on another set of doors. 'This is the executive suite,' he puffed, pushing open the doors and leading them past yet another receptionist and, finally, into Durkan's office itself.

'Gentlemen, welcome.' The small balding man who approached

246

them with a smile as fake as Hitler's Diaries looked nothing like the little hoodlum that Carlyle remembered. Then again, they had both changed a lot over the last thirty-odd years. 'I am Gerry Durkan. My most sincere apologies for keeping you waiting. Did Balthazar explain?'

'Yes, thank you.' Carlyle was relieved that Hunter seemed happy to leave the small talk to him. While introducing them both, the inspector quickly scanned the room, taking in the tumbler lying on the carpet by the window as well as the bottle of Scotch, minus its cap, on the sideboard.

It's a bit early to be starting on the hard stuff, the inspector reflected.

Durkan gestured towards a pair of chairs that stood in front of his desk. 'Please, gentlemen, take a seat. Would you like a drink?'

'We're good.' While Carlyle sat down, Hunter stayed on his feet, taking in the view.

'Not bad, is it?' said Durkan, dismissing Quant with a wave of his hand. 'It's not the clearest of days, but you can still see the Olympic Stadium over there.'

Never much interested in the Olympics, Carlyle was keen to get down to business. 'Joseph Isaacs.'

'Joseph Issacs,' Durkan repeated. 'What about him?' Still smiling, he slipped behind his desk and sat down, studiously ignoring the way in which Hunter had begun prowling around the room like a caged animal.

'Does he work for you?' Hunter demanded as he inspected a range of framed antique maps hanging on the wall.

So much for letting me take the lead, Carlyle thought.

'Yes. He's a consultant.'

'What does he consult on?' The menace in Hunter's voice was growing. He turned away from the maps and picked up a magazine that had been sitting on the sideboard. Rolling it up in his hand, it looked like he wanted to beat Durkan around the head with it. Thank God he hasn't got his gun, Carlyle thought.

'Security matters.' Durkan glanced at the inspector, knowing well enough that a two-word explanation would not be deemed sufficient.

'Can you be a bit more specific?' Carlyle asked.

'Well, that would include anything from making sure that our IT systems don't get hacked, through to having protection in place for executives travelling to difficult cities abroad.'

'Would it include killing people?' Hunter snarled.

'What?' Durkan's surprise seemed genuine enough.

Carlyle jumped to his feet, as much to be able to block a lunge by Hunter as to intimidate Durkan. 'Where is Mr Isaacs right now?'

'I would have to check.' Shifting uncomfortably in his seat, Durkan began to wonder if he might not have been better off taking his chances with Biswas and Manny. 'What has happened?'

Carlyle kept it simple. 'Isaacs rented a flat near Old Street. Four people turned up dead in it this morning.'

Durkan took a moment to process the information he had been given . . . and the information he hadn't. 'Joe's dead?' he asked finally.

'No.' Carlyle shook his head. 'But we need to talk to him – like right now.'

'I understand that, gentlemen. But, if you don't mind me asking, what's all this got to do with me?'

'He used an MCS credit card to rent the flat,' Hunter advised. 'Which means you could very well be an accessory to murder.'

TWENTY-EIGHT

'Jesus!' Gerry Durkan leaned forward in his chair, rubbing his temples, playing for time as he tried to calculate the likely odds on the identity of the various victims. After a few moments, he reached for the sleek grey phone sitting on his desk. 'Let me try and find out where he is.'

'Good idea.' Carlyle waited patiently while his host dialled the number.

After letting it ring, Durkan made a face. 'Voicemail.'

'Keep it simple,' Carlyle instructed. 'Don't mention that we're here.'

Durkan nodded. 'Joe, this is me. I need to speak to you as a matter of some urgency. Call me when you get this.' Dropping the handset back on its cradle, he looked at the inspector.

'How long does it usually take him to respond?'

'It depends,' Durkan said airily. 'He's a freelancer, we don't take a hundred per cent of his time. If he's working for another client at the moment, he could be just about anywhere.'

'Do you know who else Isaacs works for?'

Carlyle glanced at Hunter, still gripping the magazine tightly. Focused on the financier, the captain showed no sign of acknowledging his presence.

'No, sorry. Not my business.'

'You'd better give me his number.'

'Of course.' Picking up an expensive-looking pen, Durkan scribbled the details on a sheet of notepaper. 'Here you go.'

Getting to his feet, he walked round the desk and handed it to the inspector.

Carlyle folded the piece of paper and placed it in his jacket pocket. 'Do you know where he lives?'

Durkan raised an eyebrow. 'I thought you said he rented a place in Old Street.'

'He didn't live there.'

'Well, whatever details we have, HR will have on file.'

Carlyle changed tack. 'Why did Isaacs rent the flat?'

Durkan spread his arms wide, innocence personified. 'You're asking me?'

'You didn't tell him to do it?'

I sure as hell didn't tell him to use the company credit card, Durkan thought. 'No.'

'He used your credit card.'

'That, I have to admit, sounds like a breach of our corporate card policy. We will look into it.'

'What do you think he was up to?'

'You tell me.' Resting his arse on the edge of the desk, Durkan folded his arms. He could handle this Q&A crap all night and all day. The cop would get nothing.

'To hell with this!' Hunter flew past Carlyle in a blur. Setting upon Durkan, he began smashing him around the skull with the rolled-up mag. 'What the fuck is going on here?'

'Ow! Gerroff!' Durkan tried to retreat behind the desk, covering his head as the blows came thick and fast.

The scene was fairly comic; the inspector had to restrain a chuckle. 'Dan!' He placed a hand on Hunter's arm but was shrugged off with ease. Stumbling backwards, he went sprawling across the carpet.

'Tell me what you know, you fucker, or I will chuck you out the bloody window.'

A nasty-looking gash opened up above Durkan's left eye. Falling to the floor, he adopted a foetal position. 'You can't,' he bleated, 'it's bullet-resistant glass.'

Hunter gave him another smack across the shoulderblades. 'Shall we test it out?'

Durkan whimpered as he pulled himself into a tighter ball.

You're not such a hard man these days, Carlyle thought, are you? Sitting on his backside, he was vaguely aware of voices outside. As Hunter prepared to land another fierce blow, the office door few open.

'What in God's name is going on here?' Inspector Sarah Ward stood in the doorway, her mouth agape, unable to believe the tableau in front of her.

I never thought I'd be happy to see you, Carlyle thought. Sheepishly, he tried to keep out of her line of vision as he struggled to his feet. Standing behind Ward were a couple of uniforms. Next to them, Balthazar Quant looked rather queasy as he stood at the head of a rapidly growing crowd of gawkers.

Even the boys and girls on the trading floor couldn't help but be distracted by the latest developments, Carlyle observed. Always one to dig himself deeper into a hole, particularly when there was a crowd present, the inspector couldn't resist a quip. 'Just like the old days, eh, Gerry?'

'Shut it, Carlyle,' Ward snapped.

Gingerly touching his wound, Durkan said nothing.

Taking control of the situation, Ward moved into the centre of the room. 'Captain Hunter, put your weapon down.'

After some internal deliberation, Hunter took a step away from his victim, keeping the magazine in his hand.

'Put it down!'

Reluctantly, Hunter tossed the magazine at Carlyle's feet. Looking down, the inspector saw that it had landed face up, so that he could see the title: *Professional Jeweller*. The cover was dominated by a picture of a model wearing a diamond necklace and not very much else. Durkan's blood was smeared across the woman's backside.

'Don't touch that,' Ward commanded. 'It's evidence.'

'Wouldn't dream of it,' Carlyle said politely.

Ward signalled to the uniforms who stepped forward and escorted a compliant Hunter out of the office. 'Wait out there.' She turned to Carlyle. The expression on her face was almost as hostile as Hunter's had been, moments before. She pointed at the open door. 'You too.'

I don't think so. The inspector stood his ground. 'How did you know we were here?'

'You're not the only one who can follow a lead, you know,' she replied tartly.

Pressing a paper napkin to his forehead, Gerry Durkan was rapidly regaining his composure. 'Bloody Met,' he muttered, his Irish accent now considerably more noticeable than it had been when Carlyle had first walked into his office. 'Always the same. You'll be hearing from my lawyers.'

'I am very sorry for what happened, sir,' Ward replied, trying her best to adopt something approaching a bedside manner, 'but that gentleman,' she gestured in the direction of Hunter, 'is not a policeman.'

Not interested in the details, Durkan stalked over to the whisky bottle, pouring a large measure into a fresh glass. 'You're all a bunch of fuckers, so ye are.' Gulping down the scotch in a single go, he refilled the glass and retreated behind his desk. 'I'm gonna sue the lot of you.'

'Good luck with that,' Carlyle replied. He was conscious that his patience with all of them had run out. Ward or no Ward, he was going to walk out of the building with some useful information. Fuck her. If she didn't like it, she could go crying to Simpson for a second time.

'Whaddya mean?' Durkan caught sight of Balthazar hovering in the doorway and dismissed him with a curt wave of the hand.

Ward made to speak but Carlyle cut her off. 'Who would ever award a murdering terrorist bastard like you any compo?'

'Ah, so you're gonna play the ancient history card, is that it?' Durkan took a more genteel sip of his drink. Carlyle could see, however, that his hands were still shaking.

'It's hardly ancient history.'

'It is to me.'

Carlyle shook his head. 'You won't remember me, but our paths have crossed before.'

'Have they indeed?' Durkan placed his glass on the table.

'Remember the MacDermott Arms in Kentish Town?'

A wry smile played across Durkan's lips. 'Vaguely.'

'I was on duty, the day you walked out of there.' Carlyle tutted. 'Right under our bloody noses.'

'A lifetime ago.' Durkan turned to Ward. 'I bet you weren't even born then, eh love?'

Ward bristled but said nothing.

Durkan turned back to Carlyle. 'Have you been up there recently?'

'Nah,' Carlyle said. 'Not for a long time. Not my patch.'

'The MacDermott Arms is gone. Some developer turned it into flats.'

'That's what happens,' Carlyle observed.

'I suppose so. Even Kentish Town is yuppie territory now, or whatever the equivalent of yuppies is these days. It's progress, of a sort.' Durkan pondered. 'So you were at the MacDermott Arms, eh? You'll have to forgive me if I don't recall individuals. There were so many coppers there that day.'

'It was quite an operation,' Carlyle admitted.

'I got away with it on that occasion, but my luck ran out soon enough.'

'It usually does.'

'Aye well. So you were one of Maggie's boot boys?'

'Kind of,' Carlyle shrugged. 'I signed up to be a policeman, not some paramilitary thug. First there was the miners' strike, then you lot.'

Ward rolled her eyes. The look on her face said, *Put a sock in it, Grandad.*

Catching her expression, Durkan began wagging his finger in mock disapproval. 'You should know your history, girl.'

Ward gave a dissenting moue; apparently unsure of how best to proceed, she seemed content to remain silent and for the conversation to meander.

For his part, Durkan seemed to be putting his beating behind him. The cut above his eye still gaped, but at least the bleeding had stopped. 'That's the thing about people today,' he added, warming to his theme. 'You mention the *War on Terror* and all they think about is Al Qaeda. We were there first.'

'True enough,' Carlyle agreed. 'I remember that my dad was always rather disappointed you didn't manage to blow Thatcher to Kingdom Come.' Recalling the package he had yet to deliver to his father, the kernel of an idea popped into his head. He quickly stored it away for later review. 'She really wound him up. He had a foam brick that he would throw at the telly every time she came on.'

'Ah well,' Durkan said, 'the funny thing now is that I'm very glad that I *didn't* blow her to Kingdom Come.'

'People did die though,' Carlyle reminded him, his nostalgia belatedly mingling with disgust.

'Casualties of war.'

'That's one way of putting it.'

Durkan slowly recited a list of the victims. 'Sir Anthony Berry, Eric Taylor, Jean Shattock, Muriel Maclean, Roberta Wakeham. Who else even remembers their names?'

'Their families, for a start.'

'Look, I'm not defending what happened. But we were only after the one person. And, ironically, if we had succeeded, things would have turned out a whole lot worse for me.' He spread his arms wide. 'Without her, none of this would be possible. She was a great woman; I have no doubt that history will treat her kindly.'

I don't know about that, Carlyle thought.

Not interested one way or the other, Ward yawned expressively.

'The benefits of hindsight, eh? Durkan said. 'Anyway, that was all decades ago. We move on.'

Carlyle squirmed at the thought of how old he had become. 'It's not that far in the past really.'

'You don't think so? To me, it's about as relevant to us as – I dunno,' he contemplated a comparison, 'as the Vikings were to the Victorians. I find it hard to believe that the young fella doing all those things back then was even me.'

But it was, Carlyle thought. You can't shrug off your past that easily. He glanced through the open doors of the office. Outside, most of the onlookers had drifted back to their computer screens. Standing between the two police officers, Hunter stared into the middle distance. He looked like a man who was planning his next move.

This game is far from over, the inspector reflected.

'Don't you wish that you could go back and tell your younger self some home truths?' Durkan asked. 'I know I do.'

'Of course,' Carlyle said, 'although I could probably think of some better uses for time travel.'

Their middle-aged musing was finally interrupted by the shrill ring of the phone on the desk. Eyes fixed on Carlyle, Durkan grabbed the handset. 'Yes?'

The voice on the other end of the line was calm. 'Is there a problem?'

'I thought I told you that I was not to be interrupted,' Durkan snapped. 'I'll call you back.'

'No. I'll call you.'

'Okay.'

The line went dead.

Putting down the phone, he said, 'That was my secretary . . .'

Out of the corner of his eye, the inspector could see Durkan's PA in the antechamber outside. Happily chatting to one of the lingering rubberneckers, the woman was nowhere near a phone.

Yes, this game was very far from over.

Keen to pre-empt any further reminiscing, Ward stepped across to the desk and handed Durkan a business card. 'Let's wrap this up. Do you want to press charges over the assault?'

Durkan glanced in the direction of his attacker. 'The man clearly has problems. I don't want to add to them. On the other hand, you simply can't behave like that.'

Says the man who casually killed five innocent people in a Brighton hotel and maimed others for life. The inspector said nothing.

'Let me think about it.'

'In the meantime,' Carlyle reminded him, 'we still need to speak to Mr Isaacs urgently.'

Durkan gave an obedient nod. 'I understand.'

Heading for the door, Carlyle paused. 'One last thing.'

Durkan and Ward glared at him in unison.

'Ryan Fortune.'

'Who?' Durkan made a performance of consulting his memory banks. 'I don't know the name.'

Big surprise, Carlyle thought.

'Why do you ask?'

'If you don't know him,' said Carlyle sharply, 'it doesn't matter.'

TWENTY-NINE

Thirty yards from the main entrance to Thatcher Towers, Joseph Isaacs watched an angry-looking cloud hovering over the South Dock. Not for the first time, he gave himself a pat on the back for investing in a Homburg from the wonderful Bates Hats on Jermyn Street. In his opinion, the Homburg was the most elegant of headwear, and perfect for such an inclement climate to boot.

Almost immediately, he saw the first drops of rain splash the nearby paving stones. One thing the security consultant wasn't going to miss about London was the lousy weather. He hadn't yet decided on his next port of call, but it would definitely be somewhere warmer: Lisbon, maybe, or perhaps Valencia. While he waited, Isaacs ran through possible locations in his head, ending up with a 'long list' of thirty-two cities around the globe. The biggest problem, he concluded, was too much choice.

Standing in the shadow of a green-liveried flower delivery van, Isaacs dropped his cigarette end on to the kerb and kicked it into a drain with the toe of his brogues. Placing a fresh smoke between his lips, he fumbled in the pocket of his jacket for a lighter. Before he could locate it, two uniformed police emerged from the building. Isaacs' eyes narrowed. Quant had told him that a total of five cops were in Durkan's office. He wanted to make sure that they had all left the building before making his next move.

Between the two uniforms was a tall, well-built man, who moved like he was in a daze. That would be Hunter. Isaacs felt his sphincter twitch at being in the presence of a man whose whole family had perished at the hands of one of Isaacs' own associates. The security consultant had protested about Fortune's choice of Andrew Carson as the final member of his team from the very start. Unfortunately, he had not protested vigorously enough. Well, shit happened. Isaacs could live with it, just as long as the husband didn't catch up with him.

Relaxing slightly, he watched the Military Policeman allow himself to be bundled into a waiting silver Astra, shuffling on to the middle of the back seat to let the uniforms squeeze in on either side of him.

Where were the others?

A few moments later, he observed as a man and a woman came out of the building and approached the car. Even at this distance it was clear that they were engaged in quite a violent argument. The man pointed towards Hunter, provoking some angry gestures from the woman, who stalked round the vehicle and jumped into the front passenger seat.

'Five cops,' Isaacs muttered to himself. 'Perfect.'

Watching the Astra pull away, the fifth officer took out his mobile and made a short call. Shoving the phone back in his pocket, he headed off along the South Colonnade in the direction of the tube station. Hands in pockets, head bowed, shoulders slouched, the man looked deep in thought as he disappeared into the crowd. Lighting his cigarette, Isaacs took a deep drag, resting his backside on the bonnet of the van before taking a battered mobile from his jacket. Clicking the back off the phone, he removed the battery and then the sim card, before tossing the card into the sewer. Fumbling in his pocket, he pulled out the £10 sim he had bought an hour earlier at a nearby newsagents. Sticking the sim in the slot, he reassembled the device and switched it on, enjoying another couple of puffs while it found the network.

Wreathed in a halo of pale blue smoke, he dialled the number from memory and let it ring until he got an answer.

'They've gone,' Durkan said tensely.

'I know. Just remember to keep this conversation short and vanilla. No details.'

'Where are you?' Durkan hissed.

'I'm gonna have to lie low for a while.'

'You can say that again. What the hell were you playing at with the credit card?'

'Short and vanilla, Gerry. Short and vanilla.' Isaacs sighed to himself. The financier was truly an analogue man in a digital world. He thought that just because he had his office swept for bugs every fortnight, no one could be listening in on his conversations. Edward Snowden's revelations had gone straight over his head; he just couldn't grasp the idea that the technological advances of the last fifteen years had made the forces of law and order omnipresent. In Gerry's world, you were only in trouble when the British Army came kicking your door in at three o'clock in the morning.

'Ye can stuff yer vanilla shite up yer arse!'

Whatever. Isaacs scratched his head as he watched a bright red Porsche roll down the street in front of him. His boss was right, it was a schoolboy error. 'I was put on the spot. With the benefit of hindsight, it was a mistake.'

'They asked about you.'

'Obviously.'

'I had to give them your mobile number.'

'That doesn't matter. I've changed it.'

'They also asked about Fortune.'

Fucking hell, how many times? 'Not on the phone. Ten minutes. Usual place.'

At least the rain had stopped. Sitting on a bench, Isaacs sniffed the air tentatively. The brief downpour had done little to improve the air quality, which had recently been plagued by high levels of pollution – a mixture of local car emissions and dust carried from the Sahara Desert. Air quality – that was another factor to take into consideration when choosing a new place to live.

He spotted Durkan approaching from the direction of Thatcher Towers. The Irishman looked less than happy to be out and about. Over one eye he wore a large plaster. You're looking old, Isaacs thought, too old for this game, at least. He let his gaze fall on the giant video screen on the far side of Canada Square Park. It was showing an advert for a car – or rather, it was an advert for a driving machine, the kind of toy all the bankers that worked in the surrounding offices liked to splash their bonuses on – speeding up a mountain road without another vehicle in sight. Man and machine in perfect harmony.

Not quite like Commercial Road in the rush hour then.

Durkan approached the bench and sat down with a heavy sigh. Isaacs gestured towards the plaster. 'What happened to you?'

'It's nothing,' Durkan grunted.

Tiring of the small talk, Isaacs moved straight to the point. 'Fortune's dead.'

'Eh?' Gerry Durkan almost dumped the contents of his coffee cup right into his lap.

'Carson shot him and did a runner with the diamonds. That's what it looks like, anyway.'

'The little shite . . . after all we've done for him.'

'That's what happens when the sub-contractors start sub-contracting,' Isaacs observed.

'The cops said there were four bodies. Who were the others?'

'Woman and her two little kids. The family of the big guy who was in your office.'

Durkan blanched. 'Jesus H Christ!' He gingerly fingered the plaster above his left eye.

'Give you a smack, did he?' Isaacs grinned.

'He was like a fucking zombie on crack.' Durkan didn't feel the need to go into any more detail.

'Lucky for you they have no idea. Otherwise Daniel Hunter would have torn you limb from limb.'

'Hunter?' Durkan scowled. 'Why does that name ring a bell?'

'Hunter is the Military Policeman who took Carson down for shooting a pair of Taliban soldiers after they'd surrendered,' Isaacs explained. He wondered if they shouldn't have had this conversation earlier, say, around the time Durkan had hatched his 'risk-free' plan to rip off Bob Biswas and, in the process, collapse the Hydra joint venture business that was threatening to bleed him dry.

'Political correctness gone mad,' was Durkan's take on the Taliban situation. 'People are so . . . sensitive these days. Who are they trying to kid? Shoot to Kill is hardly new. Think about The Rock, for a start.' The reference to the 1988 fatal shooting of three members of the IRA by members of the SAS on the forecourt of a Gibraltar petrol station meant nothing to Isaacs, but Durkan failed to notice. 'It's only bloody murder when the Establishment says so.'

'It was the technology that did for Carson,' Isaacs commented. 'A video camera on another soldier's helmet. It's a lot harder to do things unnoticed than it was.' He was about to add '*in your day*' but thought better of it.

'I wouldn't want to be a soldier these days, right enough.'

Soldier? Isaacs let it slide. He had no desire to start arguing about Durkan's attempts at rewriting history. 'By all accounts, Hunter is a solid citizen. He might have had a run-in with Colinson, Fortune's sidekick, at some point as well but I'm not sure about that.'

'They should have left him alone.'

'Yes, they should. But they didn't want him coming after Carson a second time, so they nabbed his wife and kids to try and keep him in his box.'

The look on Gerry Durkan's face suggested a man trying to pass a bowling ball anally. 'Which genius decided that was a good idea?'

'Not me,' Isaacs said flatly. 'Carson obviously didn't want

Hunter in the game; Fortune thought it was something they needed to manage.'

'Fucking idiots,' Durkan scoffed, 'they've fucking managed it all right.'

'When we let them loose,' Isaacs offered, 'we have to accept that they . . . do things.'

'They end up shooting a woman and her fucking kids,' Durkan struggled to keep his voice under control, 'and you put that down to them using their bloody initiative?'

'Carson's gone a bit crazy.' Isaacs reached for his cigarettes then decided against it.

'Fuck me,' Durkan wheezed, 'that's the understatement of the fucking year.'

'It's done now.'

'You can say that again,' Durkan grieved. 'This is turning into a right fucking mess.'

'We just have to move on. I'll find Carson. Recover the diamonds.'

'You'd better. And sooner rather than later.' Durkan shot his security consultant a sideways glance. 'I still know people, you know.'

Yeah, geriatric people. Isaacs was careful not to sneer. 'I will deal with it,' he reiterated.

'Do you know where Carson is?'

'I know where to find him.' Isaacs let his gaze return to the massive video screen. Now it was running an almost identical advert for a different car.

'How?'

Isaacs ignored the question. 'Once I find him – and deal with him – I'm out of here.'

'Fair enough.' Durkan took the hint not to ask too many questions. 'Once it's done, I wouldn't hang around.'

'No.'

'That stupid fucker Carson has taken a simple job and turned it into a total bloodbath. Make sure he suffers.'

'There's no need for that,' Isaacs replied, looking mildly disgusted. 'Just let me do it my way – oh, and I will expect a bonus on completion.'

'Fine.' Durkan knew this was not the time to quibble about money.

'I need some travel expenses.' Isaacs mentioned a figure.

Durkan nodded. 'There's just one other thing.' He quickly ran through the highlights of his earlier meeting with Bob Biswas.

'You'll have to sort that out yourself,' was Isaacs' cool response.

'Story of my life.'

This time Isaacs did smile. 'But you know people,' he said quietly, 'so it shouldn't be a problem.'

'Oh no,' Durkan said hastily. 'No problem at all.'

'Good. I'll call you later when the Carson thing's done.' Isaacs got to his feet. 'Stay close to your phone. This can't be allowed to drag on.'

Not waiting for a reply, Isaacs walked briskly away. There was work to be done and no time to waste. One way or another, he had every intention of being on a flight out of the country within the next seventy-two hours. The basic question remained, however: where precisely should he go?

THIRTY

'Mum!'

Sitting in the shade of her eucalyptus tree, Becky Carson looked up from her copy of *More!* magazine and squinted at her daughter.

With a scowl on her face that made her look about three years old, Lucinda walked towards her, arm outstretched, mobile phone in hand. 'It's Dad. He wants to talk to you.'

'Bloody hell!' Jumping up from her chair, Becky chucked the magazine aside and snatched the handset, sticking it to her ear. 'What are you doing, calling here?' she screeched. 'The bloody police could be back at any minute.'

Not wanting to be party to yet another parental row, Lucinda retreated inside the house.

'Don't start,' Carson shot back. 'I called on Lucinda's phone, didn't I? No one will be listening in to that.'

'Let's hope not,' Becky muttered. 'Anyway, make it short.'

'I'm okay,' he told her. 'Thanks for asking.'

'Good,' Becky said grudgingly, her mind starting to focus on what she needed to get out of this conversation.

'I'll have to lie low for a bit though.'

Yeah, for something like thirty years at least. Walking over to the swimming pool, Becky felt sun-warmed paving stones on the soles of her feet. 'You can't come here.' Extending a leg, she dipped a toe in the water.

'I know that,' Carson snapped. 'I'm not stupid.'

That's a matter of opinion.

'What I'm gonna do is—'

'Andy! Not over the sodding phone.'

'Yeah, well, you know the place we used to go to, before the kids were born?'

Adjusting her bikini top with her free hand, Becky frowned. 'Which one?'

'It was when I had that old Escort. The green one with the racing stripes.'

'The one that got nicked?'

'Yeah. Remember when we used to go off in the Escort, in the days before I joined up?'

It took a few moments longer but, finally, she recalled the cottage on Mersea Island where they had gone for their summer holidays. She had gotten pregnant with Liam there, the first time Andy had refused to use a condom. By the time the boy was born, they were married, Andy had joined the Army and she was effectively starting a twenty-year stretch as a single mother.

Happy memories.

'Oh, yeah, right, I remember.'

'I've fixed it and I'm gonna lie low there for a while,' he told her. 'It'll be nice and quiet. I think I might do some fishing.'

Yeah, Becky thought sourly, a nice little holiday on the run.

'I'll give you a shout when I've planned my next move.'

'What next move?'

'Like, where I'll go next.'

Becky felt a monster headache coming on. 'Okay.'

There was an awkward pause while he digested the obvious lack of enthusiasm in her voice. 'We're gonna be fine, girl, we really are. And guess what? I've only gone and played a blinder.'

'Good.' The pain behind her eyes was growing. Becky didn't know whether she wanted to cry or to puke. 'I'm glad.'

'I'll call you soon.'

'Okay.'

'Give the kids a kiss from me.'

'Will do.'

'I love you.'

'Mm.'

'Becks?'

'I love you too.'

It wasn't much of a declaration but he knew that it was all he was going to get. 'Okay, well, bye then.'

'Bye.' Bending down, Becky placed the phone carefully by the side of the pool. Taking off her sunglasses, she folded them and placed them next to the phone. Stifling a sob, she took a deep breath and did a forward roll into the water, diving down towards the bottom in the hope that her problems would somehow be gone by the time she resurfaced.

'This is my day off, you know. What do you want?' Sitting in the middle of a busy café near Victoria bus station, Noah Templeton bit his lower lip as he eyed the FitzGibbbon's bag lying on the table between them. When the inspector offered up nothing more than an innocent smile, the young officer leaned forward and hissed, 'And if that's what I think it is, what the fuck is it doing here?'

'I'm giving it back to you.'

'Eh?' Templeton scratched at his chest through his T-shirt as he scowled at the drawing of the Aberdeen Angus cattle on the bag. It looked as if he had just rolled out of bed to make their appointment. His face was puffy, his eyes unfocused and there was a day's growth of stubble on his chin. The gash on his forehead – caused by the run-in with the flower box – was still clearly visible. Although it appeared to be healing nicely, the wound looked like it would leave a scar.

That would not necessarily be a bad thing, Carlyle thought – give the boy's face some much-needed character.

'Take it.'

A look of panic descended on Templeton's face as he scanned the other tables, in search of someone waiting to pounce and arrest him. 'Is this a set-up?'

'Not at all. All I want you to do is to deliver the stuff you stole from West End Central to Lucio Spargo, as per your original plan. Nothing could be more simple.'

'I don't know what the hell you're talking about,' Templeton huffed.

The smile disappeared from Carlyle's face. 'Don't fuck me around, sonny,' he warned. 'I have more than enough to bury you.' He was about to launch into more detail when a waitress appeared at the table, shutting him up. She was a wrinkled fifty-something with shocking purple hair and a Siouxsie & the Banshees T-shirt. As she lifted Carlyle's empty demitasse from the table, the inspector caught a flash of untrimmed armpit hair and winced. Unconcerned at his discomfort, she shot him an enquiring look. 'Want another one, love?'

'No, I'm good, thanks.' Carlyle tried his best to smile.

The woman turned to the young constable, who was keeping a firm hand on his empty Coke can. 'I'm fine too.'

Clearly not happy with the pair of squatters at her table, the waitress pointed at the paper bag. 'You want me to take that away?'

'No, no,' they choused.

Her eyes narrowed as she inspected Carlyle. 'You can't eat that in here, you know. Only food bought on the premises can be consumed at the tables. There's a sign by the front door.'

'I know,' Carlyle said. 'Don't worry.'

'Otherwise I'll have to charge you for it.'

'It's not food.'

The waitress made a half-hearted attempt to peer inside before being called over to a nearby table by a well-dressed woman.

'If only she knew,' Templeton said grimly.

'I want you to do it today,' said Carlyle, quickly returning to the order of business.

'I've got plans,' the boy said unconvincingly.

'Fuck your plans. If you want to still be in a job by the end of the day, make sure that the gear is in Spargo's office by six at the latest.'

'What if he's not around? He quite often likes to ride along with Montrose on his rounds.'

'Montrose?'

'Peter Montrose,' Templeton explained, 'the American heavy. Was in the Special Forces, or something like that. So he says anyway.'

A thought popped into Carlyle's head. 'He's not armed, is he?'

'Hardly,' Templeton sneered. 'That would be way over the top. The guy just has to walk into a room and most people are shitting themselves. Mr Spargo's not stupid, he knows that the prospect of serious injury is as effective as actual bodily harm, ninety-nine point nine per cent of the time.'

Mr Spargo. 'You think he's a genius, eh?'

'Not necessarily a genius,' Templeton said, 'just successful.'

'Does your mum know you work for him?'

'No, and she doesn't need to know, right? She thinks it's great that I'm a policeman. There's no need for her to know about any of this.'

'Why did you hook up with him?'

'He asked me. I bumped into him in a pub not long after I'd started at Savile Row. Had a bit of a chat. He said he'd had no one as good working for him since my dad died, but maybe I could do a few things for him here and there. Freelance stuff.'

'Freelance,' Carlyle repeated heavily.

'Why not?' Templeton shrugged. 'The money's good.'

'I bet it is, when you're selling drugs.' Carlyle gestured towards the bag. 'How much will he give you for that?'

'Depends.'

'On what?'

'On how much he gets for it, obviously,' said the boy, narked at such a stupid question.

'Who does he sell it to?'

Templeton shook his head. 'Not my area. Nothing to do with me.'

'Not really his area either, is it? I mean, he's supposed to be a property developer.'

'Mr Spargo likes to dabble. He sees himself as a bit of a wheeler-dealer. Easy cash is always welcome.'

Another question popped into Carlyle's head. 'How did you know the stuff was there?'

'It was just luck. I have what Mr Spargo calls a "watching brief"; keeping an eye on the local gallery owners.' He smiled proudly. 'If I see something I think we can use, I have discretion to act on it. That's basically what happened in this case.'

'So you see yourself as working for Spargo first and the Met second?' Carlyle began to wonder if the boy had any future on the Force at all. 'Isn't that the wrong way round?'

Templeton thought about it for several moments. 'I work for myself,' he said finally, 'first, second and always.' Pleased with the answer, he sat back in his chair.

'Even if that means fitting up innocent businessmen?'

'From what I hear about your mate Mr Silver,' Templeton leered, 'he's hardly an innocent businessman.'

'He's not my mate.' Over the hum of the traffic outside, Carlyle fancied he heard a cock crowing in the distance.

His denial brought a snort of derision. 'Bollocks. I asked around. You two are famous among the old-timers.'

'Yeah, right.'

'You were cops together, years ago. He went off to become a drugs dealer and you watched his back.' The grin on Templeton's ugly mug grew so wide it looked like it was going to split his face in two. 'How much does *he* pay *you,* then? I bet you're far more bent than I am.'

The next thing Carlyle knew, he was on his feet, a hand round the youngster's throat. He squeezed hard, until Templeton's smirk was replaced by a look of genuine concern. 'I have never taken a fucking penny piece, from Dominic Silver or anyone else – understand, you little shit?'

Templeton held up both hands in surrender. 'Okay, okay,' he croaked, his face beginning to turn puce. 'My mistake.'

'Too fucking right.' Looking round the café, Carlyle realized

269

that 90 per cent of the other patrons were staring at him. As his rage lifted, he released his grip and slowly dropped back into his seat.

With a frown on her face and the bill in her hand, the purple-haired waitress made her way quickly over to their table.

'Gentlemen,' she said, 'if you don't want anything else, I think it is time for you to leave.' Slapping their bill on the table, she bent down and picked up the FitzGibbbon's bag which had fallen on to the floor in the kerfuffle, along with Templeton's Coke can. Placing the bag back on the table, she crushed the empty can in her hand. 'Pay at the till. And if there's any more trouble, I'll call the police.'

'Sorry,' Carlyle muttered as she stalked off.

The boy gingerly massaged his throat as his face slowly returned to something approaching a more normal colour. 'You wanker,' he muttered, sotto voce, so that the waitress did not hear their continuing argument. 'Do that again and I'll fucking kill you.'

Ignoring the youthful bravado, Carlyle inspected his fingerprints, which were still clearly visible on the boy's throat. 'Just because you happen to have crossed the line, don't assume that the same applies to other people.'

'What fucking line?'

Not interested in an ethics debate, the inspector waved away the question. 'Deliver the stuff to Spargo by six o'clock at the latest. As soon as it's done, let me know.'

'And what happens then?'

'You just go about your business. If you can reinvent yourself as an ordinary copper, you won't get any more hassle from me.'

'What about Mr Spargo?'

Carlyle sighed. 'You just have to walk away from him, Noah.'

'What if he shops me?'

What is this? Twenty fucking Questions? 'Don't worry about that. I will deal with Spargo. There will be no comeback to you.'

'I'm not letting you set me up.'

'I am not setting *you* up,' Carlyle said impatiently.

'Fuck off. Do it yourself.'

'Listen, you little wanker. Maybe you don't care about getting kicked off the Force but that'll just be the start.'

'Bollocks.'

Carlyle folded his arms. It was time to play his Joker. 'Nice little council flat your mum has.' He gestured towards the street outside. 'How many bedrooms does it have?'

Templeton frowned. 'Three. Why?'

'Because, since they changed the law, that's two more than she's entitled to have.'

'Whaddya mean?'

'Don't you read the papers?' Carlyle immediately realized that it was a stupid question. 'The government introduced a law limiting the number of bedrooms you can have in your council house, or flat. If you have too many bedrooms, you have to move.' It was a rather simplified version of the situation, but close enough. 'Anyway, I checked with the council; the bedroom tax people haven't got round to reviewing Blefuscu Gardens Estate yet. They might never get round to it. On the other hand, if someone was to make Darbourne House a priority case . . .'

'You sneaky bastard fucker.'

'I can imagine that would be very tough on your mum.' He would never dream of shopping the poor woman to the bedroom tax fascists, but the boy didn't know that, and leverage was leverage. 'On the other hand, I'm sure that there's a nice family of refugees from Romania or Somalia or somewhere that are in real need of it.'

'But it's *our* home,' Templeton wailed.

'Says who?' Carlyle happily turned the knife. 'Is it really right for you and your mum to he hogging that property?'

'We're not hogging anything.'

'It's all about priorities. Put yourself in the position of some poor, overworked Housing Officer from the council,' Carlyle smirked. 'They have to manage all these competing demands.

It will be a total nightmare, worrying about making the right decisions, especially with property prices being what they are. It must be worth a bomb, your place.'

'The one downstairs recently went for £860,000. It's smaller though.' The boy looked like he was about to cry. He glanced at the bag containing the drugs, reviewing his options. 'Mum always said that Dad should have tried to buy it when he had the chance. Can't afford it now.'

'Come on, Noah,' Carlyle said gently. 'Fair's fair. The way to look at it is that you've had a good run. Been in the place a long time. It's time for someone else to use it. You just have to move on. Funnily enough, I have a good contact in the Housing Department. I can have a word with her and, with a bit of luck, we can get your mum relocated to a cosy little one-bedroom place. You won't have any of this uncertainty hanging over you any more.' He paused. 'Of course, the new place won't be in Central London.'

Noah stifled a sob. 'She ain't moving to Enfield or nowhere like that.'

Carlyle said sadly, 'I was thinking somewhere more like Hull. Or maybe Middlesbrough.'

The boy couldn't have looked any more horrified if he had mentioned Warsaw. Or Mogadishu. 'You wouldn't . . .'

' 'Fraid so,' Carlyle smiled. 'In a heartbeat. So don't fuck me around, Noah. Go and see Spargo, give him the stuff, and call me when it's done.' Getting to his feet, he gestured at the small slip of paper next to the bag as he moved towards the door. 'And make sure you leave a big tip when you pay the bill.'

THIRTY-ONE

Back at Charing Cross, Carlyle purchased two green teas and a couple of Mars Bars from the canteen and headed up to the third floor. Approaching Roche's desk, he put the paper cups down next to her keyboard, along with one of the chocolate bars.

'About time,' Roche said, not looking up from her screen. 'I've been trying to get hold of you for ages.'

'I brought you a tea,' Carlyle pointed out, as if that would be enough to keep him in the clear. 'And a Mars Bar.' Ripping the wrapper off his own bar, he took a large bite and began chewing voraciously.

'God!' Roche exclaimed. 'Keep that damn thing away from me. If I eat any more bloody chocolate I'm gonna explode.'

Perching on the edge of the next desk, Carlyle looked her over, trying not to be too obvious about it. She looked pretty much like the same old Roche to him. If he didn't know, he wouldn't necessarily have pegged her as pregnant. 'You're looking good,' he offered.

Roche's grunt by way of response could have signalled her disapproval of his comment on various grounds: inappropriate, unprofessional, untrue, sexist. Or, more likely, all of the above at the same time.

Feeling suitably chastened, Carlyle licked some crumbs of chocolate from his lips and concentrated on eating the remains of his Mars Bar.

'I spoke to the Chief Inspector in charge of the diamond

robbery case.' Reaching for one of the cups, Roche mentioned the name of a woman he had never heard of.

'I bet she's having nightmares at the moment,' the inspector said ruefully, 'watching her career go down the pan. Why did it take them so long to respond to the incident?'

'There was some computer problem on the night, apparently,' Roche said, 'combined with a lack of bodies as a result of West Ham playing at home.'

'West Ham?' the inspector scowled. 'What have they got to do with anything?'

'That's what I heard. Anyway, it was hardly the Chief Inspector's fault.'

'That won't help her much,' Carlyle predicted. 'Murder and mayhem on the streets of London and the perpetrators get away with it; someone's going to have to pay for that.'

'There but for the Grace of God.'

'Speak for yourself,' said Carlyle haughtily.

'Yeah, like you've never been hung out to dry.'

'I'm not worth hanging out to dry,' he observed.

'Shit!' Grimacing, the sergeant shifted in her chair.

Unwell pregnant woman alert! Carlyle froze. 'Are you okay?'

'Yeah. It's nothing.' Roche took a few deep breaths. 'Just a twinge.'

'Have you seen your doctor?'

'Of course I've seen a doctor, you berk. I'm having a bloody baby.'

'Fair point.' Looking away, the inspector waited for her discomfort to clear. There was no one else around; the rest of the office was like a morgue. Let's hope they're all out catching criminals, he thought. Somehow, that seemed unlikely.

After a further spell of controlled breathing, Roche regained her composure. 'They are really struggling with this case, right enough. Bodies all over the place, but still no sign of the stolen diamonds. And apparently, that Inspector Ward is being a right pain in the arse.'

'That sounds like Ward, all right.' Finishing the Mars Bar, Carlyle walked over to the recycling bin in the corner of the room and dropped the wrapper inside. 'She's tight with Simpson, it seems.'

'I don't know about "tight".' Removing the lid from one of the cups, Roche blew on her tea before taking a sip. 'Thanks, by the way.'

'No problem.'

'Simpson knows Ward through the Women in Policing Forum, but I don't think that they're close, particularly.'

The Women in Policing Forum? Carlyle knew he should keep his own counsel, but he couldn't quite manage it. 'Are you a member?'

'You don't really join.' Reaching across the table, Roche picked up the Mars Bar. 'You just turn up. Some people see it as good for networking. I've been to one or two events over the years but never really found it to be my thing.' Thinking better of it, she let the chocolate fall back on to the desk.

'Are you going to eat that?' Carlyle asked, licking his lips.

'I might have a nibble,' Roche teased. 'Why? Are you still hungry?'

'No, no.' Carlyle reached over and took his cup of tea. 'Just asking.'

'Mm.'

'So, what have we got?' He took a mouthful of tea and grimaced. The bag had been in for too long.

'What have we got . . .' Roche shuffled the papers on her desk, coming up with a small Moleskine notebook. Flipping through the pages, she said sheepishly, 'My bloody handwriting, what a joke! Sorry, hold on. Here we go. I checked with the HR people at MCS. They claimed to have bugger-all on Joseph Isaacs, other than his bank account details, which they won't give us without a warrant.'

The inspector shook his head sadly. 'It's great the way people always fall over themselves to co-operate with us.'

275

'However,' Roche continued, 'the woman I spoke to did let slip that it was an offshore bank account. Jersey.'

Carlyle reflected on that for a moment. 'And what does that tell us?'

'Not sure. However,' her face brightened, 'I did some digging and found a paper that Joseph Isaacs gave to the Royal Institute of International Affairs. I spoke to a nice lady there who managed to locate a bio for him.'

'Well done,' said Carlyle, genuinely chuffed.

'It seems that Isaacs has been a "security consultant" for around a decade. Before that, he was a Major in the Army.'

A thought began to grow in the inspector's brain. 'Check in with them, see if you can pull his service record.'

'Already done that,' she said triumphantly. 'His last posting before leaving the Service was Iraq, where he served with—'

'Andy Carson!' Carlyle chorused.

The smile on Roche's face grew wider. 'No.'

'Oh.' Wishing he had kept his mouth shut, Carlyle waited for her to enlighten him.

'Adrian Colinson spent nine months in Basra as part of a unit headed up by Major Isaacs.'

The inspector struggled to place the name. 'Who?'

'Colinson was the getaway driver.'

'The guy who drove the Range Rover into the concrete pillar?'

Roche nodded.

'Not exactly Jeremy Clarkson,' Carlyle noted.

'It's a link.'

'It certainly is.' Putting the lid back on his tea, Carlyle said, 'I wonder if Daniel Hunter knows about this?'

'Dunno. Where is he?'

Carlyle stood up. 'As far as I know, Ward still has him down at West End Central.'

'She really has got it in for him,' Roche said ruefully. 'It's not right. Poor bloke.'

'That's the understatement of the century.' Carlyle began heading for the stairs.

'One other thing,' Roche called after him.

'Yeah?' Carlyle turned.

'Bob Biswas.'

'Yeah, yeah, yeah. Gerry Durkan's client.'

'He's an even more colourful character than Isaacs. Started out as an illegal bookmaker in Mumbai. Now he runs a diamond-trading business in Antwerp.'

'Diamonds? I thought that was a Jewish business.'

'Times change. Apparently it's dominated by Indians these days. Anyway, it was Biswas' diamonds that were nicked at City airport.'

'Really?' Carlyle pondered the significance of this new information.

'Yup. The kid that was shot at the airport was his nephew.'

'Bloody hell!' Carlyle scratched his head. 'So why would you go and see Mr Durkan right after you'd been hit by a double whammy like that?'

'That's a good question.'

'To which we need an answer.' As Carlyle turned again to take his leave, he gave his final instruction: 'Keep digging.'

Affecting an air of professional detachment, Colonel Trevor Naylor watched as the female police officer scribbled her signature on the bottom of a sheet of green paper.

Tossing the biro on to the desk, Inspector Ward then handed him the release form.

'Are we done?' Naylor asked.

Ward glanced at Hunter, who was busy retrieving his personal effects from a brown A4 envelope. 'He's all yours.'

Folding the paper into quarters, Naylor stuffed it into his pocket. 'Good luck with the rest of the investigation.'

Uttering something incomprehensible, Ward stalked down the corridor and disappeared into the bowels of West End Central.

'You know what?' Naylor grinned. 'I think she likes you.'

Taking his wallet from the envelope, Hunter did not smile.

The Colonel felt a stab of embarrassment for attempting to be humorous. 'Sorry. This is no time to be trying to make jokes.'

'No.'

Naylor considered a poster on the wall, appealing for witnesses in a murder investigation. 'I know you must be knackered but there's a lot still to deal with.'

'I had a kip in the cells,' Hunter lied. Five hours spent staring at the mould growing on the ceiling had done nothing to clear his head or refresh his body. He felt eviscerated.

'It's absolutely disgraceful the way you've been treated here,' Naylor fumed. 'I will be having words.'

'She's only doing her job,' said Hunter dully.

'Yes, but still.'

'Don't worry about it.' Hunter couldn't give a fig about making a complaint; he still had an open case to bring to an end. 'Have there been any developments?'

'Not of any significance. It looks like Carson's gone to ground.'

'He could have left the country.'

'I doubt it. We're watching all the ports and airports. He won't be able to get through.'

I can think of quite a few ways, Hunter reflected.

'And, even if he did, we'll catch up with him sooner or later.'

' "Sooner or later" isn't good enough.'

'I know, Dan. I know. Everyone is making this their number one priority. We'll get him for you.'

'I want to get him myself.'

A pained expression crossed Naylor's face. When he spoke, his voice showed signs of cracking. 'You have to look after your family.'

'My family is dead.' Hunter's words bounced off the walls, like ricocheting bullets, each one ripping a wound in his shattered being. For a moment, he thought he might collapse but, before his knees could buckle, he felt the envelope start to vibrate

278

in his hand. It took him a moment to realize that someone was calling his mobile, still inside. Taking out the phone, he threw back his shoulders, standing upright as he considered the unfamiliar number on the screen.

After a moment, he lifted the handset to his ear.

'Hunter.'

There was no reply. Straining to hear, Hunter imagined that he could make out someone breathing on the other end of the line – slow, shallow breaths, like someone struggling to bring their heart-rate under control.

'Hello?' Slowly walking away from Naylor, Hunter stepped through the doors of the police station and into the cool night air. Standing on the pavement, a couple of uniforms were enjoying a cigarette as they chatted about last night's television. Moving to his left, the phone still clamped to his ear, Hunter took up a position under a streetlight.

'Captain Hunter?' a female voice said finally. 'Are you still there?'

'I'm still here,' he said, keeping his voice even, trying not to sound too eager. 'Who am I speaking to?' He thought he knew the answer to his question but needed it to be confirmed.

'It's Becky Carson.'

'Becky.' Hunter felt a wave of serenity wash over him.

'Andy Carson's wife.'

'I remember.' Closing his eyes, Hunter brought up a mental picture of Carson trooping out of his house in handcuffs, head bowed, followed by a scrawny blonde woman shouting insults at the young Redcaps leading him towards the waiting people carrier. In the background, the kids stood in the doorway, seemingly more embarrassed by their mum's invective than by their father's arrest.

'Are you still looking for him?'

Holding his breath, Hunter opened his eyes. Then said: 'Yes, I'm still looking for him.'

A bus rolled slowly down the other side of the street, coming to a temporary halt opposite the lamppost. On the side was an advert for the latest Jason Statham action flick. From the depths of his memory, Hunter recalled reading somewhere that the plot revolved around a diamond heist of some sort. Was that life imitating art, or the other way round? Unable to work it out, his gaze dropped to the lower deck, focusing on a young black woman with a giant afro. Her hair was so large, his first impression was that it had to be a wig. The woman was nodding gently in time to the music coming from a large pair of red headphones clamped to her skull. Briefly their eyes met. The woman didn't smile; instead she looked through Hunter as if he wasn't there.

That's all I am now, he thought, a ghost.

For a few moments, he almost forgot the woman on the other end of the phone.

Then, after a delicious pause, Becky Carson spoke again.

'I know where he is.'

THIRTY-TWO

When it was done, Becky Carson let the phone fall on the bed and stared at her naked self in the floor-to-ceiling mirror on the bedroom wall. The woman looking back at her was in reasonable shape; there was some inevitable southward drift here and there, but overall she didn't look too bad, all things considered. She certainly wasn't ready for the scrapheap just yet. There was reason to believe that her post-Andy life could consist of more than just gardening and gin.

Becky's mind drifted towards thoughts of the pretty policeman, Inspector Nikos Jones. The boy with the English father and Greek mother. Or was it the other way round? Either way, he was a decent-looking bloke. And interested. Definitely interested. She had picked up the vibes when he had been standing in her kitchen. The guy was a player.

She had his number; the cute cop's card was still in her bag, unlike that of Daniel Hunter, which was already in the rubbish. Maybe she would give Nikos a call and see if he fancied a drink; make it clear that there were no strings. The kids would give her grief about it – not to mention her mother – but Becky could handle that. From down the corridor, she could hear the comforting sound of music coming from Lucinda's room. Downstairs, her mum would be tucked up in bed, doing a crossword or reading the latest Martina Cole. Liam was out somewhere with his girlfriend. The Carson family unit, narrowly defined, was functioning normally; fairly normally anyway. Despite being stuck in this nightmare situation, everyone was doing a decent job of getting on with their life. That seemed the only sensible thing. She would do the same. At some point, once Andy had been caught, they would have to go back to England. Apart from anything else, the kids couldn't bunk off school for ever. In the meantime, however, they should make the most of the sunshine – and everything else that Crete had to offer.

Grabbing a T-shirt from the bed, she pulled it over her head before reaching for the glass of white wine that had been left on the bedside table. With the best part of a bottle of Ino Moschofilero inside her, Becky knew that she was well on the way to being really rather pissed. Tomorrow morning, she would no doubt have a very nasty hangover. There was no point in worrying about that now though. Raising the almost empty glass to the mirror, she offered a mock toast to her absent husband.

'Good luck, Andy,' she giggled. 'You're gonna need it.'

Lifting his gaze from the gutter, Hunter contemplated the warm glow coming from the café across the road. The people sitting inside were enjoying their lattes, chatting, playing on their Apple laptops and generally just watching the world go by. An older guy by the window glanced up from the book he was reading and smiled.

Hunter let his gaze drift down the street. When it returned to the café, the man had returned to his tome. A blonde woman had taken up a seat nearby, sipping occasionally on her coffee as she rummaged through her outsized shoulder bag. The whole scene looked so . . . civilized. For several moments, the Redcap had to fight an almost overwhelming urge to join the café's patrons, to flop into one of its chairs, indulge in a spot of casual people-watching and try to pretend that he still had a normal life of his own. Instead, Hunter looked at the address Becky Carson had given him, which he had scribbled down on the back of the envelope from the police station containing his personal effects.

Mersea Island? He had never heard of the place. Still, it only took a few seconds of tapping on his phone to discover not only its location – on the Essex coast – but also the most efficient way of driving there: 62.7 miles – estimated journey time just under two and a half hours.

Hunter wondered about Becky giving her husband up. Maybe the woman wasn't so dumb, after all. By shopping her old man, she was bringing the whole mess to its inevitable conclusion faster than otherwise would be the case; save everyone a bit of grief. Two and a half hours. He checked the time on his phone. This thing could be finished tonight.

Hunter quickly ran through a mental check list: pick up some stuff from the flat, recover the gun that he'd wisely stashed before heading over to Thatcher Towers, and hire a car. Taking another look at the phone, he scanned the map kindly provided by Google. Just north of Mersea Island was the port of Felixstowe. 'That'll do,' he mumbled to himself. The idea that had been floating around his brain began to take shape.

Bookmarking the web page, Hunter cleared his call log and placed the phone back in his pocket. Removing some small change from the envelope, he then ripped it up and dropped it into a nearby waste bin. For a moment, he tried to imagine his life a year from now. After some prompting, his mind presented an image of himself sitting on a bed in a sunlit room. Stripped to the waist, he was breaking down an assault rifle, working quickly, mechanically, laying the parts on the bed in order, the concentration on his face total. Moving his mind's eye away from the bed, he tried to see what else was in the room but it was impossible. All he could see was the image of the man with the gun.

A small road-sweeping van rumbled past in the gutter, bringing Hunter back to the here and now. Heading towards him, a man walking a poodle went past the entrance to the police station. The uniforms who had been enjoying a smoke when Hunter first came out on to the street had now retreated inside.

It was time to go.

Struck by a momentary paralysis, however, Hunter hovered on the pavement. He thought about Naylor waiting for him and all the bureaucracy he would have to deal with.

The bureaucracy of bereavement: the death certificates, the insurance policies, the council tax, the school . . . an endless stream of paperwork and empty condolences.

An image of Mel, Susie and Rob in that bedroom flashed through his brain. Crying out, he fought back a sob. The dog-walker gave him a funny look before dragging his poodle away from the nutter hovering beside the lamppost.

Biting his lip, Hunter struggled to pull up an earlier image of his family, one from a time when they were all together, happy. Bowing his head, he crossed the road and started to walk down the street.

Sitting in the Arcade Café, Joseph Isaacs closed his book, placing it on the bench in front of him as he watched Hunter consult his phone. Even at this distance, he could see that the man was in some distress. That was understandable, was it not? The security consultant was not a family man himself but that did not mean he was incapable of empathy. The day's trauma must be placing a crushing weight on Captain Hunter's frame.

Isaacs half-expected the man to step off the far pavement and jump in front of the next taxi barrelling down the street. Instead, after an extended period of deliberation, he began walking away from the police station in the direction of Piccadilly Circus.

Giving him a ten-yard start, Isaacs slipped from his seat, heading for the door.

'Excuse me!'

Feeling a tap on his shoulder, he wheeled around to face a pretty blonde woman who, on first glance, could have been anywhere in age between twenty-two and thirty-five. Smiling, she picked up the discarded paperback and offered it to him. 'You left your book.'

'It's okay,' he replied, trying not to be rude. 'I'm finished with it. Feel free to take it.' He hoped that she wasn't one of those wretched creatures who only read e-books. 'I like to think of it as recycling.'

Turning the paperback in her hand, the woman looked at the cover doubtfully. '*Heart of Darkness*? What's it about?'

Isaacs glanced down the street. Hunter was still in sight. The man didn't seem to be in a major hurry to get anywhere. Perhaps he had no immediate destination in mind. In his dazed state, that wouldn't be such a surprise. He smiled at the girl. 'Where to begin?'

The woman looked hesitant as she read the blurb on the back cover. It reminded Isaacs of a child being offered a new flavour of ice cream. Would it be better than chocolate? Grabbing the handle, he pulled open the door.

'Is it any good?' she asked, still unable to make up her mind unaided.

'Oh, yes,' Isaacs replied, talking over his shoulder as he headed into the street. 'It's an acknowledged classic. Definitely worth the read.'

Perched on his chair, Lucio Spargo studiously ignored the FitzGibbon's bag sitting on his desk and glared at the unwelcome visitor. 'I know you,' he hissed. 'You were at the Molby-Nicol Gallery.' Lifting an arm, he clicked his fingers as if summoning a waiter. 'The guy who runs it.' There was more clicking as he tried to remember. 'What's his name?'

'Silver.' Standing under a large framed black and white print of a seascape hanging on the far wall, Peter Montrose lifted his handcuffs to his face and scratched his nose. The serene look on the heavy's face suggested that this wasn't the first time he had ever been arrested. He certainly didn't seem fazed by the experience. 'Dominic Silver.'

'That's right – Silver. Smug bastard. Thinks he knows everything about everything.'

The inspector stifled a grin.

'Thinks he can pretend his previous career never existed,' Spargo spat out. 'Everyone's bent and everyone tries to pretend that they're not. Anyway, how do you know him?'

'I know a lot of people,' Carlyle observed airily. 'It's part of my job, after all.'

Spargo's eyes narrowed. 'Are you in his pocket? Is he paying you to do this? I should have expected something like this from the little shit.'

'Harder than putting the frighteners on some old granny, eh?''

Spargo ignored the reference to Sally-Anne Mason. 'How much is he paying you?' he demanded.

'He isn't paying me anything. I don't work for Dom— Mr Silver.'

'Crap,' snorted Montrose.

'Corruption is a very serious accusation,' Carlyle said stiffly.

'Don't worry.' Spargo gave him a sickly smile. 'We won't be making a formal complaint.'

'But,' Montrose added, taking a step towards Carlyle, 'when I get out . . .'

Waving away the threat, the inspector called in the two uniforms who were standing in the hall and told them to take the heavy to the van that was parked outside.

Spargo waited until they were alone. 'How much is Silver paying you?' he asked again. 'I can pay more, much more. Put you on a retainer, as well. After all, in my business, there are always issues that need to be . . . managed.'

Carlyle shook his head. 'It doesn't work like that.'

Spargo looked at him with contempt. 'I have to say that, in my experience, it invariably does.'

'Speaking of Noah Templeton . . .'

A look of disgust crept across Spargo's face. 'That little shit was in on this, was he?'

'Leave him out of it,' Carlyle said firmly. 'Noah's just a boy, who you've exploited. He's made a big mistake but there's no reason why he can't have a second chance.' He was feeling a little

286

warmer towards Templeton now that the kid had finally delivered Spargo. In the event, he had missed Carlyle's deadline by the best part of two hours. The inspector had just about convinced himself that Noah was going to bottle it when the text finally arrived:

Job done.

Better late than never.

'If you don't take my offer, you're the one making the mistake,' Spargo snapped.

'Story of my life,' Carlyle chuckled. Removing a pair of handcuffs from his back pocket, he dangled them from the index finger of his right hand.

'Bastard!' Spargo slammed a palm on the desk.

'Look,' said Carlyle evenly. 'We can do this the hard way, or the easy way, it's up to you. You can walk out of here under your own steam, without these on, *after* you've spoken to your lawyer, and it all gets done by the book.'

'By the book. Ha!'

'In this case,' Carlyle said slowly, 'by the book means that I write up my report and walk away, job done. You take your chances with the CPS and – if your lawyer kicks up enough of a fuss – it might not even come to court. Just another chapter in the colourful history of Lucio Spargo – adding to the legend, if you like.' Spargo started to say something, but Carlyle lifted a hand to cut him off. 'Even if you walk though, I want you to lay off Dominic Silver. If I hear that Molby-Nicol has got any problems, I will *really* come after you.'

'What's the big deal?' Spargo whined. 'It's only a bloody gallery. I'm trying to create something special here; a quality development. It's not as if he can't go and set up round the corner.'

'Dom wants to stay,' said Carlyle. 'It's his call.'

'And if I don't play ball?'

Carlyle affected the air of a man who didn't much care one way or the other. 'In that case, you can stew in the cells overnight, without access to your brief. Meanwhile, we will ring round every news desk in town, telling them that you have been arrested for possession with intent to supply. The main investors in your Cork Street project will all get a personal visit from me and I would be very surprised if at least some of them are not taken in for questioning.'

Spargo's face hardened. 'I'd like to see you try that.'

'In that case,' Carlyle gave the handcuffs another jiggle, 'feel free to call my bluff.'

Spargo lifted his eyes to the ceiling, as if hoping that some divine intervention might rid him of this troublesome cop. None was forthcoming. Finally, he acknowledged the illegal drugs sitting on his desk. 'This is nothing to do with me.'

'No one's interested in the details,' Carlyle sighed. He began reciting the words he knew better than the Lord's Prayer. 'You have the right to remain silent. However . . .'

'Spare me,' Spargo interrupted. 'I know the details.'

'Fair enough,' Carlyle shrugged. 'Now, it's decision time. Which way do you want to do this?'

Gritting his teeth, Spargo reached for the phone sitting on his desk. 'Okay, okay. You win. Let's get this pantomime over with. I'll make the call to the lawyer and then we can go.'

THIRTY-THREE

After carefully composing an arrest report which was as short as it was anodyne, Carlyle booked the contents of the FitzGibbon's bag into the Evidence Room at Charing Cross before calling it a day. Leaving Lucio Spargo deep in conversation with his lawyer in one of the station's basement interview rooms, he headed out into the Covent Garden night.

Sniffing the polluted air, the inspector realized that he had a taste for some whiskey. He also had jobs to do. Resisting the temptation to pop into The Globe for a quick Jameson's or two, he headed straight back to Winter Garden House.

Arriving home, he discovered that Helen had not yet returned from work. Approaching the living room, he hovered in the doorway. Sprawled across the sofa, mobile phone clamped to her ear, Alice remained oblivious to his arrival. The TV was on, tuned to one of the numerous music channels kindly piped into the living room by their cable provider.

'I can't do that!' Alice exclaimed, over the sound of what the inspector vaguely recognized as a Nirvana song. 'Edward would have a fit!' Belatedly sensing her father's presence, a look of mild annoyance crossed her face. Quickly sitting upright, she added: 'Look, I've gotta go. We can sort it out later. Yes. Sure. Bye!' Ending the call, she launched a professional scowl at her father. 'How long have you been standing there, spying on me?'

Nice to see you too, Carlyle thought wearily. 'I wasn't spying on you.' Grabbing the remote, he muted Kurt Cobain. 'Boy trouble?'

'No.' As she frowned, Alice's brows knitted together in a way that made her look so perfectly like her mother that Carlyle almost gasped. 'Why do you ask?'

'I just thought,' Carlyle tossed the remote on to the sofa, 'that with you having to play the imaginary boyfriend card, that you were having to fob someone off again.' He was still struggling to come to terms with the idea of boyfriends, whether real or imaginary; at the current rate of progress, he expected to have gotten over his reservations by the time Alice was about thirty-five.

Or maybe forty.

Dodging his attempt to plant a kiss on her forehead, she said, 'Mum told you about that, eh?'

'Yeah.' Stepping away from her personal space, he bowed his head, relieved that she hadn't gone ballistic about the two of them gossiping behind her back.

'In fact, that worked quite well. But this one is a *real* Edward.'

'Eh?'

'He's the brother of Katarina.'

Katarina. The name vaguely rang a bell. After a couple of moments' reflection, he recalled Helen telling him about a Swedish girl who had arrived in Alice's class at the beginning of the current school year. 'Older or younger?'

'Older, only by a year though.'

That was something, Carlyle thought. The last thing they needed right now was Alice falling for some predatory twenty year old.

'He's really cute. Got a nice bum.'

That's way too much information. Carlyle tried to hide his embarrassment behind a feeble cough.

'We started officially going out together yesterday.'

Yesterday? 'What happened to . . .' Carlyle couldn't quite remember the name of the last one.

'Oliver and I simply weren't compatible,' Alice announced. 'We had a good talk about it and decided to call it a day.'

'I see.'

'That's the mature thing to do, isn't it?' Picking up the remote, Alice unmuted the TV and the room was filled by the sound of a band he didn't recognize. Their conversation about relationships was now officially over. 'What are you going to do?' she asked, her attention firmly fixed on the screen.

'Don't worry, I'm not going to cramp your style.' Carlyle reversed towards the door. 'I need to go back out.'

Alice muttered her approval.

'I'm off to see Grandpa.'

When she looked up from the TV screen, he could see that the concern on his daughter's face was genuine. 'How's he doing?' she asked.

'Fine, I think. Under the circumstances. He has a nurse coming in every few days to check if he needs anything, and he has a hotline to call if there is a problem.'

'How long do you think he'll be able to keep living on his own?' Alice wanted to know.

'Dunno.' Carlyle knew that Alexander would fight as long as possible to keep his independence. Once he had to leave the flat, the Doomsday Clock would start ticking. He dreaded the day he would have to put his father into care. That really would be the beginning of the end.

'Give him our love.'

'Will do.'

'Me and Mum will be over to see him at the weekend. Ask him if he wants us to bring anything when we come.'

'Okay.'

Retreating into the kitchen, Carlyle went through the now familiar routine of taking down Helen's luxury muesli from the cupboard. Removing the bag of cereal from the box, he closed his hand round the small packet, about half the size of a paperback book, that had been stored in the bottom. Before returning what he had come to think of as *Spargo's drugs* to Noah Templeton, the inspector had removed maybe 30 per cent of the pills from the original package. With the benefit of hindsight, it had been a canny move, getting Dom to acquire the drugs. The way things were turning out, he would be able to deal with two problems at once – both Spargo and his father.

The inspector weighed the packet in his hand. It was worth the equivalent of a month's salary, maybe more. He guessed he had kept back enough of the pills to keep his father in pain relief for six weeks or so. That would leave Dom plenty of time to source whatever additional supplies that might be required thereafter.

Placing the now drug-free muesli back in the cupboard, he rooted out a small Waterstones plastic bag from the ever-expanding collection that Helen stored under the sink. Putting the pills inside, he took his leave of Alice and headed off to Fulham.

Letting himself into the flat, Carlyle found his father sitting in the kitchen. In contrast to the previous time, Alexander was looking remarkably chipper. Bathed and shaved, and wearing a new cardigan, bought for him by Helen, over a check shirt left open at the neck, he appeared relaxed, if a little frail. His eyes were clear and some of the colour had returned to his cheeks. The empty plate on the table suggested that some of his appetite had returned as well. In his hands he grasped a faded Fulham mug, three-quarters full of milky tea.

Alexander watched his son place the small package in front of him. 'What's that?' he asked.

'The best pain relief money can buy,' Carlyle said cheerily. 'A little something for when you need it. Put it somewhere safe and make sure that the nurse doesn't see it when she comes in.'

The old man reverted to grumbling mode. 'It's a bit late in the day for me to be getting into the drugs business.'

'It's a bit late in the day for both of us,' Carlyle said, more than a little miffed at his father's lack of enthusiasm. After all the risks he'd taken, he would have appreciated rather more gratitude from his old man.

'I've got my pills,' Alexander pointed out. 'And when I go into the hospital, they'll give me a drip.'

'This is about keeping you up and about for as long as possible.' Carlyle ran through Dom's advice on how to take the tablets. 'It's to keep the pain manageable and give you some kind of quality of life.'

'Quality of life,' the old fella scoffed. 'They never had that in my day.'

'It still is your day – just about.'

'Face facts, son. I'm done.'

'What'll we do, then?' Carlyle gestured in the direction of the Fulham Road. 'Head out and I'll nudge you under a bus?'

'Dinnae be daft,' Alexander scolded.

Carlyle tried a change of tack. 'This is the best stuff.'

'Why don't they give it to me at the hospital, then?'

'They have to play by the rules.'

Alexander looked at his son for what seemed like the longest moment. 'That was always your problem – you always thought the rules were for other people.'

'Don't be soft,' Carlyle responded, bridling at his father's comment. 'I spend my whole life playing by the bloody rules.'

'Aye.' Alexander gestured towards the bag with his chin. 'Like right now.'

Carlyle had to resist the temptation to grab the bag and smack his old man over the head with it. 'Look,' he spluttered, failing to hide his exasperation, 'I realize that we find ourselves in an interesting situation, but can we save the moral philosophy debate for some other time? All you need to do is keep this stuff somewhere safe and sound. If the medication you do get from the hospital isn't working, try a little.'

'We'll see, we'll see.' The old man eyed the illegal drugs suspiciously.

'And if these don't work, I'm sure we can try something else.'

'Like what? Horse tranquillisers?'

'Now there's a thought.'

'You're gonna turn me into a right old junkie at this rate,' Alexander complained.

'Dad! You're gonna be dead! What does it matter?'

For several moments, they glared sullenly at each other.

It's just like the old days, Carlyle thought. He recalled the night – more than half a lifetime ago – when he had come home and announced he was joining the police. The news had gone down like a lead balloon. Even now, he could hear his mother scolding his father that he should *do something about it* before stalking off to bed to leave them to have a man-to-man talk.

The same looks exchanged over the same table.

'What does it matter?' he repeated. Scooping up the packet, the inspector opened a succession of cupboards before dropping it in a large saucepan and covering it with the lid. 'Don't forget it's there. And like I said, don't go showing it to anyone. This is strictly between us.'

'It's breaking the law.'

'I'm perfectly well aware of that.'

'We're outlaws.' Alexander chuckled suddenly. 'Like Audie Murphy. Or John Wayne.'

Carlyle tried to recall the name of another sixties cowboy actor. 'Jack Palance.'

They grinned at each other.

'Outlaws,' his father repeated.

'Think of it as father-son bonding.'

'We didn't have that in my day either.'

Tell me about it, Carlyle thought. 'There's lots of things they didn't have in your day.'

'Aye, right enough.'

'We did okay though.'

'You think?'

'Sure.' Closing the cupboard door, the inspector caught a glimpse of a half-full bottle of Bell's, hiding behind the bread bin.

Not as much to his taste as Jameson's but perfectly acceptable. For the second time this evening, he desired a drink. Equally, he knew that he would regret it come the morning. Resisting temptation once again, he took a seat opposite his father.

'Is it a regret?' Alexander asked out of the blue.

'What?'

'Not having a boy.' A serious note entered the old man's voice. 'Do you regret not having a son?'

Carlyle shook his head. 'No, not at all. I'm very happy with my lot.' It was true. From the moment his daughter had been born, he had felt his life was complete; it had never crossed his mind that he might want a boy.

'Aye. Alice is a grand girl, right enough.' Alexander took a slurp of his tea. 'What if I'm raided?'

Carlyle was beginning to feel dizzy at the zigzags in the conversation. 'Why would you be raided?'

'It happens.'

'Not to terminally ill pensioners with no criminal record to their name.' Carlyle gave his father a pleading look. 'It's there,' he said quietly, 'if . . . *when* you need it. Just give it a go. If it works, we can get you some more, just so long as you don't go blabbing to anyone about it.'

A thought popped straight out of his father's mouth. 'You're not stealing it from the police station, are you?'

'Of course not.'

'Where did you get it from then?'

'You don't need to know.'

'It might not be safe,' the old man reflected. 'This kind of thing can be adulterated, can't it? You read about it in the papers, don't you?'

Carlyle threw up his arms in exasperation. They could go round in circles like this all night. 'You've got more pressing things to worry about, don't you think?'

'You don't know what goes in those pills,' his father said stubbornly.

Carlyle gestured towards the cupboard. 'This is good stuff. Dom got it for you. It'll get you high – that's the whole point. Pain relief. It'll only kill you if you take it all at once.'

A thoughtful look passed across his father's face.

'Do *not* go there,' Carlyle admonished him. 'Don't even think about it.'

THIRTY-FOUR

Monkey Beach had history. The place got its name from an incident in the Napoleonic Wars when a French ship was wrecked off the coast. A monkey who survived the wreck was washed up on shore, only to be hanged by the locals who feared it was an enemy spy. It was a local legend that was repeated in various places along the east coast, all the way up to Peterhead in the north of Scotland. However, the good people of Essex were the first to name a beach in honour of the luckless primate.

Around 150 yards or so from where the hapless chimp allegedly met its fate stood Andros Cottage. Originally built for local farmworkers, it now served as a holiday home for Londoners who couldn't be bothered to schlep over to Brittany. Before leaving London, Hunter had checked on its availability online. According to the owner's website, the property was currently vacant, on offer for a rental of £750 a week. Three hours later, sitting in the darkness of his rented Ford Fusion, the captain contemplated the light coming from one of the ground-floor windows. 'Looks like Becky was telling the truth,' he said to himself as he slipped on a pair of latex gloves.

Outside, the air was decidedly chilly. After his time in London, the sea breeze was fresh and invigorating. Closing the car door gently, not bothering to lock it, Hunter looked around. On one side of the single-track road was pasture, on the other scrubland, leading down to the beach. A couple of cars were parked down the road but, otherwise, the place appeared deserted. Aside from the cottage, there were no other properties within half a mile. Nor was there any street lighting on this stretch of road.

Hunter stepped off the tarmac to take a piss. That done, he took a short stroll along the road, away from the cottage, and then back again, in order to shake some of the stiffness from his legs. In the distance, behind the cottage, the lights of West Mersea Yacht Club twinkled serenely. Hunter checked his watch. It was almost 4 a.m. There would never be a better time for him to do the job. Removing the SIG Sauer from his pocket, he released the safety and began walking towards his target.

From the front room came the sound of an explosion, followed by the staccato stutter of automatic weapons fire. Standing in the hallway, Hunter watched Carson sitting on the floor, with his back to the half-open door. Hunched in front of the TV, 'Soldier A' grunted as he shot a succession of alien invaders coming at him on the screen.

Lifting his arm, Hunter pointed the semi-automatic at the back of Carson's head. Wrapping his finger around the trigger, he steadily increased the pressure.

Grunting, Carson continued to pound the game controller with his thumbs. On the screen, another attacker came towards him, only for Carson to remove his head with a spray of bullets. 'Shuffle off this mortal coil, you wanker!'

'Hello, Andy.'

Still playing the game, Carson looked over his shoulder. 'Oh fuck!' Letting the console slip from his fingers he pushed himself up and threw himself towards Hunter. It was a hopeless gesture; his arse was barely a foot off the floor by the time the first bullet slammed into his face.

For a split second, it was like Carson was hanging in mid-air, then the next shot sent him tumbling backwards, taking the TV with him as he crashed to the floor.

Stepping over the body, Hunter watched the aliens swarming across the screen, now covered in the remains of Carson's head.

298

'I guess that's game over.' Putting the gun back into his pocket, he began searching the room.

It took him less than five minutes to find the diamonds, sitting in an open holdall on a bed in one of the upstairs rooms. 'Time to leave,' he muttered to himself. Dropping the SIG Sauer inside, he clasped the handles and turned for the door.

'I think I'll take that, if you don't mind.'

Hunter recognized the smile immediately. This time, however, the man from the Arcade Café had a gun in his hand.

'Toss the bag over here.'

With a rueful shake of the head, Hunter did as requested. 'I guess this really is game over.'

'What?'

'Nothing. I suppose you must be Isaacs.'

'Very good, very good.'

'How did you find me?'

'It wasn't that difficult.' With his free hand, Isaacs fished a couple of scraps of brown paper from his jacket pocket and waved them at Hunter. 'After all, you very kindly wrote the address down for me.'

Hunter sat down on the bed. To his surprise, looking down the barrel of Isaacs' gun, he experienced what could only be described as a moment of euphoria. In a few seconds, all of his problems would be over.

'That was an unfortunate mistake in what has otherwise been an impressive performance.' Isaacs shoved the scraps of paper back into his pocket. 'I have to say, Captain Hunter, you are one hell of an operator. I wish I'd come across you when I was working in Basra. You could have made my life a lot easier, back then.'

'I've made your life easier now,' Hunter smiled, 'haven't I?'

'Yes, you have indeed. The Army will be much the poorer for your . . . departure.' Keeping the gun trained on the Redcap, he carefully guided the bag towards the door with his foot. 'Are all the stones in there?'

'As far as I know,' Hunter replied.

'Excellent.'

'I've been through the house. It's not like Andy was hiding anything.'

At mention of Carson's name, Isaacs' face clouded. 'We should never have got involved with that useless little shit. I'm genuinely very sorry about what happened to your family. It was completely unnecessary. Totally unprofessional.'

Hunter shot him an empty look. 'At this stage of the game, an apology makes fuck-all difference, as I'm sure you can imagine.'

'I know.' Isaacs sighed as he bent down to pick up the bag. 'But I truly am sorry. It was inexcusable. Base criminality of the worst kind. If I'd had the chance to intervene, I would never have allowed it.'

Listening to the older man's knees crack, it crossed Hunter's mind that if he launched himself from the bed he could drive Isaacs through the door and send him tumbling back down the stairs before he had the chance to get a shot off. But what was the point? Sitting back on the bed, he watched the man straighten up, the gun still aimed at his head.

'Get on with it.'

'You think I'm going to kill you?' Isaacs frowned. 'Why would I do that?'

'Do it.' Hunter licked his lips. His mouth was dry and there was a buzzing noise in his head which was getting louder. 'Do it now, or I'll come after you. Track you down, like Carson. Wherever you go, I'll find you.'

'I don't think so.' The smile returned to Isaacs' face. 'With that body downstairs, you've crossed the line. You can't go back. I know that better than anyone. We're both outlaws now.'

Hunter stared at his gloved hands.

'However painful it may be,' Isaacs continued, 'you have to move on to the next stage of your life. And take my advice – go somewhere warm.'

* * *

Listening to Isaacs retreat down the stairs, Hunter closed his eyes and fell back on the bed. As the footsteps faded away, he felt his chest heave but the sobs would not come. In the distance, he heard the sound of a car engine start up, before slowly disappearing into the night.

Pushing himself off the bed, he waited for the dizziness to clear before slowly heading for the door. Apparently, there were different kinds of dead. For better or worse, it looked like it wasn't game over, after all.

THIRTY-FIVE

Yawning, Carlyle watched as a pair of workmen struggled to remove one of the mega-dams prints from the wall of the gallery. Lowering it to the floor, they quickly swaddled the frame in bubble wrap before moving on to the next one.

An elegant middle-aged woman appeared at his shoulder. 'What do you think? This is your last chance to buy one.'

'Eva.' Quickly composing himself, he turned to give Dominic Silver's wife a peck on the cheek. 'Good to see you.'

'Put her down,' Dom instructed as he walked through the door. 'She's here to work.'

'That's right,' Eva groaned. Dropping her bag on the desk, she took a drink from the outsized coffee cup in her hand before adding: 'Fiona quit last night.'

'Apparently her tutor left his wife,' Dom chuckled, 'and they've run off to Marrakech.'

Eva shot her husband a dismayed look. 'Middle-aged men can be *so* embarrassing.'

'You have to say though,' the inspector ventured, 'as mid-life crises go, it's fairly impressive. Better than buying a sports car, at least.'

'I'm not sure Helen would find that a particularly impressive take on the situation,' Eva observed.

'Helen has nothing to worry about on that score,' Carlyle said hastily.

'Anyway,' Dom went on, 'it's bloody inconvenient. The timing couldn't be worse.' He gestured around the room. 'We have this lot to get out and then the bloody Jankowski exhibition is due to open in a fortnight.'

Carlyle knew better than to ask about the Jankowski exhibition.

Eva took another sip of her coffee. 'Just as well then you have muggins here to stand in until you find another receptionist.'

'I'm sure it won't take too long.' Stepping between them, Dom placed a hand on Carlyle's shoulder. 'At least we've got Lucio Spargo off our back,' he said quietly. 'That is a big help. Thank you.'

Eva murmured her assent.

'Me?' Carlyle made a mime of his modesty. 'I did nothing. The guy just pushed his luck too far and got caught. Happens all the time.'

'And you just happened to be there to catch him,' Dom mused. 'Anonymous tip-off.'

'I read in the paper,' said Eva, 'that some of Mr Spargo's backers have pulled out of the development next door following his rather unfortunate arrest.'

'Apparently so,' the inspector replied. 'I think he'll probably escape jail but perhaps retirement beckons. At the very least, the Cork Street development looks to have stalled for the foreseeable future.'

'Thank you,' Dom repeated. 'I owe you one.'

'Hardly,' Carlyle countered. 'Not after your help for my dad.'

'And how is Alexander?' Eva asked.

'It is what it is.' Carlyle bit his lower lip. He had already explained to Dom that not all of the drugs had been planted on Spargo and that some tablets had been kept back for his father's medicinal use.

There was a crash, followed by the sound of broken glass.

The workmen stood, matching horrified looks on their faces, contemplating a frame – which lay face down on the floor.

'Bloody hell!' Eva squawked as she rushed over to inspect the damage. 'That's already been paid for.'

'We can get it fixed,' Dom pointed out. 'Don't worry.'

'But it's supposed to go to Miami tomorrow,' Eva fretted. 'The shipping's all arranged.'

'We can fix it,' Dom repeated before returning his attention to Carlyle. 'How's your dad getting on with the, er, stuff?'

'I don't think he's actually used any of it yet.'

'Well, if it doesn't work, I've got another idea – magic mushrooms.'

Carlyle raised an eyebrow.

'I've been reading about doctors in America who have been testing psilocybin with terminally ill cancer patients. Apparently, it induces visions which help them rise above the illness and—'

The inspector stopped him with a raised hand. 'Thank you, Timothy Leary. Let's cross that bridge if we get to it, shall we?'

'It was just an idea.'

Carlyle's response was stifled by the phone vibrating in his pocket. Pulling it out, he hit the receive button: 'Hello?'

'Where are you?'

Recoiling from the dour tones of Inspector Sarah Ward, Carlyle stepped away from Dom. 'I'm in the West End.' He braced himself for a lecture about how he shouldn't have ventured again on to her patch; about how he should have let *her* nick Spargo.

'That soldier has turned up,' she said tonelessly. 'Dead. Two bullets in the face.'

It took him a moment to process what she was saying; another moment to frame his careful initial response. 'Which soldier are we talking about?'

'Andrew Carson. I'm standing here looking at him now. Not a pretty sight.'

'No, I can imagine.' Carlyle made a half-hearted attempt to summon up some sympathy for a fellow human being cut off in his prime. In the event, the best he could manage was to try and avoid sounding too gleeful. 'On the other hand, it's not the world's greatest surprise. What else do we know?'

Realizing that this was not going to be a quick call, Dom slipped off to help Eva clean up.

'Carson. Also known as "Soldier A".' It sounded like Ward was reading from notes. 'An associate of Ryan Fortune and Adrian Colinson, both recently deceased; both suspected of having sprung Carson from prison. All three wanted in connection with the diamond robbery at City airport. Carson is also a suspect in the murder of Fortune and also the murders of Melanie Hunter and her two children.'

Jesus Christ, Carlyle thought, what a list.

'Carson died of gunshot wounds to the head. The murder weapon has not been found. There are no witnesses.'

'Sounds like a professional job,' Carlyle decided. 'Tying up loose ends.'

'Quite. I don't suppose you know anything about it, do you?'

'No. Why?'

'Because it looks very much like it was your mate Hunter who killed him.'

Good for him, Carlyle thought. 'What makes you think that?' he asked. 'Have you got him in custody?'

'What did I just say?' Ward snapped. 'No murder weapon, no witnesses, no perpetrator.'

You never said the last bit, Carlyle observed. He let it slide. The inspector was obviously having a bad day.

'Carson was hiding out in a house on the Essex coast,' Ward explained. 'It's a bit off the beaten track but not that remote. Someone must have tipped Hunter off about his location. It looks like he drove up here, popped him, and then jumped on a ferry. He rented a car in Paddington and dumped it in a car park in Felixstowe. According to Belgian Border Security he went through customs in Zeebrugge yesterday morning. Fuck knows where he is now.'

Carlyle hesitated, unsure as to what he should say next. Stepping over to the window, he watched as a tramp shuffled down Cork Street, pushing all of his worldly possessions in front of him in a shopping trolley while eating a badly bruised banana. 'Well,' he said finally, 'thanks for the heads-up.'

'This isn't a heads-up.'

'Oh? What is it, then?'

'It's a warning. If I find out you had anything to do with this, Carlyle—'

'Don't worry on that score,' he replied, surprised at how easily he was keeping control of his temper in the face of her attempts to needle him. 'It's nothing to do with me.' He thought about mentioning his alibi – he was probably arresting Spargo around the time Hunter was tracking down Carson – but decided to leave it. 'I appreciate the call,' he said evenly, 'but shouldn't you be more focused on tracking down Hunter? I mean, given that he seems to be your prime suspect.'

'If he tries to get in touch with you,' Ward said tersely, 'let me know *immediately*.'

'I doubt that there's much chance of that . . .' It took the inspector a moment to realize that she was no longer there. Letting the phone fall to his side, he watched the tramp as he continued down the road, heading in the direction of St James's. Somewhere behind him, Eva and Dom bickered good-naturedly about the effectiveness of the latter's efforts to remove the last of the broken glass from the floor. Tuning out their squabbling, Carlyle's thoughts quickly returned to Hunter and his new life on the run. 'Good luck to you, Captain,' he said to himself, 'wherever you are, wherever you go.'

EPILOGUE

Balthazar Quant burst into the office, unannounced, saying breathlessly, 'Did you just see the email from Bianca?'

Sitting behind his desk, Gerry Durkan was busy studying the form for the upcoming Cheltenham Gold Cup. Tapping on his iPad, he affected to ignore the arrival of his minion.

'Bianca's email,' Balthazar repeated. He sounded as hyped-up as a five year old at 3 a.m. on Christmas morning.

'No, I haven't read it,' Gerry grunted. 'What's it say?' Reluctantly leaving thoughts of the turf behind, he watched Balthazar hop from foot to foot in excitement. Calm down, he thought, don't piss on the carpet.

'Looks like Bianca'll be back from Indonesia the day after tomorrow,' Balthazar squealed. 'She says she's raised just over 290 million dollars from new investors.' He did a little jig of joy. Surely now, the bonuses would start to flow again. 'That should just about cover our shortfall.'

'More than cover it,' Gerry corrected him. 'Given that; the joint venture from Hell, the Hydra SPV, has just gone tits up, and we don't have to throw any more money into that black hole, we should be quids in.'

'Crisis averted.' Balthazar, his face flooded with relief, looked as if he was on the point of tears.

'Indeed.' Returning to the screen, Gerry pondered the merits of a flutter on Sands of Time at 14 to 1. He'd been hearing good things about the thoroughbred and the odds had already started to shorten. His luck with the bookies hadn't been great recently but that, too, could change.

It was amazing how much the business outlook could brighten in a matter of weeks, or even days. Earlier in the month, he had been facing not only financial ruin but also bodily harm: a trip to A&E at St Margaret's Hospital, courtesy of Manny, had seemed inevitable. Now, however, both his physical and economic security seemed assured. He might not have the diamonds, but no matter. They were small beer compared to the money Bianca had raised. Macroom Castlebar Salle's finances were stabilizing; even Nathanial Ridley of the Ridley Cranes empire was making noises about coming back into the fold. Gerry was having lunch with the boy next week. A couple of bottles of Krug and a visit to Madame Lo's Gentleman's Club in Bruton Place and Nat doubtless would be fully reintegrated into the MCS family. Less amenable to rejoining the fold, Bob Biswas had taken his Ghatak Commando and retreated to Antwerp in order to plot some form of revenge. Biswas was still convinced that Durkan had been the brains behind the City airport robbery, but threats of retribution from the other side of the North Sea rang hollow. And Gerry would not sit around waiting for Biswas to strike back. He, more than most, knew that attack was the best form of defence.

As Mrs T herself might very well have said: *never complain, never back down and never, ever, stop fighting.*

He would deal with Biswas in good time. First things first, however. Taking five thousand pounds from his online betting account, he backed Sands of Time. On the nose. 'Was there anything else?'

Finishing his little dance, Balthazar stepped in front of the desk.

'The new security guy.' Balthazar mentioned the name of Joe Isaacs' replacement. Durkan had chosen him personally; a very nice guy with a quiet manner and a stellar CV. The new guy had worked for both MI5 and also a Chinese telecoms giant that was busy taking over critical infrastructure projects all over the world, giving him a good understanding of both the past and the future.

'What about him?'

'He wants to know if he can speak to Isaacs about his operating protocols.'

'Protocols?' Frowning, Durkan glanced at the postcard on his desk. It had arrived this morning. On the front was a selection of images of the Historic Quarter of Valparaiso. On the back, in careful script, was a simple message: *Thank you and goodnight*. A nice analogue touch in a digital world, it made the terrorist-turned-financier smile. Tonight, Delia would put it in the confidential shredding bin before going home, and then it would be gone for ever. 'As far as I'm aware, Joe didn't have any "protocols".' Durkan tapped his temple with an index finger. 'He kept it all up here.'

A look of dismay descended on Balthazar's face. 'So what do you want me to tell the new guy?' he asked.

'Tell him he's in charge,' Durkan smiled. 'If he wants to start from scratch, that's fine by me.'

'Okay.' Balthazar retreated from the desk.

'And one other thing,' Durkan murmured, returning to the horses. 'Find out who he would use for some rather sensitive work in Belgium.'

On Drury Lane, the refuse collectors were going about their Sisyphean task. As the inspector approached, he caught the eye of his near neighbour from Stukeley Street.

'Lost anything today, Inspector?' the bin man chuckled, lobbing a large green sack into the back of the lorry as it idled outside The Sun pub.

'Not as far as I know,' Carlyle grinned.

'You can still give us a hand, if you want.'

'It's okay.' Carlyle paused on the kerb, waiting for a taxi to pass. 'Thanks for the offer though.' Shoving a hand into the pocket of his jeans, his fingers brushed against something small and hard, like a piece of grit. Taking it out, he was surprised to see it sparkle in the weak sunlight. Then he remembered the tiny diamond he had recovered from the flat on Goswell Road. To his untutored eye, the object in his hand looked pretty much like a piece of ordinary glass; certainly it was not worth all the bloodshed and pain that he had seen over the last few weeks. Stepping into the road, he tossed the stone into the back of the rubbish truck and continued on his way.

Sitting on his bed, stripped to the waist, Legionnaire Second Class Daniel Hunter idly watched the sunlight streaming through the window. Beside him sat a FAMAS assault rifle, waiting to be cleaned, a small bottle of pure alcohol and a selection of clean rags. In the far corner of the room, a group of new arrivals were laughing and joking in a language that Hunter didn't immediately recognize. Otherwise the barracks was empty. It was a rare day off and most of his comrades had already left the base to sample the delights of nearby Castelnaudary, such as they were. Hunter had no interest in joining them. Picking up the weapon, he let his mind empty of all thought and began stripping it down.